I0534502

LOW FLYING

John Reynolds

Starblaze Publications
Auckland, New Zealand

This is a work of fiction. Names, characters, places and incidents either are the product of the author's imagination or are used fictitiously, and any resemblance to actual persons, living or dead, or events, is entirely coincidental.

Published by Starblaze Publications
10A Law Street, Torbay 0630, Auckland, New Zealand
Email: jbess@xtra.co.nz
Website: https://tinyurl.com/yyyqe5oy

A catalogue record for this book is available from the National Library of New Zealand.

To Bess

My constant and abiding muse

Chapter 1

Fleur Lassiter shifted in her chair and suppressed a yawn. Tutorials were supposed to be a time of sharing, debating and disputing between students, under the guidance of their tutor. But this young woman was hopeless; nervous, unsure, and her smile of encouragement was more akin to a sickly simper.

"Surely someone must have an idea."

Her eyes panned pleadingly around the group seeking a response, any response from one of the ten faces. The two large flies, droning fitfully in the small tutorial room, complemented the buzzing of the cicadas outside in the university garden.

She glanced at the list on her lap. "How about you, er, Fleur?" She looked round the group and caught the brief upward tilt of Fleur's head. "Have you ever been in that sort of situation?"

"Not that I'll admit to," replied Fleur. She glanced around the room and back at the tutor. "Don't want to corrupt the younger ones."

"Oh, come on Fleur," responded Heather, a pretty second year student. "We're not that young   "

"And you're not that old," chuckled her neighbour Dave, a thin young man with heavily rimmed spectacles, responding to her angry look with a wide grin.

Fleur Lassiter smiled wryly. She'd been attending university part-time in pursuit of what she often referred to as 'the world's longest arts degree'. She had started in her early twenties and then, persuaded by a girlfriend, she'd spent three years on an OE in England and Europe. Returning to Auckland she'd taken assorted administrative positions while trying to fulfil her ambition to become a freelance writer. After a year she decided to return to university to complete her degree, hoping that an English major would enhance her writing knowledge and skills.

1

Now in her final year she was less than impressed with the efforts of their young tutor in provoking a discussion on the works of Restoration female writer Aphra Benn.

"OK," said Fleur, "so you're saying that Benn's apparent bisexuality was the key factor in her writings."

"Yes," responded the tutor, obviously relieved that the possibility of a discussion appeared to be stuttering into life.

"If you want my opinion," Fleur paused and the tutor nodded encouragingly. "I think that's irrelevant. Furthermore, anyone whose chief focus is on Benn's real or imagined bisexuality seems to me an indication of trying to legitimise their own behaviour."

The tutor's head jerked back. "Who are you referring to?"

"To whom am I referring?" responded Fleur, rewarded by the shuffles of interest from her fellow students. "No one in particular, but if the cap fits…" She completed the sentence with a gentle shrug and a winsome smile.

The buzzing flies and the backing vocals of the cicadas appeared to go up several notches in the sudden silence that engulfed the room. The tutor's gaze lingered on Fleur for a long moment before switching abruptly to the clock on the back wall.

"I think that will do us for today." She rose hurriedly. "Good luck for your finals."

The students by the door hastily drew back as the young tutor swept from the room. All eyes then turned to Fleur.

"Hey, guys what did I do?" she enquired.

"Good thing for you all the essays have been marked. She could have turned nasty," commented Heather.

"I'm sure she adheres strictly to the concept of grading the essay and not the person," responded Fleur.

"Who cares? The woman was a complete bore. No idea how to run an interesting tutorial." Dave smiled. "I'm told that she's hoping to become a secondary school teacher."

"She certainly has all the right attributes." The speaker was Matt Bullock, former rugby captain of the Kings College First

XV, whose looks, talents and academic record marked him as a future leader.

The laughter echoed round the room as the students exited noisily into the warm spring sunshine.

Fleur turned as a hand touched her arm.

"Do you have time for a coffee?" asked Matt.

She hesitated and, seeing the look in his eyes, nodded. "Why not. The ferry doesn't leave for an hour. Here or downtown?"

"Downtown."

Using the pedestrian crossing opposite the clock tower they walked through Albert Park towards the centre of the city.

"You know what I want to talk to you about, don't you." It was a statement not a question.

"I have an inkling." She smiled. "Let's wait until the coffee lubricates your throat."

They walked in silence until Matt slowed and turned abruptly. "Fleur, I need you and I to—"

She placed a hand gently on his chest and gave a small push. "Coffee, Matt. Downtown."

He sighed, shrugged, and continued walking.

Chapter 2

The young Asian waiter placed two cappuccinos in front of them.

"Sure you don't want anything else, Matt?"

He shrugged. "Not particularly hungry at the moment."

He took a preliminary sip and, as he returned the cup to its saucer, Fleur laughed.

"What's funny?"

"You've got a rim of cream on your lips. Here." She reached forward and gently wiped it off with a paper serviette.

"Thanks, mother." His smile was thin.

"Uncalled for, Matt."

"Maybe it bloody was," he responded, his face colouring.

"Look, Matt, you know how fond I am of you."

"Fond! Aren't I Mr Lucky?" His voice began to rise. "Suppose that's what all you bloody cougars say when you want to discard your latest plaything."

Heads turned towards their table.

"Matt, keep your voice down." She reached forward and put her hand over his. "I've already said I'd come out to the aerodrome with you. I do want to see your first solo flight."

His hand twisted round and gripped hers.

"You sure?"

"Of course. We agreed last time, when we…" Her voice tailed off and then she smiled. "It was lovely, wasn't it, Matt."

"Yes. Christ, Fleur, have you any idea?"

"How much do you want me to come to the airfield with you?" She paused. "Will anyone else be there?"

The grip on her hand tightened and she grimaced.

"You mean like family or parents? People who might ask awkward bloody questions?"

"Well, you said that your parents were paying for your flying lessons and so I thought that they'd—"

"No they won't be there. I haven't told them. Just wanted it to be special for the two of us."

As his grip relaxed, she withdrew her hand, maintaining her smile while flexing her hand under the table to ease the pain.

"Ok, Matt. Pick you up tomorrow?"

"No, I can take you in the morning. I've booked the motel again for tonight."

She hesitated. His expression was a mixture of anger and pleading.

"But," she began, "I'm not prepared for an overnight–."

"You can use my toothbrush."

His boyish smile of anticipation was irresistible. She took his outstretched hand and they left together.

Chapter 3

"Beautiful day for it," Matt exclaimed, pointing up above the rim of the windscreen at two circling aircraft.

"Solo flyers?" she asked.

"Possibly, or just flying the circuit, practicing their take-offs and landings with their instructors, prior to flying solo."

"Looks like great fun."

Matt slowed down his blue BMW Z3 convertible as they approached the motorway turnoff to the airfield.

"You said it's taken you six months to get to this point – solo flying."

"Yes, big day. Even had to take a medical before they'd let me go up alone. Doc said I was fit and healthy in every aspect."

She turned and smiled playfully. "I could vouch for that."

"God, Fleur, I do—"

"Flying, Matt. That's your focus today."

"Yes, but last night—"

"Focus on flying, Matt. Don't want to witness you pranging the kite."

"Christ, surely you're not of the Biggles generation?"

"No, but my dad was a fan. Used to read the exploits of Biggles and Ginger to me when I was little. Pretty weird slang, but some of the stories were good – if you like that sort of thing."

"I love flying but those two with their faith in God, King and Empire were a bit much for me."

They swung left off the motorway and after a brief drive through pleasant dairy pastureland, arrived at the small airfield, which was buzzing with activity.

"Sunday's always popular," Matt explained. "Lots of people come out to practice or take pleasure trips."

As they entered the reception area a tall good-looking man dressed in dark trousers and the lapelled shirt of a flight instructor came forward with outstretched hand.

"Matt, the big day at last. All set to go?"

"Yeah, all set." He turned to Fleur. "Oh, Fleur, meet my instructor Jason Collins. Jason, this is Fleur. She's come to see my first solo."

Jason's smile was warm and confident as he took Fleur's hand. She smiled back noting the full head of dark hair tinged with light grey streaks.

"Fleur. Lovely name. Welcome."

He held her hand for a little longer than necessary.

"Hullo, Jason. Do you think Matt's ready?"

"Of course." He paused. "You a friend of the family?"

Seeing that Matt was about to speak Fleur quickly replied, "In a manner of speaking. I'm looking forward to seeing the flight."

"You can watch it from upstairs – there's a balcony in the lounge where you'll get a good view."

"Thanks."

Matt took a step forward, pushing his face towards her.

"Wish me luck, Fleur."

Deftly slipping her head to his right she kissed him lightly on the cheek.

"Good luck." She stepped back and smiled. "Oh, one final thing."

"What's that?"

"Try not to prang the kite."

With a smile at both men she turned and headed towards the stairs.

The tarmac was busy with several pilots carrying out pre-flight checks on their Cessnas and Robins prior to taking off for a day's outing. Two pairs of instructors and trainee pilots were also pre-flighting prior to flying the circuit – which involved taking off, flying around the airfield, landing and taking off again – known as 'touch and go'.

"Solo today, Matt?" called one instructor.

"Yeah," responded Matt with a wave and feigned casualness.

"Good luck, mate. Hope to follow you soon," called the trainee pilot.

"Thanks, Mike. I'm sure you will."

The pair walked towards the Robin with the TZG identification markings on the fuselage.

"Feeling OK?"

"Yeah. I'll be right."

Matt stepped up onto the wing, pulled back the canopy and placed his helmet with built-in microphone on the seat.

"Want to follow me as I do the pre-flight?" he asked.

"Sure. Away you go."

To a predetermined sequence, Matt unscrewed the fuel tank cover, pulled out the thin metal dipstick, and checked the fuel level before moving to the ailerons and raising them up and down by hand to check for stability and smoothness of movement. Satisfied, he moved to the rear of the plane to check the cables and the rudder.

"Pretty woman," said Collins.

Curious, Matt turned and looked around.

"Where?"

"Not here. Fleur. About the right age, too."

"Right age?" His eyes narrowed. "What do you mean?"

"Not for you of course. Who is she? A relative. If so I'd like—"

The younger man took a step towards his instructor.

"Listen, Jason, you're here to teach me to fly this plane. OK?"

Collins took a step backwards. "Take it easy, Matt. I only said that Fleur was an attractive looking woman and—"

"And nothing. Fleur is none of your business. Now follow me through the rest of the pre-flight and I'll get on with flying the bloody plane. Understood?"

8

Suppressing the urge to grin, Collins drew his eyebrows together and adopted a moderately contrite expression.

"OK, Matt. No offence. Now, let's check the oil and the prop." He looked skywards as a plane, having briefly touched down, was soaring above the trees at the far end of the airfield. "Plenty of traffic today so you'll need to be vigilant with your radio calls and look outs."

"As always."

"Yes I know that, Matt. But you'll be more keyed up today and so just take extra care not to become distracted."

Matt grunted, clambered into the cockpit, and pulled the overhead canopy shut before his instructor could respond. Collins hesitated and then, with a shrug, turned and walked towards the clubhouse.

Commencing interior pre-flight checks Matt pumped the throttle and turned the key. After a second attempt the engine sputtered into life. The aircraft began to move forward and having tested the brakes he made the standard radio check as he taxied towards a wide area near the runway. He halted and began his run-up procedures that included bringing the engine up to 1800 rpm and checking to see that all the instruments were responding normally.

Taxiing out to the point near the beginning of the runway he pressed the call button on the top of his joystick.

"North Shore Traffic. Tango Zulu Golf. Lining up Runway Two One."

The empty runway stretched ahead of him. As he'd been taught, he looked ahead at a point at the far end and thrust the throttle fully forward. The plane shuddered and then responded with a rising roar, rapidly gathering speed as it headed down the runway. Controlling the rudders with his feet he kept it on a steady course before easing back on the stick. The aircraft began lifting slowly from the tarmac. As they passed the balcony in front of the clubhouse Matt glanced right, preparing to give Fleur a quick wave.

She was leaning on the balustrade. Matt started to raise his right hand when he saw her turn away to greet Jason Collins as he came up behind her and put his arm across her shoulder.

Chapter 4

"Smooth enough take-off," Collins remarked, leaning on the rail beside her.

"Looked fine to me, not that I'm anything of an expert." Fleur looked up to where TZG was continuing to climb. "Beautiful day for his first solo. Has Matt been a good pupil?"

"Yes. I remember the first day I met him. Came here with his parents for an introductory test flight – for his twenty-first birthday I think it was." He paused. "Always good to start the learning processes when you're still just a young man."

He looked searchingly at Fleur, but she looked quickly away.

They both watched as the plane levelled off and continued south of the airfield.

"He enrolled for flying straight away, I believe."

"Yes, after we came back from the introductory flight there was a quick confab with his parents and then Matt signed up. His old man paid with his credit card – obviously well heeled. They said their goodbyes and then left in a late model Jag. I got the impression that like a chip off the old block the boy is used to having his own way."

The emphasis on 'boy' was too obvious to ignore.

"He's a university student and growing up fast."

"I'm sure he is. He's learning to fly planes and…" his voice tailed off.

"And what?"

"Possibly developing a preference for older women."

Showing no reaction, she glanced skywards. "Look, he's turning."

From the wall behind them Matt's voice crackled from the external speaker that transmitted all radio calls.

"Tango Zulu Golf, downwind Runway Two One."

"That's Matt."

"What does that mean?"

"Just telling us where he is and what he intends doing – in his case coming downwind prior to turning at right angles for his final approach."

"He'll be OK?"

"Yes. Wouldn't have let him fly otherwise."

Leaning on the rail together they watched the plane dip and make its final turn.

"It's a wonderful experience to fly your own plane. Not as comfortable as the big planes, of course, but the views are great and you're the one in charge."

"Is it difficult?"

"No, not really. It's a matter of gradually learning each of the steps, assisted by an experienced instructor."

"Like yourself presumably."

"Yes." He paused and smiled. "Why don't you try it? I could take you up for an hour or so. We could fly over the city, the harbour, Rangitoto Island. You'd love it. No cost. My treat."

"You're sure?"

"Absolutely. And afterwards—"

"Tango, Zulu, Golf, final Runway Two One," crackled the speaker.

"Look, he's coming in now."

The little plane was approaching low over the trees towards the runway.

"He's a bit fast," muttered Collins. "Easy Matt."

Barely missing the treetops, the Robin, its fuselage flashing, headed towards the runway. Just at the point where it appeared that the whirring prop at the front of the nose would dig into the tarmac the plane jerked upwards and flew parallel to the runway before the wheels, with a harsh shriek and puff of smoke, hit the tar seal. It rose slightly, bounced twice, slewed right, half corrected itself and then slid to a shuddering halt at an awkward angle near the end of the runway.

"Christ, for a moment I thought he wasn't going to bloody make it! What's the matter with him? He's landed twenty or more times with me."

*

Matt sat in the cockpit with his foot still jammed hard on the brake. It was a lousy landing. He knew he could have done far better, particularly in front of Fleur, but the sight of his instructor distracting her from his take-off had infuriated him. When he'd taken to the air and commenced his circuit he'd told himself to calm down and concentrate on the flight, but as he'd returned for his downwind approach he'd been able to clearly make out Fleur's red dress and the male figure close beside her on the viewing platform.

At first the age difference between Fleur and him had been exciting – a relationship with an attractive older woman. However, he'd now become involved with her to the point where he needed her constant reassurance – which seemed to be waning.

Taking a deep breath, he lifted his feet off the brake pedals and taxied the plane towards its allocated place in front of the hangar. Afraid of what he might see, he resisted the temptation to look across at the clubhouse and concentrated on manoeuvring the Robin into position before pulling the mixture control to cut off the idling engine.

"He looks OK." She frowned. "Funny that he didn't look our way as he went past."

"Probably aware of his lousy landing. He'll be right. Happens to the best of us."

"Maybe. But he'll be upset. Let's go down and greet him."

Without waiting for a reply Fleur turned, walked across the lounge area and headed downstairs.

Clambering out of the cockpit Matt, with helmet, logbook and keys in hand, headed towards the clubhouse. Standing by the gate that carried the sign 'Authorised Personnel Only', he saw Fleur. He was about to lift his arm in tentative greeting when Collins quickly came up behind her.

"Well done, Matt. Bit hairy but you did it, mate," called Dan, the instructor who was walking past him to the tarmac. Matt ignored him as he quickened his stride.

Reaching the gate, he lifted the latch. Fleur was standing directly in front of it, smiling a welcome.

"Matt, congratulations. You—"

She stepped back hastily as he shoved the gate towards her and thrust his face in front of a startled Jason Collins.

"Couldn't bloody wait, could you! I'd only just got off the ground when you were making a move, you randy bastard!"

"Matt, don't be a bloody fool."

"Fool? Not me. I know your type. One sniff and you're on to it like a bloody mongrel on heat."

A flush of anger spread rapidly over Collins' face as he met Matt's furious glare.

"Listen to me you stupid young bastard, don't think that your lack of maturity can excuse—"

"Sorry pilot officer, sir, but I'll now follow your example – actions rather than words."

Swinging the helmet in his right hand he caught Collins' head a glancing blow, causing the older man to stagger backwards. Quickly recovering, Collins launched himself at Matt, hitting him squarely in the face. The force of the blow sent the young man staggering through the open gate onto the edge of the tarmac.

"Jason, no!" shouted Fleur, trying to seize his arm as he charged through the gate intent on following up his blow.

Matt, blood streaming from his nose, flung his helmet, key and logbook onto the grass. He ducked under Collins' roundhouse right hook and punched him in the stomach, sending him to his knees.

"Not so mature now, you bastard," rasped Matt as Collins tried to regain his feet.

"Stop this, both of you!" Chris Winstone the General Manager and Dale Salmond the Chief Flying Instructor, having witnessed the start of the brawl from the office area, had come rushing out onto the tarmac followed by several other men. Two of them seized Matt's arms while another two, having hauled Collins to his feet, held him tightly.

"Completely unprovoked!" Collins shouted. "Stupid young bastard made a mess of his first solo landing and decided to take it out on me!"

"There's more to it than that and you know it!" retorted Matt.

"Here," said Fleur, pushing through the group. "His nose is bleeding." She stood in front of Matt, spat onto a small handkerchief and began to dab at the trickle of blood that was now dripping off his chin.

"Who's she?" asked Winstone.

"Maybe his mother," muttered Salmond.

A murmur of amusement came from the other men. Matt's angry response was stifled by Fleur's handkerchief being quickly pressed into his lips. Turning to Dale she said, "I think it's best if I get him away from here now."

"Good idea. Take the heat out of the situation."

"What about my flight?" The men had loosened their hold on him and he was attempting to wipe the blood off his face with his right sleeve.

"It'll be recorded."

"Normally we take a photo at the end of a first solo for the club magazine," said Dale, "but under the circumstances..." His smile was mirthless.

"Take him home," said the General Manager, and turning to Collins he said quietly, "There'll be an enquiry into this incident of course, Collins."

"I understand," was the subdued response.

15

Chapter 5

Fleur had insisted on driving. She had pulled the hood down, swung out of the parking lot and headed towards the motorway. For the first ten minutes the journey proceeded in silence.

Finally, Matt, after wriggling and clearly his throat a few times, looked sideways at his companion.

"Fleur, I'm sorry."

Keeping her eyes on the road Fleur showed no reaction.

"It was going to be a great day. Now it's all just a fucking mess."

"Well, at least that's something we can agree on."

"He had no business moving in on you like that as soon as..."

"Listen to yourself, you stupid young idiot. You make me sound like a helpless female who was completely vulnerable to the advances of any man who takes a fancy to me."

"That's not—"

"And as for your flying," ploughed on Fleur relentlessly. "You let your own foul mood put not only yourself in danger, but also everyone in the vicinity – not to mention the potential of writing off the plane. I don't know much about flying but I do know how important it is for a pilot to keep calm and professional whatever the circumstances. You, on a beautiful day, with a cloudless sky and no wind, nearly wiped yourself out – and why? Because Jason and I were on the terrace, talking to each other."

"Fleur, I—"

She swung round angrily. "Matt, shut the fuck up! Do I make myself clear? I don't want to hear another word from you until we reach your place."

He opened his mouth as if to speak, thought better of it and lapsed into a sullen silence for the remainder of the journey.

The afternoon sun was starting its slow descent as the Z3 pulled up outside Matt's home. Without a word Fleur pulled on the handbrake and turned off the engine. She opened the door, stepped out and stood looking down at the still sullen Matt.

"I'll take a taxi home." She shut the door firmly. "A word of advice, Matt Bullock. Even boys from privileged backgrounds can't get everything they want when they want it."

Matt winced, but continued to sit in the seat, listening to the sound of the boot being slammed shut and then watching Fleur's trim figure walk determinedly down the street until she disappeared around the corner.

Chapter 6

"Is Jason Collins available please?"

"Jason," responded Yvonne the aero club receptionist. "I think so. Just a moment, please."

A long pause followed. Fleur was just about to hang up when a voice said, "Jason Collins speaking."

"Jason, it's Fleur. Fleur Lassiter."

"Fleur? Good God. Fleur. How are you?"

"Fine. More to the point, how are you?"

"I'm OK. Still here, just."

"Just?"

"Yes, there was an in-house inquiry. I was cleared although they suggested I'd let the young fool go for his solo flight too prematurely."

"Can't help feeling that I'm somehow responsible."

"Put it down to everyone being in the wrong place at the wrong time."

"I'm glad you were cleared. You're still teaching flying?"

"Yes, although I get the impression that I'm having to prove myself again. No one's actually said anything but, well, you know."

"Yes." She paused and took a deep breath. "You remember when we talked on the terrace, you offered to take me up for a flight."

"I do."

"Is it still a possibility? I mean, if it would cause any problem then—."

"No, of course not. Might raise a couple of eyebrows and feed the gossip machine, but as long as we follow procedures there'll be no difficulty."

"Great."

"So, when would suit you? You free during the day?"

"Next Friday. How would that do?"

"Just a moment I'll check on the computer." A pause. "Looks OK. How would four o'clock suit? You'll be my last appointment for the day. We could have a drink afterwards if you like."

"Four o'clock on Friday. Lovely. I'll see you then."

"Oh, Fleur, one other thing. What happened when you took Matt home?"

"Nothing. I dropped him off and we haven't been in touch since."

A fleeting smile preceded his response.

"See you Friday then."

Chapter 7

"Can't you do anything, Dad?"

"Not sure what you want me to do, Matt."

"I know he's mixed up in some deal or other but I'm not sure what. During my training he talked about making extra money. Don't know whether or not he's boasting, but I don't think he's short of cash."

Ray Bullock eased himself out of his leather chair and reaching for the decanter, poured himself another Glenfiddich whisky. He looked inquiringly at his son seated opposite him.

The study was cosy and, as always, immaculate. The cleaning lady was instructed to never enter it as his father insisted that he and he alone would be responsible for its cleaning. On the gleaming top of the native timber desk was a small neat stack of papers, an iPhone and the latest Apple notebook.

Outside came the shouts of splashing and laughter from Matt's younger sister Helen and her friends as they leapt in and out of the large family swimming pool.

"No thanks, Dad. Match on Saturday."

"Of course."

His father replaced the stopper in the decanter and looked up.

"Matt, you know I've got plenty of connections…"

"Yeah, I know that, Dad. That's why I'm asking." His face darkened. "That bastard has to be taught a lesson."

"Don't let your personal antipathy cloud your judgement, son. You've told me that he's let you down badly as a flight instructor."

"Yeah. For sure."

"Yet the level of your dislike suggests that there's something deeper."

"Well I'm sure he's mixed up in some sort of illegal business."

"Maybe, but you've no proof. However," he held up his hand, "here's what I'll do for starters. I have a man who's totally trustworthy and discreet."

"A private investigator?"

"Something like that. Be assured, he'll check Jason Collins out thoroughly. If there's dirt to be found he'll drag it to the surface. If he can't find it then," he shrugged, "it doesn't exist."

"Thanks, Dad." Matt stood up. "There's still some daylight left so I'll go for a training run."

"OK, son. Close the door behind you, please."

As the door clicked shut Bullock reached for his iPhone and told Siri to make a call. It was answered after the second ring.

"Zhukov."

"Bullock here. I've another assignment for you."

"Of course, Mr Bullock. What sort of assignment?"

"Investigation of an individual. Any dirt you can find – financial, sexual, past errors, any illegal activities. You know the sort of thing."

"I do, Mr Bullock. You have details?"

"Only his name and workplace."

"He is local?"

"Yes. Auckland based."

"No problem. Ready when you are."

The information was exchanged and, having received an assurance of rapid action, Bullock ended the call. Zhukov was expensive but efficient. Over the past few years the Russian had provided him with muscle for his clubs and debt collecting for recalcitrant clients – without him having to concern himself about the sordid details. Where a debt had been incurred, after the application of appropriate pressure, it was always quickly repaid.

Bullock was puzzled by Matt's attitude that seemed to border on obsession but at least a report on Collins would put the boy's mind at ease. Strange about the flying though; he'd loved it from the start and his enthusiasm hadn't waned – until last week.

Bullock shrugged. His son's teenage years had not always gone smoothly – his short temper and flashes of resentment at any criticism had not endeared himself to either of his parents. However, he was doing well at university, and on this basis, Bullock had started to provide his son with information on the operation of his businesses. He hadn't glossed over the heavy tactics required in dealing with debtors and had even sent Matt out with Zhukov's muscle on debt-collecting forays on the basis that a dose of realism would harden him up. Hopefully, with more maturity, his son could start to play an active role in developing Bullock's business interests.

His speculation was interrupted by a token knock at the door that was then opened by Maryanne.

"Sorry to interrupt, Ray. Just wanted to let you know I'll be out at the school's Arts Federation dinner tonight. Helen's receiving an award."

"Fine, Maryanne. Will they be expecting another donation?"

"No, Ray. They're still babbling their gratitude over our last one. Sure you don't want to change your mind and come?"

"No, I've got some business matters to attend to. If Helen does receive an award tell her to come and see me when you both get home."

"I will." She paused and her voice was sharper. "You know, of course, that if it had been Matt you would have been there."

She shut the door firmly before he could reply. He smiled wryly. A trophy wife without a doubt, but her good looks were increasingly reliant on trips to beauty parlours and God knew where else. She'd produced a son and a daughter, and she still looked attractive on his arm at corporate dinners and conferences, but…

He gave a brief sigh. Matt was showing an increasing grasp of business and entrepreneurial principles and practices and Ray had high hopes for him. However, Helen had inherited her mother's looks, showed little interest in her school studies apart from art, and several teachers had raised concerns about her disruptive classroom behaviour. When household tensions flared Helen always took her mother's side and was becoming increasingly resentful whenever her father complimented Matt. Consequently, the tensions between husband and wife were mirrored in a deteriorating relationship between son and daughter. He'd thought of raising the issue with Maryanne, but their rare in-depth discussions on emotional issues invariably descended into mutual recriminations.

By unspoken agreement, what they did in their spare time was never discussed and the conjugal bed was no longer used. Not that he'd missed out in that department. Dismissing thoughts of family tensions, he smiled, reached for his phone, and activated Siri again.

A soft familiar voice answered after several rings.

"Hullo."

"This weekend, you busy?"

"As a matter of fact..." the voice paused teasingly.

"Yes?"

"No, no I'm not." She chuckled. "What did you have in mind, Raymond?"

"Queenstown. A conference."

"Another one. You are a busy man."

"Will email you your ticket. See you then, sweetheart."

"Bye, baby."

He terminated the call. Not that Maryanne would give a damn but there were some aspects of his life his wife, let alone his children, didn't need to stumble upon.

He glanced at his watch, took a remote from his desk drawer, and turned on his wall mounted television screen.

Westminster Investments, a company he had floated five years ago, had been his first venture into the investment business. He'd operated a loan company for several years, catering for people who were unable to obtain finance from banks, and the

23

high interest rates he charged had given him a healthy return. An investment company gave him more prestige and respectability in the business community. It had started well but needed to raise its profile in order to increase the financial returns. Consequently, he had bought prime time advertising slots including several on the early evening news. A preview of the key stories appeared on the screen and was then replaced by the image of a building fronted by tall Greek pillars and a sign in Gothic-style lettering that read 'Westminster Investments', backed by a stirring brass theme. In a cross-fade Rex Leonard, a former TV One newsreader, replaced the image. Dressed in a dark pinstriped suit and holding a leather portfolio he stood confidently in front of the Westminster Investments logo. From a slightly low angle he looked directly into the camera and in a voice that was familiar nationwide he began to intone the merits of investing with Westminster Investments. As he concluded with, "Your wealth is our priority," the camera tracked into a close-up on a face that exemplified sincerity and trust. The theme ended on a series of resounding chords and a graphic containing contact details that were intoned as a voiceover.

Bullock reached for the remote and muted the sound as the evening news began to unfold on the screen. He lay back in his chair twirling his glass and nodding his head appreciatively. Using the former newsreader was a touch of genius. He had driven a hard bargain, but the advertising agency pointed out that the man had a high trust rating. Although acknowledging that reading autocues with words written by other people wasn't exactly the epitome of trustworthy behaviour, Bullock accepted the accuracy of the agency's analysis, and he had to admit that the newsreader certainly looked and sounded the part. The proof, of course, would be in the numbers of punters who signed up for shares offering very attractive dividends – designed to bring in badly needed liquidity.

As the world had begun to recover from the recent economic downturn Westminster Investments was banking on people becoming more adventurous with their surplus capital – or capital that they could borrow from their bank and invest at a high rate of interest. The public had short memories and it was very easy to appeal to people's greed by using television commercials laced with attractive phrases such as "low risk, high yield", "exceptional opportunities" and "fast growing business platform" backed up by glossy prospectuses and well-designed websites. Bullock was aware that he had a reputation in the city as a sharp trader and while some would shake their heads in disapproval, for others his position was an attraction. An advertising campaign designed with trust as its central theme would provide positive reassurance to wavering investors.

Not that the company was in dire straits – far from it. However, his increasing personal expenses required regular replenishing. As long as the books passed muster with the tame accountants there was no real cause for alarm, and Bullock revelled in the maintenance of a lavish lifestyle. And, in any case, where Westminster Investments couldn't supply his fiscal needs, he was cultivating other options where the increased risk was commensurate with lucrative financial rewards.

The sun was going down and with it the noises from the pool subsided. He was reaching for the mute on the remote control, when he heard a soft footfall followed by a tap on his office door.

"Come in," he called.

Matt entered, barefoot with a towel thrown over his shoulder, and closing the door behind him, stood in the centre of the room. The fading remnants of the late afternoon sun highlighted his well-muscled body, the result of years of competitive sport and regular visits to the gym.

"You're looking good, son. I'm sure the ladies think so, too."

Matt's worried expression remained unaltered as he asked hesitantly, "Dad, did you—?"

"All taken care of, Matt."

"Who did you—?"

His father held up the palm of his hand.

"The less you know the better. I'll inform you when the next stage is completed."

With a dismissive nod Bullock pulled some papers on the desk towards him and picked up his pen. He frowned and looked back up at his son.

"All taken care of Matt. OK?"

"OK." Matt turned, opened the study door and hesitated.

"Oh, Dad?"

"Yes, Matt?" There was a hint of irritation.

"Thanks."

Bullock grinned. "You're welcome, son. And always remember," he smiled.

"Remember?"

"Your interests are my interests."

Chapter 8

Ray Bullock had been tall and solidly built for his age and consequently, when he was seventeen, he had been able to gain entrance into an Auckland strip club accompanied by a couple of former school mates. The atmosphere immediately excited him – the low lighting, the garish decor, the bar with an enticing display of liquor, and the clientele who varied from those in elegant suits to those whose wardrobe bordered on scruffy. But what really aroused him were the scantily-clad girls curling themselves provocatively around tall poles and those who, to a burst of techno music, appeared in bikini style costumes with long high heeled boots, and proceeded to remove their garments while gyrating to the rhythm of the music. When, in a final flourish, they exposed their breasts and their pubic area he leapt out of his seat and cheered loudly before being hauled back by one of his companions.

Later in the evening his delight was further enhanced when one of the strippers sashayed over, stood above him for a long moment before smiling and lowering herself astride him where she commenced the teasing delights of lap dancing, for which one of his mates had paid. He'd been warned about the no touching rule and so just closed his eyes and enjoyed the fantasy that her gyrating body created. When at the prompting of his mates he gingerly inserted a $50 note into her G-string and was rewarded with a kiss and a smile, he felt a delicious ripple of pleasure.

In the small hours, when they were informed that closing time was approaching, he went to the manager's office and asked about employment opportunities. The manager questioned him, while sizing up his physique and self-confidence, and then offered him a position as a trainee security man, which Bullock immediately accepted.

The ensuing months had their highs and lows. While the heady mixture of liquor, money, music and naked women maintained their attraction, the major part of his work involved standing outside the door and checking those seeking admission. This invariably led to confrontations with males deemed too young, too scruffy, or too drunk, or a combination of all three. He was always paired with another well-built bouncer, and they were usually able to quickly box in and firmly steer the rejected hopefuls on their way. In extreme cases a blow to the solar plexus rapidly reduced their belligerence. And in any case, no-one wanted to be arrested in a strip club.

Aggressive women required a different approach. If a female began swinging punches, the men had to try to grab, restrain, and calm her down before showing her the exit. Bullock and his colleagues were warned any violence by them towards women would not be tolerated.

Being stationed outside the club meant he couldn't enjoy the inside attractions but he was told if he did his job well, he could gain promotion to an inside position, so he set his mind to the task and quite enjoyed the power that his role gave him.

The strippers generally exhibited a tough, devil-may-care persona. Their role was primarily to arouse men by getting naked and take their money, without having sex with them. It had been made very clear to him that the girls employed by the club were not perks for male employees, and initially he'd kept his distance. However, as they came and went, they exchanged greetings or chatted to him when he escorted them to their vehicles at the end of their shifts. Inevitably, he struck up a relationship with one or two, outside of the club's environs. He discovered that these girls were not sex maniacs, but were seeking a relationship in which sex, although part of it, was not paramount.

His youth failed him with the first two girls who were in their twenties, but with his increasing cash flow he was able to take the dark-haired Olga, with an East-European accent, away

28

for the weekend to the west coast suburb of Piha where they walked along the wide black-sanded beach and swam between the flags as the breakers completed their long journey across the Pacific Ocean and collapsed in roars and spumes on the hard sand. She loved the wild and free environment and their lovemaking was uninhibited, with no obligations on either party.

When it became clear that Bullock wasn't interested in a long-term relationship, Olga moved on as did he – to the inside of the club. His conscientious approach to his work on the door had impressed his boss who promoted him to security chief. His predecessor had started to rough up one of the girls in a dressing room, but her piercing screams of outrage had brought the boss and several other security men running. The man had been instantly dismissed, the girl given a week's paid leave to recover, and Bullock a promotion.

He enjoyed his new role. He always arrived well before opening time to ensure everyone was present, the place clean and neat, the lighting and sound crew in place and the performers on time – and had left any emotional baggage at the door. Although the girls were well paid, the required performance was demanding, particularly to the mixed and often noisy clientele. Prior to start time the dim lights created a dark and expectant atmosphere, as the patrons took their seats and ordered their pricey drinks and food. Bullock always marvelled at the transformation of the place when with a flick of a few switches the club became transformed into a magical darkened pit illuminated by sparkling red, white and blue lights that projected swirling, ever-changing patterns flowing across the stage. The newly cleaned and polished poles gleamed and as the music flowed out of the speakers the scantily clad dancers appeared to shouts of appreciation. It was show time.

His work inside the club also gave him the opportunity to cultivate men with influence in the city. While many of them came for R & R and preferred to maintain a level of anonymity, others were ready to talk about themselves and their businesses to a bright, ambitious young man who seemed comfortable in the 'entertainment business'. When he told them that he was undertaking a business management degree they nodded approvingly.

One night, just as the dancers had finished their final performances, Bullock felt a tap on his shoulder. He turned to see a smiling Jonathan Harris who asked him if he had time for a drink.

Harris was a man in his forties whose speech matched his high standard of dress. Over the ensuing weeks he and Bullock had chatted and in the course the conversations it became clear that Harris was a successful businessman who was keen to expand his business empire. Bullock had also noted that Harris seemed interested in his background, experience and business acumen.

"Yes, over here," Bullock suggested, pointing to a small booth. "What will you have?"

"G and T," replied Harris, and Bullock signalled to a passing waiter.

"I'll get straight to the point, Ray," said Harris. "I'm in the process of establishing an inner-city night club, called the Toulouse, and need an experienced, reliable and ambitious manager. Are you interested?"

Bullock tried to remain calm, but his widening eyes betrayed his eagerness.

"Is this a new club, Mr Harris?"

"Please call me Jonathan. Yes, brand new and designed for an upmarket clientele with discerning tastes."

"Sounds exciting, er, Jonathan. Do you have an opening date?"

"Two months from now. I'd need you to join the team within a fortnight so that you can be part of the planning process."

"A fortnight," said Bullock, taken aback.

"Yes. I'd start you on an annual salary of $100,000 and, once the club is underway, we can discuss performance bonus payments." Harris smiled. "Sound attractive?'

Ray Bullock would always remember that moment as a turning point in his career. He'd made an effort to save his earnings from the strip club and had begun to build a reasonable nest egg. However, once under Jonathan Harris's wing, his earnings expanded exponentially as did his expertise in the management and operation of an upmarket night club.

Inevitably he increased his range of contacts and, with an eye on enhancing his reputation, he romanced and married Maryanne Chambers, the attractive daughter of a prominent Auckland businessman. His earnings, supplemented by a substantial loan from a friendly banker, enabled him to purchase a property in Parnell and to cultivate the image of a wealthy and respected member of the wider Auckland community.

After several years Harris offered him a partnership in the Toulouse and he also began investing in the local commercial and domestic property market where the flow of tenants' rents, coupled with some creative accountancy, considerably increased his cash flow.

He'd accumulated sufficient capital to buy the strip club, and after several years, to make Harris an offer that resulted in his becoming the sole owner of Toulouse. The two clubs continued to provide him with a steady revenue stream, although the strip club security was a continual worry. As owner he had insufficient time to supervise the bouncers and the other security personnel and was forced to fire several of them for petty thieving.

One evening, near closing time, he was seated in the small strip club bar enjoying a quiet Drambuie when a large man with a craggy face approached him.

"Mr Bullock?"

"Yes," said Bullock, looking up and smiling automatically.

The man hesitated and then said, "Could I have, please, moment of your time?"

"Of course." He indicated the seat next to him.

"Thank you." The man eased himself into the seat and took a deep breath. "Thank you, Mr Bullock for giving me time," he began. "My name is Vladimir Zhukov. I come from St Petersburg in Russia and am now living in your country."

"How long have you been here?"

"Five years.

"Do you like it here?"

The Russian nodded vigorously. "Yes, I do, sir."

"What work do you do here?"

The Russian paused before replying. "That is what I talk to you about, Mr Bullock. I am in security services."

"Do you want a job here?"

The Russian laughed briefly. "No, Mr Bullock, I have men who work for me. I give security services to other people," he gave a brief expansive gesture, "people like yourself. I employ Russian and Polish men. They are tough, reliable, honest and trust, er trust…"

"Trustworthy," suggested Bullock.

"Da, yes, trustworthy." He hurried on. "I offer very good price for my honest and trustworthy services. The men report to me and they do not try any funny business."

Bullock suppressed a smile. "And, are they all legally in New Zealand?"

Zhukov wiped his hand over his craggy features, glanced briefly at Bullock before looking away.

"I give you very good price for security services, Mr Bullock. And all with no trouble for you."

After some further negotiations, Bullock, deciding not to inquire into the legal status of Zhukov's employees, agreed to hire his services on a trial basis. The stony-faced, solidly-build men who accompanied Zhukov to the strip club the following week exhibited an agreeable degree of deference to Bullock and were soon able to show a high standard of efficiency in dealing with potential troublemakers. Zhukov was also able to offer additional services involving debt collection and the surreptitious gleaning of information on suspect clients in both clubs. The information was valuable, and Bullock was happy to pay as the decline in security problems and the flow of revenue and information all increased the turnover and profitability of his clubs.

Yet he was always haunted by his poor beginnings. The continual tension in the West Auckland state house where his impoverished mother, who'd been deserted by her husband, attempted to raise three troublesome children, and his high school where, as an academic underachiever, he'd felt that other students looked down on him. They rarely criticized him to his face, his athletic build being a sufficient deterrent, but the occasional sideways looks and snide comments had made their opinions clear.

His low level of academic achievement had often handicapped his relationships with his school's female students. His position as front row prop in the school's First XV rugby team attracted some girls, but on occasions when he'd tried to date the female prefects or other high achievers, they'd turned him down.

His strip club employment had done little to expand his romantic opportunities. His sexual needs had been well met, and his subsequent marriage to Maryanne had been a boost to his ego, but he still felt the need for reaffirmation, with the result that he'd indulged in regular extra-marital affairs; his wealth, good looks, and brash attitude endeared him particularly to women who'd had cosseted upbringings.

His increasing affluence had enabled him to create a lifestyle for his wife and two children that he had never enjoyed. However, he was always aware that his prosperity was founded on shifting sands. His expensive house was still heavily mortgaged, and his car and launch were leased. Although his businesses were showing a steady profit, his lifestyle was a constant drain and consequently Bullock's accountant had to bring all his skills into play to keep his substantial tax bill to a minimum. Other sources of revenue needed to be found.

Chapter 9

"Listen, tovarich, this man is one of my best clients. He pays what we are asking, and always on dot."

His companion smiled. "The dot," he corrected.

"You know what I mean, Gregory?"

"Yes, of course."

"That is enough, yes?"

"Yes, Vladimir."

"You think you are smart because you have qualifications at local university? I ask you again the question – how much big money have you made?"

"You know the answer, Vladimir. Finding good work is not easy for us, even with local qualifications."

"But for me you have right qualifications. Active NKVD service in Chechnya."

"And Georgia. Intimidation does not require too many brains. Just a strong stomach."

A cynical grunt made him turn his head.

"And you, Tony. What you think?"

Tony Foster as always, found the two East Europeans an intriguing pair. Vladimir Zhukov epitomised every cliché of the Russian gangster – large, loud and, after an excess of vodka, lugubrious. In spite of a murky past, forged papers had ensured his seamless entry into New Zealand followed by a recent granting of permanent residency. Over the ensuing months he had maintained an appropriate level of respectability and covered his tracks well. Gregory Atanashvilli, a native of Georgia, had joined the Russian army at a young age, and was ultimately recruited into the NKVD. When Premier Putin had sent his army into the Georgian cities of Abkhazia and South Ossetia, Gregory had been responsible for infiltrating Georgian Army intelligence and betraying a number of his fellow countrymen.

Whether or not his motivation for joining Zhukov in New Zealand was due to the post-war death threats against him was unclear. However, he and his partner in crime seemed to be finding their adopted country provided them with a fecund environment in which to ply their nefarious trade. They had both admitted to Tony that adapting their methods to work undetected in a small democracy with one of the lowest levels of corruption in the world had been a challenge. Nevertheless, in all countries there are opportunities for men prepared to carry out criminal activity for generous financial gain and New Zealand was no exception.

Tony had initially encountered Zhukov in an Auckland waterfront bar. A mate whom he'd met in Auckland's Mt Eden Prison, where they'd both done time for possession and distribution, had introduced him. Tony had found life as a full-time university student financially challenging and had sought to supplement his income by dealing in drugs. His initial success had made him cocky and careless, which had been his downfall.

Tony's solid build had attracted Zhukov who had asked him if he was interested in doing "a few little jobs for cash". He'd begun with debt collection that required little more than stand-over tactics and intimidation. The Russian paid promptly and well and although the subsequent jobs required an increasingly amount of ruthlessness, the financial rewards improved exponentially. Yet clearly this new assignment was moving to another level – in terms of risk and money.

"Tony!"

Tony blinked and met Zhukov's glare.

"To you I am talking."

"Yea, sorry Vladimir, miles away."

"Miles away?"

"I mean that I was thinking about some other things, but now…."

"You have how you say, the cold feet?" The Russian's voice was hard.

"No," responded Tony shifting uneasily. "No, of course not. The target has been identified, the money's guaranteed, and the plan looks fool proof. I'm up for it."

"*Da*." Zhukov relaxed his craggy features, tapped a cigarette on the back of a pack of Camels, placed it between his lips and lit it with the flame of a Zippo lighter. He inhaled and blew a long thin stream of smoke in Tony's direction. "Loyalty to me is always well rewarded. Betrayal or failure..."

"Yes, Vladimir, you've said so many times and I understand."

"Good."

The big Russian grunted, opened the folder on his mahogany desk and leaned forward in his high-backed leather chair.

"Now to business. Come, look."

The two men pulled up chairs as Zhukov extracted several 8 x10 coloured photographs from the folder and placed them on the table. He stabbed a nicotine-stained forefinger on the middle photograph. "Your target. Here. Name, age, occupation, address and any other information are written down. I have made same copies of all."

"Duplicates, Vladimir."

"Da, Gregory, as you say, 'duplicates'."

"When do you want—?" began Tony.

Zhukov held up his hand.

"Wait. You are to do nothing without first talking to me. You will observe the target over next two weeks. You are not to be seen and not to be heard. Yes?"

"I understand."

Zhukov grunted and, fixing his eyes on Tony, leaned forward. Unhurriedly, he took two final drags on his cigarette and thrust it into an overflowing ashtray.

"Tony."

"Yes, Vladimir?"

Tony always had difficulty maintaining a calm outward appearance when the Russian addressed him directly. Aware that the man's constant exuberant show of affability masked an instinctive brutality he was always on edge as he strove to provide the appropriate responses to Zhukov's questions.

"Yours is more difficult job. First you must study information carefully."

Tony nodded, meeting the Russian's direct gaze.

"You have any questions?"

Tony hesitated as a siren emerged from the noise of the traffic that drifted from Karangahape Road up to the second-floor office.

"I'll study the information, and come up with a plan as you ask." He hesitated. "I do have two questions."

"Yes?"

"Firstly, do you want me to come up with a budget?"

To his surprise the big Russian threw his head back. His bellow of laughter echoed round the office.

"A budget. Have I not told you that our client is very rich man? Anything you need, it will be paid for. Yes?"

"Yes, of course, Vladimir." He flushed with anger at his own naivety. He should have realised that money would not be an issue, but he had always had a hard job shaking off his previous years of hard graft for limited reward – which is why he'd started dealing in drugs, resulting in a stretch inside.

Zhukov lit another cigarette.

"You had second question?"

"Yes." He hesitated. "You haven't really explained—"

"Explained what?"

Another stream of smoke was directed at him but turning his head to one side he went on.

"Explained the object of this job. The target – what's the point?"

"The point?"

"I think, Vladimir, that he's asking about what is going to happen to the target," said Gregory.

The big Russian's smile contained no hint of mirth.

38

"Are you with us one hundred per cent, Tony?"

"Yes, Vladimir, of course. I am only asking."

"Excellent. From now on, Tony," the end of his cigarette glowed in response to his long drag, "from now on the only questions that you ask me or Gregory are questions that you need to know to do your job. No other questions."

Tony met the man's gaze with difficulty.

"No other questions," Zhukov repeated. "I am making myself clear, yes?"

"Yes, Vladimir. Perfectly clear."

"Good. We have additional information on target that I give to you. Wait here."

He jerked his head at Gregory and the two men left the office.

Tony gave a long sigh, closed his eyes and stretched out his legs. The money was good, but Christ, dealing with Zhukov was bloody stressful. He opened his eyes and looked round the large office. The walls were bare except for two large paintings of young women mounted opposite Zhukov's desk. Gregory had informed him that they were Russian originals from the Soviet era. One was of an attractive woman with short dark hair, sitting naked and cross-legged on a couch, knitting with a skein of yellow wool. Her body was partially concealed by the knitting that was held level with her left breast. Her expression was one of deep concentration seemingly oblivious to anything other than her knitting.

The other showed a woman younger and prettier than the knitter. She was seated sideways, looking directly at the viewer, seemingly aware that she was being observed. Her back was naked, its contours highlighted by gentle patches of light, and her breasts partially covered by a blanket held in place with her left hand. What intrigued Tony was her expression of complete indifference. It always put him in mind of the lyrics of Mean Woman Blues made famous by Elvis Presley.

'She makes love without a smile.

Ooh, hot dog, that drives me wild.'

The door swung open and Zhukov, followed by Gregory, entered. He moved his eyes swiftly from Tony's face to the paintings and gave a knowing smile.

"You not get lonely, Tony?"

Tony felt his face redden as he quickly replied, "No, Vladimir."

The big man chuckled mirthlessly and handed Tony an envelope.

"More details of your target and location. Keep them safe."

"He means the details, not the target, of course," grinned Gregory.

Ignoring Zhukov's puzzled look Tony gave a weak smile, stood up, took the envelope and with a nod of thanks, left the room.

Chapter 10

"Hi, I'm Jason Collins."

The firmness of the man's grasp matched his strong build.

"Hi. Tony Foster."

"I'll be taking you on your trial flight, Tony. Special occasion is it?"

"Special occasion?"

"It's just that people often take these flights to celebrate a birthday or something," smiled Collins.

"Oh, I see." The man laughed nervously. "No, it's just something I've always wanted to do, so thought I'd give it a go."

"You thinking of taking up flying?"

"Yes, could do. We'll see how we go today."

"Of course." He glanced out the window of the aero club. "Certainly a beautiful day for it. Been flying before?"

"Only a couple of Air New Zealand trips to Australia."

"Today it'll be a little different," smiled Collins, "but I'm sure you'll enjoy it. Excuse me a moment while I just fill in the details and collect our helmets."

Tony had driven up to the aerodrome an hour before the appointed time and watched the planes taking off and landing. He was surprised at the amount of noise they made and concerned at their relatively small size. He hadn't given it much thought, but then he'd never imagined that he'd ever be flying in a light two-seater aircraft. He'd had two trips with the family to Australia and he still remembered his older brother Ian's jeering remarks when, in a weak moment, he'd confessed that he felt scared at the prospect of flying. When Ian had immediately told his parents, they had expressed surprise. His mother had assured him that he'd be fine and that he could sit next to her on the plane. By contrast his father had told him not be "a bloody girl" and that he should be "bloody grateful considering the amount of bloody money it was bloody costing to fly him to Surfers

Paradise". After that he kept his fears to himself but even now he could still remember the film of sweat that had seeped out across his skin when the big jet had lifted skywards.

He heaved a long sigh. Now he was required to fly in a tiny, noisy aircraft and attempt to befriend the instructor at the same time; Christ, the last bloody thing he'd imagined he'd have to do.

"Here's your helmet, Tony. It has a microphone built into it."

Tony turned the helmet over in his hands. "Why?"

"It's too noisy inside the cockpit for us to hear each other."

The palms of Tony's hands moistened as he nodded his understanding.

Collins turned towards the door. "So, Tony, let's go and do the pre-flight and then we'll take off."

"Hi Jason."

Both men paused and turned at the sound of the woman's voice. As she stepped forward and went on tiptoe to plant a kiss on Collins' cheek, Tony took in the details of her long legs, small waist and well-rounded breasts.

"Fleur, this is Tony. I'm taking him up for a trial flight."

"Hi, Tony." She held out her hand. "You'll enjoy it." Her eyes flicked momentarily at Collins. "He's certainly a man who knows what he's doing."

The combination of the woman's attractiveness and his apprehension at the forthcoming flight resulted in Tony only managing to smile and nod as he took her soft hand.

She smiled up at him. "Have a good flight." She turned to Collins. "I'll still be here, upstairs in the clubhouse."

He touched her arm before turning to Tony.

"OK, Tony, let's go."

They crossed the tarmac, passing several small Robin aircraft being inspected.

"We have a number of these Robins. They're a popular aircraft for beginning and recreational pilots. Easy to fly and easy to maintain."

"Easy to fly?"

"Well, once you know how, of course," smiled Collins as he waved to a pilot who was about to clamber into the cockpit of an adjacent blue Robin. "There's ours just ahead."

The plane that he indicated was red with the identification TZG prominently displayed on its fuselage.

"Before we take off there are a number of safety checks that we have to undertake.

"Safety checks?" asked Tony quickly.

"Yes. Safety is a number one priority in flying. These checks are done prior to any take off, just as there are also safety procedures which have to be done prior to landing."

Watching Collins as he walked round the plane carefully checking the rudders, ailerons, propeller, inlets, oil and fuel levels made Tony feel marginally calmer. However, his feelings of foreboding increased when in response to Collins' instructions he gingerly climbed up onto the wing, lowered himself into the seat on the left side of the small cabin and fitted on his helmet. When Collins sat down in the adjacent seat and pulled the cockpit roof shut, the confining environment increased his apprehension and he was hardly aware of the pilot's voice in his helmet outlining the interior pre-flight procedures. When, with a noisy roar, the engine fired and the propeller commenced whirring, he clamped his hands together, trying to suppress their twitching.

"Do you want to see anything special?" Collins' voice crackled in his headphones above the noise of the Robin as it taxied towards the take off point.

Tony turned towards Collins and shook his head, but realising that the other man was concentrating on taxiing the plane, made an effort to calm himself and replied, "Not really. Just sort of fly around."

"Sure," he responded. "It's a great day so we'll fly east over the peninsula and then over the sea towards Rangitoto Island. It's a favourite spot on introductory flights."

The noisy, rattling take-off down the runway tested the limits of Tony's self-control. Having reached the required height, the Robin levelled off and Tony, his hands gripped tightly together, made a conscious effort to take a series of slow deep breaths.

"You OK?" asked Collins.

"Yes."

"Heard your deep breathing through the headphones. Are you trying—?"

Concentrating on keeping his voice steady, Tony responded, "Just getting used to this confined space in a small noisy plane, that's all."

Collins laughed. "A common reaction. It's totally different from being a passenger on a big jet aircraft."

Tony smiled wryly. "That's for sure." Realising that he'd been hunched forward against the safety straps from the time they'd sped down the runway, he made an attempt to lean back and settle himself into the seat.

"Look to your left. That's where we're heading."

To the aircraft's left the iconic shape of Rangitoto Island nestled in the glistening waters of the Waitemata Harbour. The spectacular aerial perspective was unique to him.

"Quite a view," he murmured.

"That's what we're up here for. We'll cruise above and around the island and then head south towards the city."

While Collins was updating his position to the control tower Tony's eyes took in the stunning harbour vista. For a few moments he forgot his fear, but a sudden downwards lurch snapped him back to reality.

"Christ!"

"It's OK, just an air pocket," chuckled Jason. "Very common."

"Do you get used to them?"

"Yeah. All part of the pleasure of flying."

44

Tony made another effort to relax and reminded himself he was on a job and that Zhukov would want a progress update.

"So, air pockets are OK. What about wind, rain and other natural factors?"

"If the weather looks doubtful, if there's too much cloud cover for example, then we won't take off. Safety is always a priority."

"On a longer trip the weather could change."

"True. If it became threatening, we'd contact the nearest airfield and request an emergency landing."

"What about mechanical failure?"

"Mechanical failure is unlikely to occur without some sort of warning. If it does happen, same procedure – request the nearest emergency landing."

The little plane momentarily sank in response to another air pocket and it was a few moments before Tony was able to frame his next question.

"But there are plenty of air accidents, aren't there? I'm always reading about—."

"There are far more car accidents than air accidents. In fact, flying is a lot safer than driving. Any fool can get a car licence but a pilot needs hours of training to fly even a small plane like this. I get tired of people who go on about air accidents without knowing the first thing—"

Sensing the pilot's rising annoyance Tony cut in quickly.

"OK, OK, I'm sure you're right. I suppose air accidents look more spectacular on the TV and in the papers."

"Course they do. And it's silly bloody reporters looking for an easy story that are always eager to feature them. Makes me sick."

Tony felt his nervousness increasing rapidly. It was bad enough being cramped up in this noisy little plane without having the pilot losing his cool.

"You're right, of course, er, Jason. I completely agree with you. And, and I'm enjoying the flight."

"Good," replied the pilot, with a touch of sarcasm. "That's what we're up here for."

"Of course"

The minor outburst gave Tony a chance to evaluate the man and his character – touchy bastard who was quick to anger, even when dealing with a paying passenger. At their first meeting Tony initially had few reservations about his target – a warm, friendly welcoming guy. Now, having been on the receiving end of a flash of temper, his reservations had begun to increase. But he'd need to proceed with caution if he were going to cultivate and snare his prey.

He cleared his throat.

"It must be wonderful to fly over views like this every day. I'm sure it never loses its thrill."

"Well, I've done it a few times." The pilot laughed coarsely. "Of course there are other thrills that come with the job."

He was obviously expecting a query in response and Tony took his cue.

"Other thrills?"

"Not all the passengers I take up are males. Women also enjoy a little joyriding, or to be taken on a flight of fancy by a man in a uniform."

"And plenty of experience," responded Tony, obediently.

"Of course. I'm a very experienced pilot so I'm capable of dealing with all that Mother Nature can throw at me, and, of course, Mother Nature's daughters."

Collins' cynical laugh was becoming irritating, but Tony echoed it.

"Sounds like your job provides a regular stream of sexual opportunities," he said endeavouring to sound envious.

"For sure. Being a pilot gives me heaps of charisma, and if opportunity knocks then who am I not to answer the door?"

By this time the flight had reached Auckland city where they circled over the harbour bridge and then turned north.

"Sorry, Tony, have to return to base. Your time's up, as the actress said to the bishop."

Tony hoped he'd managed to mask his cringing reaction with the requisite laugh. "This guy's a piece of work," he thought.

"Been a great experience, Jason. I was a bit diffident at first but I think I'd like to try it again."

"That's great. Among my many talents is that of flying instructor. You might consider flying lessons."

Tony felt his stomach tighten and hoped his voice remained steady as he replied, "Yes, I'll certainly think about it."

Chapter 11

"An arrogant prick – completely full of himself. The way he talks you'd think he flies supersonic jets around the world instead of a tinny, noisy little two-seaters that are like Ladas with wings. And he sees himself as the great seducer, scoring with women on a regular basis as they swoon at the feet of the handsome aviator."

"Swoon? What is that?" Zhukov's irritation was a reminder to Tony that he had to confine his English to a relatively simple vocabulary in the presence of his paymaster.

"Ladies who think a man is wonderful and will do anything for him," responded Gregory – ever eager to take on the role of interpreter.

The big Russian grunted his comprehension. "So Jason Collins has a weakness for the women." He clapped his big hands together. "Good! Good for me! Good for you, Tony! More vodka?"

"Thank you, Vladimir."

He would have much preferred a light Kiwi pilsner, but he could do without the withering scorn that that would have elicited.

The Russian, removing the ubiquitous cigarette from his lips, leaned forward expectantly. "So, what is your move, next?"

"I need to win his confidence."

Zhukov frowned and Tony moved on quickly before Gregory could interrupt.

"I need to become better friends with him. I need to make him trust me, to think that I am his friend."

Zhukov grunted his understanding.

"You do not like the flying?"

"It's OK, Vladimir, I can hack it." The Russian frowned and he hastily clarified it with, "I do not like it but I will do it. Once Jason Collins trusts me, I can make my move."

"OK. But do not take too long. My time not…"

He paused at glanced at Gregory.

"Unlimited," offered Tony quickly.

The big Russian smiled and nodded.

"Da. unlimited." He looked at Gregory. "The young Kiwi man is getting as good as you, tovarich."

The Georgian's smile was thin.

"So I'd like to arrange another trip tomorrow afternoon. I think he's hoping that I might be interested in taking flying lessons."

"Flying lessons? You?"

"Yes, Vladimir. If he thinks I'm keen he'll keep being friendly towards me."

"Play him like fish, da," smiled Zhukov, pleased to display his knowledge of an English colloquialism. "Good idea."

Tony nodded and managed a smile. The thought of another flight in the noisy little aircraft gave him no pleasure, but the lure of the financial rewards was strong.

He picked up his cell phone and pressed the indented button at the base. He saw the two Eastern Europeans regard him quizzically, but ignoring them he said, "Phone Jason Collins."

"Calling Jason Collins," responded Siri's female voice.

The call was quickly answered and, still ignoring the watching pair, he arranged a flying lesson for the late afternoon.

"A man of action, no?"

"Just carrying out instructions like you said, Vladimir." Tony stood up. "Now, if you'll excuse me, I have to go. I'll be in touch tomorrow."

He nodded to both men and left the room.

Exiting the building he made for a nearby coffee house. He ordered a long black, and taking it to a corner table, slumped into his seat. His hands were shaking slightly but several mouthfuls helped to steady him. It had taken all his self-control to phone Collins without first asking Zhukov. It was fortunate that the pilot had a spare slot the following day, enabling him to make the arrangement quickly and efficiently, and keeping his cool when taking his leave. His action hadn't been premeditated but he now realised that he'd taken the initiative as a reaction against Zhukov's domination. He wasn't trying to anger the Russian, but he had felt the need to assert himself. Hopefully the man would now have more confidence in him.

He took another mouthful of the strong black liquid. "Hopefully," he muttered to himself.

Chapter 12

"Hullo, Tony, you here for a lesson with Jason?"

At the sound of the woman's voice he turned. She was as attractive as he remembered.

"Oh, hi, er Fleur, isn't it?"

She smiled an affirmation.

"Yes. Jason's a bit behind time. One of his pupils was running late. He's still in the air."

"Oh."

She interpreted his temporary relief for disappointment.

"Tell you what, why don't we go up to the lounge for a coffee? We can watch him land."

Nodding, he stepped aside to let her precede him up the stairs, enjoying the bonus of an uninterrupted view of her shapely legs.

"Here we are. How do you like yours?"

"Black, thanks. I'll get—"

"Next time," she smiled. She turned to the young woman behind the bar. "Two black coffees thanks, Jenny."

They sat down at a table from where they could see the runway.

"So, what are you—?"

He tailed off uncertainly and she laughed.

"What am I doing here?"

"Well, yes. Have you been flying today?"

"No, not today." A momentary frown before she continued brightly, "I love watching the planes and Jason said he was finishing early today so I drove out."

"Sorry, my fault. I took that final slot."

"No problem," she shrugged. "Are you enjoying flying?"

"I think so. It's certainly challenging." Seeking to divert the conversation from himself he asked, "What about you? Do you enjoy having Jason as your instructor?"

Her answer was a shade too quick.

"Oh, yes, of course. He's very patient and understanding." She paused. "As long as…"

"As what?"

"Well it's not really a criticism, but you have to do things his way."

He feigned surprise.

"Really? In what way?"

"Up in the air I accept that he's in charge, for safety's sake and all that. Back on the ground he still tries to continue the role, and—."

The noise of a plane touching down interrupted her.

"Oh, it's probably Jason."

"Ah."

She looked directly at him and he could see a hint of vulnerability in her eyes. "Look, Tony, what I just said—"

He touched her lightly on the arm and smiled. "You can trust me. Shan't breathe a word."

Her smile was warm as she squeezed his arm. "Thanks."

He followed her down the stairs in time to see Collins and a pretty young woman climbing out of the cockpit of a Robin. He noted the friendly way Collins chatted to her as they both walked towards the clubhouse. Perhaps that was for the benefit of the club executive members, or perhaps a clumsy attempt to demonstrate his imagined legendary charm with the female sex. Tony ventured a quick glance at Fleur and registered the transformation of her face from an irritated frown to a beaming smile, timed to greet Collins as he entered the door.

"Hullo, darling! Have a good flight?"

Grasping him by the shoulders she tilted her face and kissed his lips. Taken aback he glanced quickly at his female companion, recovered himself, and with a smile that matched Fleur's, touched her arm.

"Sandy, I'd like you to meet Fleur."

Fleur directed her beam at the attractive young woman.

"Your first time, Sandy?" she queried archly.

Somewhat overcome by the warmth of Fleur's greeting, Sandy replied, "Ah, yes. I met Jason through a friend, and he asked me if I'd like to take a flight with him." She looked quickly at Collins and back at Fleur. "That's alright isn't it?"

"Of course it is, Sandy. Jason loves to encourage young people to fly. He's been flying for years and feels he has so much to offer at his age."

Collins' interruption was abrupt. "Now, Sandy, come with me please for our post-flight briefing." Taking her firmly by the arm he led her towards a small room opposite the reception area. "Won't be a moment, Tony."

"Bastard." Fleur's voice was barely audible.

Tony turned towards her. He touched her arm. "Let's get some air."

Without protesting, she let him guide her outside the entrance to the car park where she joined him on a bench under a tree. He looked at her for a moment, realising that she was on the verge of tears. She was certainly very attractive, but he knew that to pursue a relationship would be a dangerous game on several levels. However, her temporary vulnerability, and the possibilities that could be opened up motivated him to continue.

"Are you in love with him?" He paused. "Sorry to be—"

"It's alright. I thought I was, as he can be very charming. But deep down his attitude to women is positively medieval. He demands loyalty but still wants to play the role of the great lover." She grunted. "Ageing Lothario, more like, particularly with young women." Her foot kicked out, scattering small stones. "Christ, what a bloody mess!"

"So what do you think you'll—"

"Oh, I'll keep having flying lessons. Oh yes, indeed. And if he puts a foot wrong in the air or on the ground, I'll report him." Her smile was grim. "He's already got himself into trouble around here. He needs to tread very carefully."

"Really?"

"Yes. I'll tell you about it some time."

The sound of footsteps made them turn.

"Fleur, darling. I'm sorry about that. A misunderstanding. The young woman was feeling a little upset after the flight and I needed to—"

Fleur was on her feet in an instant. "Don't be silly, darling. There's no problem."

He matched the warmth of her smile and turned to Tony.

"Sorry to keep you waiting, Tony. There's still plenty of light. Shall we go?" The smile and the voice, though brimming with warmth, did not disguise the sharp edge.

Taking a deep breath Tony replied, "Ready when you are." He turned. "See you again, Fleur."

"Yes, of course," she smiled winningly, ignoring Collins' feeble attempt to mask his annoyance. "Have a good flight, darling."

"Thanks," was the grunted response. "Let's go, Tony."

Fleur, watching them walk back towards the clubhouse, was unaware of the footsteps that approached her.

"Hullo, Fleur. Thought I'd find you here."

She spun round.

"Hullo, Matt," she said.

Chapter 13

"That's it, Tony," came Collins' voice through the headphones. "You're getting the hang of it."

"Never realised planes were steered by foot pedals," replied Tony, striving to keep the tension out of his voice. "Always thought you just opened the throttle and used a joystick or something."

"Most people do," replied Collins. "However, you're a fast learner."

Tony grunted a response. Although tense, he found that actually having to steer the plane as it taxied towards the runway gave him something to concentrate on, thereby lowering his stress level. He'd always fancied himself as a slick car driver and although the plane was noisy and clumsy by comparison, there were similarities.

This was his third lesson and his first attempt at a take-off. Collins had briefed him carefully, assuring Tony that should anything go wrong he would immediately take over the controls.

Having carefully manoeuvred the aircraft into position, Tony swallowed hard and looked inquiringly at the pilot.

Collins went through the control tower notification procedure and then addressed Tony.

"OK, now open the throttle and the plane will start to move forward. Then open it right out like you've seen me do."

Taking a deep breath, Tony pulled the throttle towards him. The engine revved loudly and the plane started to shake.

"Feed it some more."

Tony pulled further and the plane, in response to the increased fuel flow, began to move forward down the runway, rapidly gathering speed. Seeing it beginning to veer right Tony pushed down hard on the left pedal, which promptly swung the aircraft to the left.

"Easy. Don't thrust so hard."

With intense concentration Tony managed to adapt the plane's direction with his pedal pressure while at the same time watching the runway ahead as the speed increased.

"Now, ease back on the stick."

As Tony pulled the joystick back the plane lifted slowly off the runway and began an upward climb.

"Well done!"

"Thanks. That wasn't easy."

"But you did it. Now relax for a minute or so while I take it up to 1,000 feet and settle it into a straight and level position."

Tony thankfully relinquished the controls to the older man and admired the way Collins quickly manipulated the aircraft into the required position.

"Straight and level," said Collins, touching the instrument panel. "That instrument is the Attitude Indicator, or Artificial Horizon." He indicated a horizontal line that didn't move. "That line represents the horizon" He pointed to a line that was shifting slightly up and down. "The other line shows our aircraft's relationship to it. If they both match it means we're…" he looked inquiringly at Tony.

"Straight and level, I suppose," responded Tony.

"Well done," Collins smiled. "I'll fly for a little bit longer and then you can take over."

Tony nodded. Although fairly keen to extend his take-off success with further opportunities to use the controls, he was also feeling mildly nauseous after the effort of taking the aircraft off the tarmac.

"Fleur."

"Pardon?" said Tony.

"Fleur. The woman I introduced you to a couple of weeks ago and who you met again just before we took off."

"Yes, of course." Sensing the chance to glean some more personal information he looked at Collins and smiled warmly. "Attractive woman. How did you meet her?"

"She turned up accompanying a young guy who wanted to learn to fly. I took a chance and asked her to go flying with me."

"And?"

"She did. I then took her out to dinner." His smile verged on a leer. "You could say that one thing..."

"Led to another?"

"It did."

"So you're now an item?"

"I think so."

"Think?"

"Well, she's the jealous type. You might have noticed her annoyance that I was chatting warmly with my new pupil Sandy."

"Another attractive woman," replied Tony.

"In this business it's an occupational hazard."

"Fleur did seem a bit upset, but tried not to show it. But I – God!"

The plane had suddenly dropped briefly causing Tony to gasp audibly.

"Air pocket."

"Of course."

"Don't worry, you'll get used to them. Now what were you saying about Fleur being upset?"

Tony was making a desperate effort to keep down the contents of his stomach. Just when he thought he had gained control of himself the bloody plane had started to drop out of the sky. How the hell was anyone—?

"Tony, you were saying?"

The voice in the headphones had an edge to it, bringing Tony back to reality. He took three long deep breaths and tried to keep his reply steady.

"Sorry. Still getting used to the unexpected lurches."

"Yes?" was the impatient response.

"Well, all I said was that Fleur seemed annoyed at the attention you were paying to Sandy, but at the same time trying to mask it."

"So what do you make of it?"

"Me? I hardly know her. I was just making a comment."

"Which is quite insightful. Did you get the impression she was upset but she didn't want to make me angry?"

"That's pretty much sums it up."

"OK." Collins' voice had finality to it and sensing that he could be missing out on further insight, Tony quickly attempted to re-ignite the conversation.

"So we agree about Fleur's feelings. But what about any long-term plans? Are you genuinely interested in her or is she just another flying trophy?"

"You certainly have a way with words," smiled Collins.

"So?"

"I'm not sure. She's bloody attractive, good company, great in bed but I'm not entirely—"

"Three good reasons. Many a guy would be—"

"More than happy. I know. When we land, I'll track her down and make things right between us."

"Sounds good. Keep me posted."

"Why this interest in my love life?"

"No particular reason," responded Tony quickly, "but you introduced the subject."

"Fair enough. Now, you're here to learn to fly. Let's see if you can maintain straight and level."

"Straight and level," murmured Tony tightening his grip on the stick.

Chapter 14

Matt shifted awkwardly and looked down.

"I had to see you. I don't understand what went wrong between us." His voice began to rise, and she looked quickly around the car park.

"All I know is that I love you Fleur and—"

"Matt, stop." Her smile was warm, but he winced as she gripped his arm. "My car's over there. Come on."

Turning away from him she strode rapidly towards her car, beeped it open and then settled herself in the driver's seat.

Matt, quickly sliding in alongside her, opened his mouth but she cut him off.

"I warn you now, Matt, if we can't have a reasonable, adult conversation then I'll get straight out of the car and leave you to it."

"Yes, of course, Fleur." He placed his hand tentatively on her arm and, encouraged that she let it stay there, he continued rapidly. "Fleur, if any of this is my fault, then I apologise now. Please let me explain."

She smiled, nodding encouragingly. Still simmering from the sight of Collins dancing in attendance on the little bimbo, she had to admit that Matt was a handsome lad. Yes, the game had elements of danger but on the other hand she'd never rejected a challenge, particularly where sexual relations were involved.

"Fleur, did you hear what I said?" His voice was harsh with desperation.

"Of course," she smiled coyly, "but I'm not sure what you mean exactly."

"I asked if we could get back together again. I'll do anything you ask as long as you agree that we have an exclusive relationship."

He watched her with a puppy dog expression that made her inwardly cringe. However, adventure called, and, with a winning smile she placed her hand over his.

"You're right, Matt, darling. I'd love to start again."

"Oh, Fleur!" His joyful response was followed immediately by a clumsy attempt to kiss her passionately. Pushing him firmly away and maintaining her smile with difficulty, she responded, "Steady, Matt, not here. I need to freshen up, then I'll come back to the car and you can follow me."

"Follow you?"

"Yes, back to my place."

Chapter 15

The early morning sun gently caressing the waves and sand on Takapuna Beach cast a welcome calmness over Fleur as she sat on a grass mound gazing across the waters at cone-shaped Rangitoto Island. Her family home had been in central Takapuna and as a child she had often played on the beach and swum in the waters of the Waitemata Harbour. The beach's tranquillity and its comparative safety had made it a popular spot with people of all ages. However, this early hour on a Monday morning meant there were only a handful of joggers participating in their daily exercise before heading off to work, and a few elderly strollers enjoying the increased leisure retirement brings.

Fleur had insisted Matt leave early, making her point by noisily rising from beside his sleeping form at 5.30 and making him bacon, eggs and coffee – on the assumption that at his age his carnal appetite was matched by one requiring ample quantities of solid food. This was confirmed by his enthusiastic demolition of every morsel with the added bonus of making him relatively compliant when she instructed him to leave. Anticipating some reluctance on his part she embellished her farewells with promises of meeting up later in the week, and following the obligatory lingering kiss, waved him on his way with a sigh of relief.

Seeking solace in a tranquil environment she left the house, walked through the comparatively deserted Takapuna shopping centre, and found a grassy bank on the edge of the sand under the shelter of a large pohutukawa tree.

Matt and the other men in her life – she sighed deeply. As she'd done so often since her teenage years, she reviewed the key events in her mind that had led to her current situation.

The conversation she'd heard fifteen years ago between Sarah Williamson and Tania Sanders had, in her mind, been the beginning. Sitting in front of them on a bank overlooking the school sports field she'd caught details of a tense discussion concerning Mr Long, the school caretaker. His office was set in a corner of the school, and, from what she could gather, the girls had visited him from time to time where he'd rewarded them with sweets and money. Clearly the initial visitations, which had begun with a few cuddles on Long's knee, had begun to reach a worrying level, as his hands were now wandering inside their clothing and touching them intimately.

Fleur had remained absolutely still as the conversation unfolded. The parallel to her father's behaviour was unmistakable. The previous year, when she turned thirteen, he had begun to encourage her to sit on his knee in his study and had caressed her with increasing intimacy. He was a tall handsome man, quick witted and popular among a wide circle of friends. However, during her childhood, whenever she sought his help or approval his response was frequently curt and impatient. Consequently, although uncomfortable with his new behaviour, particularly when he told her that it was 'our secret', she felt grateful for this attention from the man from whom she craved love and approval.

Clearly the two girls on the bank were increasingly concerned about Mr Long's behaviour, recognising it as being unacceptable. With growing unease Fleur listened as they discussed their options, finally deciding that they would both inform their mothers that night.

The following Monday, as she was arriving early for a pre-school netball practice, a police car had passed her on the school driveway, heading out of the gates. In the back seat, accompanied by a uniformed officer, was Mr Long.

Shaken by the sight she quickly realised the complexity of her own situation. That her father's behaviour could result in police involvement was a shocking revelation. To inform on him could make her the direct cause of his arrest and possible imprisonment, an action that she could never take as the loss of her father was unthinkable.

The issue was further compounded when Mr Long went on trial and was sentenced to a jail term. It transpired that Sarah and Tania were not his only victims – that he'd been using his position at the school to entice young women into his office over several years. His behaviour was the subject of considerable gossip among the students, with both boys and girls taking the opportunity to contrive coarse humour involving word plays on 'care' and 'taker'. Fleur listened intently to all the comments but ventured no opinion, terrified that a careless word on her part could result in an investigation of her own family situation.

The weeks that followed were intolerable for her. Apart from the times when he was away on business trips her father's behaviour continued. When next her father suggested another 'dad and daughter chat' in his study her initial response was reluctance, but the anger of his response frightened her into submission and resulted in her contriving a mask of enjoyment at his advances. Increasingly she had difficulty concentrating on her homework and sleeping at night. At school where she'd always been a bright student, her inattention and negative behaviour patterns were now bringing her into conflict with her teachers. Although she continued to receive high grades in English, always her best subject, her teachers were disturbed by the increasingly bleak and introverted content of her creative writing.

Her father's threatening attitude prevented her from sharing her growing concerns with her mother. Fleur also realised that her mother could either refuse to believe her or could directly confront her husband. Her parents' marriage was characterised by frequent backbiting and snide remarks and consequently she had no way of predicting a positive outcome if she had sought her mother's help.

The knowledge that her father's behaviour was criminal increasingly disturbed her. Finally, when she reached the age of sixteen, she summoned up enough courage to tell him that he should stop. Surprisingly he agreed once she had given her assurance that it would remain 'our secret'. Although greatly relieved by his compliance she was acutely disappointed that as a result of their agreement her father's attitude towards her abruptly became one of complete indifference to any aspect of her life.

Early in her teens she had realised that she was attractive but had resisted the clumsy attempts of her male classmates to form any sort of relationship. Not long after her seventeenth birthday she had agreed to go to the school ball with the captain of the first XV rugby team – not only was he good-looking but also his position in the school enhanced her prestige with the other girls.

After the ball they'd parked up and engaged in some heavy petting. She had enjoyed it but had made a deliberate effort to encase her true emotions in a circle of indifference. As the boy became increasingly aroused, she realised that it was she who had the power to decide how far things would go, and providing that she continued to encase her emotions, she remained in control.

It was from this point on that she decided to continue to enjoy the sexual opportunities that frequently came her way, while at the same time maintaining control over the men who provided them. She had long ago decided that amateur psychologists would classify her behaviour as springing from a need to revenge herself on the male of the species for the behaviour of her father, but the grim satisfaction that she derived from the encounters had encouraged her to continue.

However, new factors were now in play. While maintaining a mask of indifference she realised that she'd been genuinely hurt by Collins' behaviour with Sandy. Furthermore, she was now aware that exploiting Matt's canine-like devotion to her was a game from which she derived diminishing pleasure. Yet she felt increasingly uneasy as to possible consequences that could result if she attempted to terminate the relationship.

A twig fell from the pohutukawa tree and landed on her knee. Idly she picked it up and began to strip the tiny leaves from the stem. The soft murmur of two voices caused her to look to her right. A young couple, holding hands and oblivious to their surroundings, walked slowly past her. A few metres further on they slowed and stopped briefly as the man kissed the woman's forehead before resuming their romantic perambulation.

Fleur gazed after their retreating figures for a few moments. Suddenly she snapped the twig in half, rose abruptly and strode in the direction of her home.

Chapter 16

Matt pulled up in front of the clubhouse, switched off the motor and sat breathing deeply as he watched a Robin coming in for a landing. Memories of his own botched landing filled his thoughts but after a lengthy phone conversation with Chris Winstone, it was agreed that he could attempt another solo flight – his previous attempt being deemed unsatisfactory. At Winstone's insistence he had selected a day when Collins would be absent from the airfield, thereby minimising any chance of a confrontation.

He would have liked Fleur to come but she pleaded a prior commitment. Initially he'd suspected that Fleur preferred not to be there, but quickly dismissed the thought. Her assurance that she'd be thinking of him enabled him to rationalise his position as being ideal – no Collins, no Fleur, just himself, drawing on his own abilities.

He closed the car door and strode resolutely towards the clubhouse.

"Hi, Matt."

The General Manager was standing in the doorway.

"Hi, Chris.

"All set to go?"

"Sure." He made an effort to smile confidently.

"Excellent. You're not scheduled to start for another fifteen minutes. Suggest you grab a coffee and I'll come and get you for the pre-flight."

"Sure," he replied and turned towards the stairs. A coffee and an opportunity to watch other planes going through the touch and go procedure could help him relax.

The lounge was almost deserted, except for a young woman pouring herself a coffee from the large Perspex pot that was available when the bar staff were off duty.

Vaguely noting that she was attractive, he nodded as he reached for the pot and gave her an obligatory "Hi".

"Hi." Her smile was warm. "You flying today?"

Although not feeling particularly talkative, common courtesy required a response.

"Yes. In about fifteen minutes. A solo circuit."

Her eyebrows shot up and she unashamedly looked him over. "Solo. That's pretty impressive at your age."

He gave a self-deprecating smile. "I had my first solo a week ago. It wasn't particularly impressive."

"So you're trying again. Good for you." She paused. " I've had four flying lessons so far."

"You enjoyed them?"

"Pretty awesome most of the time."

She paused. "Can be a bit scary, can't it?"

He sensed that her last sentence was designed to seek assurance.

"Yes, it can be. But if you persevere and listen to your instructor then it will become easier."

"Yes, that's what Jason keeps telling me."

"Jason." The sharpness of his response was instinctive.

Looking a little surprised she asked, "Do you know him?"

"Yes, he's been my instructor for all of my flying lessons."

He'd made an effort to keep his tone neutral, but the young woman had sensed his ambivalence.

"How did you find him?"

"He was sitting in the clubhouse," responded Matt.

She frowned for a moment and then laughed and touched his arm. "Very witty." She paused. "I think he's a good instructor although…"

"Although?"

She glanced quickly around. Despite the room being empty she lowered her voice. "He can be rather abrupt, you know, and he doesn't like his instructions being questioned." She paused uncertainly. "Or is that just me?"

"No it's not."

"That's a relief."

Not wishing to dwell on the subject, Matt touched her elbow and gently guided her in the direction of the chairs on the balcony that overlooked the runway.

"Let's watch the planes."

Her quick acceptance of his suggestion was accompanied by a warm smile that lit up a face framed by soft dark curls. Matt's pulse quickened, and as she was settling herself into the seat, he also noted the trimness of her figure.

She turned to him with a shy smile. "I'm Sandy, by the way."

"Matt."

She grinned. "Hi, Matt."

They sat in silence for several minutes watching the activities around the runway.

"Do you live locally, Sandy?"

"I share a flat with another girl in Mairangi Bay. It's a bit of a trip into the city each day, but I do love the east coast bays. Suburbia, with a permanent holiday atmosphere." There was a further silence and then she asked, "What about you?"

"Me?"

"Yes, do you live locally?"

"Sort of. St Heliers."

"Sounds pretty flash."

"Suppose so. It's my parents' place."

"You live at home?"

"Yes. I'm a uni student and it's cheaper, although…"

"Although?"

"Matt, time for your flight!"

They both turned to see Chris Winstone standing in the doorway.

Matt jumped up, clearly made nervous by the abrupt return to reality.

"Right. I'm coming."

As he started to move towards the door Sandy reached out and touched his wrist.

"Matt?"

He paused and looked down at her. "Yes?"

"Is it OK if I stay here and watch your flight?"

"Watch my flight? I suppose so. If you'd like to."

She smiled warmly. "And we could chat about it afterwards, perhaps."

He returned her smile. "Yes, why not."

Chapter 17

The wheels touched the tarmac, lifted off momentarily and then quickly re-settled as Matt throttled down and taxied the Robin into its parking position. The landing hadn't been perfect but compared to his earlier effort it was more than satisfactory.

His thoughts returned to Sandy. Whether or not she'd observed his take-off and landing from the balcony hadn't occurred to him at the time as he'd been determined to give the flight his full concentration. Now he'd landed he wondered if she'd bothered to stay.

"Not that it matters," he muttered to himself as he clambered out of the cockpit and on to the wing.

"Well done, Matt. A considerable improvement!"

Matt jumped down as Chris Winstone came striding out to meet him with outstretched hand.

"Thanks, Chris. I really concentrated this time."

"Obviously," Chris grinned. "Normally I'd offer to shout you a celebratory drink but," he cocked his head to one side and raised his eyebrows, "I believe that you may have a more attractive alternative."

Matt frowned.

"There." Chris pointed towards the clubhouse. "The young lady, at the gate. I think she'd be keen to down a celebratory glass or two. She and I watched your entire flight. Come on!"

Matt felt his heart rate increase as they walked briskly towards the airfield gate where Sandy was standing on the path, her smile radiating warmth and admiration. Matt had barely opened the gate when she stepped forward.

"Congratulations. Great take-off and landing."

Instinctively Matt reached out and gently grasped her right arm. "Thanks," he murmured.

For several seconds they both stood still. A discreet cough from behind caused Matt to drop his hands and turn around.

"An enthusiastic and well-deserved welcome back to terra firma."

Their laughter was spontaneous.

"Thank you, Chris," smiled Sandy. She looked up at Matt. "I'm told that the usual practice after a successful solo is a drink – right after Chris has taken the obligatory first solo photo."

Chris Winstone raised his camera. "Smile," he commanded.

Matt obliged and then jerked his head inquiringly towards Sandy.

"Of course," smiled Chris.

Matt slipped his arm across Sandy's shoulders and she smiled up at him as the shutter clicked.

"A charming photo. Away you go," Chris grinned. "I may join you later."

Matt reached out, took Sandy's hand and together they walked towards the clubhouse.

They settled down in a corner of the lounge with drinks and a large basket of wedges and dips. Matt, still buzzing over his successful flight, was delighted to be able to describe all the moments in considerable detail to somebody with a genuine interest in flying. Whenever he paused in his description, she immediately posed a question that encouraged him to keep talking. As he did so he became increasingly aware of the enjoyment he gained in not only telling her about the flight but also from the genuine pleasure that she was deriving from his re-living the experience. Her questions and comments were warm and empathetic with no trace of criticism or cynicism.

From the doorway of the lounge bar a motionless figure, with narrowing eyes and clenched fists, stood watching the young couple – completely absorbed in each other. As their mutual laughter drifted across the room, Jason Collins whirled round and strode back towards the stairs.

*

The door of the clubhouse was thrust open and, by rapidly stepping back, Fleur only just avoided being hit and colliding with the man who burst through it.

"Fuck!" he growled.

"Pardon, Jason."

Collins stopped, turned and his features morphed from anger to apology.

"Fleur. Oh, sorry. I wasn't—"

"Looking where I was going." She smiled. "You seemed to be a little preoccupied."

He looked sheepish. "Suppose so." He looked away and shifted uncomfortably for a moment. "Just some problem with a plane – mechanic hadn't done his job properly."

"But you told me that they were all first class."

"Yes, but everyone has their off days."

He was obviously lying but Fleur let it drop.

"So, what brings you out here. Do we have a lesson booked? I don't—."

"No, Jason, I just thought I'd take a drive out to, er, watch the planes."

"Or watch Matt?"

His flash of anger took her by surprise.

"Matt? Is he here today?"

"Yea. Just completed his second solo flight."

"Oh, how did it go? Successful?" She tried to sound casual, but her look was searching.

Collins shrugged. "Didn't see it myself, but Chris said it was OK." He gave a thin smile. "This time."

"That's good. I'm pleased for him."

"He's pretty pleased for himself. He's celebrating upstairs."

"Upstairs." Fleur took a step towards the door, but Jason caught her arm.

"Not a good idea, Fleur."

Fleur frowned. "Why? He's not getting drunk, is he?"

"Not on alcohol."

Her frown deepened. "Then what?"

His smile was thin. "New lady friend."

"New lady friend? Who?"

"Sandy."

"The pretty young woman that you've been teaching to fly. When did this happen?"

"She apparently watched his solo, congratulated him at the gate and they're now absorbed with each other in the bar." His top lip curled momentarily upwards. "Young love. Wonderful thing."

Fleur stood stock still for a long moment then with an effort forced a smile.

"So, high flyer, why don't we take off together? We could do a little celebrating on our own?"

The invitation was easy to read – mutual lust as a form of therapy.

"Meal and a motel?"

"Hell of an idea!"

He reached for her hand.

"Let's go."

Chapter 18

"So, how many lessons you had so far, Tony?"

The cigarette glowed fiercely as the Russian drew deeply, while maintaining unwavering eye contact with the younger man.

"Eight," replied Tony making a conscious effort to maintain a cool demeanour. "If you're worried about the cost then—"

"Cost, huh, not my money not my problem. But I want progress and action. Are you forgetting the purpose of mission – maybe enjoying the flying too much?"

"That's not fair. I'm gaining quite a lot of information from him."

"I decide what's fair. And in any case 'fair' is irr…"

"Irrelevant," prompted Gregory.

"Da, irrelevant." He savoured the word for a moment. "If job needs to be done then that is all that matters. Fairness is irrelevant."

Zhukov's thin smile was becoming familiar to Tony – always a signal that a storm was imminent and needed redirecting with some soothing assurances. The Russian increasingly pissed him off with his cheap cracks and thinly veiled threats of violence. Over the preceding months he'd gained some insight into the man's background from snippets of conversation with Gregory. Zhukov had joined the Russian army as a teenager and had been subject to the standard barrack room brutality dished out by officers and NCOs. From there he'd been part of the ill-fated Russian invasion of Afghanistan where brutality on both sides was the norm. 'Fairness' to such a man was a foreign concept.

"I've told you that I don't enjoy flying, but that I'm doing it as part of the assignment. Jason Collins is an arrogant bastard who constantly talks about himself and is quick to criticise others – including me."

Zhukov opened his mouth, but Tony hurried on.

"I have done my best to establish a friendship with him, while assessing his weaknesses. Because he loves to talk about himself I'm able to learn a lot – all I have to do is listen and utter words of encouragement to keep him going – even better when he's had a drink or two."

"So, what then have you learned?"

"He has expensive tastes and his remuneration as a flying instructor is insufficient."

"Not paid enough?" said Zhukov.

"Not for his tastes in cars, women and creature comforts."

"What is this creature comforts?"

"Fancy house, good music, books, travel, clothes, that sort of thing," said Gregory.

"And he's definitely on the take," said Tony.

"You know this. How?"

"He got drunk the other night and boasted to me how he's creaming profits off the top for himself."

The Russian grunted. "Like the milk."

"Exactly. He smuggles in medical drugs, such as vitamins, health supplements, and performance enhancements that have large profit margins. Some are duplicates of high-priced mainstream drugs, manufactured in India and China. Others are vitamins or stimulants for people trying to maintain their youth and beauty." He shrugged and grinned. "Snake oil."

"Snake oil?"

"An expression for fake medicines, Vladimir, with fancy names and labels that encourage gullible people to part with their money."

"Do those drugs give him a large enough profit margin?"

"Not quite, Gregory. His most profitable clientele are people with life-threatening conditions who need expensive drugs not subsidised by our health system. Due to a lack of hard research their effectiveness is questionable."

"So why do people buy them?"

"They're desperate. Their condition is life threatening. The approved drugs they're taking aren't working, they hear about these so-called 'miracle drugs' on social media or from other sources and are prepared to try them – often as a last resort."

"In spite of cost?"

"Yes. They feel they've nothing to lose. He also told me that the Covid 19 epidemic slowed down production in both China and India which resulted a shortage of these medical drugs."

"Was that a problem for him?"

"Not really. It meant that people were prepared to pay even higher prices to get their hands on the drugs."

Zhukov frowned thoughtfully and asked, "How does Collins smuggle these drugs in?"

"Light aircraft, from Australia across the Tasman – using remote landing strips."

Zhukov's eyes narrowed and he cocked his head enquiringly.

"We're not talking about crates of weaponry," continued Tony. "Large quantities of drugs can be packed tightly into relatively small packages."

"He would need reliable pilots and effective distribution systems," said Gregory.

"Collins arranges the transport and the distribution through his website, retail, mail order, service clubs and other outlets."

"Does he use these drugs?" asked Zhukov.

"No. He prefers alcohol."

The Russian tapped a fresh cigarette on top of the packet, inserted into his mouth and lit it with his Zippo. Through a fresh stream of smoke, he studied Tony intently.

"So, he is making big money, yes?"

"Yes," said Tony. "By smuggling the drugs he avoids the high cost of registering them with Medsafe, as well as any duty and taxes."

Zhukov stood, walked over and stared down at him. Tony recognised the attempt at intimidation but held the Russian's gaze.

"This pilot is making much money bringing in these drugs. We need to elim…"

"Eliminate."

"Da, Gregory. Eliminate him and take over his operation." Anticipating a protest from Tony he held up his hand. "Not yet, however. We first need to find out more about these drugs, where they come from, how much they cost and how they are distributed."

"What about your contract with Bullock?"

Zhukov shrugged. "I've been feeding him information on Collin's background, habits, women and also that he's probably dealing in drugs. He seems happy with this. Said he'll contact me if he wants anymore."

Gregory nodded but Tony looked worried.

"The additional information you want about the drugs and their source will take some time," Tony said.

"Time. Yes, but time is short. We need to speed up things."

"How?"

"How, my young friend?" His smile was mirthless. "We pay friendly visit to Mr Collins."

Chapter 19

A fresh downpour swept the street as the black SUV pulled up.

"Fucking rain," muttered Zhukov as he opened the passenger's door. "This the place?"

"Yeah," said Tony from the back seat.

"OK. Come on."

Tony looked apprehensively at the house but on opening the car door and feeling the force of the rain his only thought was shelter. He dashed towards the garden gate, pushed it open and ran up the steps to the front door. Zhukov and Gregory were right behind him.

"Been here before?"

"No, Vladimir. But the address is correct."

The big Russian grunted.

"Knock," he ordered.

Tony took a deep breath and then knocked loudly on the door. The trio, huddled together under the inadequate veranda, listened for a response. The only sound was the hammering of the rain on the roof.

"Again! Louder!"

Tony knocked more loudly.

Footsteps could be heard advancing towards the door. The silhouette of a figure appeared through the frosted glass.

"Who is it?"

"It's Tony, Jason."

The door chain slid back, and the door half opened. Jason Collins peered through the gap.

"Tony. What the hell…?"

Zhukov thrust the door open with his shoulder and strode into the small hallway, sending Collins staggering backwards.

"What the hell! You can't just—"

"It is wet. We are wet. We come to visit you."

He thrust his dampened face forward. "You are Jason. You are inviting us into your house, yes?"

Repulsed by the man's foul breath, Collins instinctively stepped back.

"*Spasibo*. Thank you." Zhukov marched up the passage, paused at the lounge door and entered.

"All of you, come!" he commanded.

Collins hurried after him.

"Now, listen, mate, you can't—"

The Russian turned and quickly gathered the front of Collins' shirt in his large fist.

"I am not yet your mate. Perhaps soon, but first we talk." He thrust the man back towards the leather sofa on the right-hand side of the room. "Sit."

Collins sprawled backwards onto the sofa. He opened his mouth to protest, but caught Tony's eye. The young man frowned fiercely and shook his head.

Zhukov settled into a comfortable chair opposite Collins and signalled for the other two to be seated. The trio quickly took in the main details of the room. A beautifully crafted Lladro piece, showing an 18th Century couple in an ornate coach drawn by four white horses with liveried driver and two footmen, dominated an intricately carved dresser. Several large paintings covered the walls, complemented by heavy patterned drapes and wall-to-wall Persian carpet.

"Now, Jason, thank you for inviting us into your beautiful home," began Zhukov. "You know, of course, Tony. This is my other friend Gregory. I am Vladimir Zhukov. We come to talk to you."

Collins slowly sat upright and looked intently at the three men.

"Talk. What about?"

"We have business proposition."

"Proposition?"

"Da. We have business proposition for you." He spread his arms widely and smiled. "That is all. I'm sorry if I was not polite at your doorway, but it is raining, and we were getting soaked to our skins."

"Business? What business are you in?"

"In a moment, my friend. We understand that you are an importer of very costly items that you sell for handsome profit, yes?"

Collins swung his gaze at Tony.

"What gave you the right to discuss my business with people like this?"

Tony shifted uncomfortably in his seat, but Zhukov's rapid reaction saved him having to contrive some platitudinous response.

"What you mean, 'people like this'? You think you are better than me? You think because I am bloody foreigner that I am not equal to you?" The big Russian stood and advanced towards the couch. "I come to discuss business with you. You reply with insult."

Zhukov's attempt to intimidate Collins had the opposite effect. Pushing himself off the couch he sprang upright and faced the Russian. Their eyes locked together.

"You push your way into my house, pretend friendship and now you threaten me. I have no interest in talking to you." He pointed towards the door. "Get out! Now!"

Zhukov stepped away from the angry pilot, giving a brief impression of backing down. He paused, his eyes narrowed and without shifting his gaze he murmured, "Gregory, do you see the lovely coach and horses on the large cupboard behind me?"

"Yes, Vladimir."

"Bring to me, please."

Collins' protest was cut short as Zhukov's right hand shot out, seized his throat and pressed a large thumb into his windpipe.

"Do not move, or make a sound."

He reached out with his left arm and carefully took the Lladro piece that Gregory placed in his hand. Slowly he lifted his arm high above his head. Poised like a triumphant statue, he held the piece perfectly still. Collins, whose gaze had followed the lifting of Russian's arm, stared with widening eyes and began to make whimpering noises. Zhukov smiled gently and then let the piece slip from his grasp. He winced as the coach, horses and figures hit a marble bust of a pilot and ricocheted onto a large mohair rug.

"Oops," he whispered before brutally thrusting Collins back onto the couch.

He stepped heavily to his left and the sounds of the Lladro remnants being ground under his boot filled the room.

"Now, Jason, we talk business, seriously, yes?"

Collins sprawled on the couch, his eyes flickering between Zhukov and the shattered remains of his precious Lladro.

Zhukov's voice increased in volume. "Yes?"

"Jason, what the hell's going on here?"

All eyes turned towards Fleur, standing in the doorway of the lounge.

Zhukov swung to his right. "Who is this woman?"

Fleur strode towards him. "Who the hell are you?"

"I am business associate of Jason."

Fleur held his gaze and then her eyes deliberately travelled down the rest of his body taking in his flashy double-breasted suit, the gold bangles on each arm, and the heavy rings on his stubby fingers. Her mouth curled with distaste. She took a small step backwards and feeling something crunching under her foot, looked down and gasped when she saw the shattered Lladro pieces. Her eyes flicked to the sideboard, back to the carpet and then to Zhukov. Her face showed that she was torn between incredulity and fury.

"You bastard. Did you smash the Lladro?" she demanded.

Zhukov cocked his head and sneered, "Why, lady? Is it yours?"

"A gift to me from Jason." Her fist clenched, she took a step towards Zhukov. "You are obviously some sort of foreign oaf who has stumbled out of a sewer into a home that's way out of your class."

"Nobody speaks to me like that, bitch," snarled Zhukov. He drew his right arm back and swung a blow at Fleur. She twisted sideways, but the heavy punch caught the side of her head and she staggered sideways.

"Fleur!" shouted Collins. Leaping forward he caught her in his arms, but his foot slipped on the remnants of the Lladro and he lurched to one side, colliding violently with the sideboard. His grip on Fleur loosened and she fell forward, striking her right temple on the solid sideboard edge and collapsing on the rug in front of the fireplace.

With a cry Collins crouched down next to her.

"She will be OK," growled Zhukov who appeared above him.

Collins' furious retort was cut off by an exclamation from Tony.

"Blood! From her head!"

A small but expanding pool of blood oozed from under Fleur's head onto the rug.

Collins gently lifted her head and turned it to the left. Her fair hair was rapidly becoming matted by a dark red seepage.

"Fleur," he whispered. "Can you hear me?"

The only response was a long shuddering sigh, before her head fell back and her eyes snapped open.

Collins quickly held his fingertips on the side of her neck. He shook his head slightly and taking her right wrist, again checked for a pulse. With a further shake of his head he gently placed her arm back on the carpet and remained kneeling beside her.

"Christ, she's dead," murmured Gregory.

Collins scrambled to his feet, leapt at Zhukov and smashed his fist into the side of the Russian's face.

"You fucking bastard! You've killed her! You'll pay for this!"

Tony and Gregory exchanged glances – both reading each other's thoughts. Zhukov will tear him to pieces.

The Russian staggered back and touched his left cheek. He stood stock-still for a moment, but instead of hurling himself at Collins, he walked slowly to his chair and settled himself comfortably before meeting the eyes of each of the lounge's occupants. He reached into his pocket, extracted a cigarette and lit it. He ignored Collins glowering features.

"You accuse me of killing the woman? You are a fool. Yes, she did not show me respect and I hit her. But you caught her and held her. Then you let her go. She fell and hit her head, causing her to die."

"You lying bastard!" Collins began to advance towards Zhukov, but Tony stepped in front of him.

"Wait, Jason. The police could call this a murder in which you'd both be implicated."

"He's right," agreed Gregory. He jerked his head towards the body. "We can't help her but we need to help ourselves or we'll all be in deep shit."

Each stared at the other, wrestling with their apprehensions. Finally, Zhukov spoke.

"So, who is this woman?"

Collins, clearly shaken, slowly sat down. "Her name's Fleur. I met her at flying school."

"She live with you?"

Collins glared at Zhukov. "No. Just stays some nights."

The Russian, suppressing a leer, grunted and nodded. "She have family, children, husband?"

"No children, no husband."

"Friends?"

"Only a few I think."

"You think?" asked Gregory.

Collins nodded. "I've never met any of them."

Zhukov nodded slowly. "Good. There will be very few people who will questions be asking."

"If you're thinking of—"

"What I am thinking, Jason is that you are in difficult situation. A woman has died in your lounge. On her body will be your…" he raised his right hand, wriggled his fingers and looked at Gregory.

"Fingerprints."

"Da, fingerprints. "

"But–."

"There is more. We will all say that you killed her."

"And I will say that you killed her. It was your blow that knocked her—"

"Three people with one story and one man with another, trying to say why a woman with his fingerprints on her body died in his lounge."

"I don't like the odds, Jason," murmured Tony.

"Whose fucking side are you on?"

"The strongest side, Jason. These two." He turned to Zhukov. "What should we do now?"

"We take the body away and make carpet clean, very clean. No one will know. Only the three people in this room."

"But—"

"Do not say the word 'but'," interrupted Zhukov, extracting a fresh packet of Camels from his pocket and peeling off the cellophane. "We came to you to discuss a business deal. You did not want to. You're now in big trouble. We can help you if you cooperate with us."

"We all witnessed what happened. We are all in this together. We can help you if you help us," said Gregory."

"But Fleur—"

"Is dead," continued Gregory. "Very unfortunate but nothing we do can reverse that. Vladimir can fix it so the body is taken away and no one but us will ever know anything. He will be doing you a big favour. You can repay the favour by cooperating with him and with us."

Collins slumped in his seat. The shock of the visit by the trio, the sudden death of Fleur and the bizarre nature of his dangerous position were overwhelming. He looked at Zhukov.

"How soon can you?"

"What?"

"Take Fleur away." His voice was barely audible.

"Within next hour. It's dark outside and getting late."

"Where will you take her?"

"Don't worry. No-one will ever find her."

Collins' eyes shifted from Zhukov to the body by the dresser. Fleur was a devious, calculating woman with whom he'd had a tempestuous sexual relationship. They'd used each other unashamedly for physical gratification, with feelings of warmth and friendship only a minor consideration. Yet he had grown fond of her and now suddenly she was dead. He shook his head trying to come to terms with the woman whose blood was visible on his rug and whose disposal had been taken over by a brutal Russian oaf and his henchman.

Summoning the remnants of his self-respect he glared at Zhukov.

"So what are you bloody waiting for? Get on with it!"

Chapter 20

Zhukov's suggestion that they all vacate the house for two hours met no resistance. The Russian, who had spent ten minutes murmuring into his cell phone, terminated the call with a grunt of satisfaction.

"All taken care of," he informed the other three.

"But who—?"

"Our people," interrupted Gregory. "They will also clean the carpet. Ask no more questions, Jason."

Half an hour later the four of them entered the Restaurant Smolensk in Parnell. It was obvious to Collins that Zhukov was a valued patron by the deference with which the maître d' greeted the group.

"The food here is good. Not as good as back home, but not bad for the other side of the world," Zhukov informed them expansively as they seated themselves at the large round table. "You like Russian food, Jason?"

"Black bread and undercooked cabbage, washed down with copious quantities of vodka. Not my preference."

Seeing Zhukov's head lift in anger, Gregory put a restraining hand on Collins' arm.

"I think you'll have your opinion changed for the better tonight, Jason," he said, opening the menu cover, decorated with the Romanov double-headed eagle.

Collins grunted. "About the food, maybe."

Missing the subtlety Zhukov stared questioningly at Gregory, who responded with a shake of his head and a brief smile.

"So, Vladimir, you are the expert." He flourished the menu. "Order for us the best examples of Russian cuisine."

The Russian, obviously keen to share his homeland's food with his companions, smiled broadly. "We will begin with drinks, of course. Jason, what would you like?"

"A beer."

"Beer for everyone?"

They all nodded.

Zhukov signalled to the waiter who hurried over.

After a brief whispered consultation Zhukov turned to his companions and smiled expansively.

"I have ordered Ivan Taranvo Three Bears – good strong Russian beer – five per cent alcohol."

Two waiters appeared carrying four bottles and glasses. The four men watched in silence as the caps were removed and the bottles lifted. The golden liquid flowed invitingly into each of the glasses.

Zhukov reached forward, wrapped his large fist around his glass, and nodded for the others to follow suit.

"When we drink in Russia we say, '*nostrovia*' which means in English, 'good health'."

He raised his glass with a flourish and made brief eye contact with each man.

"So, my friends, *nostrovia*!"

He put the glass to his lips, drained it and slammed it down on the tabletop.

Gregory also completely drained his glass while Tony and Collins contented themselves with a long draught.

"Good, yes?"

The cold strong beer bit deep into Collins' gullet eliciting a spontaneous response.

"Delicious." He paused and noting the Russian's expectant look, added, "Thank you."

"*Khorosho*, good." Zhukov smiled benignly at his companions before standing and patting his pockets. "I need cigarette. In this country a man cannot smoke in restaurant. Bloody stupid, no?"

Pushing his chair aside he strode to the exit, calling "More beer!" to the waiter.

Gregory stood. "I need to pee."

The departure of the pair left Tony and Collins staring at each other for a long moment. It was the latter who broke the silence.

"How the hell did you get mixed up with that Russian bastard and his mate?"

"Long story, Jason. He hired me several months ago. When he heard about your operation, he told me to take flying lessons and make friends with you."

Collins gripped edge of the table and leaned forward. "You mean…?"

"Yes. I've always been scared of flying, but Zhukov pays well and," he shrugged, "after a while I began to enjoy it – thanks to your tuition."

Collins opened his mouth, but Tony hurried on.

"Zhukov wants a piece of your operation. He has plenty of money and contacts and could help you expand – to everyone's benefit."

The sound of an interior door signalled Gregory's re-appearance.

"We'll talk some more, Jason." He reached out and gripped the other's arm. The Ukrainian sat down heavily and smiled at both men.

"You talk, yes? Everything okay, yes?"

"Yes, Gregory, we have talked and Jason now understands." He gave Collins a hard look and the other man nodded his head.

"It's obvious we're all in this together," said Gregory. He lowered his voice and leaned forward. "The woman's death was accidental but agreeing to cover it up puts us all in the same frame."

There was silence as the waiters arrived to replenish the beer. As they left Gregory said, "This is not all bad, particularly for you, Jason."

Collins glared at him. "Particularly for me. How?"

"Vladimir is a very powerful man, with very good connections – nationally and internationally. This will be of a great advantage to you. It will grow your business and you will become a very rich man."

"Just a moment. I have not agreed to—"

"I don't think you have an alternative, Jason," said Tony. "His power is matched by his ruthlessness and brutality. You've had ample demonstration of that tonight. I suggest you smile and make the most of the situation."

"Easy to say but—"

"Yes," smiled Tony reassuringly. "But you have a few cards in your deck. You've set up your system, you have the contacts, the flying knowledge, and all the other parts that make it work. All of these can be expanded for your benefit and the benefit of your partners."

"The system is functioning quite well with low risks and—"

"You have expensive tastes in housing, cars and women. You're not getting any younger and as your age increases so will your expenses. With partners on board you can expand the operation and reap a substantial increase in profits." He paused and smiled confidently. "Substantial!"

Seeing Zhukov re-entering the restaurant, Tony thrust his beer glass upwards and swept his eyes around the table.

"Substantial! Substantial profits!"

The big Russian paused behind his seat, reached for his glass, and echoed the shout.

"*Da*. Substantial profits!"

Tony raised his glass higher while sharply elbowing Collins with his left arm. After a moment's hesitation he also raised his glass and murmured, "Substantial profits."

As they lowered their glasses the waiters arrived with the main course.

"*Sharkoi*," announced Zhukov. "Traditional Russian beef stew. You will enjoy the eating and it will fill you up. So, my friends, *Preeyat nahva, a pee tee tah!*"

"Bon appetit," translated Gregory.

The stew was steaming hot, the substantial chunks of beef supplemented with potatoes, carrots, onions and peppercorns. The traumatic events of the day had given each man an appetite and they needed no further persuasion to slake their hunger. Jason, although still shaken by the image of the dead Fleur and the speed of the subsequent events, succumbed to the aroma and the generous portion that had been placed in front of him.

"Vladimir."

The Russian turned towards Gregory.

"*Da?*"

"Some red wine? It would go well with the beef."

Zhukov smiled and nodded. "Red meat, red wine. A good, ah…"

"Combination," offered Gregory.

"Of course." He looked up and shouted, "Russian River, Pinot Noir, for all!"

"Pinot Noir? From Russia?" enquired Collins.

The big Russian grinned. "Yes, my friend, from the Black Sea region. We make wine for more than two thousand years." He grunted and looked directly at Collins. "People of Russia are not all beer and vodka drinking peasants." He turned towards the two waiters hurrying over with bottles and glasses. "As you will see!"

A generous quantity of the smooth red wine was poured for each man, and following Zhukov's lead, they raised their glasses to their lips. To Collins' surprise the big Russian did not noisily gulp down his portion, but savoured it with his nose, swirled it around and then took a delicate sip – a ruthless villain and a wine aficionado – a contradictory combination.

The men ate heartily, and little was said during the meal. Once the plates had been taken away and they were all leaning back in their chairs Zhukov cleared his throat.

"Everybody is happy, yes?"

There were various affirmative grunts.

"Good." He turned to a hovering waiter and spoke rapidly in Russian. The man gave a short bow and hurried away.

"I tell him we are not to be disturbed. We are business talking."

The table fell silent and all eyes turned towards Zhukov.

"So, first thing, the problem of young woman who had accident. We were all there. This means we were all part of it. We are therefore all," he paused uncertainly, "joined together."

Seeing puzzlement on some faces Gregory quickly cut in. "What you're saying Vladimir is if one of us goes down, then we will all go down."

"*Da*, Gregory. Exactly what I mean. We keep our mouths shut. We heard nothing, we saw nothing, and we were not there. Her body is gone. Nothing will happen if each man keeps his mouth shut. If he does not, something will happen," his eyes swept around the table, "to him. Understand?"

Each nodded a firm affirmation.

He then switched his gaze to Collins.

"So, Jason, you and I are now on same team." His smile held a hint of triumph. "We are partners in criminal."

"Partners in crime, Vladimir."

The Russian grinned and savoured the phrase. "Yes, partners in crime. Is good, no?"

Collins shifted uncomfortably in his chair, feeling the pressure of Zhukov's unwavering gaze and the expectations of the other men.

"I suppose so," he murmured reluctantly.

Zhukov's enthusiastic thump on the table caused everyone to jerk back in their seats.

"Good, Jason! That is good!"

Collins took a deep breath, seeking to salvage something from the remnants of his self-respect.

"I agree we are all linked to Fleur's death." He paused and his voice hardened. "That does not automatically make us business partners."

"You come to this Russian restaurant with me. You drink beer I pay for, wine I pay for and food I pay for. You should be thanking me!"

"Thanking you!" Collins' voice rose. "Thanking you for what? You think that you can win my gratitude with some foreign booze and a plateful of stew?" His pronunciation of the final word was full of scorn. "If you want to propose any sort of partnership with me then we will meet at an appropriate time, at an appropriate place and you will make a proposal that I will consider – which will include payment for the Lladro piece that you smashed."

Zhukov thrust back his chair and stood, his eyes blazing with fury.

"I will not have—"

Collins' chair crashed on the floor as he sprang to his feet and eyeballed the Russian across the table.

"No, it is I who will not have you treat me like some lackey, some snivelling Siberian serf. I am a qualified pilot with expanding business interests. You will therefore treat me with an appropriate fucking level of respect!"

In the stunned silence the only sound was the heavy breathing of the protagonists. The others sat quite still – only their eyes moved as they shared apprehensive glances.

Suddenly Zhukov spread his arms and gave a huge smile.

"Jason, my friend, you are right. We need to sit down and talk about plans like two businessmen. I ask Gregory to make proposals, to give them to you and to make a time for us to talk about them. Is OK?"

Taken aback by this abrupt change of mood, Collins hesitated. He glanced round the table, and saw Tony nodding vigorously. He took two deep breaths, looked back at Zhukov and gave a curt nod.

"Gregory will draw up some proposals for me to consider and then we will meet?"

"Of course." Zhukov's eyes narrowed. "That is what I have just said. Do you think I would—?"

"I will draw them up tonight and contact you tomorrow," quickly interrupted Gregory. "We can then arrange a time to meet."

"At a mutually convenient time."

"Yes, Jason, of course."

"OK, I agree with this first step." Jason looked down and smiled grimly. "I still have some wine in my glass." He retrieved his chair, sat down, reached for his glass and took a sip, knowing he had gained a small advantage as it left Zhukov standing by himself.

The big man hurriedly resumed his seat. He caught Jason's eye and raised his glass, an action to which the other man silently responded.

Chapter 21

"Bullock here, Zhukov."

"Ah, Mr Bullock, good to hear from you. Are you well?"

"I haven't phoned you to discuss my state of health. I want to know about progress with our target."

"Our target? Of course, sir." He paused and swallowed. "Everything's progressing well, sir."

"Progressing well. Meaning what, exactly?"

"Taking a little longer than I thought, sir. It's important that our target is happy with my contact and does not become suspicious."

Ray Bullock answered with slow deliberation.

"You have served me well in the past, Zhukov. Your work has been fast, efficient and has left no traces. I'm expecting you to do the same with this assignment."

"Mr Bullock, of course."

"Am I making myself crystal clear, Zhukov?"

"Yes, sir. Clear as the crystal."

"In that case I will need a final report from you within seven days, when you will tell me that the task has reached a final and satisfactory conclusion."

"Of course, Mr Bullock."

"Within seven days."

"Yes, sir, within seven days."

Bullock pressed the red button and placed the iPhone on his desk. He wasn't particularly concerned about the completion of the task, but money was a little tight and he had promised Matt that he would take action, so the sooner the better for all concerned.

*

The big Russian tossed his phone onto the nearby armchair and reached for a cigarette.

"Yes, Mr Bullock, no, Mr Bullock, of course, Mr Bullock," he muttered to himself. Bullock was generous with his money and Zhukov was keen to maintain the flow, but the obsequious role that he'd been forced to adopt contradicted his nature. Men obeyed him; men deferred to him. Deference to Bullock increasingly gnawed away at his pride.

As the Zippo snapped, he turned towards the doorway.

"Gregory!"

Hurried footsteps responded to his bellow. Gregory appeared in the doorway looking anxious.

"What has happened, Vladimir? Has something gone wrong?"

"Fucking Bullock!"

Gregory remained silent. Asking questions at this point would probably trigger an abusive response.

"He talks to me like some fucking dog. He is giving the orders so I must obey. This I do not like!"

"His money's good."

"Only if I do as he says."

"And what does he say?"

"He wants job completed within seven days."

"Seven days?"

"You fucking parrot, Gregory?"

His companion flinched but remained silent.

"So, where's Tony?" demanded Zhukov.

"He's flying. He said he'd return at two."

"Two," grunted Zhukov.

Gregory resisted the temptation to paraphrase the parrot comment and merely nodded.

"You text him. Tell him we will meet here at two. Important meeting. He is not to be late. *Da*?"

"*Da*."

Gregory reached for his cell phone

95

Chapter 22

"You're gaining in confidence, Tony."

"Thanks, Jason," grinned Tony. "Like I said before, I'm now beginning to enjoy it."

Having just completed their post flight check on the Robin the two men were crossing the tarmac on the way to the clubhouse. Tony was relieved that the death of Fleur and the confrontation with Zhukov didn't appear to have affected their relationship. Given the man's volatility, he was still wary, but prepared to take it at face value in the meantime.

They walked in silence for a few moments and then Collins reached out, touched Tony's arm and paused.

"Tony, before we go into the clubhouse there's something I'd like to discuss with you."

"Oh," replied Tony cautiously. Assuming that it concerned Fleur all his senses were alert.

"I've been a flying instructor for a number of years," continued Collins. "I enjoy it but the money's not exactly spectacular."

"I see," replied Tony, relaxing a little. If it was about money and not about Fleur then it could be the breakthrough for which he'd been waiting. However, remaining cautious, he just nodded and grunted.

"You now know about my other business activities."

Tony nodded, but retained a blank expression.

"They've been expanding, and I need a partner."

"A partner," responded Tony making an effort to keep his voice neutral.

"Yes. Would you be interested?"

The noise of a small plane taking off made conversation impossible, giving Tony a moment or two before he replied.

"Why me? I'm not even qualified to fly solo."

Collins smiled. "That will happen soon, I'm sure." He paused and looked hard at Tony. "During our conversations I've gained the impression that you've had," he hesitated before continuing, "a colourful past. Therefore, my assumption is that you could be interested in making some good money in an unconventional manner."

Tony's excitement mounted but he kept his voice steady.

"You're a perceptive man, Jason. Yes, my past has been a little," he paused, "colourful." He grinned wryly before continuing. "I definitely am on the lookout for making good money, and am not worried about it being through unconventional means."

"Good," responded Collins. "I am—"

Tony held up his hand. "But having said that, I have no wish to run afoul of the law again. Once was enough."

Collins grunted and nodded. "No need to elaborate. My scheme is virtually fool proof. We are not technically breaking the law. Just bending it a little."

"Sounds ideal." The younger man smiled, and then frowned. "What about, Zhukov? What will he say?"

"Bloody Zhukov. He wants a piece of the action and, in order to keep him quiet, I might agree to involving him in some of the drop offs. But I'm not prepared to give away good money to a vicious bastard like him. That's why I need an assistant to run another arm of the operation that will be hidden from Zhukov. What he doesn't know won't concern him."

Tony frowned.

"You look worried, Tony. Look, the fact that you work for Zhukov would be an advantage for me."

"I see," murmured Tony noncommittally.

"Does he pay you well?"

"Not as much as he should. Debt collecting from unsavoury characters can be a dangerous and unpleasant business."

"I guess." He paused. "If you started working for me would that put you into conflict with Zhukov?"

"No. I don't work full-time for him. He only calls me in when he wants a job done. Rest of the time's my own."

Tony was making an effort not to appear over-eager. Being in partnership with Collins would give him a greater insight into the business and could also provide him with some real money. However, the problem now was that Zhukov had said that he wanted Collins eliminated. If the Russian succeeded in taking over the pilot's business then Tony was likely to be offered additional work – but it would always be on Zhukov's terms – as his assistant and being subject to the man's unpleasantness and bullying. A partnership with Collins could be a more attractive proposition. He frowned. Just as the golden goose was on the point of laying some high-quality eggs it could have its throat cut.

"I guess you're worried about your lack of flying skills."

"What? Oh, yeah."

"Don't worry. I'll give you extra flying and navigation lessons at no charge in order to speed up the process. You can start as soon as you've passed the solo qualification. You won't need to carry passengers – not at first, anyway."

"Will any of the flying be done at night?"

"Eventually, but in the meantime we'd confine you to daylight pickups – sometimes by plane and other times by car. The main thing is that the goods are collected sight unseen and brought back to me for distribution."

"How are they paid for?"

"Cash, only. Don't want any bank records. You'll be given the cash with clear instructions. You'll have passwords so you won't need to identify yourself by name."

Tony grinned. "All very cloak and dagger."

"'Tis a bit. But it works, and protects everyone – suppliers, couriers and receivers."

An instructor and his trainee walked past and nodded to them. As they moved out of earshot Tony asked, "You told me the other night that these are drugs people use for medical purposes – drugs they can't get from their doctors or hospitals."

"Some of the drugs are low risk health pills and powders," he smiled cynically, "for people who want to retain their youth. The actual medical drugs vary in type and purpose. Some are for people who've got a problem with alcohol – if you're addicted and want to stop drinking." He grinned. "Never felt the need myself, but there are plenty of people for whom total abstinence is impossible, and for whom organisations such as Alcoholics Anonymous have been no help. The more expensive drugs are for people with life-threatening conditions like cancer, for whom conventional medicines offer little hope and are not covered by Pharmac. They're desperate and are willing to pay accordingly."

"Do these drugs work?"

"In many cases, plus the placebo effect. Desperate people are willing to try anything."

"If they have the money."

"Exactly. And that applies to all the drugs that I bring in. Virus scares are particularly profitable; like the recent Covid 19 epidemic. People were desperate for an antidote and paid big money." Seeing Tony frown he shrugged. "I'm not a one-man charity, I'm a businessman, who has discovered a lucrative market."

He reached out his right hand. "So, Tony, are you interested?"

Tony smiled. "OK," he said as they shook hands.

Chapter 23

"I have two problems, Tony."

"Only two, Vladimir? You're a lucky man," grinned Tony.

Zhukov grunted and glared at him.

Realising his feeble attempt at humour had not been appreciated, Tony quickly adopted a concerned look. He was anticipating a tense discussion and his clumsy joke had reflected his anxiety.

"My two problems are these. One, we have to provide Bullock with some dirt on Jason Collins. Two, you have given us enough to keep Bullock happy, but I am worried that he wants to take over the operation."

"I see."

"Maybe you do, maybe you don't. We need more information from Collins. You told us what you know about the operation, but that is not enough. Has he told you anything else?"

"No," lied Tony. "He is proud of his operation but he keeps the details close to his chest."

"His chest?" frowned the big Russian stubbing out his cigarette.

"Close to his chest, like a man playing cards," responded Gregory, with a quick smirk at Tony. "The other players see nothing and know nothing." He frowned. "Time is short, Vladimir. Perhaps we should capture and beat the truth out of him."

The Russian shook his head. "Too risky. He could give us some information and then turn against us. He is the slippery bastard, but a bastard with courage." He grunted. "I enjoy beating him, of course, but I don't think it would work. His operation is too complicated, so we need to use method that will give us the big picture."

"You said you had two problems, Vladimir," said Tony. He'd already anticipated the answer, but wanted it confirmed.

"We are under orders from Bullock to provide dirt on Collins. We have only three days to the deadline."

"I can probably give you enough information to satisfy Bullock, but not enough to whet his appetite," responded Tony. Seeing Zhukov puzzled frown, he went on. "Not too much information otherwise he may try to muscle in on Collins' operation."

"You think you can give me enough to make Bullock satisfied?"

"Yes," nodded Tony. "You'll then receive the rest of your money from him and hopefully it will keep him away, leaving you to negotiate with Jason Collins."

Tony realised that commenting on Zhukov's operational intentions was well outside his role of obedient assistant but his need for the golden goose to survive had emboldened him. Expecting the usual flash of anger, or sarcastic put downs he was relieved to see his boss lean back in his chair and nod thoughtfully.

"Can you finish report by tomorrow?"

Tony nodded.

Zhukov turned to Gregory. "What you think, Gregory?"

Eager as always to agree with his boss, but irritated that Tony seemed to be trying to expand his role, his reply was cautious. "There is a risk, Vlad. If Tony's report has too much detail, then Bullock might be tempted to muscle in on Collins."

"Perhaps," responded Zhukov, reaching for his cigarettes. He slowly placed one between his lips, lit it, inhaled and looked at the other two men.

"Write your report, Tony and have it ready by noon tomorrow." He waved his hand dismissively. "Now leave me."

Chapter 24

"Dad, Mum, I'd like you to meet Sandy Anderson."

Maryanne, smiling warmly, reached out and took the young woman's hand. "We're delighted to meet you, Sandy. Aren't we, darling," she added turning to her husband.

"Yes, indeed, darling." Ray Bullock in turn took Sandy's hand. "Welcome to our home," he smiled.

"Thank you," responded Sandy shyly. She had been somewhat overwhelmed by the size of the house and the opulence of the interior. "It's lovely to meet you both. Matt has told me so much about you and—"

"Not too much, I hope," interrupted Bullock with a jovial laugh that was followed by a hearty slap on his son's back. Matt staggered forward, knowing that his father's public display of affection was being staged for Sandy's benefit.

"Hullo," said a voice from the doorway. They all looked round to see Helen Bullock entering and walking towards Sandy with a smile. "You must be Sandy. I'm Helen."

"My kid sister," added Matt unnecessarily.

"Kid sister!" she shot back. "You've only just started shaving, so don't—"

"Hey, I started shaving three years ago and—"

"Enough, you two. Sandy I apologise on behalf of my two ill-mannered children who seem to have forgotten—"

"That we have a guest," interrupted Bullock. "Now, Sandy, please have a seat and we'll arrange drinks for everyone."

Sandy smiled and sat down in the seat indicated by Maryanne. Matt quickly sat beside her muttering, "Sorry about my sister, but—"

Her touch on his arm and her warm smile caused him to stop and squeeze her hand affectionately. He took a deep breath. This was the first time he'd officially brought a girl home and he was keen to make a good impression.

His father, meanwhile, had been appraising Sandy. Her pretty face, shy but warm smile, and her obvious attraction to his son, impressed him. His wife, also running a practised eye over Sandy, noted with approval the cut of the light summer dress, the cashmere cardigan and the low-heeled shoes; obviously a young woman with an excellent taste in clothes.

"It's a lovely warm day, today, isn't it, Sandy. What would you like to drink, dear?"

"Oh," replied Sandy, "I'll just have a fruit juice, er, apple if that's alright."

"Of course it is. Helen?"

"The same thanks."

"And you, darling?" she asked, smiling warmly at her husband.

"A beer for me, thanks, darling. A pilsner."

"Matt?"

"I'll keep you company, dad. Put some hair on my chest."

"And your chin," muttered his sister sotto voce.

Bullock turned quickly to Sandy. "I believe you and Matt met at the flying club, Sandy. Do you enjoy flying?"

"Oh yes, I do, although it can be challenging at times."

"Are the instructors helpful?"

"Yes, they are." She hesitated and then continued. "One or two of them can be a bit bossy, sometimes they like to put you down—"

"Because you're a young woman?" interrupted Helen.

Sandy glanced at Matt who shrugged and smiled. She took it as a sign to continue.

"Possibly, yes. I'm one of the youngest flying students and one of the instructors, I think, sort of resents me," she screwed up her face, "possibly because I'm a young woman."

"Maybe he fancies you," grinned Helen. "Is he good looking?"

"Only if you like older men, and he's certainly not my type."

"What's his name?"

"Helen," cut in Matt, "I don't really think that's relevant."

"Why not?"

"His name's Jason Collins. He's not all that bad. Just a bit full of himself, that's all."

Matt briefly caught his father's quizzical look and knew there'd be a follow up discussion with him before the end of the day. He'd wanted Sandy's first visit to the family to be successful and had considered asking her not to mention Jason Collins but had quickly realised that this could result in her asking some innocent, but awkward questions. He could deal with his father later, but now, rapid intervention was called for.

He saw his mother was about to speak and reaching out for Sandy's hand he turned to the rest of the family.

"Sandy really is good at flying. She's had several instructors and she impresses them all. She should be going for her solo qualification in a couple of months. We could eventually go on trips together to different parts of the country."

"You won't be able to take passengers will you, dear?" asked his mother.

"Not immediately. We'll need additional qualifications for that. But I don't see that being a problem." He looked directly at Sandy and smiled. "Do you, babe?"

The use of the endearment had been deliberate – a clear signal to the family that the relationship was serious, and also focusing attention on them as a couple, thereby diverting any further discussion on Jason Collins.

Sandy, a little startled, gave him a warm smile. "No, Matt, we both love the sport and we seem to be progressing well." She turned to the others. "Perhaps in the future we'll be able to take all of you away on trips – day or overnight."

Matt noticed that both his parents flinched but then quickly adopted warm smiles of approval. He found the friction between them unsettling but was grateful that they'd been prepared to make an effort to provide a family welcome for Sandy. But then, he thought to himself, surely they'd approve of his choice – a beautiful, intelligent girl with a warm personality. What could possibly go wrong?

Chapter 25

"Close the door, son."

It was more of a command than a request and Matt quickly complied. His father seated behind his immaculate desk, signalled for him to sit down facing him.

"Jason Collins."

"Yes, Dad."

"The last time we spoke about him you were adamant you wanted him dealt with. Remember?"

"Yes, Dad, but—"

His father held up his hand. "Wait. You'll recall at the time I didn't ask too many questions. Angry and upset, you'd come to me for help – help that involved getting heavy with Collins. Right?"

"Yes, Dad."

"Although I didn't inquire too much, I assumed a woman was involved. Was it Sandy?"

"No Dad. This was before Sandy came on the scene."

His father nodded. "You're obviously very taken with Sandy. Don't blame you. She's a lovely young woman." He paused and sighed. "Can I assume that punishing Collins is no longer a priority with you?"

Matt shuffled in his seat and ran his left hand over his mouth. "Actually, Dad, I haven't given Jason Collins much thought over the past couple of weeks. When I met Sandy, I decided she was exactly what I wanted in a girl. As you say, she lovely, talented—"

"What you mean is you were so bloody obsessed with the girl that you completely forgot that you'd asked me to arrange for Collins to be taught a lesson he'd never forget." He leaned forward with his arms on the desk. "Right?"

Matt's face turned plum coloured.

"Yes, Dad. I did forget. I had other things on my mind. Sorry."

"Sorry will get you nowhere fast in the corporate world, son. You need to plan, and then execute boldly." He sighed. "I'll need to contact Zhukov. I presume you're no longer interested in punishing Collins."

"No, Dad. There's no point."

"So tell me this. Was some woman the real cause of the problem?"

Matt paused and frowned. "I know he's mixed up in something shady, and I was angry about his involvement with a woman."

"Cherchez la bloody femme," muttered his father. "So," he demanded, "does this woman have a name?"

"Fleur. She was in my tutor class at uni." He shuffled in his seat. "She's a bit older than me."

"You slept with her."

Matt nodded then raised his head in alarm. "Sandy knows nothing about Fleur. Please don't—"

"Oh, for Christ's sake, Matt, I'm just pleased you dipped your wick in an older woman. Hope you learned something. Have you broken it off with her?"

"Suppose so. I haven't seen her for a while."

"Was she also screwing Collins?"

Matt shrugged. "Looks like it. He was keen – she's an attractive woman and that's all the excuse he usually needs."

"So let him get on with it, and you get on with Sandy. I'll get hold of the Russian."

"OK. Thanks, Dad." He rose and turned to leave.

"And one more thing, son."

Matt looked back. "Yes, Dad?"

"Sandy. Your mother approves and so do I. Well done."

Matt's smile was one of relief.

Chapter 26

"Oh, good morning, Mr Bullock. I was just about to phone you."

"Saved you the trouble. Listen, Zhukov, a change of plan. You will leave Jason Collins alone."

"Leave alone? I do not understand."

"I don't need any dirt on him."

"You don't?" Zhukov's voice was incredulous.

"That's right. The situation has changed. Just leave him alone."

"But, Mr Bullock—"

"I will pay the amount that we discussed. I'll transfer the money later today, signalling the end of the contract."

The only response on the other end of the phone was a long expulsion of breath followed by silence.

"You there, Zhukov?"

"Yes, but I am not understanding. You say to me that you want lots of information on this man. I spend time and money preparing for this – takes long time. Now you tell me that contract is ended. You give no reason for this."

"I don't need to give you a reason, Zhukov," replied Bullock, with irritation. "I have said I will pay you the agreed amount. If you have spent additional time and money, then I will add an extra ten per cent to the agreed amount. Agreed?"

Zhukov paused for a moment. He had no wish to lose Bullock – a client who always paid promptly and generously. Making a conscious effort he replied in a conciliatory tone.

"Yes, Mr Bullock, an extra ten per cent. And thank you, sir, for giving assignment to me. Always happy to be of service."

"That's OK then," replied Bullock, a little mollified. "As I said, you'll get your money later today and we will consider the matter as closed."

"As you say, Mr Bullock, the matter is now closed. Thank you, sir."

A click terminated the call. Zhukov sat at his desk for a long moment, reached for his packet of cigarettes and bellowed, "Tony! Gregory!"

Chapter 27

"So, that's the story of Fleur."

Sandy stared at him for a long moment, sighed and then smiled.

"Quite a story, Matt."

Matt gazed out the window at the other cars in the airfield car park and grunted ruefully. "True. I thought I should tell you as I knew you were puzzled by some of the comments you'd heard around the clubrooms."

"I suppose I'd guessed Fleur and Jason were an item but never quite understood why you didn't like him. You'd said he was arrogant but that still didn't add up to your really negative attitude towards him."

Matt shrugged. He knew that telling Sandy about his affair with Fleur was a calculated risk, but decided she'd appreciate his honesty.

"Well, now you know." He took his hands off the steering wheel, took both her hands and smiled warmly. "I have absolutely no interest in Fleur. Since I met you, Sandy, she's become a bad memory."

Sandy paused and studied his eyes. "I accept that, Matt. However, you did say that at one stage you thought you were in love with her. Having some sort of liaison with a woman is one thing but believing you're genuinely in love is a whole different level."

"I believed at one stage I was in love with her, but I now know I was just flattered by the attention of an attractive older woman."

"Hmm," she murmured.

"What's 'hmm' supposed to mean?"

She shrugged and gazed out of the car window.

"Sandy, surely you believe me when I say that I'm in love with you. Surely you don't bloody think that—"

"I'm not sure what I bloody think, Matt. I know that sort of thing goes on all the time, but your story's a bit close to home. I need a little time to think about it."

"Sandy, for Christ's sake—"

"No, Matt, for my sake. I said I need a little time. That's all. Not much to ask is it?"

She turned to fix him with an intense stare.

"No."

"No what?"

"No, Sandy, it's not much to ask."

Sandy broke the long silence that followed. "Your flight's booked to start in thirty minutes. You need to get going."

He gave her a long hard look before he wrenched open the car door, climbed out, and, without looking back, headed straight for the clubhouse.

Sandy remained seated, gazing at his departing figure. It had all been overwhelming – the revelations of Matt's affair, her need to think it through, and his angry reaction. Surely, he could see that it had been a shock to her. But on the other hand, he had trusted her with the revelation. He could have kept it to himself, knowing she'd be unlikely to find out. But then he should have trusted her with the information, accepted her reaction, and agreed to her reasonable request for some time to think it over.

She sighed heavily. "Bloody men."

Then she noticed that he'd left the keys in the ignition.

*

Matt strode into the small club bar where he noticed with relief that it was empty. As he approached the bar, Jenny, the bar manager looked up with the smile.

"Hi, Matt? What can I get you?"

"Lager. Pint."

The abrupt response from the usually friendly young man surprised her. However, having had experience in dealing with a wide variety of bar patrons she confined herself to the task in hand.

"There you go," she said briskly, placing the full glass on the bar.

"On my tab," he responded, seizing the handle, turning away and heading for a vacant table in a far corner.

He took a long draught of the cool liquid, leaned back in the chair and stared unseeingly at the contents of the glass. What a bloody shambles! The meeting-the-parents exercise had gone well enough, and although his father had subsequently agreed to lay off Jason Collins, Matt had still felt foolish. Seeking some comfort, he'd decided to confide in Sandy only to be confronted with a 'need more time' reaction. Did this mean that she didn't trust him, or even love him? He reached for his glass. God, women were so bloody complicated.

A shadow fell across the table and he looked up to see Jason Collins standing above him.

"Hi," said the older man.

"Hi," responded Matt after a moment's hesitation.

"Mind if I join you?"

Matt noticed that Collins had a glass of fruit juice in his hand. "Day's work not yet over?" he asked.

Taking the comment as an invitation Collins pulled out a chair.

"Still got a couple of lessons to go." He nodded at Matt's glass. "Not flying, obviously."

Matt shook his head and took another long drink. "Was going to. Changed my mind."

"So, are you just here as a spectator?"

Matt glared at the other man. "Look, Jason, I'm not sure what your motives are but…"

Collins threw up both his hands in a surrender gesture and smiled. "Just trying to be friendly." He leaned forward. "Look, Matt, we had our differences in the past but you've obviously moved on with Sandy, and I presume that Fleur is only a memory. We have a mutual interest in flying so let's concentrate on that."

Matt shrugged. "Yeah, guess so." He drained his glass and stared morosely at the empty dregs.

"Another?"

"What? Oh yeah, er thanks."

In response to a signal from Collins, Jenny brought another pint to the table. Matt's perfunctory thanks caused Collins to shrug apologetically to Jenny as his companion seized the glass and quaffed greedily.

He thumped the glass back on the table and burped loudly.

"S'cuse me," he muttered.

"Tell me to mind my own bloody business, mate, but you don't look too happy."

"No, I'm not. Sandy…" his voice trailed away.

"Sandy. Is there a problem with her?"

"Yeah. Probably my own bloody fault." He hiccupped, wiped his left hand across his mouth and muttered, "I told her about…"

"About?" echoed Collins encouragingly.

"About Fleur and me."

"Fucking hell! What did you do that for?"

"Dunno. Clear the air, I suppose."

"Clear the air? Why? Had she found out?"

"No. Just thought that eventually she might."

"Find out? How?"

Matt shrugged and reached out for his glass. Collins seized his wrist and locked eyes with him.

"Listen you silly young bastard. I'm going to give you some advice about women. Never confess anything – ever. If they find out, then always have some credible explanation in your hip pocket."

"S'pose you're right," shrugged Matt.

"'Course I am. Did she come with you, today?"

"Yes, she did," said a voice from the doorway.

Both men looked up to see Sandy striding towards them.

"A cosy little twosome; an ageing Lothario and his grubby apprentice."

"Sandy, listen," cried Matt, pushing back his chair and beginning to stand. Unfortunately, the quantity of beer he'd consumed in a relatively short time caused him to stagger and reach out to Sandy for support. Instinctively she stepped back resulting in his crashing against the side of the table and sprawling on the floor, as the remaining contents of his glass spilled over his shirt.

Chapter 28

"C'mon, get on your feet, you stupid young bastard."

Collins hooked his right arm under Matt's left armpit and with relatively ease hauled him upright and dumped him back into his chair.

"You've made a right bloody mess."

"Where's Sandy?" Matt looked around the bar but the only woman he saw was Jenny, glaring at him with a look that showed that she wasn't going to be the one cleaning up the pool of beer on the floor.

"Buggered off. Straight away. Didn't look back."

The sound of a car starting, motor revving, tyres squealing and the fading growl of a high-revving engine floated up through the open windows.

"Probably her," grinned Collins.

"In my bloody sports car!" He started to rise from his seat, but Jason shoved him back down.

"Sit down and shut up. It's no more than you deserve. And when you've sobered up a little, go and ask Jenny for a bucket and mop to clean up the little lake you left." He stood. "I'll leave you to it."

Matt looked across to see Jenny nodding in agreement.

He carefully rose from his chair and approached her.

"Sorry about the mess, Jenny. My fault of course. Bloody idiot. Have you got a bucket and mop I could use?"

Jenny nodded and pointed behind the bar where the two items were propped up in the corner.

"Oh, thanks." With head lowered he fetched them and headed towards the seat just as the doors opened and several club members came bursting in. They paused and regarded him with amusement.

"Hi, Matt. You Mrs. Mops today?"

"Watch out, Jenny, he'll be after your job."

Responding to the chuckles with a sickly leer Matt vigorously applied the mop and squeezed the contents into the bucket until the area around the table was gleaming.

With eyes still downcast he picked up the bucket and walked back towards the bar.

"Good job, Matt. Done it before, have you?"

Matt shrugged.

"Here," she smiled. "I'll empty it. You've obviously had a hard day."

He looked up and grinned nervously.

"Thanks, Jenny. Thanks a lot. It hasn't been a good day at all."

"Here, have one on the house. It's our fruit juice special."

As she poured the contents into a tall glass, added ice, and handed it to him, Matt noticed how dry his mouth was. The drink he took was long and slow.

"Delicious, Jenny." He grinned. "Done it before, have you?"

Their joint chuckle caused surprised heads to turn.

"Once or twice."

"So how long have you worked here?"

"Couple of years. The hours are part-time which suits me."

"Part-time?" he enquired as he drained his glass.

"I'm finishing my uni degree. This job supports me in the meantime." She reached for his glass. "Another?"

"Yes, please."

As she turned away his eyes flicked over her, with renewed interest – pretty girl, nice figure, a cheerful smile, and brains.

"What are you studying?"

"Bachelor of Forensic Science, final year."

His eyebrows shot up in surprise. "Wow! That sounds impressive."

She smiled. "Depends on my results. It's hard work but I'm enjoying it."

"Forensics. Is that part of crime solving?" he asked a little uncertainly.

"It can be. I'm certainly interested in its application to criminology – drug detection, crime scene analysis, that sort of thing."

"So you'll complete your degree at the end of this year."

"Hopefully."

"Could you go on to further study?"

"Yes, a master's degree and," she shrugged, "who knows?"

"Awesome. You'll be—"

A piano riff in his pocket interrupted him.

"Sorry."

He pulled his iPhone out of his shirt pocket.

"Yes?"

"It's me."

He gave Jenny an apologetic smile and moved to the nearest corner.

"Where's my car?" he demanded.

"Albany bus terminal, in the car park. I left it there and caught a bus home. Listen, Matt—"

"Did you lock it?"

"No. I put the key under the front left wheel. Look, Matt—"

"Brilliant! Why didn't you just leave a note on the windscreen saying, 'Help yourself'. I'll need to go and pick it up straight away before some bastard nicks it."

He terminated the call.

"You ok, Matt?"

Jenny's voice broke into his thoughts.

Pocketing his phone, he stepped back to the bar.

"My car's in the Albany bus terminal. I need to pick it up. It's unlocked."

"How will you get there?"

"It's not too far. I'll phone for a taxi."

She looked at her watch.

"I'm knocking off in ten minutes. I could give you a lift."

Matt thought rapidly. It would probably take at least ten minutes for a taxi to arrive and a lift from Jenny would certainly be more pleasant.

"If you're sure."

"I'm sure," she smiled.

Chapter 29

"How come your car's at Albany?" she asked as she guided her rather noisy Toyota out of the airfield car park.

"Bit of a long story."

"OK. None of my business – just happy to help."

"Yea, thanks Jenny. It's much appreciated."

She smiled and nodded, keeping her eyes on the road.

They drove in silence through the pleasant rural countryside until they reached the motorway on ramp.

"What sort of car do you have?"

"A BMW sports. A Z3."

"Unlocked in a public car park. I can see why you're worried."

"Sandy left it there," he offered after a pause.

"Emergency, was it?"

"No, nastiness. She took off with it – we had a row on the way here, then she came into the bar, saw me talking to Jason, stormed out and drove off with my car."

"With Jason? What was wrong with that?"

Matt sighed. "Well," he began.

"Well?"

"It was really over another woman."

"Another woman," she echoed. "Who?"

"You can keep a secret?"

"Of course."

"Fleur. Fleur Lassiter."

"You and Jason—."

"And Fleur. All over now, for me. Trouble is I told Sandy."

"Ah." She paused and then looked across at him. "You've been a busy boy, Matt."

"Yeah. Should have kept my mouth shut."

"Or your fly zipped." Jenny spun the wheel and entered the car park. "And here we are, lover boy."

Chapter 30

"Tonight, is it, Tony?"

"Yes, Vladimir, the pickup is all planned and ready to go."

"Where?"

"A private landing strip. About two hundred kilometres north of Auckland."

"You have details?"

"I have the location, the time and the people involved."

"Are you involved?" asked Zhukov.

"Yes. I'm flying up early this evening with Jason. We'll unload the plane when it lands from its trans-Tasman trip. Some of the consignment will be loaded onto our plane."

"The drugs?"

"Yes."

The Russian grunted and nodded. "Continue."

"Yes, well, like I said, some of the goods will be loaded onto our plane and the rest onto two separate pickup trucks for distribution to other locations."

"What will your role be?"

"Nothing specific, Vladimir. Jason just wants me to accompany him so that I can gain an understanding of the process."

"So what you think we should do?"

"At this point, nothing. There will be other opportunities, so leaving me a free hand to watch and learn would be very valuable."

Zhukov stood and walked over to where Tony was seated. Tony lifted his head and met the Russian's direct glare.

"So it is free hand that you are wanting, yes?"

Tony grunted and nodded.

"Why you think I should give this to you?"

Tony pretended to be confused. "Give what to me?" he asked.

"The free hand, to do as you bloody wish with nobody to be there to watch you."

Tony held his gaze for several seconds before responding with deliberate slowness.

"I have spent a long time carefully following your orders, Vladimir. I took flying lessons even though I had a fear of flying. I overcame that fear. I did very well with my flying and will be qualified very soon. I made a friend of Jason Collins, an arrogant prick, but I kept smiling and earned his trust, so much so that he offered me the opportunity to participate in his operation. Do you understand me, Vladimir, the opportunity to participate, to be part of what he does, to reveal the key points of his operation to me?" His pace remained the same, but his voice rose. "You do not give me a free hand – I have earned a free hand, the right to use my own judgement in this operation and the right to your trust as a colleague, as a partner of your team, not as some snivelling little sycophant who has to ask your permission to fart."

Zhukov had taken a step back, his stare changing from challenge to puzzlement.

"And one more thing!" barked Tony.

"Yes?"

"Do not ever again blow your cigarette smoke in my face. It's a disgusting thing to do to anyone, particularly a colleague." He paused and spat out the next word. "*Ponimayu?*"

It was the first time Tony had ever spoken a Russian word to his boss. The grammar wasn't perfect, but the challenge was unmistakable – Do you understand?

Zhukov stared at him for a long moment before nodding and muttering, "*Da, ya ponimayu.*"

"Excellent!" Tony pushed his chair back and stood. With an effort he smiled broadly at Zhukov. "Now we both understand each other."

"Vlad, surely this does not mean that he can operate on his own?" Gregory was obviously stunned by the sudden turn of events and could see a potential threat to his own position.

"Enough, Gregory! What Tony said is true. He followed my orders and has been successful. He will go to the rendezvous alone." He looked at his watch. "What time you leave?"

"Now, would be best. I'm driving to the airfield where I'm meeting Jason. We'll tell anyone who asks that he's taking me for a night flying practice – a common enough occurrence."

"Good," grunted Zhukov. He reached for his cigarettes and then appeared to change his mind. "I give you good wishes for tonight." His stretched out and shook the other man's hand. He then turned and looked at the Georgian.

"Gregory!"

"Yes, Vlad?"

"You will also give Tony your good wishes, please."

Gregory hesitated and then stretched out his hand.

"Good luck, Tony. Be interested to hear the details when you return."

Tony hoped that he'd suppressed any hint of triumph in his smile.

"Thanks, Gregory." He swept up his keys, and with a brief nod to both men, was gone.

Chapter 31

"On time and on target," said Collins' voice through the headphones as the Cessna 172SP lifted off above the club's landing strip. He'd explained that they were using this in preference to a Robin aircraft as it had a larger baggage compartment.

The plane swung into a half turn and headed north. Behind them the city's lights were still burning as dawn was two hours away.

"Rendezvous in a couple of hours?"

"That's the plan, young man. The two pickups should be in position and the lights ready to be turned on as we approach. We're timed to arrive thirty minutes before the plane comes in from Sydney."

"You said that it's a private landing strip."

"Yea, they're all over the country, especially in farming areas where the local cow cocky can use his plane for transporting goods and personnel, or some recreational flying. Ideal from my position as the take-offs and landings aren't monitored very rigorously – particularly if the landing strip's been there for a few years."

"You know the owner?"

"Yeah. Taught him to fly a few years back. I pay him well for the use of the strip and he knows better than to ask too many questions."

"How about the pickup drivers?"

"Couple of local boys. Have links with local gangs further north. Medical drugs are an increasing source of revenue for them and they're willing to take my money, deliver the supplies, and keep their mouths shut."

"You sure?"

"As sure as it's possible to be in this business. I pay well and they know that there's a high chance of further business"

"So a portion of the goods will be delivered to other contacts in your network and you'll take the rest."

"Correct. If everyone's on time the whole process should take less than an hour. After that we return home and unload the packages into my van."

"What if anyone sees us? Won't they ask questions?"

"We'll be back before the club opens for the day, so there'll only be a security guard on duty. I've already informed him that we're transporting some parts and equipment. He just shrugged and said okay, so no problems there."

The sky was completely dark and apart from occasional glimpses of the moon the only other light sources came from buildings, settlements and towns. Tony had been nervous about the night flight but his successful confrontation with Zhukov and his keenness to view the operation in action had overcome his fear – and the constantly changing vista was spectacular. It promised to be an exciting trip.

He smiled as he settled back into his seat. He hadn't planned to confront Zhukov but had decided that the best approach would be to present him with a clear description of the rendezvous and that he should be left to proceed on his own. However, when the man had reacted by deliberately standing over him it had triggered off a reaction that was the end result of a cumulative effect of the condescension and rudeness that he'd experienced over the preceding weeks. The cigarette smoke issue had also been completely unplanned but looking back on the incident he surmised that his brain had decided that he might as well go for broke.

A shiver went through him as he imagined what would have resulted from a negative reaction by the brutal Russian. But it had been worth the risk. He'd made his point and caused the arrogant bastard to back down. He smiled and nodded to himself.

"There's Whangarei coming up on our left. We'll swing forty degrees west which should get us to the rendezvous point in thirty minutes."

"Great."

Twenty-five minutes later Collins, having established radio contact, simply stated, "Rendezvous, repeat, rendezvous." Almost immediately a patch of lights appeared in the distance.

"That's the strip. Here we go."

The plane began to slowly descend and the shape of the landing strip, outlined by powerful landing lights around its perimeter, became clearer. As they touched down and throttled back, Tony noticed two pickups parked at the far end with several men standing nearby.

The plane landed smoothly, and Collins guided it off to the left of the airstrip near the pickups before switching off the engine.

"OK, out we get."

Following his lead Tony opened his door, stepped onto the wing and dropped to the ground. The pair walked towards the group.

"G'day," said a tall man. "Good flight?"

"All went smoothly."

"The Aussie kite just radioed in. They're about fifteen minutes away."

"Must have picked up a tailwind across the Tasman. Good."

Tony noticed that although the tall man and Jason appeared to know each other, neither made any attempt to make any introductions – obviously all part of the ethos. Two burly young Maori men were standing back from the rest of the group, seeming to prefer the security of the shadows. They wore identical leather jackets with gang insignias on the right sleeve. Tony assumed larger insignias would be on the back of the jacket, but it was too dark to see. The taller of the two wore a broad brimmed black hat, and his companion's heavy beard was complemented by a generous growth of black hair, kept in place by a dark red bandana.

Although the surrounding area was farmland, a few hundred metres away stood a large patch of natural bush. Silenced by the plane's arrival, the nocturnal sounds of crickets, cicadas, owls and other creatures began to re-emerge in a gentle cacophony. Tony, who'd spent his early years in the country, endeavoured to identify some of them.

"Aircraft coming," said the tall man.

From the distance could be seen points of light and the emerging sound of an aircraft's engines slowing down in preparation for landing.

"It's a Cherokee 6," explained Collins. "Ideal for us as it has a baggage compartment in the nose between the cockpit and the engine compartment and a large double door in the back for easy loading of cargo."

"And can go the distance?"

"Yes, its Australian departure point is Lord Howe Island. It has four long range fuel tanks and reduced power settings to save fuel if required."

The Cherokee 6 landed smoothly. The pilot guided it in a half circle so that it faced back down the empty airstrip before turning off the engine and, with his co-pilot, clambering out of the cabin. He and Collins shook hands, and after a minimum of pleasantries, the side of the plane was opened. The pilot produced a manifest as Collins signalled to the two Maori men to approach.

The co-pilot walked round to the large fuel drum, wheeled it over to the plane, unlocked the fuel cap and began to refuel the aircraft.

Collins briefly explained that the manifest contained a complete list of the cargo's contents and that it had already been divided into two separate groups, one for Collins and the other for the Maori men.

"Here you go," said Collins to the two men. "All your cargo is in these two crates."

The bearded man gave the document a perfunctory glance. "What's listed here is what's in the crates, right?"

"Right. I've told your boss and he's agreed to take my word for it. If you wanted to cross-check everything now it would take some time."

"Yeah, he told us." The man paused and looked squarely at Collins. "I wouldn't try to fool him if I was you. Doesn't like being crossed."

"That's for sure," echoed his companion.

Collins kept his voice steady. "Your boss and I have done business before, to our mutual benefit. I value our relationship and want it to continue. To try to fool him might give me a short-term gain, but it would result in a long-term loss."

"'Specially for you, eh, bro," replied the hat wearer.

"Nobody would win, not your boss, not you and not me. Now, are you prepared to accept my word that all the items in the manifest are in the crates?" Both men exchanged glances then nodded. "Good. Do you want a hand to carry them?"

"Not necessary, bro."

Reaching into the fuselage, the bearded man swung the first crate round and placed his hands underneath the leading edges. His companion did the same and together they lifted and walked it over to the pickup.

"Christ," murmured the Australian pilot, "those boys are all muscle."

The pair returned and lifted the second crate.

"All set?" asked the bearded man.

"All set," nodded Collins.

"OK. See you, bro," and they were gone.

"I think we'll need a hand," smiled Tony to the pilot and the tall man.

"Thought you would," grinned the pilot. "Not all you Kiwis are muscle men."

"Except when the All Blacks play you lot at rugby."

"Yeah, whatever. Let's just get this stuff shifted."

With four men to each crate the aircraft was loaded with comparative ease. In response to a nod from Collins, Tony

127

climbed up onto the wing, but before lowering himself into the cabin, he paused and looked back over the scene of one of the strangest evenings he'd ever experienced. The pickups had already left, and he noticed that Collins, prior to shaking hands with the other pilot, had handed over a bulky envelope. Then, repeating the procedure with the tall man, he walked over to the plane. Outside the darkness was slowly surrendering to the advance of the morning light.

"OK, we'll let the Aussie take off first to make sure he's safely in the air."

"Makes sense. You happy with the way it all went?"

"Yeah, no problems. The lights came on as requested, and everyone rendezvoused at the right time."

"The two Maori guys looked a bit intimidating."

"You think so?"

"Yeah, with their grim faces and gang patches."

"Not the sort of guys you see round the clubhouse, you mean?"

"Yeah, suppose so."

"Yet I'd rather deal with them than many of the Pakeha characters that I meet on a daily basis. Treat them fairly and they'll reciprocate."

Collins put on his headset and Tony followed suit.

"OK, but what was all that stuff about not crossing their boss?" he asked as the engine turned over and fired.

"Supports what I'm saying. Don't cross us and we won't cross you. Easy to deal with guys with that attitude."

Tony nodded slowly.

"Makes sense. Met a few of them when I was," he paused, "inside. They tended to keep together, had a strong group loyalty, but I don't remember anyone complaining about being screwed over unfairly by any of them."

"So there you go. This group is part of the network – I play fair by them and it's reciprocated – to our mutual advantage."

"Is 'mutual advantage' one of your guiding principles?"

Collins smiled as he positioned the plane for take-off.

"Yeah. If the clients feel that they're being fairly treated they won't try to rip me off." He grinned. "Worked well so far."

"And if anyone tries to do the dirty on you?"

"Haven't struck that yet. If I do," he grinned, "I know people."

While they'd been talking the Australian pilot had taken off and was lifting his plane into the night sky.

"The Aussie pilot? A mate of yours?"

"Yeah, from way back. We were instructors in the same club in Brisbane and became good mates. Had some great times together, but then I had to leave."

"Had to?"

"Yeah. Women. Story of my bloody life."

"Oh, surprise, surprise."

Both men's eyes followed the aircraft as it slowly turned east heading for Australia.

"How do they manage to avoid customs and all the formalities?"

"They fly low, under the radar."

"Really? As in wartime. Isn't it risky?"

"Not really. From here they'll go to Kerikeri Airport in order to conform with the flight plan and avoid the hassles they could get at a larger airfield. Then they'll fly back to Aussie, via Lord Howe Island." He indicated the deserted landing strip and smirked. "There'll be no record of their landing and take-off from here."

Tony grunted and nodded. "Neatly planned, Jason."

"A key factor is the pilot. My mate and his co-pilot are first class and would be capable of responding to any unforeseen circumstances."

"I presume they're well paid."

Collins smiled wryly. "Oh yes, their compensation is generous."

"So the cargo they bring would need to fetch a high price."

"It would, and it does. It's a lucrative operation, which is why all parties are at pains to cover their tracks." He paused and leaned forward. "Speaking of which, we need to get going."

Tony watched Collins as he eased the throttle open.

"So, are you interested?" asked Collins.

"Yeah. You've obviously organised a system that works very smoothly, based on efficient organisation with advantages for all participants, and mutual trust."

He paused while Collins increased the engine revs and the plane began to shudder in anticipation.

With a quick wave to the tall man Collins thrust his aircraft down the runway and lifted it into the air. As they rose Tony noticed that the runway lights were immediately extinguished.

"So you'd be prepared to play a more active role on future occasions?"

"Yes, I would. My only reservation would be..." he hesitated.

"Zhukov?"

"Yes, we'd need to carefully sort out how we manage that relationship. He thinks he owns me, and that whatever I do will be done on his behalf. At this stage he wants me to report back on tonight's activities, and if my comments are positive, he'll be very keen to have a large piece of the action – at your expense."

"So, Tony, where does your loyalty truly lie?" The question was posed with slow deliberation.

"Tonight was the clincher for me, Jason. I owe Zhukov nothing. My loyalty is to you."

Chapter 32

"How's the flying going, Matt?"

Accepting the beer that his father handed him, Matt smiled.

"Going well, Dad. I'm enjoying it and making steady progress."

"Good." Bullock took a sip from his glass and placed it on his study table.

"Jason Collins. Apart from the problem with the woman, do you know much else about him?"

Matt, relaxing in the depth of the leather armchair, straightened up.

"In what way?" he responded cautiously.

"I've had information that suggests he's involved in some sort of smuggling racket, possibly connected with drugs."

"Christ! It's been rumoured round the club that he's had to supplement his flying instructor's income to maintain his expensive lifestyle, but there's been no mention of drugs."

His father nodded, reached for his glass and took a long swig.

"Why the interest, Dad?"

"What I'm about to tell you is strictly confidential." He lowered his glass and looked hard at his son. "Strictly confidential."

"Sure."

Bullock shifted his position, gave a heavy sigh and began slowly.

"My business, although quite prosperous, is not doing as well as I'd like. It's sound enough but the cash flow's drying up a little, which is starting to cause me a few financial problems." He smiled mirthlessly. "Like Jason Collins, I too enjoy the good life, but unlike him, my expenses are heavier." He spread his arms briefly. "This house, my two children and your mother. It all costs money. You all enjoy a very pleasant lifestyle, but it's dependent on my generating a regular cash flow, which now needs a little extra injection."

He paused and Matt, now sitting bolt upright, stared at him.

"Hell, Dad, does this mean that you're going broke, that you'll have to sell the house and—"

His father held up his hand.

"No it doesn't. I just need to generate more revenue, more ready cash."

"But what's this got to do with Collins and his activities? What he's doing is certainly illegal and—"

His voice trailed away as a realisation dawned on him.

"Jesus! Are you interested in Collins because you want to be part of what he's doing?"

His father's response was controlled. "Matt, I'm seeking to expand my business activities, particularly where a cash flow can be directly generated. You've indicated that Collins may be involved in a business that fits my needs. If it's on the edge of the law, so be it. If the money's good it'll be worth the risk."

"Even if it's illegal?"

His father took another mouthful and slowly ran his fingers around the rim of the glass.

"Business has many grey areas where the interpretation of legal and illegal is open to question." He smiled sardonically. "That's why we need lawyers. Consequently, it's always been a guiding principle of mine to look at all business opportunities and, if they can avoid close scrutiny by the authorities, to take advantage of what's on offer. In the case of Jason Collins, if he's making money and there's a way of becoming part of his operation, or even taking it over, then I'd like to consider it."

Matt showed no sign of wanting to respond.

"So, son, whatever is in my interests is also in yours. If I increase my profits, then you'll benefit. If I don't, if things become tight, then your lifestyle will have to be curtailed."

"Curtailed?"

"Yes. You'd have to drop some of your more expensive activities, and on top of the list would be…" his father's voice tailed off and he raised his eyebrows.

"Flying?"

"'Fraid so, Matt."

"Fuck!"

"Fuck indeed. But it needn't happen if you can find out some more information about Collins and his activities."

Matt stared at his father for a long moment. The recent incident in the club bar had been embarrassing for him, but Collins had made the initial no-hard-feelings approach. As the man loved to boast about his achievements perhaps he could use flattery to gain further information.

"Could be tricky. And if I did get the information you wanted, what then?"

"You can leave it with me. I have people who'll be able to, ah, actively follow him up."

"You mean beat him up and take over his operation."

"Not necessarily. Just a little gentle persuasion."

"If I agree to do so, can I keep flying?"

His father smiled warmly. "Of course. I'm not exactly facing penury, Matt. I can still finance your flying and any expenses that your investigation could incur –within reason." He tilted his head upwards. "Think you can do it?"

Matt nodded slowly. "Yes, but I'll need to think it through."

"Fine by me, Matt." He raised his glass. "To a successful father and son enterprise."

They finished their drinks over some small talk and then Matt excused himself. His father reached for the whisky decanter, poured a generous drink and leaning back in his chair, smiled. He'd paid off Zhukov and assumed that was the end of the matter. However, that morning he'd received a package that contained a brief report on Jason Collins' activities. A hand-written note accompanied the package. "Dear Mr Bullock. This report was finished when you rang. You paid for it so I send it to you. Thank you again for your business". It was signed by Vladimir Zhukov.

Bullock had already searched Jason Collins on the Internet, so was familiar with his background and appearance. Zhukov's additional information, although short on specifics, showed Collins was involved in the importing of drugs using light aircraft, and he appeared to be making very good money. Bullock had decided to share this information with Matt and to stress his need to generate an increased cash flow, thereby motivating him to further expand the information already contained in the report. It was something of a juggling act but worth the risk.

He frowned as he reached for his glass. There was clearly an element of danger. He took a mouthful of the soothing liquid. Matt would have to tread carefully.

Chapter 33

The luxury cruise ship *Ovation of the Seas* made its stately way past Rangitoto Island towards the docks. The water on Auckland's Waitemata Harbour parted gracefully as the vessel, attended by two tugs, slowly turned to starboard. The beautiful day with a gentle breeze had attracted yachts of all sizes – some of which were competing in nautical races, while others were sailing towards the many islands in the Hauraki Gulf.

"Never get tired of watching those big ships."

"Me neither. Would be great to climb on board and sail away into the wild blue yonder, leaving it all behind."

"Sounds pretty heartfelt, Sandy. Are you just fantasising or do you really mean it?"

Sandy reached up quickly to clap her hand on her sunhat before a sudden gust swept it away. She and her friend Lucy Marshall were seated on a grass embankment on top of Mount Victoria that offered a panoramic view of the city. Along with many inhabitants they had climbed the tall Devonport hill to view the yachts, the other craft and the giant cruise ship. Summer was the cruise ship season, providing Auckland inhabitants with a continual stream of vessels that in turn provided a continual stream of revenue to New Zealand's largest city.

"Dunno. Way I'm feeling at the moment I'd be ready to chuck it all in and just bugger off."

"Even your flying lessons?"

"Huh! Particularly my flying lessons."

"But the last time we met you told me they were awesome – you loved flying and your instructors had said that you showed promise."

Her friend didn't reply but just stared out to sea.

"And you also said you'd met a great guy who also likes flying, and you'd even been to his Remuera home to meet his parents."

"Yeah, well."

"Yeah, well what? Is he the reason you're feeling pissed off?"

Sandy nodded.

"How come?"

"It's complicated."

"It generally is where men are concerned. But it might help to talk about it."

Sandy reached down, picked a large daisy from the grass embankment and began plucking the petals.

"OK, it might help me make sense of the whole mess." She took a deep breath. "His name's Matt, couple of years older than me. He's also learning to fly and is doing well."

"What's he like? Good looking?"

"Yeah, tallish, dark hair and blue eyes. His shyness mixed with genuine warmth initially attracted me. Initially, anyway."

"But you've changed your mind?"

"Yeah, probably."

"Why?"

"My first flying instructor was a dude called Jason Collins, an older man, good looking who fancied himself with the women. Apparently some found him attractive, but I found him creepy. Anyway, he was having an affair with one of his pupils, a woman called Fleur – in her mid-thirties, attractive but hard."

"With you so far, but what's this got to do with—?"

"Patience." She took another deep breath. "For some reason, Matt didn't like Jason Collins. They'd even had a fistfight on the clubhouse tarmac."

"Really?"

"Yes, I discovered this just recently. Anyway, Matt and I had been going out for about a month, and I'd met his parents—"

"What were they like?"

"His little sister's pretty aggressive and I don't think his parents get on, but they did their best to make me welcome – in their opulent house."

"Opulent?"

"Yes, very." She paused and sighed. "But getting on with the story, a couple of days ago Matt and I drove out to the airfield where he parked his car and said he wanted to talk about something important, before we went inside. He then confessed that he'd been having an affair with the Fleur woman."

Lucy stared at her. "At the same time as the flight instructor?"

"Yeah, the real reason why they didn't like each other."

"Is the affair over?"

"He assured me it was, he truly loved me and that he'd never behave like that again."

"What did you say?"

"I told him it was all a big shock and I'd need time to think it over before I could give him an answer."

"Fair enough."

"Not for him it wasn't. He jumped out of the car, slammed the door and strode into the clubrooms without looking back. I sat there for about fifteen minutes before finally deciding to go in. I went upstairs into the lounge and there was Matt drinking beer with bloody Jason Collins."

"Oh, my god! What did you do?"

"I marched over to the table, and made a caustic comment about an ageing lothario and his grubby apprentice. Matt, who'd obviously been drinking, tried to stand, slipped, crashed into the table, fell on the floor and the beer from his glass spilt all over him. I marched out, went down to the car park, got back into his car, drove to the Albany bus terminal, parked it, phoned him to let him know where his car was, and caught a bus home. Haven't heard from him since."

Lucy gaped at her for a long moment. "Wow! Can I use that scenario for my script writing class at uni?"

"Be my guest."

The two young women sat in silence watching the giant cruise liner coming to a stop within the inner harbour. Too large to fit into any of the berths and having been anchored firmly fore and aft, the vessel floated majestically in the stream. Passengers crowded the rails watching as orange lighters appeared alongside, ready to ferry them ashore.

"Flying's for the birds," said Sandy. "Perhaps I'll take a sea voyage."

Chapter 34

"Hi Matt."

About to enter the aero club entrance Matt turned to see Tony walking towards him.

"Oh, hi Tony. How's things?"

"Good. You flying today?"

"Already had a morning flight. Thought I'd have a bite of lunch." He smiled. "Care to join me?"

"Why not?" shrugged Tony. "Lead the way."

The pair climbed the stairs to the lounge nodding at several club members who were relaxing over drinks.

"My shout. What are you having, Matt?"

"Just a light beer."

Tony turned towards the bar where Jenny was serving two men. She looked up, nodded at him and then caught Matt's eye. She favoured him with a broad grin.

Tony returned to their table and sat down. "Jenny said she'd bring them over."

"Of course," Matt grinned, watching Jenny walking towards them with two long glasses of lager.

"Hi, Matt. You're looking happy," she said.

"And you're looking good, Jenny," he responded as she placed the glasses on the table. "What time do you finish tonight?"

"Not till late. It's Saturday night, remember."

"I know," grinned Matt.

"Staying for lunch?"

"Yeah."

"Menu's on the blackboard."

"Thanks, Jenny. We'll let you know."

Jenny smiled and both men watched as she walked back to the bar.

"Pretty girl," commented Tony.

Matt raised his eyebrows and nodded and lifted his glass.

"Cheers."

"Cheers."

They both drank deep and put their glasses back on the table.

"Have you seen Jason today?" asked Matt.

"Not this morning. I think he's got a couple of student flights booked for this afternoon. Why?"

"You know him pretty well, don't you?"

"Suppose I do. He taught me to fly."

"Me too. We had a bit of a falling out, but we're OK now."

Tony grinned. "Yes I did hear about that. Glad it's all smoothed over."

"Reason I asked is that," he paused, "I need a bit of information."

"Yeah?"

Matt took another drink and putting the glass down, slowly looked to his right and left.

"Jason likes to live the high life and to do that he needs a good income."

Tony frowned and nodded.

"But, I don't think being a flying instructor would give him enough cash to live his kind of lifestyle."

Tony nodded again making an effort to maintain a neutral expression.

"He boasted to me about his female conquests but he also hinted he's making additional money on the side."

"Did he?"

"Yeah. He didn't say much more than that, so I just wondered if you knew anything about it."

Tony's eyes narrowed.

"Why do you think I would?"

"Oh, no special reason," said Matt hurriedly. "I just thought he might have mentioned—."

"Why do you want to know?"

Matt made a poor attempt at nonchalance.

140

"Oh, I just thought if there was money to be made..."

"I thought you had a wealthy father. Has he got financial problems?"

"What? God no! It's just that—"

Tony reached out, grasped Matt's wrist and squeezed hard.

"Take my advice and leave well alone."

Shocked by the pain and the change in tone Matt reddened and nodded his head several times.

"Yes. Of course."

Tony relaxed his grip and favoured Matt with a warm smile.

"Good. Now let's order lunch from the lovely Jenny."

Chapter 35

"Hi Jason, it's Tony."

"Hi Tony. What's up?"

"It may be nothing, but I thought you should know I had lunch with Matt at the clubhouse and he started asking questions."

"What sort of questions?"

"About your extra income sources."

"Christ!"

"He didn't seem to know much, but had guessed that you made extra money outside of your regular job."

"Why was he so interested?"

"Before I shut him down he hinted that his father could be having financial problems and was looking for an increased income flow. I pushed him further, but he very quickly denied it, which increased my suspicions."

"Interesting."

"He was actually hoping to see you – wanted to ask you some questions about your extracurricular activities. Said you'd already mentioned them to him." He paused and then he added, "Had you?"

"Christ Almighty, why don't I just post it all on Facebook and invite people to bloody invest? One minute I'm quietly running a profitable operation on the quiet and the next minute a Russian oaf and now a Kiwi rich-lister wants to muscle in. This is getting fucking serious, mate."

"Yeah. The question is what are you going to do about it?"

Chapter 36

The sound of the evening traffic on Karangahape Road drifted past his apartment's windows but Vladimir Zhukov barely noticed. He'd dimmed the lights, switched off his cell phone, and opened a fresh bottle of vodka and a pack of cigarettes. He was in no mood for company – male or female.

The cold weather always increased his back pain. The cigarettes helped to confine the pain to a dull ache, but a drop in temperature invariably meant a heightening of the discomfort and an increase in the frequency of the spasms. His thoughts dragged him back to St Petersburg, formerly Leningrad – a city devastated by the Nazi invasion.

During the immediate post-war period paranoia was sweeping through the Soviet Union. Joseph Stalin imagined internal enemies on all sides, particularly the Leningrad industrial managers, scientists and academics. Under what became known as the Leningrad Affair there were widespread arrests and trials held behind closed doors. Leading officials were sentenced to death and a further two thousand disappeared into the maw of the Gulag Archipelago whose prison camps sprawled through the Siberian wastes.

During this period his parents had met at Leningrad University. His father had gained a postgraduate degree in English in the same year that his mother had gained her English undergraduate qualification. They had married in 1958 and their son was born a year later. Soon after their marriage his father had been posted to the KGB, his primary roles being document translation and improving the English language skills of trainee spies and diplomats.

A year later a trusted colleague had given Zhukov's father a copy of George Orwell's recently published Animal Farm. *Intrigued by the allegorical content he'd mentioned this to a trusted colleague. Two days later he was arrested. It was the last time his wife and infant son ever saw him again.*

Although the death of Stalin in 1953 and the subsequent reforms probably saved her from sharing her husband's fate, she nevertheless lost her government position and was forced out of their comfortable apartment. From a one-room flat in a poorer part of the city she tried to make do with menial work such as cleaning houses and taking in washing. Living a hand to mouth existence, and unable to provide more than the absolute bare necessities for her son, she started to teach him English, speaking softly in their flat and during their walks in the local parks. The little boy was bright and showed an interest in what his mother called their 'shared secret', talking together in English and only conversing in Russian when in the hearing of other people.

Sickness and disease continued taking its toll and although medication slowly became more widely available, the Party apparatchiks and their families had priority. Medical assistance for the wife and child of an exiled intellectual was almost impossible to obtain. When he was six years old his mother contracted pneumonia. In the ensuing days her terrified son watched helplessly as her hacking cough and trembling increased until, one dark night in a midst of a howling blizzard, she reached out for his hand, gave a final moan of despair and ceased to breathe. A neighbour found him the following morning, traumatised and cold, lying across his mother's lifeless form still holding her hand.

The rest of his family had perished in the war and with no one else prepared to claim him, the authorities put him into a state orphanage. Life there was strict with brutal punishments for even minor misdemeanours, particularly for a boy whose father was an enemy of the state.

The only positive side was a steady supply of food, the result of government policy in a country that had lost millions of its citizens, where the rearing of the next generation was given

144

priority. Bread, gruel and small portions of unspecified meat were the standard fare, eaten in silence in the food hall. Older boys patrolled between the aisles to strictly enforce the 'no talking' rule – disobedience always resulting in cuffs to the side of the head. Repeated flouting of the rule was punished by brutal canings with long rods on the bare backside and back – but only after the culprit had finished his food; the orphanage's mantra being 'healthy bodies and obedient minds'.

Bullying was widespread. Although not officially encouraged, it was generally ignored by the authorities with the result that a pecking order based on strength became well established. Younger and weaker boys had to defer to those older and stronger, staying at the back when they all huddled round the fireplaces in the winter, and surrendering warmer bedclothes and items of clothing on demand. Parcels sent to boys fortunate enough to have relatives on the outside were immediately seized by the self-appointed committee of older boys who then distributed the contents to their cronies. The official recipient of the parcel would be unlikely to enjoy any part of the contents, particularly if he was a younger or weaker boy.

One late afternoon, in his sixteenth year, Zhukov was hurrying across the courtyard during a heavy snowfall when he slipped on the icy surface. As he fell to the ground he shouted, "Shit!" He started to pick himself when another boy crouched down beside him. "What did you say?" he whispered in English. Zhukov stared at him for a long moment and then, in the same language, replied, "I said, shit. Do you speak English?"

"Yes," muttered the other boy. "My father worked in England as a diplomat."

Zhukov looked around the deserted courtyard. He seized the boy by the arm and pulled him into a nearby alcove.

"Vladimir. My father is English teacher."

"Sergei." He frowned. "If your father is alive, why are you here?"

Zhukov's eyes dropped. "He is prisoner, in the camps."

Sergei nodded. "Mine too." He shrugged. "I think he's dead, like my mother."

"And mine."

Both boys shared an empathetic silence until Sergei spoke.

"If they catch us speaking English they might beat us."

Zhukov nodded.

"Yes. But is good to speak with someone like you."

"But what can we do?"

Zhukov paused.

"I think of something. At dinner, watch me. When I leave, follow me."

Two hours later the boys were huddled together in the alcove. The winter sky had darkened, and the plummeting temperature had discouraged anyone else from venturing outside.

"I have idea. We should volunteer for latrine duty," said Zhukov.

"Volunteer?"

"Yes, say that we will do it. Clean the toilets."

"Ugh! Why?"

"Nobody likes the job so they offer extra food. People will leave us alone and we can talk English together."

Sergei had finally agreed and the next day they approached the fatigues officer. Initially suspicious he was finally impressed by the boys' seemingly high level of motivation and agreed that they could start their duties the following day.

The task was unpleasant but for two boys raised in the privations of post-war Russia, it was tolerable, and the opportunity to practice their English and the extra rations provided sufficient incentive to persevere. Although limited by their own knowledge of English vocabulary and grammar, the chance to practice and increase the speed of their oral communication was exciting.

Zhukov was big for his age and, although initially a target for bullying, had soon grasped the essentials of the system, and

146

began offering his support and services to the older boys. He would fetch and carry and on orders beat up any of his peers who needed to be 'taught a lesson'.

In spite of the strict discipline imposed in the classroom, he enjoyed the lessons. His teachers, noting his enthusiasm for learning, treated him favourably in class and as the years went by, he was consistently in the top ten in all subjects.

He and Sergei continued their latrine duties and other boys soon learned that any attempt to mock him was liable to be met with swift and brutal retaliation. Consequently, the pair was left alone to continue their unpleasant task.

One evening, two years later, as they were completing the washing of their buckets and mops, the dinner bell echoed through the halls.

"Just in time for dinner," said Zhukov.

"Yes, I'm hungry," replied Sergei.

They both turned to walk to the dining room and stopped abruptly. Confronting them was Ivan Stepanov, a fatigues officer.

"What language were you speaking?" he demanded.

The two boys exchanged glances and Zhukov replied, "English, sir. We only know a little."

"Where did you learn it?"

Both boys exchanged glances.

"Answer me!"

"From our parents, sir," said Zhukov.

"Your parents."

"Yes, sir. They are both dead."

His hard expression softened a little.

"Return to your duties."

They continued with their latrine duties for the ensuing months but restricted themselves to occasional whispered exchanges of English phrases – after they'd checked to see if anyone was in the vicinity.

Over the ensuing years Zhukov systematically worked himself into leadership roles and by his eighteenth birthday, he was enjoying the special privileges that he regarded as his right.

But he went too far.

One bitter winter's night during a particularly nasty blizzard, the temperature in the dormitory plummeted. He awoke just after midnight feeling the cold crawling through his body. He lay shivering for a few moments before flinging off his bedclothes and striding down the dormitory to where the younger boys slept. He stopped by a bed where a boy was sleeping and grasping the two top blankets, began to pull them off the bed. The boy, waking instantly, clutched them tightly, shouting, "Leave my blankets alone!"

"Let them go! I want them!" responded Zhukov, pulling the boy and his blankets off the bed. Scrambling upright the boy sprang forward. He threw a right hook that caught Zhukov on the left cheek, sending him staggering. Furious at this show of rebellion he dropped the blankets and felled the other boy with left and right hooks. As the boy fell his head connected with the bed's iron frame. He slid to the floor, moaned once and lay still. Zhukov, still angry, began to kick the boy in the ribs with the side of his right foot until arms seized him.

"You crazy fool," a boy's voice shouted above the sound of the blizzard. "His head's bleeding!"

Zhukov ceased struggling and stared down.

Two sheets of lightning showed two other boys kneeling and lifting the limp body of the younger boy. Blood seeped from the head wound and dripped onto the dormitory's wooden floor. The older boy checked the pulse and heartbeat before looking up at Zhukov.

"He's dead." He shook his head slowly. "You're finished, Zhukov."

Retribution was swift. While the authorities turned a blind eye to bullying, a death was a completely different matter. That night Zhukov was seized by senior staff members, hauled roughly

148

downstairs and flung into a tiny cell where he was knocked to the floor and kicked in the ribs by heavy boots. Clad only in his pyjamas, he was left moaning and bleeding for the remainder of the night. The next morning, barely conscious, dressed in standard orphanage issue clothing he was forced upstairs where he was ordered to stand to attention outside a door and wait until summoned.

After thirty minutes he was roughly ushered into the room where three men sat facing him behind a large desk. Ordered to stand to attention he did so and then started to look around the room. A blow to the back of his head was accompanied by, "Face straight ahead, Zhukov!" He staggered and quickly resumed his stance, fixing his eyes on the man in the centre of the trio.

"Vladimir Zhukov," intoned the man. "you have been found guilty of murdering Anatoly Sokolov."

"Murder! I only hit him with my fists and—."

A heavier blow to his head sent him staggering to his knees. He was immediately dragged upright and ordered to stand to attention. The ringing in his ears meant that he had difficulty hearing the next utterance.

"You have two choices – the reform school for older boys or enlistment in the Russian Armed Services operating in Afghanistan."

Zhukov grunted and reached for another cigarette. He well remembered the multitude of confusing thoughts that swirled round in his head confronted by the questioning looks on the faces of the trio. He remembered thinking that reform school would certainly be worse than his present environment and the army option could provide him with a life of action and possibly adventure. He had no idea where Afghanistan was, so that wasn't a factor in his decision.

"The Russian Armed Services."

"Say, sir, you scum," hissed a voice behind him.

Bracing his shoulders, he loudly repeated, "Sir, the Russian Armed Services, sir!"

The trio exchanged glances and nodded.

The central figure shrugged and smiled grimly. "Be it on your head, Zhukov. Take him away!"

Zhukov took a deep drag on his cigarette and expelled a stream of smoke with a long sigh. It had been a momentous decision. His only regret on leaving the school was that he had no time to say goodbye to his friend Sergei. From time to time he wondered what had happened to him.

Two days later, dressed in khaki army fatigues, a cap and ill-fitting boots, he'd been transported at dawn by truck to Leningrad's Moskovsky Railway Station and thrust onto a train filled with young men, all heading for the Afghanistan border. No band had been playing on the station platform and the only personnel to farewell them had been cursing army officers who reinforced their orders with heavy blows from short sticks. As Zhukov slumped on the carriage's seat surrounded by sullen and fearful young men, a shiver of premonition went through him as he contemplated his future.

Later in the day large numbers of smartly dressed soldiers, laughing and talking loudly, had filled the remaining carriages. No stick-wielding officers had been in evidence.

The three thousand kilometres trip from Leningrad to Afghanistan confirmed his fears. He lost count of the days he spent on the train, eating half-cold food and sleeping intermittently. When the train stopped for any length of time the occupants of his carriage were herded out onto the far end of the platform, isolated from the regular soldiers. They were permitted to walk up and down, under the watchful eye of soldiers armed with Kalashnikovs. Talking on the platform was forbidden, a rule swiftly reinforced by officers carrying the now familiar short sticks.

From spasmodic conversations with the other young men Zhukov realised that they had all been given the option of joining the army or going to a reform school or prison. Clearly that explained their harsh treatment.

Early one morning Zhukov felt the train slow. Looking out the window he saw a row of buildings, large groups of soldiers, assorted vehicles and several T55 tanks. As the train reached the end of the row, he saw a large sign that read 'Afghanistan'. They had crossed the border.

Their arrival was less than welcoming. Housed in barracks that were warmed by a single wood stove, their first two weeks consisted of repetitive drills, obstacle courses that involved crawling through mud under layers of barbed wire, wading through waist-high freezing water, and scrambling over high walls – all to the accompaniment of relentless abuse and frequent use of sticks by army NCOs.

Battered, bruised and cowed, they returned to their barracks every night and collapsed into their bunks hoping to catch enough sleep to enable them to face whatever taste of hell the following day would bring.

Zhukov stretched, yawned and walked to the window where he looked down on the busy street scene below. Those weeks had been an enduring nightmare from which there appeared to be no respite. The initial damage to his back had come from the beating in the school cell and had increased during the brutal repetitive drills. Yet he'd known better than to report his pain, knowing that the NCOs would have then targeted his back.

A release had come from an unexpected source. He grunted as he recalled the occasion.

It had been a cold, dark morning when, once again, they stood to attention awaiting their orders for the day. He noticed an officer had marched onto the parade ground and, after returning the sergeant's salute, had briefly conversed with him. The officer had then nodded and stepped one pace back.

"Zhukov, Vladimir!" shouted the sergeant. "Step forward!"

He smiled grimly as he remembered the icy shiver of fear that went through him. This must be a mistake? Surely…

"Zhukov, Vladimir! Step forward immediately!"

He noticed several heads turning towards him and realising that he had no choice, marched forward and came to attention in front of the sergeant, expecting the worst.

"Private Zhukov, you are to go with Captain Kuznetsov," barked the sergeant.

Zhukov looked nervously at the officer who, jerking his head, turned and marched towards the administrative block. His mind overlapping with dire possibilities, Zhukov followed.

Five minutes later, having entered the main building, he found himself being conducted into a large office. Behind a polished wooden desk sat a grey-haired officer whose lined face seemed to bear testimony to the rigours of military life. On the wall behind him was the logo of the GRU (Russian Military Intelligence) – a black bat hovering over a blue globe. Zhukov suppressed a gasp as he saw that the man wore a triangle of golden stars denoting the rank of Colonel.

"Colonel Mikhailov, I present Private Zhukov."

"Thank you, Captain." The colonel's raised his eyes and studied the young man for a long moment before he smiled.

"Private Zhukov, I have been reviewing your file."

Zhukov, noting an open folder on the desk, could only nod.

"I see that you speak English, private."

Feeling as though he was about to seal his own fate he coughed and replied, "Yes, a little, colonel."

"Where did you learn English?" The question was in English.

"From my mother, sir," he replied in English.

"And your father, he was in the KGB as a translator and teacher?"

A denial would have been futile, so Zhukov nodded.

The colonel indicated a large leather chair in front of the desk.

"Sit down, private."

Surprised, he sat down gingerly on the edge of the chair.

"You have had no news of your father since he was, er, sent away?"

"No, sir."

"And your mother died about ten years ago?"

"Yes, sir," he murmured.

"Life has been difficult for you, hasn't it?"

Sensing a hint of sympathy he nodded. "Yes, sir, it has."

The colonel returned to the file for a long moment before he looked up again.

"This murder charge—"

"Not murder, sir! I punched boy and as he fell, he hit his head on side of bed and—"

The colonel held up his hand, and gave him a sympathetic smile.

"Yes, your testimony is on the record. I just wanted to test if your explanation is still the same."

"It is, sir, and—"

"Let that be an end to the matter," interrupted the colonel. He smiled. "Now," he continued, "be honest. How good is your English?"

Still shaken by the mention of the murder charge, and then by the abrupt change in the questions, Zhukov decided to give an honest answer.

"I think I have good understanding of English basics, sir, although I have trouble with order of words. And I cannot practice my written English very much."

The colonel nodded slowly.

"I see. If you were given the opportunity to practice your oral and written English, would you be interested in doing so?"

Zhukov grunted and feeling a back spasm, lit another cigarette. He would never forget his astonishment at the colonel's question and its life changing consequences.

Chapter 37

Events had moved swiftly. He was told that he would be transferred to a branch of Army Intelligence that specialised in dealing with monitoring and intercepting messages in English from 'foreign powers'. During his initial training period he would be spending eight hours a day receiving English language tuition and reading English language books, newspapers and periodicals. At the end of this period he would begin his translation assignments.

He had readily agreed and in a dreamlike state had signed some papers and exchanged a welcoming handshake with Colonel Mikhailov. He was then introduced to Lieutenant Gorsky, a friendly young soldier who wore the black bat insignia on his right shoulder. Gorsky took him to the clothing stores where an attentive corporal fitted him with a new army uniform and comfortable boots. From there he was taken to a cluster of huts on the edge of the compound. They had walked along a row until Gorsky paused outside one and opening the door, indicated that Zhukov was to enter.

The room had a table and four chairs in the centre and a desk, chair and shelving in the corner near a wood stove in which a fire was burning. Through an interior door Zhukov saw a bedroom with a single bed, a bookcase, a chest of drawers and a closet for clothes.

Puzzled, he turned to Gorsky. "Who lives here?"

"You," was the smiling reply.

"Me? And who else?"

The other man shook his head.

"No one. These are your private quarters."

"But, surely private quarters are only for officers?"

Gorsky raised his eyebrows and smiled.

"Yes," he replied. "You will be on one month's probation. If your work is satisfactory you will be promoted to officer rank in the Intelligence division."

Zhukov stretched and yawned. The traffic on the street below was diminishing. The late hour and the vodka had made him sleepy, so he climbed into bed. His body was tired, but his mind continued to be filled with memories of his time in the military, particularly the role that had been assigned to him. He lay back with his hands behind his head and let his mind drift over the key events that had unfolded.

"Congratulations, Lieutenant Zhukov!"

Colonel Mikhailov raised his glass of vodka and the other officers followed suit.

"Nostrovia!" they chorused, downing the liquid in one swallow.

Zhukov, wearing his new uniform with the GRU insignia on the right shoulder, accepted the congratulations of his fellow officers in a haze of bemused delight. During the previous month he had diligently applied himself to improving his written English and had begun the challenging task of translating messages that had been intercepted by the GRU – requiring him to extend his knowledge of military terms and weaponry.

The bulk of the messages were transmitted from the United States Army to the fierce mujahideen guerrilla forces fighting the Russian troops in the mountainous areas. The Soviet army was particularly concerned at the amount of sophisticated weaponry that flowed into Afghanistan from the USA, frequently dropped by air into mountainous strongholds that were difficult to access. Of particular concern was the supply of shoulder-fired Stinger missile launchers that enabled one man to shoot down a plane or helicopter.

"It is vital that we immediately monitor and translate all messages related to the Stinger," stressed Colonel Mikhailov. "Our losses in the air are far too high."

This had been conveyed to him at a briefing session held several months later when he'd been introduced to the Lisa (the Fox) translation team. Hundreds of messages were intercepted by the GRU on a daily basis. All those that referred to Stingers were immediately forwarded to Lisa. Although Zhukov's reading of English was improving, the pressure of translating was intense, knowing that the lives of men and their machines were at stake. Sometimes the team members were able to work in pairs, but when a large volume of documents arrived, pressure was on the individual members to get through the work alone.

In spite of the official line that claimed constant military success, Zhukov soon realised that the Russian armed forces, in spite of their superiority in men and weapons, were fighting a losing battle against the guerrilla army.

Lisa team members were allowed one free day every ten days. Six months after he'd begun his translation duties, he had decided to spend his free day paying a visit to the railway terminus. He knew that all rail traffic to and from the various fronts passed through this terminus, and therefore could provide him with a greater insight into the military situation. Seeking some refreshment, he'd strolled into the main concourse and ordered a black coffee in the café. Taking his drink, he went through the entrance gates to the main platform and walked to the end. He'd sat on a bench, stretched out his legs, sipped his coffee and relaxed in the relative tranquillity of the semi-deserted station. The pressure of his work gave him little time for reflection and consequently, as he relaxed, his mind drifted over the events of the previous months. The winter sun shining through the clouds onto his sheltered corner of the platform provided him with welcome warmth. He closed his eyes and drifted off to sleep.

The sound of an approaching train woke him.

Zhukov grunted and screwed up his face at the memory. He'd grown up enduring many hardships and had seen his share of brutality, but nothing had prepared him for the sight that met his eyes.

A long train hissed its way alongside the platform and wreathed in smoke and steam, shuddered to a stop. Immediately men and women in medical uniforms swarmed onto the platform. The shouting of instructions mingled with the wheezing of the train, but as the carriage doors opened Zhukov heard chilling new sounds added to the cacophony –the piteous moans and cries of men. From out of the carriages lurched soldiers in filthy uniforms whose seeping wounds were crudely bandaged. The most distressing sights were those being assisted from the carriages with bloodied bandages wrapped around the stumps of missing limbs or covering their eyes.

Stretchers carrying inert bodies that could have been alive or dead followed them.

Carriage after carriage disgorged their terrible cargo while the medical personnel, clearly overwhelmed by the numbers, struggled to cope. Zhukov slowly stood and stared in horror at the unfolding scene of suffering.

A heavy hand gripped his shoulder.

"Lieutenant, you are not permitted to be here. You must leave immediately!"

Zhukov spun round to be confronted by a lieutenant backed by five hard-eyed soldiers carrying Kalashnikovs.

Zhukov stared at him. "This sight. It's hideous."

"Take him!"

Zhukov was immediately seized by two of the soldiers who twisted his arms behind his back.

"Who gives you the authority, lieutenant?" shouted Zhukov. "I'm a lieutenant in the intelligence—."

The officer leaned down and thrusting his face in front of Zhukov's hissed, "Shut your mouth! You have no authority here. My men will escort you from the station and you will not return." He nodded to the two soldiers who jerked Zhukov's arms higher causing him to flinch in pain. "Understand, lieutenant?"

"Yes," he gasped.

In a series of swift movements, he was thrust through the exit gate, now heavily guarded, out through the main concourse and onto the street.

The lieutenant confronted him again. "You will not return and you will not speak of this to anyone. Understand?"

The two men stood eye to eye. Zhukov, outraged at his treatment by a man of the same rank, took a deep breath and clenched both his fists. Mindful of the five soldiers' half circle he slowly looked the other man up and down, nodded abruptly, spun round and walked away.

As he paused on the kerb he noticed that on his left a double line of armed troops, facing outwards, had formed up by a station exit. Behind them he could see glimpses of wounded men and others on stretchers shuffling towards a line of ambulances, also ringed with soldiers. The nature and extent of the Russian army's casualties was clearly not for public consumption.

Hearing a scraping of feet, he turned his head and seeing the lieutenant starting to move towards him, quickly crossed the street and disappeared among the stalls of the local market.

Zhukov sighed and rolled on his side. Sleep always eluded him whenever his mind drifted back to Afghanistan. The personal cruelty he'd experienced, his abrupt change of fortune, the pressure of delivering fast, accurate translation, the dreadful sights he'd seen at the railway station and the realisation that the army was losing the war, had occurred in a relatively short space of time, leaving him mentally and physically drained.

Although his officer rank and his desk job had spared him from front line duty where the casualty rate mounted daily, it had left him with little loyalty to the army. He'd experienced the cruelty inflicted on those in punishment battalions and had seen daily reminders as trucks containing men with despairing eyes, were driven out to engage the mujahideen.

As a result of his experience at the railway station he had decided that at the earliest opportunity, he would leave the army and quit Russia. He knew that English speakers populated the most prosperous countries and was confident that his linguist skills would enable him to be absorbed in an affluent English-speaking country.

Zhukov smiled mirthlessly at the memory of his naivety.

Chapter 38

"The price will be high."

"I know. But I'm prepared to pay."

The other man nodded.

"Very well. It shall be done."

He winced as Zhukov seized his upper right arm and squeezed.

"I will give you half now and half on satisfactory completion of the documents, Brusilov." He maintained the pressure on the man's arm. "Do not betray me."

"You have my word," was the gasping reply. "Please let go of my arm."

Zhukov slowly released his grip.

"Good. You will meet me here at the same time next week, da?"

"Da," nodded Brusilov, grimacing as he rubbed his arm.

Zhukov had initially met Brusilov in the Rumochnaya Bar near St Petersburg's city centre. Seated on a bar stool he noted that the man next to him, although not flashily dressed, wore high quality clothes. He also noted that when the man stretched his right hand out to take his glass of vodka from the barman, his fingers were stained – not with nicotine but with a dark blue colouring. This sparked Zhukov's interest, and after cautious questioning and answering by both men, Brusilov acknowledged that he specialised in what he euphemistically called 'document creation'. The samples that he subsequently produced were impressive and an agreement was made.

Zhukov reached into an inner jacket pocket and withdrew an envelope. "Here is the first half," he said.

The other took the envelope, nodded, turned and hurried away across the sand as twilight settled over central St Petersburg.

Zhukov remained by the outer wall on the banks of the Neva River in the shadow of the Peter and Paul Fortress – where the remains of Tzar Nicolas II and his immediate family would be re-interred in 1998. He and Nicolai Brusilov had met on a beach area, popular in the summer but, with winter approaching, the likelihood of anyone seeing them was now remote.

Like the Americans in Viet Nam, the Soviet Russian army had withdrawn from Afghanistan having failed to win the hearts and minds of its fierce and patriotic inhabitants, but refusing to admit that it was a defeat. Zhukov had been part of the 1989 withdrawal and had been quick to accept the offer of discharge. He'd been vigilant in saving his officer's pay and therefore was able to set himself up in a small central St Petersburg apartment. Through a process of visiting bars and nightclubs, carefully screening those with whom he came into conversation, he'd found himself a niche in the city's burgeoning underworld.

The Afghanistan failure had been followed by the collapse of the Soviet Union, and during the chaos that followed, opportunities for ruthless men abounded. Zhukov had joined a criminal coterie that had engineered a takeover of state assets that included a power station, and the financial returns were lucrative. However, the men in the group had limited loyalty to each other and consequently everyone ran the risk of being eliminated by someone else who was seeking a greater share of the riches. It was time to move on.

Brusilov had driven a hard bargain, but Zhukov had sufficient funds to meet the price. He trusted the man to deliver forged documents that would pass official scrutiny. As a precaution he had obtained copies of genuine documents that he compared with the first set supplied by Brusilov. The forgeries were pristine.

Nevertheless, he had still decided a little physical intimidation of the forger would increase his security. It was unlikely that Brusilov would try to cheat him, due to the amount of money he was being paid. Even in the dog-eat-dog St Petersburg underworld, Zhukov hadn't made any real enemies and therefore was working on the principle that there would be no one prepared to pay for his elimination.

The following week at the same time he made his way along the banks of the Neva River towards the Peter and Paul Fortress. It had been a cold day and a soft fall of snow was starting to clad the city in a white evening coat. He had arranged to meet Brusilov in the usual place from where they would walk together to Zhukov's nearby apartment to scrutinise the documents.

He approached the wall and saw his contact leaning against it; his back turned away from the falling snow. At Zhukov's crunching approach he swung round, their eyes met, and he nodded.

"Show me," commanded Zhukov.

Brusilov reached into his heavy coat and pulled out a large envelope.

"Good. Come."

On reaching the entrance to his apartment building Zhukov stepped aside and signalled that Brusilov should go first. He paused in the doorway, checked the street and then entered.

Once inside Zhukov indicated the dining room table. Extracting the envelope Brusilov laid the contents carefully on the surface and stood back.

"Pour yourself a coffee," said Zhukov as he sat down and pulled the documents towards him. The Russian passport with his photograph passed his scrutiny. He'd requested a passport that looked a little worn, his own name with the occupation 'Lecturer', and with three UK entry stamps dated several months apart. He was also pleased with his Master's degree in Russian and English from the Leningrad State University, the Russian exit documents and the UK work visa.

162

Brusilov, who had been watching him anxiously, sighed with relief when Zhukov lifted his head, smiled and nodded.

"Excellent work. Thank you, Brusilov."

He tucked the documents into his jacket pocket and turned to go.

"Just a moment."

He turned and looked the forger up and down.

"Yes?"

"You still owe me the additional half of the payment."

Zhukov's smile had no mirth.

"I have already paid you the agreed amount. I owe you nothing."

Angrily Brusilov stepped forward, his face inches from Zhukov, who promptly seized him by the lapels of his coat, slammed his forehead sharply forward and let Brusilov collapse to the floor where he sprawled, moaning and clutching his shattered nose.

Zhukov looked down at the whimpering forger.

"I owe you nothing."

He swiftly exited leaving the man on the floor glowering after him with a look of pure hatred.

Zhukov had already booked a passage to London on a cruise ship due to dock in St Petersburg the following morning. He phoned for a taxi and ten minutes later he was on his way to the Pushka Inn Hotel where he would spend his last night in Russia. He leaned back in the seat and smiled at the prospect.

Zhukov had selected New Zealand for two reasons; it was on the opposite side of the world to Russia, and was a small, benign nation with a low crime rate. The prospects for rich pickings looked promising and he assumed that emigrating via England would be easier than directly from Russia. His assumption had proved correct – his documentation impressed the New Zealand immigration authorities, as did his ability to lie with credible sincerity and fluency during the interview. Consequently in 1999 his passenger plane had touched down at Auckland International Airport.

He'd made useful contacts and kept on the right side of the law. He'd established a small import company, sourcing goods from Eastern Europe, and using a reputable accountancy firm, maintained a scrupulous set of books. This legitimate front enabled him to operate other profitable income sources with clients such as Ray Bullock. However, these were intermittent. The newest prospect, based on Jason Collins' smuggling operations, looked promising. However, there were too many hands reaching into that particular pot and competition would be fierce. The Russian proverb, "If you're afraid of wolves, don't go to the woods" occurred to him and he grunted.

He was not afraid, and the woods were waiting.

Chapter 39

Reaching out, he picked up the ringing extension phone.

"Chris, there's a call for you."

"Thanks, Yvonne." He paused and then said, "Chris Winstone."

"Mr Winstone. My name is Detective Sergeant Burton."

"Oh," replied Chris. "No problem with the club is there?"

"Not in so many words, Mr Winstone. We're trying to trace a missing person who may have spent time at your club. Her name's Fleur Lassiter."

"Fleur Lassiter. Yes, she was a flying student here a couple of months ago. Haven't seen her for a while. Missing, you say?"

"Yes, a friend reported her as missing. We've been checking her friends, acquaintances and places that she frequented. Your club was one of them."

"She could have left the country."

"We checked. There's no record of that." He paused. "I'd like to come out tomorrow to visit your club and talk to you. Would around three o'clock suit?"

"Yes, that's fine. In the meantime, I'll ask around among my colleagues and club members."

"Actually, Mr Winstone, I'd rather you didn't."

"Really? Surely you're not saying that one of our club—"

"I'm not saying anything or making any assumptions. It's just that starting speculation and rumours could muddy the waters. I'm sure you understand."

"OK, if you think that's best. But I really don't think—"

"Thank you, Mr Winstone. I'll see you at three tomorrow."

The phone went dead. Chris held it in his hand for a long moment before slowly replacing it and then tapping '0'. Yvonne answered. He asked her if she'd seen Dale Salmond, the Chief Flying Instructor. She told him that Dale had just arrived and was in the equipment room.

"Morning, Dale."

Salmond looked up from the first aid kits he'd been checking and smiled.

"Morning, Chris." He nodded at the kits. "My monthly task."

Winstone nodded. Salmond, a man with a ready smile and an unassuming manner, took his job seriously. Fortunately, accidents at the club were few, but flying had its risks, and having a man as conscientious as Dale was an asset.

Winstone turned, closed the door, and sat down in a nearby chair.

"Need to talk to you," he said.

"Serious?" asked Salmond.

"Not sure. I've just had a phone call from a detective sergeant."

"Hands in the till again, Chris?" grinned Salmond.

"Not funny, mate. You remember Fleur Lassiter, the woman—"

"Everyone remembers Fleur Lassiter." He smiled at the mental picture that her name conjured up. "Tall, dark hair, long legs, bedroom eyes—"

"Silly of me to ask. Anyway, apparently, she's been reported missing. The police are checking her friends, places of work and our club. They're coming tomorrow but have asked me not to say anything to anyone."

"Except me, apparently. Why?"

"Just wanted to run over a couple of things with you. That stoush between Jason and young Matt – it was over her, right?"

Salmond nodded slowly. "Yes. But so what?"

"If the police find out…"

"They'll investigate further."

"Jason fancies himself as a lady's man and works pretty hard at it. It can be a dangerous game, so he could possibly be mixed up in her disappearance."

Salmond frowned.

"If she has actually disappeared. She may have just moved away somewhere or gone overseas."

"The cops have checked. She hasn't left the country."

"So how much do we tell them?"

"Why do you ask?"

"Well, if Jason or Matt are mixed up in her disappearance it could be tricky. Jason's on the staff and Matt's a club member." He shrugged. "Or maybe we tell them all that we know. If something nasty's happened to Fleur, then they need to have all the facts at their fingertips." He looked at Winstone. "They're taking this pretty seriously, aren't they?"

"Yeah. The sergeant will be here tomorrow at three o'clock."

*

The following afternoon a black Holden Commodore pulled into the car park and a middle-aged man and a younger woman, dressed in civilian clothes, climbed out. They paused and looked at the clubhouse, the buildings and the landing strip before entering the main door and approaching the reception desk.

Yvonne had been forewarned.

"You'll be from the police, here to see Mr Winstone."

Both nodded as she picked up her phone.

"Your visitors are here, Chris."

She turned to the pair. "He'll be right with you."

Moments later Winstone strode through the door.

"Chris Winstone."

"Detective Sergeant Burton, Mr Winstone, and Detective Constable Young."

Both showed their badges. Winstone glanced quickly at them, nodded and they shook hands.

"We'll talk in my office," he said. "Would you like tea or coffee?"

The detectives exchanged glances.

167

"Two coffees would be good. White, no sugar," replied the sergeant.

"Coming right up," responded Yvonne.

Winstone indicated the two seats and sat down behind his desk. He studied the pair. Burton, who he estimated was in his early fifties, had a full head of carefully combed dark hair, with streaks of grey. His suit was smart and complemented by a striped business shirt. Young wore a red jacket, knee length black skirt, and held a notebook with pen at the ready.

"Thank you for making the time to see us, Mr Winstone. I'm sure the responsibilities of running an aero club keep you busy."

"We have our moments." Winstone nodded, and smiled as he heard the sound of a plane touching down, revving its engine and taking off again. "Touch and go," he explained to the inquiring look from the pair. "A student flyer practising landing and takeoff."

"You have many students?"

"Yes, a steady stream. Mostly adults, but some in their late teens."

"I imagine the parents would be paying for the teenagers."

"Yes," he smiled, "it's a bit more expensive than rugby or netball."

"What percentage are female?" asked DC Young.

Chris paused and frowned. Before he could reply there was a tap at the door and Yvonne entered with three coffees.

"Thanks," said Chris, as she took them off the tray. "Yvonne do you know our current percentage of female students?"

Yvonne placed the third coffee on the table and paused.

"About twenty per cent at present. Been a steady increase over the last five years."

"What age group?" asked Burton.

"Mostly between twenty and forty."

Burton nodded. "Thank you, Yvonne."

"You're welcome," she smiled before exiting.

"So, Mr Winstone, what can you tell us about Fleur Lassiter?" asked Burton.

"I checked the records after your phone call, sergeant," replied Winstone. "She had seven flying lessons, the last one being four weeks ago."

"Has she been back to the club since then?"

"I don't believe so."

"Did she have the same flying instructor?"

"Yes."

Burton frowned. "His name, please."

"Jason Collins."

"Were there any problems between him and Fleur Lassiter?"

"There was an altercation between Jason and a younger member," said Winstone, carefully choosing his words. "They came to blows on the edge of the runway. We had to separate them."

Burton and Young exchanged glances before the older man continued.

"What had that to do with Ms Lassiter?"

"The fight was over her. Two men and one woman – the usual stuff." Winstone tried to smile but it quickly faded when he saw Burton's grim expression and Young scribbling in her notebook.

"And the other man?" asked Young.

"Matt Bullock."

"Was she to blame for this quarrel?"

"Hard to say," said Winstone. "She was an attractive woman and rather flirtatious. She could have been leading both of them on."

"Or sleeping with them," suggested Young.

"That would certainly cause a problem," said Burton. "We'll need to speak to both these men."

"Matt's a student pilot. He's not here today. Jason has two days' leave. He'll return on Wednesday."

"What about other staff members?"

"You've met Yvonne. You could talk to her of course."

"Anyone else?"

"We have two other instructors on duty today, but they're both in the air." Seeing the look of frustration on Burton's face he added, "You could try Jenny Cater, our bar manager. She's a bright young woman, and popular with the instructors and male students. She might be able to help."

"Thanks, we'll do that. We'll also need contact details for Jason Collins and Matt Bullock. And we'll probably want to talk to you again."

Chapter 40

"Jenny Cater?"

Jenny smiled at the two figures standing in front of her.

"Yes. What can I get you?"

"Possibly some information. I'm Detective Sergeant Burton and this is Detective Young."

As they both showed their badges Jenny's smile quickly faded.

"Police," she said slowly.

"We're making inquiries about Fleur Lassiter."

"Fleur," said Jenny cautiously.

"Yes. You knew her, presumably?"

"Yes, I served her in the bar a few times."

"When did you last see her?"

"About a month ago." She frowned. "Why, is she in trouble?"

"She's gone missing, Ms. Cater." Burton looked round the room. Two men in the far corner were poring over some maps. "You don't seem very busy." He nodded to the opposite corner. "Could we sit down over there for a few minutes?"

"Sure," replied Jenny and led the way to the corner where they seated themselves round a circular table.

"What can you tell us about Fleur Lassiter?" began Burton.

Jenny, considering her words carefully, answered slowly. "She's a snazzy dresser who takes care with her appearance."

"Any particular reason?" asked Burton.

"I think she just likes to look attractive."

Young grinned.

"To men?"

Jenny shrugged. "Could be."

"Men such as Jason Collins?"

"He wasn't the only one."

"Oh?"

171

"Look, I don't want to get anyone into trouble."

"You won't Ms. Cater," said Burton. "We're just seeking background information."

Jenny nodded. "Well, Matt Bullock was also attracted to her."

"And was his instructor Jason Collins?"

Jenny nodded.

"And we're told that it resulted in problems."

"Yes, a fist-fight by the runway."

"Did you see it?"

"I heard shouting and looked out the window just in time to see Jason hit Matt. He staggered back and then knocked Jason to the ground. The General Manager and some others separated them."

"Fleur Lassiter was there?"

"Yes."

"And?"

"I couldn't hear much, but it seemed pretty clear from others that the fight was over her."

The pair exchanged glances.

"And you say that she seems to have disappeared," said Jenny. "So, you think there's a connection?"

"Do you think so, Ms. Cater?" asked Burton.

Jenny did not reply immediately. She was aware that her dislike of Jason Collins could influence any personal speculation regarding his involvement in Fleur's disappearance. However, it intrigued her to know that this was now the subject of a police inquiry.

"It's worth following up, don't you think?"

"How do you mean?"

"Obviously you'll be talking to Jason and Matt regarding Fleur. Either or both of them could be involved in her disappearance but, until you have actual proof, you could be stymied. So, from my observations of Jason, Matt's and Fleur's

172

behaviour it does seem clear that she was having some sort of relationship with both men."

"Which you didn't like?"

"I would have said it wasn't any of my business, but when Jason Collins started coming on to me it made my skin crawl."

"When was this?"

Jenny frowned before replying, "Fairly recently. As I hadn't seen Fleur around, I assumed fresh conquests were his aim."

"So what did you do?"

"Fixed on my plastic smile, and served his drinks. I enjoy the job and need the money."

"Good for you," said Young and started closing her notebook.

"You'll be continuing your investigation of the relationship between the two men and Fleur Lassiter, will you?" asked Jenny, her face a picture of innocence.

"We'll have to consider all the facts, of course," replied Burton.

"In the hope of finding the truth?"

"Always, Ms. Cater," smiled Young. "Thank you for your assistance. If we need further information I'll be in touch."

"Or me," added Burton curtly. "Let's go, Young."

Jenny smiled as she watched the two leave the bar.

Chapter 41

"Beer, please, Jenny."

"Steinlager?" she asked, fixing a bright smile to her face.

"Yeah." He paused. "You're looking particularly attractive today, Jenny."

She turned away and grimaced as she opened the sliding door to the liquor cabinets. When she'd first met Jason Collins, she'd responded positively to his good looks and quick humour. However, over the past weeks his comments on her appearance and clothes had become irritatingly suggestive.

"You're looking pretty pleased with yourself, Jason." She forced a smile as she placed the glass of beer on the counter.

Collins lifted his shoulders and preened himself.

"Yes, you could say that, Jenny."

"Oh?" Flipping the top off the bottle, she placed it on the bar and adopted an air of innocent interest.

Collins looked around the empty room and then leaned closer into her. Jenny, managing not to recoil from the nearness of his visage, smiled.

"I've got a little operation going on the side. It's bringing me a little extra revenue."

"A little extra revenue?"

"Well, quite a lot actually. I'm flying in small but valuable items from overseas. They sell very well."

"Your own import business?" asked Jenny, her interest piqued.

"Yes, but can't tell you more than that. But as I said, the money's good. In fact, I took a delivery last week and was intending to celebrate with a weekend away in a fancy resort." His right hand reached across the bar and touched her arm. "I'd love you to join me. You and I could have a great romp together."

Jenny moved back a step and swallowed. The snippet of information was interesting, but the man was really quite repulsive. Aware of his lascivious stare she swallowed, took a deep breath and smiled warmly.

"I've been meaning to ask you, Jason," she began.

"Ask me?" he leered. "About a wicked weekend together?"

"No, about your friend Fleur."

His head jerked back.

"Fleur?"

"Yes. She was your pupil and your girlfriend, wasn't she?"

"My pupil for a while, and," he shrugged, "we went out a couple of times. That's all."

"Oh, I thought it was more serious than that."

"Look," he glared, "why the questions?"

Jenny smiled. "Oh, no particular reason. Haven't seen her around and wondered what had happened to her."

"Nothing's happened to her," he replied quickly, and then made an effort to smile. "She just decided she didn't want to fly anymore."

"Interesting."

"What's so bloody interesting? She's gone and—"

"Two people were here yesterday making enquiries about her. Wanted to know if I knew her and if I'd seen her recently."

Collins stood stock still, his lips moving uncertainly before responding.

"Who were they?"

"Police detectives." She shrugged. "I wasn't able to tell them much."

"Christ! Detectives." Collins had gone pale. Leaning forward he demanded, "What did you tell them?"

"Just said that you were her instructor and you also seemed to be good friends."

Collins stared at her, a range of emotions reflected in his face, until he abruptly swept up and drained his glass, slammed it back on the bar counter and strode out of the room.

Chapter 42

'Zhukov."

"Vladimir, it's Jason Collins."

"Jason. Where are you? It sounds like there is wind around you."

Collins pressed his phone closer to his mouth and looked nervously around the club car park. He started to walk towards the east side corner that was sheltered by a grove of pittosporums.

"Sorry, Vladimir. It's a bit windy. Is this better?"

"Yes, I can hear you well. Why are you telephoning me? Some problem?"

"Possibly, Vladimir. I've just been told that the police visited the flying club yesterday and asked questions about Fleur Lassiter and me."

There was no response.

In spite of the coolness of the early spring day Collins could feel the sweat forming on his forehead and beginning to spread through his body. "Vladimir, you still there?"

"Da. The police. Not good. Not good at all. You will come to my place tonight and we will talk together about this."

"But—"

"We are not to talk about this on phone. Tonight, we will talk further. Here, eight o'clock."

A click terminated the call. Collins stood stock still feeling fear spreading through his body. The police interest in him was cause enough for alarm, but the thought of meeting the unpredictable Russian on his own patch was a prospect that filled him with foreboding. His mind raced. Zhukov was a ruthless bastard who cared for nothing and no one. If the police began to suspect a link between him and Fleur's disappearance, then further investigation could also uncover his relationship with Zhukov. He could swear that he would never reveal the relationship to the police, but he knew that the Russian would treat this with scorn. There was no way that Zhukov would want to become a suspect in Fleur's disappearance. So, what would be his reaction? The answer was obvious. Jason would be eliminated.

He felt his legs trembling. He needed a drink. He took two steps towards the clubhouse and stopped. If Jenny knew about the police visit, then surely Chris Winstone would know. In fact, he'd probably told the police about the fracas by the tarmac. Chances were the whole club now knew and would start asking him questions. Christ, what a bloody mess!

The sound of an approaching car made him look up. Matt's BMW Z3 – the last person he wanted to talk to. He spun round and strode towards his car, ignoring the toot from the young man's vehicle. Quickly opening his door, he slid into the driver's seat, started the engine and sped out of the car park leaving an astonished Matt silhouetted against the sky with his arm half raised in greeting.

Driving at speed he quickly reached the motorway. He moved into the right-hand lane and headed south at a steady 100 kilometres per hour. The traffic was light and the steady hum of the tyres and the reliable rhythm of the car's engine soothed him a little.

He took several deep breaths and began to consider the alternatives. The first, return to the clubhouse, tell anyone who asked that he hadn't heard from Fleur for several weeks and had no idea where she was. If pressed, he could explain that their brief romance had broken up and he'd seen no reason to make any further contact. That could dampen down the rumours but inevitably he'd have to talk to the police who'd be unlikely to shrug, thank him and walk away.

And as for Zhukov and his cohorts, that would bring him nothing but grief, pain and possibly his death. He would need to immediately cut off all further contact with the Russian. In fact, no further contact with anyone would be his best bet in the short term. Yes, he'd swing by his apartment, pack a suitcase, grab his passport, head for the airport and catch a plane. Where to – Australia, one of the Pacific Island nations, Asia or Europe? His choice. He had money and flying qualifications that could provide him with a new start.

He laughed out loud. Of course, a brand-new beginning in an exciting new location far from New Zealand, the police and Vladimir Zhukov.

He swung his car off the motorway drove up the steep incline of Parnell Road, swung left at the Parnell Cathedral, then right before he turned into Tohunga Crescent and stopped outside his house. Motivated by the feasibility of his escape plan he stepped out of his car, strode up the short pathway to the front entrance and reached forward to punch the code into the security pad.

Hearing a soft footfall behind him, he spun round.

"Going somewhere, Jason?" asked Vladimir Zhukov.

Chapter 43

Collins slowly opened his eyes and lifted his head. He gasped as it began to spin. He tried to lift his hands to his forehead, but his arms wouldn't move. He tried again and realised that they were tied to the back of a chair. He told himself to breathe slowly and as the dizziness began to subside, he tentatively looked around. He was in a low-ceilinged building with wooden walls. Through a nearby window he saw green paddocks with a few grazing sheep. His slow breaths brought an aroma to his nostrils that triggered memories from boyhood holidays on his uncle's farm; wool, lanolin and sheep dung – a shearing shed.

He tried to lean forward but the rope was tight. With a growing feeling of panic, he tried to stand. Impossible. His feet were tightly roped to the front of the chair. What the hell was going on? He cast his mind back. He remembered Zhukov outside his front door and a strong-smelling cloth being clamped over his mouth and nose. He remembered nothing more.

He opened his mouth to yell for help but shut it again as he realised the futility of such an action. In any case he probably couldn't do more than croak, as his throat and mouth were parched. He wondered why he hadn't been gagged but quickly assumed that the remoteness of the location meant that the only creatures likely to react to any shouting would be the sheep. He shuddered. Drugged and tied up in a remote sheep farm – little cause for optimism.

Another wave of dizziness hit him. He lowered his head, which helped a little, and tried to concentrate on breathing slowly. The dizziness passed and he fell into an exhausted sleep.

*

A stinging blow on his left cheek jerked him awake and he lifted his head to see Zhukov's face inches above his.

"Zhukov, you bastard."

The Russian swung his arm and the palm of his hand connected with Collins' other cheek, nearly tipping him over.

"You speak only when I give you permission, you traitorous scum."

Collins turned his head to one side to avoid the man's foul breath. Tony Foster and Gregory Atanashvilli were standing to one side gazing at him impassively. He turned his head back to face Zhukov and gave a low moan. Zhukov stared at him for a long moment.

"You want water?"

Collins nodded.

"Tony, some water." A thin smile flickered briefly over his craggy features. "I want him to speak clearly when I begin to question him."

Tony pressed a large glass of water to Collins' lips.

"Easy mate,' he murmured.

Collins gulped its entire contents before throwing his head back, groaning and nodding his thanks. The liquid had moistened his mouth, but he knew that this relief was only temporary. He wanted to start explaining but both his cheeks were stinging painfully, his head was throbbing, and he didn't want to give Zhukov an excuse to hit him again.

The buzzing of blowflies and the occasional bleating of sheep backed the sound of Zhukov's heavy breathing as the man stood staring down at him.

He began speaking softly.

"So, Jason, you have been talking to the police. You have been telling them about me, and about Fleur."

Collins met his stare, opened his mouth, thought better of it and vigorously shook his head.

"No? You have not been talking to police?"

Collins shook his head again.

The Russian scowled and smacked his right hand across Collins' left cheek.

"You shake your head when I say you have not been talking to the police. So you have been talking, you bastard!"

The blow had triggered off another wave of dizziness causing Collins to close his eyes and suck in air with gasping breaths. As his breathing pattern began to settle, he opened his eyes to see Zhukov still staring at him. Taking a chance, he spoke quietly.

"No, Vladimir, I have not been talking to the police."

Zhukov started to swing his arm back.

"Wait! Let him explain further. If you keep hitting him, he won't be able to speak at all!"

The Russian glared at Tony, grunted, and lowering his arm addressed Collins.

"Speak!"

Collins took another deep breath and began speaking slowly. "This morning I talked to Jenny at the bar. She told me that two police officers had been at the club the day before asking questions about Fleur Lassiter. She had told them that I was her flying instructor and that we had a brief liaison." He licked his dry lips. "I didn't know what to do so I phoned you. Then I left the club. I did not speak to the police and they have not been in contact with me."

A sheep bleated and the blowflies buzzed in the long silence that followed.

Zhukov smiled and slowly nodded his head.

"OK. I believe you."

Collins' attempt at an answering smile was merely a sickly leer.

"But, there are other problems that we have to ad…."

"Address, Vlad," prompted Gregory.

"*Da*. The barmaid has big mouth. Police now know that you and Fleur Lassiter were flying and fucking." He chuckled mirthlessly at his crude juxtaposition. "They will soon discover link between you and me and will start asking me questions. That I not like."

181

"No, Vlad, that would never happen. I had already decided…" his voice trailed away, and his head slumped.

"You already decide to run away, yes. Suitcase, money and passport with next stop airport, I think."

"I was going to tell you that."

"Liar! You tried to escape like a rat. Leaving us to face police."

"With me gone, there'd be no links to you that the police could investigate. That's why I decided to leave the country. To help you."

Even though he tried to keep his voice even, he was aware of the increase in pitch.

The blow sent him sprawling sideways on the shearing shed floor. The shooting pains in his arms and legs as the ropes bit into them matched the pain on the side of his face. He lay shaking and whimpering. Clearly any hope of reasoning with the Russian was out of the question. He had compromised Zhukov, and he knew that the retaliation would be ruthless. Zhukov's booted feet planted themselves in front of his face and knowing that he'd be unable to avoid the next assault his whimpering increased.

"Vladimir! Enough!" It was Tony's voice. He saw the booted feet turn sideways.

"Shut your mouth, Tony. This man is a filthy traitor. He must be punished!"

"No, Vlad," came Gregory's voice. "Yes, he's a bloody idiot but he's not a traitor. He has told the police nothing. Beating him senseless will not solve anything. We need to keep him alive and well while we consider our next move."

Aware that the response could decide his fate, Collins lay motionless. The feet shuffled and the sound of heavy breathing increased. Finally, after loudly clearing his throat, Zhukov spoke.

"OK. Drag the bastard up. Take him to house, and put him upstairs, under guard."

The two men cut him free and hauled him to his feet. Although his legs trembled and he had a blinding headache, he made a major effort to re-establish some modicum of self-respect. Forcing his eyes open he eyeballed the Russian.

"You called me a traitor." His voice trembled and he took a deep breath. "I'm no traitor but you are a coward." Zhukov took a step towards him, but he pressed on. "You tied me to a chair so that I could not defend myself. Then you hit me repeatedly. That is the action of a coward." His voice faded but he managed to croak, "Shame on you, Vladimir Zhukov!"

Zhukov's eyes swept over his two companions who flanked Collins. Their faces were expressionless, but he noted that they started to move their bodies protectively across Collins. His face showed no emotion as he snarled, "Take the bastard away!"

Chapter 44

Collins lay on top of a bed gazing at the ceiling. Through the window came the gentle sounds of night insects and the occasional hoot of a ruru, the small brown native owl. The sky was beginning to lighten with the approach of dawn.

Gregory and Tony had assisted him out of the woolshed. Although his legs were trembling, aware of Zhukov's presence, he'd made a conscious effort to hold his head up and to walk forward with minimal assistance from the other two. They'd taken him to an adjacent house, helped him onto the bed and left the room. Outside the window was dark sky. He'd obviously had a long sleep.

He'd awoken with a thumping head and a dry mouth. With his hands he'd explored his face. Both his cheeks were painful to his touch but his jaw, although sore, was intact and his teeth were still in place. He tried to lift his head, but the room began to spin, and he fell back onto his pillow. His situation, considered from all angles, seemed desperate. He had no idea where he was – obviously in some farmland area, but how far away was the nearest town? Uppermost in his mind were thoughts of revenge against Zhukov. However, in his weakened state, any physical retaliation was out of the question. Yet, he was still alive. Zhukov could have easily killed him and disposed of his body, yet he'd let him live. The reprieve, for whatever reason, was too good an opportunity to miss; but it would need careful thought.

As he lay on the bed an idea began forming in his mind and, in spite of his headache, he smiled.

"How are you feeling, Jason?"

He turned his head to see Tony entering carrying a bowl.

"I've brought you some soup."

He put the bowl on an adjacent table, reached across to position two pillows behind Collins' back and helped him to sit upright. With his left hand he lifted the bowl in front of Collins' face, and with his right hand dipped a spoon into the steaming liquid.

"Chicken and mushroom. Open wide."

Collins complied and Tony carefully fed him the entire contents of the bowl.

"Feel a little better?"

Collins closed his eyes and nodded. "A little. Thanks."

"Sorry we couldn't find you a better-looking nurse, Jason."

Opening his eyes, he saw Gregory enter with a glass of water in one hand and a small packet in the other.

"Codeine, for your head."

From the packet he extracted three tablets and dropped them into the water. Watched closely by Collins they drifted to the bottom of the glass, leaving a white trail in their wake. Gregory swirled the glass around to increase the absorption process then handed it to Collins.

"Drink up."

Collins folded his arms and fixed Gregory with a stony stare.

"How do I know that it's codeine?"

Gregory shrugged and showed him the packet.

"Says so right here."

"Doesn't prove anything."

Grabbing the packet from Gregory, Tony pulled out the small tray of tablets from which three tablets had been removed.

"See for yourself, mate. All individually sealed with 'codeine' stamped on the foil."

Collins stared at the tray.

"Look, mate," continued Tony, "was the soup OK?"

Collins nodded.

"Did it make you feel better?"

"A little."

"Good. These codeine tablets will help to take away your headache."

Collins shuddered as another wave of pain passed through his head. Slowly he stretched out his hand and grasped the glass.

185

"Good man," smiled Tony as Collins downed the white liquid in two gulps. "That will help you—"

The glass hit the far wall with a splintering crash.

"Help me!" snarled Collins. "You kidnapped me, tied me to a chair and stood by while that fucking Russian beat the shit out of me. Yeah, you two were a great bloody help."

Exhausted by the effort of speaking, he fell back on the pillows and closed his eyes.

The two men looked at each other uncertainly. When Tony finally spoke, his voice was soft.

"Jason, we're both sorry for the way you were treated. It was cruel and unnecessary." Receiving no response, he continued cautiously. "But you were the one who tried to skip the country without telling Vladimir. That wasn't very smart."

Collins opened his eyes and took a series of deep breaths. A smile flickered across his face and he cleared his throat.

"You say that you're sorry for the way that Zhukov treated me."

Both men nodded.

"Then you will be willing to help me."

"To some extent," was Gregory's cautious reply.

"Good." He looked at his watch. "Tell Zhukov I want a meeting with him."

"A meeting. When?"

"I need to sleep some more. Tell him to meet me at eleven."

"What do you want?"

"My business." He eyeballed both men. "You will also be there."

"Where?"

"Here. At eleven."

The pair looked uncertainly at each other.

"Tell him!"

*

Collins woke to the now familiar sounds of sheep bleating. Through the open window he saw small white clouds drifting past against a backdrop of blue sky.

He lay still, checking his condition. His fierce headache had been reduced to an occasional throb. The pain in his jaw had also largely subsided. Gingerly he swung his legs out of the bed and stood upright. He flexed his arms and walked backwards and forwards across the room with increasing confidence. He went over to the window and looked out at the tranquil rural setting. He took several deep breaths and, to test his voice, spoke out loud.

"Here's to the future, to hell with the past. Out of my way, I'm moving on fast."

He had no time to contemplate his spontaneous doggerel as the sound of footsteps preceded the opening of his door by Tony.

"Up and about. That's good," he said.

"Time for a couple more codeines," said Gregory, following close behind, carrying a full glass of water. "Are you feeling better?"

"Better and hungry," responded Collins.

"Bacon, eggs and coffee suit you?"

"Sounds bloody good."

The pair nodded and disappeared.

The meal lifted Collins' spirits. After pouring a second cup of coffee he again walked over to the window where he continued to hone the idea that had come to him the previous night.

*

Precisely at eleven o'clock the door swung open and Zhukov swept into the room. He glared at Collins who was sitting on a chair behind the table. An empty chair was placed opposite him.

"What do you want?"

"Sit down, Zhukov, and shut up!"

187

"You dare to tell—"

"You will not lay a finger on me again, you cowardly bastard. Now sit down, keep your mouth shut and listen carefully."

Collins pointed to the empty chair. Zhukov, his face twisted with anger, hesitated and then seated himself. Tony and Gregory, who'd followed the big Russian, immediately sat on the side of the bed.

"What is it you wish to—?"

"I've told you to keep your mouth shut." The bruises on Jason's face were beginning to darken but his eyes were bright. "You will not speak again until I give you my permission." He locked eyes with Zhukov who finally looked away, reached into his coat pocket and extracted a packet of cigarettes.

"No smoking!"

Before the Russian could respond, Collins continued speaking.

"You're all well aware of my operation that imports medical drugs using light aircraft. I've no idea why you've brought me here, or what you intended doing with me, but I do know that you, Zhukov, had expressed interest in the operation. I've scheduled another drop off to take place in three weeks' time, but only if I contact all the key personnel. If you think you can force me to provide their names, you'd be wasting your time. They'll only respond if they hear my voice giving them details such as cargo, dates and touchdown times."

He paused and looked at Gregory. "Could I have another glass of water, please?"

Gregory filled a glass from the jug, and Collins gulped it down. He grunted his thanks, placed the glass on the desk, and looked at each of his silent listeners.

"As you know, the police have been asking questions, so I need to lie low for a time. I will be happy to stay here as long as I have good food, alcohol and a phone. I am prepared to offer a percentage of my profits as a return from a financial investment

188

that you, Zhukov, will make in my operation. I have plans to expand but need additional capital. Therefore, I'm willing to consider any reasonable offer."

Seeing that Zhukov was about to speak, Jason held up his hand.

"This agreement can only take place if four conditions are met. The first is that I will continue as director of all operations. I'm not offering a partnership, just an investment opportunity. Secondly, I will be treated with respect; Zhukov or anyone else associated with him will make no physical threats or take no physical actions against me. Thirdly, my cell phone, passport and wallet will be returned to me, with its contents untouched."

A long silence followed before Tony spoke. "You said there were four conditions."

Collins smiled thinly. "There will be no smoking in my presence."

"This is my house! You do not tell me—"

"If you want to be part of my operation you will do things my way," barked Collins.

"You cannot—"

"My way!"

There was a tense silence as the two men sat glowering at each other. A quiet scrunching sound caused Collins to look down. His features remained passive and did not betray his quiet satisfaction that the Camel cigarette packet, which had remained in Zhukov's right hand, had been crushed into a shapeless mass. Hatred flashed in the big Russian's eye before he opened his mouth, and with an obvious effort, spoke calmly.

"Interesting proposal. You are wanting your passport returned. That means that you still wish to leave country."

Collins shook his head. "It doesn't. I panicked when I heard that the police were asking questions about me. That was bloody stupid. I now intend to stay, to keep out of sight here at this farm, and continue to run my operation until things die down."

"How can we guarantee that?"

"You can't. But you have my word and I'm also offering you a chance to invest in my operation, which has considerable financial possibilities."

"If you don't return to your position at the flying club, that will make the police very suspicious," said Gregory.

"Probably. I'm due for some leave so I'll send a message to the club. I won't give them any other information and if they assume that I could be leaving the country that's OK with me."

He looked around the room.

"Does this bedroom have an adjacent kitchen and bathroom?" he asked.

Zhukov grunted and nodded.

"And an office and a lounge?"

"There is an office and a small area by the kitchen for meetings," said Gregory.

"Is this the upstairs part of the house?"

"Yes. There are other unoccupied rooms further along the corridor."

"How far is this farm from Auckland city?"

"About an hour's drive."

Collins nodded slowly before carefully standing upright.

"Good. Show me round and I will tell you of any additional resources that I will need." He looked at Zhukov. "Then you and I will discuss your investment in my operation."

The Russian, who was staring at his crushed cigarette packet, looked up.

"Tell these two what you want. I talk to you in ten minutes."

He turned and abruptly exited the bedroom.

"While he's satisfying his craving for Madame Nicotine, shall we inspect the facilities?"

Tony and Gregory followed Collins as he walked towards the door.

Chapter 45

Vladimir Zhukov expelled a long stream of tobacco smoke and watched it curl upwards before dissipating into the atmosphere. The pain in his back had started to throb and the cigarette had, as always, helped to dull the ache. However, the physical pain was of little importance when compared to the tightness in his stomach as he contemplated his humiliation at Jason Collins' hands. The man had treated him in the same way as he'd been treated during his early army service days – with complete contempt. Taken aback by the confrontation, he had reverted to his early role of submissive recruit who had no rights or authority. Furthermore, although he'd been able to give Collins the beating he deserved, the man still had a distinct advantage over him – he had the information that was vital to the operation's smooth running.

He took another long drag and grunted.

St Petersburg's post-Communist period had necessitated the rapid honing of his skills in order to make a profitable living in the jungle inhabited by ruthless criminals each of whom was striving to gain a share of the new riches that had resulted from the Communist state's collapse. Gaining his share had meant calling upon all the cunning and ruthlessness that he'd amassed during his orphanage and army years and, although he'd been well satisfied with the wealth he'd amassed, he was also well aware of the enemies he'd made, any one of whom would have been happy to permanently eliminate him. Hence his decision to take his wealth, permanently leave Russia and re-establish himself in a more benign environment.

And he'd been well satisfied with his decision. New Zealand's pleasant southern Pacific democracy had been an ideal environment in which to ply his variety of trades – intimidation, debt collection, robbery and forgery. He'd invested his considerable capital in various funds that, in spite of the relatively low interest rates, provided him a steady income. But he needed to increase it. He enjoyed the usual accoutrements of success – restaurants, cars and women, but above all, he enjoyed the power – the ability to control and manipulate others, to have them defer to him, the fear and uncertainty obvious from their speech and demeanour. He'd spent his earlier years being bullied and intimidated. Now it was his turn.

Or was it? Jason Collins was a generation younger than him, and in spite of the beating, he'd recovered quickly and had displayed the ability to intimidate the older man. So, should he just shrug, release Collins and walk off into a comfortable sunset? He stubbed out his cigarette, stretched and studied the tranquil scene through the window. For a long moment he was tempted, but then the vision of Fleur Lassiter's lifeless body sprawled on the lounge carpet flashed into his consciousness. He and Collins had shared knowledge of her death and either man had the potential to rat on the other. Walking away and giving Collins a free hand would mean that he'd be constantly worried at every knock on the door or ringing of his phone. He needed to keep the man where he could watch him.

He stood, stretched, lit a fresh cigarette and bellowed, "Gregory!"

Chapter 46

Jenny, with a tray full of empty glasses, looked up as a young woman who looked vaguely familiar entered the bar.

"Hi," Jenny smiled. "Can I get you anything?"

The young woman looked around the bar and nodded. "A glass of white wine."

"Take a seat and I'll bring the wine. You have a preference?"

"The house Chard'd be fine."

Jenny put the glasses on the kitchen bench behind the bar, selected a bottle of Villa Maria Chardonnay and poured it into a glass.

"Haven't seen you in here before."

"No, first time. I've always wanted to learn to fly and finally decided to do something about it. They told me at reception that all the instructors are out flying and suggested I come up here and watch the action from the balcony."

"Good idea. I'm Jenny by the way."

"Sue – nice to meet you. Do you run the bar?"

"Yes. Been here for the last couple of years."

Sue took a sip of the wine, nodded approvingly and asked, "Are there many women flyers in the aero club?"

"They're in a minority, but the number's increasing steadily."

"That's encouraging. A friend of mine told me that she was considering flying lessons at this club. Wondered if she had. Her name's Fleur Lassiter."

Jenny was instantly on the alert.

"Fleur Lassiter," she responded slowly.

"Yes. We were in the same class at Auckland Uni."

"I thought you looked familiar. I've seen you there."

"Yes, in the library."

Jenny nodded and smiled. "So what's your connection with Fleur?"

"She and I graduated in English together. I've been working in Singapore for the past couple of years and we lost touch. Wondered if she'd taken any lessons."

"Did you try to track her down when you returned from Singapore?"

"That's the funny thing."

"What is?"

"I tried phoning her but there was no reply, so I went round to her flat. I knocked, there was no answer, so I tried the door and it opened."

Jenny's raised her eyebrows.

"I'm not a burglar. I called her name before entering."

"And?"

"The place was very neat, typical Fleur, her bed was carefully made, plenty of clothes in the closet, but…" Sue paused and frowned.

"But what?"

"It didn't look as though anyone lived there – thin layers of dust on the benches and tables; most unlike Fleur. It was like she'd left in a hurry, or just disappeared. The only clue was an address written on a pad by her bed – 25 Tohunga Crescent, Parnell.

"Did you know it?"

Sue shook her head.

"You said the door was unlocked."

"Yes. Again, unlike Fleur." Sue took another sip before asking, "So, did Fleur have any flying lessons here?"

Jenny nodded slowly before replying. "Yes, she did, up until about three months ago with instructor Jason Collins. Then she stopped coming."

"Just stopped coming?"

"Yes." She nodded towards Sue's glass. "You'd better have another mouthful before I continue."

"Good god, has something happened to her?"

"A couple of weeks ago two detectives turned up inquiring about her. She's been reported as missing."

"Really?" Sue drained her glass. "Have they any idea what's happened to her?"

"Apparently not." Jenny refilled the empty glass. "But you may have provided a lead."

"A lead?"

"Yes, the Parnell address. You didn't go there?"

"No. Do you think…?"

"It's certainly worth following up."

"So you'll phone the police?"

"When we have something of interest to tell them. All we have at the moment is an Auckland address."

"We?"

"Yes, we. Are you interested in finding your friend Fleur?"

"Of course," replied Sue.

"So am I. And I want the opportunity to put my knowledge into action."

"Meaning?"

"I'm completing a Bachelor of Forensic Science this year – plenty of theory but not a lot of practical work. Maybe now's my chance."

"Yes, but…."

"What work did you do in Singapore?"

Sue smiled briefly. "Actually I was on secondment to the Singapore Ministry of Defence – Legal Service Department. Advised them on courts martial, military and civil law. Also did some practical training, surveillance, undercover work, that sort of thing."

Jenny, clearly impressed, held out her hand. "The fates have smiled upon us. We'll investigate the Parnell address and if we find anything, we'll notify the police. Deal?"

After a brief hesitation, Sue shook her hand. "Deal."

Chapter 47

Tohunga Crescent, a narrow street in upmarket Parnell, looks east over Hobson Bay and the Waitemata Harbour. The sun had already set when Jenny drove slowly past number 25 and parked twenty metres further down the darkened street.

"No point in alerting the inhabitants."

"Didn't see any lights on, so maybe no-one's home," replied Sue.

"The aerial photo shows trees all around the property which hopefully shelters it from prying neighbours."

"Got your special tools?"

Sue lifted a small tool bag from beside the seat.

"OK. Let's proceed with caution."

The pair climbed out of the car, which Jenny locked, and they walked slowly in the direction of number 25. Further up the street a man came out of a property with a dog on a lead and started walking towards them.

"Slow down a little," murmured Sue. "Streetlight ahead."

The dog walker passed under the streetlight, wished the pair a "Good evening" and continued his stroll. His dog, taking a cue from the master, gave both women a peremptory sniff.

"Good thinking," said Jenny. She looked quickly round. "All clear. Come on."

Three quick strides and they turned into the house's entrance where the view of the grounds was obscured by tall trees and a high hedge on both sides. Ahead of them a short path led to the front door. The imposing two-storied house stood silent and still. Its peaked roof with two tall chimneys covered a white Tudor-style dwelling with lead-light windows and black crisscrossed beams. There was no sign of life.

Keeping close to the hedge the two women moved towards the back of the house, pausing several times to check for any reactions. Without incident they reached the back door, which was in the shadow of a tall pine.

"You start, I'll keep watch."

Sue nodded and unzipping her tool bag, extracted several small implements.

"A couple of military policemen in Singapore showed me a trick or two with door locks. The time has come to test their teaching ability."

She crouched by the door and opened a pocketknife with a variety of blades and probes. She selected one and inserted it into the lock spending about a minute in manipulation before pulling it out.

"I'll try another one," she muttered.

Jenny, who had enthusiastically suggested exploring the house, was now having second thoughts. They were breaking and entering and if caught, tried and convicted, her dreams of a forensics career in the Ministry of Justice would be doomed. Around her the hedge and tall trees made a variety of rustling and creaking sounds, while the occasional breeze moved the branches, causing shadows to flit across the back of the house, adding to her mounting trepidation. She took a step towards Sue, whose hunched figure was absorbed in the task of trying to pick the lock.

"Sue, I—"

Click!

"Done it!" Sue looked up with a grin of triumph as she pushed the door open. "Come on. But shoes off first. Don't want to leave any clues of our visit."

The back door opened into a kitchen, comparatively small by modern standards. Jenny switched on her torch and keeping the beam below the windows slowly swept it around the kitchen. It was clean and neat and gave no indication of being recently used.

Exiting the kitchen, they paused at the entrance to what their torch showed was a dining room. The clean and neat appearance was repeated. After poking around in the corners of the room and finding nothing of interest they moved onto the next room, the lounge.

The beam of Jenny's torch swung round the perimeters of the large room and paused at a Welsh dresser.

"Photos," murmured Jenny.

She moved closer and gasped.

"It's Jason Collins!"

"The flying instructor at the aero club?"

"That's the one."

A variety of photos showed a grinning Collins standing in front of various small planes, drinking with other men and, in a corner of the shelf, a photo of him with his arm around a woman.

"Fleur," they said simultaneously.

"So was Fleur having flying lessons from Jason?"

"Yes, and as this photograph suggests, there were fringe benefits for both of them."

"So, has anyone asked him about Fleur's disappearance?"

"I did."

"And?"

"He stormed angrily out of the bar. Haven't seen him since."

"When was this?"

"Last week."

Jenny pointed to a nearby couch and they both sat down. Apart from the movement of the trees, and the occasional noises from nocturnal creatures, the house was silent.

"So the flying instructor..."

"Jason Collins..."

"Could be involved in Fleur's disappearance."

"Wouldn't surprise me. He's pretty repulsive."

Sue started to lean back and put her hands behind her head. Suddenly, with a short cry of pain she lurched forward, groping behind her.

"What the matter?"

"Something sharp. This."

She held up a piece of broken pottery, whose sharp edge had dug into her.

Jenny shone the torch on the piece while Sue turned it over in her hand.

"It's Lladro. Look at the detail."

The piece depicted a headless man in a long coat and boots clutching the ornate bridle of a horse, minus its torso and legs. The details of the man's coat and boots, the horse's teeth, eyes and mane, and the intricacies of the bridle showed meticulous craftsmanship.

"How did it get on the couch?"

"First, how did it get broken? It was obviously a valuable piece – probably quite large."

"A fit of fury, a fight?"

"In which case, where's the rest of it?"

"You tell me, Miss Forensics."

Jenny grunted and knelt on the carpet.

"If there was a fight, and a piece of Lladro was smashed, then it probably happened near the couch. Let's see what this mohair carpet reveals."

The two women crouched side by side in front of the couch and, using the torch, began a meticulous inspection of the carpet. Its long fibres made the task more difficult but also added to the chances of items, no matter how small, being concealed.

"Ouch!" exclaimed Sue.

"What?"

"A little prick."

"You've found Jason Collins?"

"Very funny. No, my hand found something sharp that's made my finger bleed."

She gingerly combed the fibres with her other hand and pulled out a small piece of pottery. The light of the torch revealed a female head with the jagged remains of an ornate bonnet.

"Lladro again?"

"Definitely," replied Sue. "But something's not right here."

"Go on."

"The two remnants we found are almost certainly from a larger piece, with possibly a coach, horses and various people. If they'd been dropped or deliberately smashed, then the pieces would still be here."

"Unless the perpetrators cleaned up the pieces but missed the one hidden by the fibres and the other that presumably shot over to the couch."

Jenny swung her torch around at eye level before pausing by a marble bust of a flyer in helmet and goggles.

"Collins, in marble! What a wanker."

"But a marble surface from which a piece of crockery could ricochet. Bring the torch over."

A brief inspection of the bust showed a white score on top of the skull.

"Down went the Lladro, hit Jason Collins and shattered on the carpet, except for one bit that landed on the couch."

Jenny nodded. "I think we're on to something," she said.

Chapter 48

With a sigh of contentment Maryanne Bullock poured herself a cup of tea, picked up the latest copy of *Hello* magazine, and settled down for an in-depth scrutiny of the royals, the rich, and the famous.

The sound of the front doorbell echoed through the house. Maryanne groaned with exasperation.

"Helen, can you see who's at the front door!" she called.

"I'm busy, Mum," came the sharp response from the end of the passage. "Can't someone—"

"Helen, answer the bloody door!"

After a brief pause Maryanne heard angry footsteps make their way to the front door and the door opening, followed by the murmur of male voices. Moments later Helen appeared.

"Mum, there's two police officers at the door. They want to speak to Matt."

"Good God! Why?"

Helen shrugged and gave a thin smile.

"Dunno. They didn't say." Her smile held a hint of schadenfreude. "Maybe he's in trouble."

"Don't be ridiculous," responded her mother rising rapidly to her feet and striding down the passage.

"Good afternoon, madam. I'm Detective Sergeant Burton and this is my colleague Detective Young. We'd like to talk to Matt Bullock. Are you his mother?"

"I am." She glared at the detective. "What's this about, Mr Burton?"

"We'd prefer to speak to Matt Bullock, madam. Is he at home?

"Yes," responded Helen, standing behind her mother. "He's out by the pool. I'll get him for you." She turned and then paused. "Ask them in, Mother," she grinned. "I'll bring Matt."

She hurried out to the pool area where Matt was sprawled on a canvas recliner reading a novel.

"Matt, two people have arrived."

"And so?" replied her brother, annoyed at being disturbed.

"They want to talk to you."

"Me. What about?"

Her grin was gleeful.

"They're police. Maybe you know better than me."

"Jesus!" Matt stood abruptly.

"Mum's invited them in. There's no escape, Matt!"

"Don't be so bloody stupid, Helen!" He paused, shrugged and muttered, "No idea what they want. I'd better go and find out."

"Yes, you'd better. Let's go."

"No, Helen. We are not going anywhere. I am going to talk to them, and you will make yourself scarce."

She was forced to jump aside as he strode towards the house.

As he entered the lounge Burton and Young rose from the couch.

"Matt Bullock?"

"Yes,"

"I'm Detective Sergeant Burton and this is my colleague Detective Young. We'd like to ask you a few questions."

The two looked up as Helen entered the room.

"I'm Helen, Matt's sister." Ignoring Matt's glare, she smiled at the two detectives. "Will you want to talk to me, too?"

"No, Helen, that won't be necessary," replied Burton. He looked at Maryanne. "We'd prefer to see him alone. Perhaps another room would be more acceptable."

"Alone, why, what's he done?" responded Maryanne. "Matt needs—."

"It's alright, Mum. We'll go down by the pool." He turned to Burton. "Is that OK?"

"Fine. Lead the way, Matt."

"But—"

"It's OK, Mum. I'm not being arrested." He looked at Burton. "Am I?"

"No. We just have some questions that we'd like answered."

"See, Mum."

Matt, more puzzled than frightened, smiled reassuringly at his mother before leading the pair out the door and down to the pool. He quickly arranged three chairs under the large black sun umbrella and the trio seated themselves. Matt looked inquiringly at Burton.

"We need to have a conversation concerning Fleur Lassiter. An acquaintance of yours, I believe."

"Yes," he responded cautiously, "I've met Fleur."

"I think you've known her for some time, Matt."

"OK, I have. That's not a crime."

Burton's eyes narrowed. "Why did you use the word 'crime', Matt?"

"No reason. It's just an expression."

"I see. Fleur Lassiter has been reported missing, and we've begun making inquiries."

"Missing. Why would she go missing? Perhaps she's left the country."

"She hasn't. We've checked," said Young.

"Well, maybe she's just gone on holiday somewhere remote and not told anyone."

"Why do you think she'd do that, Matt?"

"Dunno. Just an idea."

"When was the last time you saw Fleur Lassiter?"

"A couple of months ago. She'd been taking flying lessons at the North Shore Aero Club but then she stopped coming."

The pair exchanged glances and Burton nodded.

Young's voice was soft. "You had a sexual relationship with her, Matt."

The abruptness of the statement caught him off-guard. Why the hell was the female cop asking him this? None of her bloody business.

"Did you hear my question, Matt?"

"Yes, I heard it, but I don't know why you asked it."

"We said that Fleur Lassiter is missing," responded Burton. "We're making inquiries. That means that we're questioning anyone who knew her – including you."

"OK, I had an affair with Fleur, but it was over months ago." He looked at both officers in turn. "She was also having an affair with the flying instructor Jason Collins. I hope he's on your list."

"He is. You say you haven't seen her for a couple of months."

"That's right."

"Have you had any communication with her during that time – phone call, letter, email, text?"

"No."

"And do you have any idea where she might have gone?"

"No, I don't."

"Do you know any friends of hers that could help us with information?"

"No. I've never met any of her friends."

Burton paused before continuing and Matt could feel sweat forming on his brow that was not caused by the bright sun hovering over the pool.

"How did you meet her?"

"At uni, we were in the same tutorial together."

"And you never met any of her university friends?"

"No."

"That's a little unusual."

"Look, she was a little bit older than me and she preferred to keep our relationship secret."

"I see. What was your age difference?"

"Um, about eight years."

Young raised her eyebrows. "That's rather a gap, isn't it, Matt?" she asked.

Matt's growing feeling of trepidation was abruptly replaced by anger.

"Look, I don't know what the hell this has to do with Fleur's disappearance. I already told you we broke off several months ago. I have a new girlfriend."

"The same age as you?" interrupted Burton smoothly.

"Yes, she is." He took a deep breath. "I'm sorry Fleur's missing and I hope you find her. But her disappearance is nothing to do with me."

A long silence was broken by Burton rising to his feet, followed by Young.

"OK, Matt, we'll leave it there for now. We may need to talk to you again, but in the meantime, I want your promise you'll phone me if you hear anything about Fleur that could be pertinent to her disappearance." He reached inside his jacket and produced a card, which he handed to Matt. "Here are my contact details."

Matt suppressed a sigh of relief as he accepted the proffered card.

"Thank you. I will contact you if I hear anything."

They both nodded and walked towards the front gate. Matt breathed deeply and as he began to sink back into his recliner, he saw his mother and sister staring at him from the large window that overlooked the pool area.

Chapter 49

Matt slumped back into his seat. Fleur missing, relationship questions, reference to a crime, possibility of further questions and, of course, the inevitable grilling from his parents. Christ, what a mess!

When he was tense, he often dived into the pool and swam a series of lengths. He stood and started to pull his t-shirt over his head, just as his cell phone trilled. He let the t-shirt drop and picked up the vibrating device. The number looked vaguely familiar, so he pressed the button.

"Hullo."

"Matt?"

"Yes."

"Matt, it's Jenny."

"Jenny?"

"From the aero club bar."

He relaxed a little.

"Hi, Jenny. Do you need a hand to clean the floor again?"

"No," laughed Jenny, "but we would like to have a chat to you."

"We?"

"Oh, sorry. I mean Sue and I. We met at the club a couple of weeks ago. She's a friend of Fleur Lassiter. As you may know…"

"She's missing. The cops have just been here. They tried to imply that I had something to do with her disappearance."

"Actually Sue and I have been investigating Fleur's disappearance. We've made some interesting discoveries. We'd like to talk to you about them."

"Why me?"

"We've found a link with Jason Collins."

"Hardly surprising."

"And we've uncovered some evidence that could have sinister implications."

"Sinister? What do you mean?"

"Look, Matt, it's nothing for you to be concerned about but we think you can help us. Jason took a fortnight's annual leave last month but then he never showed up and no-one knows where he's gone."

"Maybe he's hooked up with Fleur."

"Doubt it. The police had been looking for her a couple of weeks before he disappeared. As I said, Sue and I have been doing some investigating of our own and we need your help. Can you meet us both in town for a drink at the Commons in Takapuna, Wednesday night?"

"I guess so. Just one thing."

"What?"

"I'd like to bring my girlfriend Sandy."

"Sandy? The student flyer?"

"Yeah."

"OK, don't see why not. Eight o'clock suit you?"

Hearing footsteps approaching he looked up to see his mother and sister bearing down on him.

"Sure. See you then," he said and terminated the call.

He watched as the pair sat down in the seats previously occupied by the two detectives.

"So, Matt, what was all that about?" His mother's demeanour was cold and her gaze unwavering, but he noticed her hands were trembling.

He shrugged. "Nothing much, really. One of the aero club members has gone missing and they wanted to know if I could tell them anything."

"Why you?"

"I'd met the person a few times, but not recently."

"How long has he been missing?"

"She."

"She?" His sister's eyes were bright with anticipation. "Was she your lover?"

"Helen!" snapped her mother.

207

"No she bloody wasn't, Helen!"

"Was it Sandy, that girl you brought to dinner?"

"No."

"I'm relieved to hear that," said Maryanne. "Are the police taking this any further?"

"They'll continue making inquiries, but they were satisfied that I knew nothing."

"That's a relief. It's very upsetting to have the police coming to our home. At least they weren't in a police car and didn't wear uniforms."

"So your good name is still intact, Mother," said Matt, smiling sardonically.

"That's enough of your sarcasm, young man. Your father won't be pleased to hear of the police visit."

"There's no need to tell him, Mum. I told you, the police are satisfied that I know nothing about the person's disappearance."

"Of course your father will need to be informed."

"Yes, of course he will," echoed Helen, smiling sweetly at him. "If the police are satisfied that you're not involved, there's no need to be worried."

Chapter 50

"Thanks for agreeing to join me."

Sandy's expression was neutral as she studied the menu.

"So," said Matt brightly, "what do you fancy?"

"Fish of the day will be fine, thanks."

"Good idea," he responded, maintaining his smile. "And a white wine would be best wouldn't it?"

"Chardonnay thanks."

"Good choice."

He looked round, caught the waiter's eye and placed the order. The pair sat in silence for a long moment until Matt took a deep breath.

"Sandy, I was a bloody fool and I sincerely apologise."

"Matt, the tale of your sordid affair threw me, and when I asked for more time to think about it you stormed out of the car. Pretty immature."

Matt took a deep breath, quelled an angry rejoinder and replied in a soft voice. "I agree. I handled it badly. Clearly it was insensitive of me. But, Sandy, I'm truly sorry." He paused, deciding that if he kept going, he could start babbling. Finally, Sandy spoke.

"OK, Matt, I heard what you've said and I accept your apology."

Matt felt a wave of relief but kept his reply steady.

"Thanks, Sandy. Appreciate it."

He was about to stretch out and take her hand when the waiter arrived with the two glasses of wine. Matt picked up his glass, smiled and raised it.

"To us."

Sandy, after a moment's hesitation, raised her glass.

"To us," she echoed.

The arrival of the fish left little room for meaningful conversation, which was a relief to Matt who was content to confine the conversation to small talk. Soon both of them were smiling and laughing.

Over coffee Matt reached out and took her hand.

"Sandy, I'd like you to come with me to a meeting."

"A meeting," she frowned. "What about?"

"It's not anything formal. Yesterday I had a phone call from Jenny at the aero club."

"The bar manager?"

"Yes. She and her friend are investigating the disappearance of Fleur Lassiter."

Sandy paused, her coffee cup in mid-air.

"Fleur Lassiter again. She seems to appear—"

"Sandy, this has nothing to do with my previous relationship." He hurried on. "A month ago she was reported as missing, and the police are treating it seriously. But the real reason Jenny phoned me was that Jason Collins also seems to have disappeared."

"Jason?"

"Apparently."

"So why did Jenny contact you?"

"She's teamed up with Sue, a friend from uni. They've been doing some unofficial investigating on both disappearances and want to discuss it with me. Jenny's completing a Bachelor of Forensic Science so I think she could be worth listening to. I thought that you might be interested."

"So are the police investigating Fleur Lassiter's disappearance?"

"Yes."

"Have they questioned you?"

"Yes, a week ago. They came to our place and spent about half an hour grilling me. I told them I knew nothing about her disappearance, and they seemed satisfied."

"Bet your family wasn't happy with a police visit."

"Mother was upset and my little sister was bloody delighted."

"And your father?"

"I haven't told him. I thought Mum would but so far she hasn't said anything."

"And your sister?"

"She'd love to tell Dad but I think Mum's warned her off."

"Sounds like a river of tensions is running through your family."

Matt shrugged. "Nothing new. I know we probably tried to put on a good show for you when you came to dinner but..."

"I did realise that you were not a blissfully happy suburban family cocooned in a bubble of wealth and prosperity."

Matt smiled ruefully. "You've got a keen insight, Sandy."

She shrugged. "Thanks, but it didn't take much effort to read the signs."

There was a pause before Sandy continued. "You promise me that this has nothing to do with your previous affair."

"Absolutely. I told that you I was completely finished with her and that…"

He hesitated.

"And that what?"

"That I love you, Sandy."

"Not now, Matt." She paused. "When's the meeting?"

"The Commons, in Takapuna, Thursday, eight o'clock. I could pick you up."

"That's fine. At seven. That will give us time to talk before the meeting."

*

Promptly at seven Matt pressed the chime button on Sandy's front door. When she opened it her smile was warm.

"Hi, Matt."

She leaned forward offering her right cheek for a brief kiss.

"You look lovely, Sandy."

"Thanks. Shall we go?"

211

He reached out, took her hand and they walked to his car. He opened the passenger's door; she slipped in and smiled her thanks. He hurried round into the driver's seat, started the car and eased it out into the light traffic.

"Sandy, I think you need some background before the meeting."

"OK, as long as it's not a rehash of your ill-fated relationship with Fleur Lassiter."

Matt winced before shaking his head. "No way. I need to tell you about Jason Collins and his operation."

"Operation – has he been in hospital?"

"No, an operation that he's been running on the side. It involves flying drugs into the country."

"Drugs? You're sure?"

"Yes. Not hard drugs – medical drugs that are not supported by Pharmac's government funding but which rich people with life-threatening conditions can afford."

"Diseased, desperate, but not destitute."

"Exactly. It has high risks but provides high returns. I don't know all the details, but my father has asked me to find out more."

"Your father?"

"Yeah. He wants a piece of the action."

"But why would he want to take the risk?"

"He's short of money. Yes, he's rich but he has a lifestyle that requires a considerable cash flow, that needs topping up."

Sandy nodded slowly before continuing.

"I see. But how is this linked to the disappearance of Fleur and Jason?"

"Not sure." He sighed heavily. "But it could have implications for him," he paused, "and for me."

"I can see why you want to hear what Jenny and her friend have discovered." She locked eyes with him. "Once we've heard what they have to say and shared our information we can decide where we go from there."

The use of 'we', although ambiguous, was not lost on Matt who smiled.

"You're right, of course. As they say, information is power," he said as he pulled into the restaurant parking area.

Chapter 51

As Sandy and Matt entered the Commons, they saw Jenny waving from a booth in a far corner. She and her companion rose to meet them.

"Sandy, Matt, meet my friend Sue. Sue, meet Sandy and Matt."

Smiles and hugs were exchanged and the four of them settled into the comfortable seats around the large wooden table.

"Pleasant spot," said Sandy, looking at the high ceilings and large windows, framed outside by a variety of trees and shrubs.

"It's midweek so not too crowded," said Jenny. "We picked this corner so hopefully we won't be disturbed. How about we order drinks and food before we tell our story?"

Drinks were ordered first, glasses of Chardonnay for the women and a beer for Matt and, after a lively discussion of the food offered on the menu, they all selected seafood dishes. The drinks arrived promptly, and Jenny raised her glass.

"Here's to an enjoyable and informative evening."

They all touched glasses, sipped their drinks and echoed her toast.

"I'll start with an update on our progress."

The others nodded in agreement and Jenny began by describing her initial meeting with Sue, their mutual acquaintance with Fleur, Sue's search of Fleur's flat, her discovery of the Parnell address, and their decision to visit it.

"Visit it? Did you know who lived there?" asked Sandy.

"Not at that stage."

"And what if no-one was home?"

"Fleur had disappeared and so strong action was called for."

"If no-one was home we'd already decided to have a look round," added Sue.

"I believe it's called breaking and entering," said Matt, looking round to ensure that no customers had moved near their table.

"It is and we did. We went at night. It was a two-storied house surrounded by trees – quite spooky. Sue picked the lock and we entered."

Matt looked at Sue. "You picked the lock?"

"Yes, I worked with the Singapore Ministry of Defence – learnt a few tricks."

"Obviously," said Matt. "What did you find?"

"The house belonged to Jason Collins," said Jenny.

"Jason Collins?" Matt's eyes were wide.

"Classy place. We found a bust of him in flying helmet and goggles, a photo of Fleur and some smashed bits of an expensive Lladro piece."

"And the occupant?" asked Sandy.

"Negative. The house showed no signs of recent habitation."

"Maybe he skipped the country with Fleur in tow?" said Sandy.

"The police said there's no record of Fleur having gone overseas," said Matt. "Not sure about Jason."

"Matt, you said you and Jenny had some additional info."

"Yes, Sandy. It appears that Jason was engaged in some activities involving importing medicinal supplies across the Tasman using light aircraft. Apparently a fairly lucrative operation."

"And now he's disappeared. Do you have any other information?"

"My father had asked me to investigate Jason's operation." Matt hesitated as he searched for the appropriate words. "He was interested in becoming part of it."

"Your father? Why?" asked Jenny.

"Is it legal?" added Sue.

"He wants to increase his cash flow. He admitted it was on the edge of the law. I said I'd make a few inquiries, but," he

215

shrugged, "now Jason Collins has vanished I'm becoming more wary about his operations."

Seeing the women were about to speak he held up his hand. "I suspect my father knows more than he's told me so far. I'm pretty sure he knows a man who intimidates people for a fee. This man could be linked with Fleur and Jason."

Sandy stared at him. "You never said anything about this to me. Your father in cahoots with some hired gorilla!"

"I've been joining the dots while Jenny was talking. The smashed Lladro suggests there was some heavy intimidation. And two people are missing. They may be dead. Clearly something has to be done."

"We could go to the police," said Sandy.

Matt rounded on her.

"No! I don't want the police questioning Dad. I'll look into it." He looked at Jenny and Sue. "You two have done pretty well so far. Let's keep the momentum going before we involve the law."

"Which we may have broken by entering Jason's house. Heads down at this point I think," said Sue.

Jenny and Matt nodded in agreement, but Sandy showed no reaction.

"You've a problem with that, Sandy?"

"No, Matt, but we need to be very clear as to the where, how and why, and the common sharing of information as it comes to hand."

"Otherwise we could all wind up with the common sharing of a cell," muttered Jenny.

"Exactly."

Two waitresses arrived at the table with their seafood orders. Welcoming the brief break from their deliberations the group began to eat.

Matt broke the silence. "There could be another link in the story. Dad's gorilla could be a dude called Zhukov."

"Sounds Russian," said Sue.

"It is."

"Sounds dangerous."

"He is."

"How do you know?"

"My dad hinted at it. Told me Zhukov is good at taking care of business."

"Sounds like a line from a gangster movie," muttered Sandy.

"You feel this Zhukov guy is worth following up? That he could be involved in the disappearances?"

Matt nodded.

"Why do you think that?"

Matt reached for his glass and slowly drank the rest of his beer, giving himself time to collect his thoughts. He didn't want to relate how his father had hired Zhukov to intimidate Collins at his request. He already sensed Sandy's disapproval at the seamier side of his family and was reluctant to expand further.

He put his glass down and looked at each of his companion's faces.

"My dad used Zhukov to help collect money owed by clients who were a little slow in making payments."

"Did your father ever mention Fleur Lassiter?" asked Jenny.

"No."

"But there could be a link between her, Zhukov and Collins," said Sandy.

Matt shrugged his shoulders and took another sip.

"There's no proof at this stage, but I guess it's a possibility," he said.

"As I see it," began Jenny, "we need to know more about this Zhukov character. If the Lladro had been deliberately ground into the lounge carpet it fits the concept of violent and intimidating behaviour by Zhukov."

The others nodded their agreement and Matt, still worried his father's link with Zhukov would be further explored, spoke up quickly.

"Yes, you're right. I'll try to find out as much as I can about Zhukov, full name, address, and background, known associates, that sort of thing. As my father's made use of his services he's bound to have information that could provide us with further clues."

"You're going to ask him direct?" asked Sandy, her eyebrows raised in disbelief.

"I said I'd find out as much as I can. Let's leave it at that."

His eyes travelled round the group and it was obvious to the three women that further questioning would be futile.

"OK," said Jenny, "I'm happy to leave it to Matt in the meantime. How long will it take to get the info?"

"Give me until this time next week. If I have enough stuff we could meet here again to plan our next move."

Jenny and Sue exchanged glances, and then nodded their agreement.

Sandy's eyes narrowed.

"Look," she said, "I don't want to spoil your fun, but we could be moving into dangerous waters. Two people have disappeared, some Russian hood who intimidates people could be involved, there's possible smuggling of illegal medical supplies, the police have already contacted Matt and Jenny, yet you all seem keen to proceed without notifying them. Don't you realise the risk you're taking?"

Sue broke the silence that followed.

"What you say is valid, Sandy, but when Jenny told me my friend Fleur had disappeared and described her involvement with Jason Collins, I decided I should do something about it. To date, all the police seem to have done is go around asking questions but making very little progress."

"You don't know this," said Sandy.

"Maybe not," cut in Jenny, "but if they had found additional evidence I'm sure they would have come back to me for further questioning. I didn't know Fleur that well, but she always seemed friendly, whereas Jason Collins was a first-class creep. If he's involved in her disappearance, then I believe we have to do something. We've already decided to contact the police when we have more evidence but so far all we have are suspicions. We need more."

"Agree," said Matt. He turned to Sandy. "Sandy, if my dad's involved in some shady dealings then I want to find out about them and warn him off. If he's done anything illegal and the police charge him, it will ruin him."

All eyes focussed on Sandy who sat for a long moment drumming the fingers of her right hand on the table. She stopped, lifted her head and nodded.

"OK, I hear what you're saying. I agree Jason Collins is a slime ball. As for Fleur Lassiter," she looked at Matt who glanced away quickly, "if she's missing then clearly steps have to be taken to find her. Jenny's said you'll contact the police once you have more evidence, which is fair enough. And I also take Matt's point about protecting his dad."

"So, are you with us?" asked Jenny.

"At this stage, yes. As long as we agree we won't do anything foolish or engage in any actions of false bravado. OK, Matt?"

"Moi?" grinned Matt. "No, of course not." Noting that Sandy did not return his grin he reached out and took her hand. "Seriously, Sandy, I don't want any trouble with the law or with Zhukov and his mates. I promise I'll proceed with caution."

"And in the final analysis," said Jenny, "the challenge is worth a few risks."

Chapter 52

Matt sat in the lounge flicking through a flying magazine and listening carefully to the sounds in the house. His father was away at a two-day conference, his sister Helen was going for a sleepover at a friend's place, and Maryanne had said she'd drop her off on the way to meeting some girlfriends for drinks. He had only to wait.

He'd been surprised neither of them had said anything to his father about the visit by the police. He'd have bet money that Helen would have wasted no time in ratting on him and revelling in their father's angry reaction. He could only assume their mother had threatened her with dire consequences if she didn't keep her mouth shut. He'd been aware for months that his parents' love for each other had long ceased. However, the current arrangement appeared to suit them both, and clearly his mother had no wish to disturb her version of domestic bliss. That didn't mean that the two women would continue to maintain their silence – another reason why he had to move fast in obtaining any relevant information.

"Helen! Get a move on!"

The clatter of footsteps was followed by his mother's "Bye, Matt!" to which he responded with a friendly, "See you, Mum!"

He listened as the doors slammed and the car made its way down the drive. He waited, then rose, opened the front door and looked out. The drive was empty.

He moved quickly into his father's study, drew the curtains and turned on the desk light. In the middle of the desk was his father's latest model MacBook Pro. Ray Bullock had an identical model that he took on business trips – rationalising that the one left in his office would always receive up to the minute information that may not be available in other locations. Matt had suggested this was needless extravagance, but his father was adamant, and hopefully tonight it would work to Matt's advantage.

Matt sat down in his father's well-padded swivel chair and pressed the 'On' button. It requested the password and Matt tapped in 'Bigbucks 99'. The screen lit up with a photograph of an attractive fulsome blonde in a low-cut evening dress. Matt studied the image for a long moment, grunted, "Current bimbo, lucky bastard," and tapped Return. The screen responded with a wide range of options.

Moving quickly to Documents, Matt took a deep breath and typed in 'Zhukov'. A blue file folder appeared, and his click revealed two Word document symbols. He clicked on the first. It revealed a summary of Vladimir Zhukov's background – some of it copied and pasted from various sites. The passages in Russian had translations underneath. The information covered Zhukov's birth, his service in the Russian military, and his application and acceptance papers for New Zealand residency. Clearly his father had reliable sources.

The second file contained Zhukov's contact details, including his email address, phone number and two residential addresses – one at Karangahape Road in Auckland city and the other near the rural town of Riverhead, about thirty kilometres north of Auckland.

Matt switched to email and sent a message to his own email address, attaching both folders. He then deleted the message from the Sent list. He typed 'Zhukov' into the email search and was rewarded with ten emails. The first few were instructions from his father to the Russian for jobs involving the collection of debts from various individuals. In each case his father had been rapidly reimbursed in full as shown in subsequent emails to Zhukov with details of the collection fees paid to the Russian.

In the final email he struck gold. It was from Zhukov with an attachment. Opening it, Matt read with growing fascination the Russian's report on Jason Collins' drug importing operation. He forwarded it to himself, deleted it from the Sent folder, and leaned back in the chair. Zhukov's comprehensive report had clearly triggered his father's interest in Collins. Yet, given Zhukov's seedy background, surely he too would be interested in the operations. Therefore, was the Russian involved in the pilot's disappearance? Had Collins been kidnapped and forced to hand over the operation to Zhukov and his cronies? And if so, had Zhukov then murdered him? And what about Fleur? Was she caught up in all this? And if so, how and why?

On the Word file he clicked Open Recent and clicked Clear Recent. Satisfied that any trace of his computer use had disappeared into cyberspace, he turned it off, switched off the desk light, opened the curtains and exited the study, closing the door behind him.

From the fridge he took out a bottle of Stella Artois, opened it, took a long swig, picked up his phone and gave instructions to Siri.

When the call was answered he paused, before he said, "Hi, Sandy, I have some information you will certainly want to hear. Free anytime tomorrow?"

Chapter 53

"Visit Zhukov? Are you mad?"

"Not entirely," replied Jenny holding up the palms of her hands as if to ward off the reactions of the other three. "We've all agreed that we need more info on Jason and Fleur and that Zhukov probably has it."

"So what's your plan? We storm the place, capture him and beat the truth out of him?" responded Sandy.

Jenny took a deep breath and looked at each of the trio in turn. "OK, hear me out. From my understanding, the Russian is a dude who would answer force with greater force. Therefore, we need a more subtle approach. What I'm suggesting is that two of us pay him a visit explaining that we need his help. We smile warmly and flatter him. He's a big ugly bastard who probably doesn't get many compliments from attractive women so it's worth a try."

"I still don't see the point—"

"Hang on, Sandy, let me finish. We explain that we're trying to find information on Fleur Lassiter, a missing friend of ours. Point out that the police have had no success in finding her and so we've decided to see what we can find."

"Jenny, won't he want to know why we think he has information that we need?" asked Matt.

"And if he's involved in her disappearance he could turn nasty," added Sandy.

'I've thought of that. We can explain that we're friends with Matt Bullock, Ray Bullock's son and that Matt thought he might know something about Fleur."

"That could increase his suspicions."

"It's more likely to increase our credibility. Keep smiling and playing the role of two naïve young women trying to locate their friend. If he turns nasty, we'll just act surprised and then leave."

"You keep saying 'we', Jenny," said Matt. "Are you volunteering to be one of the pair?"

"Yes. And you'll need to be parked in the street outside. We'll all have our cell phones on speed dial in case there's any signs of trouble."

"It could work," said Matt. "So who's the other one of the pair?"

"I'm suggesting that Sandy stays in the car with you while Sue and I pay Zhukov a visit. OK, Sue?"

The two women exchanged glances and Sue shrugged.

"It's a bit of a risk, but on the other hand we may be able to gain some information from him." She made a chopping movement with her right arm. "And if he or his thugs try anything it'll give me the chance to demonstrate my Singapore combat skills." She grinned. "And it could be quite exciting visiting the Russian bear in his den."

Jenny nodded slowly. "OK, we've all taken a few risks and so far they've paid off. We need to keep going, so I'll be a starter."

"You're sure?"

"Yes, Matt. And you agree to be parked outside the whole time?"

"Absolutely. Although, if he appears to be making trouble you politely thank him and leave. He won't want any problems with the cops."

"If Jenny and Sue get any fresh info, then what?"

"We'll decide on our next move, Sandy. OK?"

Sandy looked at the other two. "You're both sure about this?"

They both nodded.

"OK, let's sort out our plan of action."

Chapter 54

The knock on the door was tentative.

Zhukov put down the *New Zealand Herald* newspaper and sighed. He could hear Gregory on the phone in the next room so reluctantly pushed himself out of his chair and ambled towards the door. He wasn't expecting any morning callers and hoped that the hesitant knock wouldn't be some earnest missionary, with pamphlets on salvation at the ready.

He twisted the handle and pulled the door open with a swift movement. He started in surprise at the two attractive young women clad in skirts, blouses and jackets, smiling warmly at him.

"Mr Zhukov?" asked the taller of the two.

Zhukov would normally have just grunted an affirmative. However, taken aback by the sight of two fresh-faced young women he replied, "Yes, I am Mr Zhukov. Can I help you?"

"Yes, sir," replied Jenny, broadening her smile. "We need some help in finding a friend of ours. May we come in?"

Normally wary of allowing unknown callers at his apartment, Zhukov found himself responding to her smile, stepping back and indicating that they could enter. The two women immediately stepped forward and paused in the hallway.

"This way, please."

He ushered them into his lounge and indicated a large couch. The furnishings looked relatively new but like the carpet, they were dotted with stains of various densities. Several low tables contained ashtrays full of cigarette butts, and empty but unwashed shot glasses.

The big Russian stood awkwardly over the pair.

"Would you like a drink?" he asked.

"A cup of tea would be nice," replied Sue, with a gentle smile.

"Tea?" he frowned.

"We don't want to put you to any trouble, sir."

"Gregory!"

Startled by his bellow the two women were further surprised by the immediate appearance of a tall young man dressed in jeans and a T-shirt bearing a logo of The Eagles. He too was obviously startled by the unfamiliar sight of two pretty women seated in Zhukov's lounge.

"Vlad?"

"Tea, Gregory. We have tea?"

Gregory shifted his gaze from Zhukov to the two young women and frowned.

"I'm sorry," said Jenny, sensing that tea was not a beverage consumed by either of the men. "We haven't introduced ourselves." She reached out her hand to Zhukov. "I'm Gladys Williams and my friend is Sylvia White."

She tried not to wince at the prospect of Zhukov's sizeable hand engulfing hers. But to her surprise he took her hand gently and brushed it with his lips.

"I am happy to meet you, Gladys."

He repeated the gesture with Sue before relaxing into his chair and turning towards Gregory, who had observed the greeting process with astonishment.

"Tea?"

Quickly recovering himself Gregory replied, "I think we have run out of tea, Vlad. I'll go to the mini-market and buy some." He turned to the two women. "My name is Gregory. What tea would you like?"

"English breakfast would be lovely, thank you, Gregory," replied Jenny, smiling shyly.

"Yes, English breakfast, if it's not too much trouble, Gregory," echoed Sue cocking her head coquettishly.

Gregory blushed. The women he generally encountered were dressed provocatively and expected to be well paid for the pleasures on offer. Demure females were well outside his experience, or his boss's for that matter.

"No, of course not." He exchanged a quizzical look with Zhukov before exiting.

Keen to commence the conversation Jenny asked, "Mr Zhukov, you came to New Zealand from Russia. Do you like living here?"

Zhukov nodded and smiled. "Yes, I do. It is peaceful country with many green open spaces and," he hesitated, and an awkward grin appeared on his craggy visage, "many pretty ladies."

Sue smiled and lowered her eyelashes for a moment before asking," What work did you do in Russia?"

"I was in Russian army for a long time."

"The army?" Jenny adopted a wide-eyed expression. "That must have been exciting."

The big Russian stared at her for a moment before throwing his head back and roaring with laughter. "Exciting! Young lady, you know nothing of army or war, yes?"

"Well, no, sir, I don't really."

"Then I tell you that life in Russian army was often very difficult for soldiers. Bad food, bad weather, and the dis...," he hesitated.

"Discipline?" offered Jenny.

"*Da*. Discipline – very harsh for private soldiers."

"And were you a private soldier, sir?" asked Sue.

"For several years." He gave a faint smile and raised his head a fraction. "But then I got a promo...."

"Promotion."

He nodded at Sue. "Yes. I became officer." He suddenly leapt to his feet, saluted and barked, "Lieutenant Vladimir Zhukov, Soviet Armed Forces!"

Jenny and Sue stared in astonishment at the ramrod figure towering over them. To their relief, Zhukov abruptly sat down and grinned at them.

"My apologies, ladies. There are some army moments I like to remember. My pro- promotion to lieutenant meant no more beatings from officers. I, Vladimir Zhukov was now one of them."

"Did you go to war, Mr Zhukov?" asked Jenny.

"War? Yes. I went with Russian army to Afghanistan. Did I enjoy it? No. It was bloody bad, horrible, men killing and being killed." He folded his arms tightly across his chest. "I hated it."

"Did you leave the army after the war?"

"Yes. I was a, er, businessman in St Petersburg for some years." He laughed mirthlessly. "That was nearly as dangerous as fighting in Afghanistan. So I decided to come as far away from Russia as I could – to New Zealand."

The two women smiled. "A good decision, I think, sir," said Sue.

Zhukov's reply was interrupted by the sound of a door closing, rapid footsteps on the stairs and the entrance of Gregory carrying a small packet.

"Ah, Gregory, you have tea."

Gregory smiled at the two women and nodded.

"Yes, Vladimir.'

"Then make it please. Four people."

Gregory seemed about to speak but changed his mind and walked into the adjoining kitchen.

"Now, ladies, you say that I can help you. I am of course happy to if I can. Please tell me."

The pair exchanged glances and Jenny nodded. Sue took a breath and began. "We are looking for a friend of ours. She went missing several weeks ago and we have not heard from her."

Zhukov frowned. "Why have you come to me?"

"Our friend Matt Bullock said that you might help us. His father is—"

"Ray Bullock?"

"Yes, that's right. Matt said that you might have contacts that could help us with our search."

Zhukov sat upright and stared at both of the pair for a long moment. "What is name of your friend?" he asked softly.

"Fleur Lassiter. She's the same age as me and—"

His response was harsh. "I do not know of such girl."

He reached for a packet of cigarettes on the nearby coffee table that had remained untouched since the women's arrival. He placed one in his mouth, his lighter flared and a puff of smoke temporarily enveloped his face.

"I ask Gregory."

He rose abruptly and left the room. The two women sat silently. From the direction of the kitchen they heard Zhukov speaking in Russian, followed by the loud rattling of crockery and a rapid and apparently tense conversation.

Several minutes later Zhukov returned, followed by Gregory who was carrying a tray with three mugs and a teapot. Although the big Russian was smiling, both women sensed the tenseness in the air.

"Gregory is sorry but he has no knowledge of your friend Fleur Lassiter."

"No knowledge at all, Vlad," said Gregory rather too loudly.

"Gregory has to leave on urgent business. We now have tea for three."

Gregory, without looking at the two women, left the room as Zhukov reached for the teapot.

"I'll pour it if you like, Mr Zhukov," volunteered Jenny.

"Is OK, you are my guest and I pour tea," he replied tersely, followed by a hastily contrived smile. Grasping the handle, he slowly poured the tea into each mug. He paused and handed one to each before taking the third mug and sitting back in his chair, his eyes exhibiting a new watchfulness.

"So, how long is friend missing?"

"I returned recently from Singapore," replied Sue. "I tried to contact Fleur but without success. I met J-, er Sylvia at the North Shore Flying Club and she told me that Fleur had been taking flying lessons but had suddenly stopped. Matt Bullock was also a trainee pilot at the club and knew Fleur, so we asked him if he could help. He hadn't seen her for about a month but suggested that we visited you due to your contacts in the city." She shrugged her shoulders and tried unsuccessfully to put on a disarming smile. "So here we are."

"What about police? If your friend is missing have police been told?"

"Yes, they've started making inquiries but haven't found anything so far."

Zhukov grunted, drained his tea in one noisy gulp, screwed his face and replaced the mug on the table.

Jenny put her mug on the table and began to rise.

"Just a moment, Miss Gladys. I have some more questions of my own. I am not sure why your friend Matt Bullock said to ask me. Why did he think I know about your missing friend?"

"He didn't say you would know about Fleur. He said that you have done some work for his father and had many contacts in the city. We have no real leads so we're trying every possibility."

Zhukov drew deeply on his cigarette and expelled the smoke in their direction.

"Well, I know nothing and neither does Gregory."

"In that case—" began Jenny.

A buzzing sound interrupted her. Zhukov pulled a cell phone from his inside pocket, studied the screen briefly and stood.

"You finish your tea. I cannot help you, so you go now."

He strode through the lounge to the front door, opened and remained beside it.

Jenny looked at Sue who nodded. Nervously the pair rose. Their hurried, "Thank you," was barely acknowledged by their now scowling host, who slammed the door shut as soon as they'd left.

Chapter 55

"Hope they're OK." Sandy looked at her phone for the umpteenth time. "How long have they been there?"

"Fifteen minutes," responded Matt. "Just keep your eyes peeled and stop worrying."

They both continued to stare down Karangahape Road, watching for Jenny and Sue to emerge from the street entrance to Zhukov's apartment. Matt had parked the car a hundred metres away on the opposite side of the street where, apart from being occasionally obscured by larger passing vehicles, it gave them clear view of the road and pavement.

Sandy gave a long sigh and shifted in her seat.

"I should never have agreed to the plan. Far too bloody risky. Now they're up in an apartment with a crazy Russian who's probably already instructed his henchmen to dispose—"

"Give it rest, Sandy! We all agreed to the plan, and they know we're here ready to immediately respond if there's any trouble."

"Respond? Yeah, but only if they're able to contact us before some bastard thrusts a bag over their heads and a knife in their throats!"

*

The echo of the slammed door sounded in the corridor as Jenny and Sue hurried towards the stairs.

"We know Matt's parked up the street," said Jenny as they began their rapid descent. "Hope they've both got their eyes on the exit."

Stepping out into Karangahape Rd they looked to their left. On the other side they saw a pair of car headlights flash.

"That's him! Come on," said Sue.

*

"They've seen us, Matt!"

"Great. Let's hope they have some positive info."

Matt and Sandy started to relax as they watched Jenny and Sue walk briskly in their direction.

They hardly noticed a black Jaguar I-Pace sweeping up to the kerb twenty metres ahead of the pair. A burly male slid out of the passenger's seat and pulled open the rear kerbside door. Another man swiftly emerged from an adjacent doorway. As the two women drew level with the vehicle they were seized, bundled into the rear seat, and immediately followed by the two men. The door slammed, the electric Jaguar powered softly away from the kerb, u-turned to the accompaniment of squealing tyres and hooting horns, raced up the street to the Pitt Street intersection and cut to the right just as the orange arrow turned red.

"Christ, Matt they've been kidnapped! Get after them!"

Matt started his car, swung out into the traffic, and sped towards the busy Pitt Street intersection. As the lights were red it left him no alternative but to swing right into the turning lane and stop.

"We have to catch them, Matt!"

"OK, Sandy, if I could press a bloody button and sprout wings I'd do so. The traffic's fairly heavy but I'll do my best. So, calm down."

He reached out and squeezed her right arm.

"I think they'll be crossing the harbour bridge and heading north to Zhukov's property near Riverhead. I copied the address from my father's computer onto my phone, so even if we lose them, we should have no trouble finding the place."

"OK. But then what? And shouldn't we contact the police?"

The arrow turned green and Matt followed the three cars in front across the intersection.

"The cops? I'm not—"

A buzzing sound interrupted him.

"Message on my cell phone," he said, pulling it from his inside jacket pocket and handing it to Sandy. "Can you check it?"

Sandy swiped and studied the screen.

"Oh God," she whispered.

"What?"

"We've got the two girls," she read aloud. "They will not be harmed as long as you do not call the police. We will contact you." She looked across at him. "There's no name, just a number."

"But how the hell did he get my number?"

"More importantly, what the hell do we do about Sue and Jenny?"

"The address is in 'Notes' on my phone, under 'Zhukov'. When you find it type it into my 'Maps' and check with Siri for directions, while I take us north."

Crossing the Auckland Harbour Bridge they headed north on the main motorway. The early afternoon traffic was building and mindful of speed cameras Matt stayed in the outside lane driving just over the 100 kilometres per hour. As expected, there was no sign of the black Jaguar.

Sandy, who'd been concentrating on loading the mobile phone with the address details, finally looked up.

"OK, all done. We're heading in the right direction. I can switch Siri to 'Go' if you need her to give you more specific details."

Matt nodded. "Thanks. So far so good."

The traffic was starting to thin and Auckland's urban sprawl was tapering off to be replaced by rolling hills dotted with patches of bush, tall trees and a variety of livestock.

"So," said Sandy, "if we do locate the place, what do we do then?"

"Not sure. But we need to check it out – houses, buildings and the surrounding area. We can't plan anything specific until we have more information."

"Easy to say, but from what we've gleaned so far, Zhukov has a sophisticated operation that we'd have a very hard time going up against."

"Maybe."

"What do you mean by 'maybe'? Matt, you're living in a fantasy world if you think you can successfully challenge that Russian and his cohort of gorillas. This morning's kidnapping had all the hallmarks of a carefully planned and executed operation. I've seen that sort of thing in American gangster movies but never thought I'd see it on an Auckland street."

"Neither did I." Matt paused and then continued, carefully measuring his words. "Look, Sandy, I know that you think I'm too impulsive. OK I've behaved like that in the past, but recent events have caused me to take more care, particularly towards those that I care for." He reached across and squeezed her hand. "You're right, Zhukov has a very smooth operation that takes no prisoners, and—"

"Except for Sue and Jenny," she murmured.

"I was speaking metaphorically," he smiled. "Please don't think that I'm imagining myself leading an all guns blazing rescue mission. But we do have options and resources. Just leave me to come up with some firm ideas once we've tracked down Zhukov's lair."

"OK, Matt, I hear you," she replied, looking doubtful. She glanced at the screen. "Take the next left at the intersection."

*

Both women, bruised and shaken, were jammed in the right-hand corner of the rear passenger seat unable to move. The bodies of the two men were pressed against them – their menacing faces effectively supplemented by the pistol that the nearest man held pointed straight at Jenny. Like his partner he wore a black tracksuit with a hood that partly concealed a dark face and glittering grey eyes.

When he spoke, it was in an East European accent full of menace.

"Do not move. If you try to escape, to signal any passing traffic or yell for help you will not live to see sun come up tomorrow morning."

His eyes flickered between the two frightened women.

"Nod if you understand," he said, positioning his pistol next to Jenny's throat.

Both women nodded vigorously. Jenny tried to pull back from the barrel, but her head was hard against the car seat.

"Excellent." He reached up and stroked Jenny's cheek. "Hmm, lovely and soft. We'd hate to damage such pretty features."

His throaty chuckle was accompanied by a malevolent leer.

The big car continued along the motorway at a brisk pace. Sue, whose face was nearest the window, noted that the windows were heavily tinted, making it unlikely that any passing motorists would notice anything untoward. Although the two men had eased back into the seat thereby reducing the pressure, the atmosphere of silent menace persisted.

At one point she took a deep breath and asked, "Where are we going?" Her query was met with two silent stares and the raising of the pistol towards her face. After that the only sounds were the humming of the tyres on the road, and the breathing of the Jaguar's five occupants.

Sue, with some difficulty, manoeuvred her left hand down between her left and Jenny's right legs, and through a series of small position shifts Jenny reciprocated. Although only a small gesture, the gentle touch of the other's hand offered both women some mutual comfort.

Although the early gestures with the pistol and the verbal threats had been frightening, their male captors had made no attempt to touch or molest them and, apart from occasional glances, had seemed content to relax in the comfortable leather seat. At one point the pistol-carrying man had slipped his weapon into an inside pocket, and catching Jenny's eye, had scowled and tapped the bulge of his hooded jacket. The message was clear – the weapon was positioned for instant usage.

As the car veered towards a motorway exit two hoods were pulled over the women's heads, accompanied by, "Keep quiet!" All they could do was note when the vehicle had slowed or swung left or right. After about 30 uncomfortable minutes they felt the car slow right down, turn a sharp left and stop. They heard the lowering of a car window and a man's voice asking, "Got both packages?" and an answering grunt. The rattle of chains and a long creaking sound suggested the opening of a large gate. The Jaguar moved swiftly forward for what seemed like a hundred metres, swung right and halted.

Footsteps came hurrying towards the car. Both back doors were pulled open, strong arms seized the women and propelled them forward.

*

Siri's instructions directed Matt and Sandy northwest through occasional vineyards where, apart from the developing country town of Kumeu, the undulating green hills continued.

On reaching the town of Riverhead, Siri instructed them to "Continue on Highway 28 where you will reach your destination in ten minutes".

"Not sure what to expect, but we need to make sure we don't draw attention to ourselves. It's my guess that Zhukov's headquarters will be back from the road so we'll approach and drive past the address at a slow but steady speed, keeping our eyes peeled," said Matt.

Sandy sighed deeply. "God, I hope Sue and Jenny are OK."

Matt nodded and they continued their journey in silence until Siri's voice said, "In five hundred metres take the next turn right."

"Here we go," muttered Matt, his hands tightening on the wheel as he slowed for the turning. Immediately Siri informed them that, "In four hundred meters your destination is on your left."

The straight road enabled them both to see clearly ahead.

"This could be it," said Sandy.

Coming into view they saw a large farm gate that was closed across the entrance to a long driveway. Leaning on the gate were two men who, on seeing the approaching car, slowly straightened up and took positions on either end, with their hands dangling by their sides. Their movement, although seemingly casual, suggested a carefully rehearsed procedure.

As Matt and Sandy drove past, both men's eyes followed them.

Sandy was about to speak when Matt held up his hand. He continued to drive for several minutes, constantly checking his rear-view mirror, before pulling up at a small layby and switching off the engine.

"Sorry, but I needed to keep my wits about me and make sure we weren't being followed."

"Fair enough," replied Sandy. "So what did we see?"

"The two men were dressed casually, but they reacted immediately to our approach and appeared to take up prearranged positions. I noted they were both wearing combat boots, and their loose-fitting jackets could easily have concealed handguns."

"At the end of the drive is a large two-storied storied house and a little further away an outbuilding that could be a shearing or milking shed," added Sandy.

"This is fairly hilly country but it seems flat in the area around the buildings."

"Yeah, so what?"

"It's given me an idea."

Chapter 56

"In here!"

Rough hands shoved the two blindfolded women forward. They collided with what appeared to be a wall and stood helplessly alongside each other.

"Turn around!"

They turned and instinctively huddled closer together.

Footsteps advanced towards them and stopped. In a smooth movement their hoods were whipped off their heads and they stood staring at one of the men with whom they'd shared the drive. The other remained by the door, pointing a revolver at them.

"Your new accommodation," said the hood remover, smiling grimly.

"You will be answering questions for us tomorrow," said his companion. "Hard questions that require truthful answers, otherwise it will not go well for either of you." He smacked his right fist into his left palm and glowered at them.

The women looked around the room. There were two beds, a desk and chair, a radio and a small TV set. On a sideboard were several stacks of magazines and books. A door on the left-hand side led to a small bathroom. The half-drawn curtains on the exterior window provided a brief glimpse of a farm with cattle and sheep peacefully grazing in nearby paddocks. The window was closed and had strong iron bars latticed across its exterior.

"As you can see, you can relax, read, watch the television or listen to radio. Meals will be brought to you, and you can make coffee and tea."

"A home away from home," muttered Jenny.

The taller of the two men reached forward and clipped Jenny on the side of her head.

"Yes, and be grateful that you are still alive!" he snarled.

Sue broke the brief silence that followed. Reaching for Jenny's hand she faced the men and addressed them in slow, measured tones.

"You're a big brave man, aren't you? Hitting women who can't hit you back. You must feel very proud."

The taller man growled and took a step towards her.

"Igor, enough!"

His companion reached out, gripped the big man's arm and slowly shook his head. Igor shrugged, glared at both women and after waving a warning forefinger at them, followed his companion from the room. The door closed, and the women heard the sound of the lock being turned.

"You OK?" asked Sue, reaching up and turning Jenny's head towards the light.

"Yeah, I'm fine. Cowardly bastard." She gave a wry smile. "You took a chance standing up to him."

"Yeah. Two armed men meant the odds were stacked against us." She grimaced. "I'm sure he would have tried to hit me again if his mate hadn't stopped him. Did he call him 'Igor'?"

"He did. Next time they visit us, we'll ask the other one his name. Could be useful."

"Anything could be useful in our situation," said Sue, walking over to the window. "Nothing much here except paddocks with sheep and cattle. Obviously a working farm, which provides a good cover for Zhukov and his cronies."

An unlocking of the door preceded the entry of Igor and his accomplice who was bearing a large tray of food. He placed it on top of the writing desk, nodded to both women and murmured, "Enjoy."

Sue smiled. "Thank you," she said and looked inquiringly at him. "My name is Sue and my friend is Jenny. Your friend is called Igor but I'm sorry I don't know your name."

The two men exchanged glances and Igor shrugged and nodded.

"Evgeni," he replied.

"Evgeni," repeated Sue, imitating his pronunciation. She smiled. "*Dobroe utro, Evgeni. Kak dela?*"

Obviously surprised, the man smiled, replied, "*Khorosho, spasibo*," and briefly tipped his head to her in acknowledgement. Igor growled with disapproval, signalled for his companion to exit immediately, followed close on his heels, slammed the door and locked it.

As the sound of their retreating footsteps faded away, Jenny reached out and hugged Sue.

"Good girl," she whispered in her ear. "That really pissed off the bully boy. What did you say?"

Sue grinned and shrugged. "I said, 'Good morning, how are you'. He replied, 'Good, thank you'. I took Russian to stage two at uni. It's a challenging language, but I've always liked the sound of it."

"Continue tomorrow when they bring breakfast," said Jenny. "Now, the food doesn't look too bad. Let's tuck in before it gets cold."

While they were eating their meals, they paused several times when they heard the sound of footsteps and male voices coming from further down the corridor, but no one came near their room.

At Sue's suggestion they turned on the six o'clock TV news but there was no mention of any incidents on Karangahape Road. During the remainder of the evening they tried news broadcasts on various radio stations. The result was the same.

"Nobody's missed us and nobody knows where we are," said Sue gazing out the window at the moonlight paddocks. "We could be on the bloody moon."

Chapter 57

The door was unlocked, pushed open and Evgeni entered, carrying a tray. Igor remained by the doorway.

"*Dobroe utro, Evgeni,*" said Sue, smiling warmly.

"*Dobroe utro, Sue*" he replied, with a shy smile. "I bring you breakfast."

"*Spasibo,*" nodded Sue.

She bent down and cleared a space on the small table in the centre of the room and nodded as he put down the tray. Their eyes met for a moment and he hesitated, as if on the point of speaking. She raised her eyebrows inquiringly and he spoke softly to her in Russian. A brief exchange of Russian followed, accompanied by smiles and nods on both sides.

"*Evgeni! Cton!*"

Evgeni looked round at Igor who was glaring at him from the doorway. He shrugged apologetically at Sue and turned to leave.

"Evgeni. Igor," said Sue.

Both men looked at her.

She indicated the breakfast and smiled warmly.

"*Spasibo za zavtrak.*"

Evgeni gave a warm smile, but Igor barely nodded before indicating that his companion should leave the room. The door was locked behind him.

"So what was that all about?" asked Jenny as the men's footsteps faded away.

"I wished him a good morning, he asked where I'd learnt Russian, I told him at university and asked him if my pronunciation was OK, and he said it was very good. Then Igor ordered him to stop and leave, so I thanked them both for the breakfast." She grinned and shrugged. "Just doing my best to promote relations between our two great nations."

"Very commendable, comrade." Jenny grinned. "And I think Evgeni fancies you."

"Nice young man, but not quite my type," murmured Sue who was studying the lock intently. She straightened up. "I think I can probably pick it," she said.

She held up her right forefinger and, reaching forward, removed a hairpin from the right side of Jenny's head.

"Looks like we're here for at least another day," she said as she held up two fingers before removing a second hairpin from Jenny's left side.

Jenny frowned at her before asking, "Now what?" as she tidied her hair.

Sue sat close to her, holding both hairpins in the palm of her left hand. "I'm going to introduce you to the gentle art of lock picking." She looked at the door. "If it works we could try to escape tonight."

"It had better bloody work, after you've mucked up my ponytail," muttered Jenny. "What about the guard?"

"I heard them both walk away. Perhaps they're happy to leave us at mealtimes. Anyway, let's make the most of it. They could be back at any time."

Sue selected one of the hairpins and bent it open until both ends were at right angles to each other. She then held the rubber tip between her fingers and tried to pull it off. It refused to budge so she put it between her teeth and tugged. The hairpin tip came out, and she removed it from her mouth. She walked quietly to the door and by inserting the tip of the second hairpin a couple of centimetres into the lock and pulling it gently sideways, created a slight hook. The other end she twisted into a handle shape.

Jenny watched as Sue placed the closed end of the hairpin about five centimetres into the lock's keyhole and applied gentle pressure in a clockwise direction. She then inserted the other hairpin into the lock and began to probe.

Tiny vibrations and clicks were accompanied by Sue's grunts of satisfaction until with a smile of triumph she extracted both the hairpins. "It's unlocked," she murmured.

Chapter 58

Collins stretched and yawned. It had been a long and frustrating night. Although for the first couple of days after his conversation with Zhukov he'd been treated well and allowed to wander through the house and the immediate surroundings, suddenly, yesterday afternoon he'd been locked in his room by two burly grim-faced armed Russians. He'd protested, demanding to see Zhukov, but they had escorted him to his room, informed him that he would be confined there until the following morning, walked out and locked the door.

At first he'd been furious, but after a whisky from his now well-stocked liquor cabinet he'd calmed down and decided that upon his release he'd demand a full explanation. As the sun was setting, he had heard the sound of a car coming down the driveway, hurried footsteps downstairs, the front door opening, car doors slamming, and footsteps entering the house. He'd moved closer to the locked door and listening with increasing interest as footsteps came up the stairs and down the corridor towards him. As they came closer and passed his room, he'd heard what sounded like low male growls and muffled female protests. These were followed by the opening of a door further along the corridor, more footsteps, and the door closing.

After that, from time to time he'd heard rapid male footsteps going to and fro along the corridor accompanied by indistinguishable mutterings. By mid-evening, apart from the odd noise drifting up from downstairs, there had been no further sounds.

He'd surmised that he'd heard two adult women being taken along the corridor, against their will. It was hard to determine their age from the muffled voices, but it seemed safe to assume that they were in their twenties or thirties. If they'd been taken for the ultimate pleasure of the male inhabitants, it was unlikely that they'd be older. But if they were sex workers why had they been forced down the corridor and locked in a room? It was more likely they'd been kidnapped. Were they being confined because they were a problem for Zhukov, or were they being held for ransom? And finally, why had he been locked in his room? Clearly Zhukov didn't want him to gain any information on the women. Perhaps…

The unlocking and opening of the door interrupted his reverie. Gregory and Tony entered and stood in front of him a little awkwardly.

"Oh, so I'm no longer a prisoner?" he asked sarcastically.

"Look, Jason, it wasn't our decision," said Gregory.

"Vlad told us that the other two were going to lock you up for the night and that we weren't to interfere," said Tony.

"So, was it some sort of petty revenge gesture by him?"

"No," replied Gregory. "We had some new arrivals last night and he didn't want you to see them."

"Who were they?"

"Sorry, Jason, but we've been told to say nothing," replied Gregory.

"Not that we know much anyway," added his companion.

"They were two women, weren't they?"

Both men exchanged surprised glances.

"I can't see through doors but my hearing's pretty good."

"OK," shrugged Tony. "Two women. But we didn't see them, so we know bugger all."

"Why are they being kept here?"

"We dunno. And we've been told to ask nothing and say nothing. Suggest you do the same."

Collins looked at the pair, and decided they were probably telling the truth. With a shrug he said, "OK. Isn't it time for breakfast?"

Gregory smiled. "Yeah. Come on."

Collins followed the pair downstairs to the dining room. Zhukov was at the head of a large table. He nodded a greeting and his eyes followed Jason as he took his seat. It was obvious the Russian was half-expecting some complaint about his confinement, but Collins decided to keep his counsel. Although curious about the two women and why he'd been kept from seeing, them he decided that showing no interest at this point would keep any heat off him.

During breakfast he laughed and made small talk with those nearest to him, conveying the impression he was relaxed and confident. Initially he noticed Zhukov watching him closely but, as breakfast progressed, the man appeared to turn his attentions elsewhere.

As he buttered his second slice of toast Collins saw two of the Russians leaving the kitchen carrying trays of food. He turned to his neighbour and started to chat to him while following the progress of the men across the dining room and towards the stairs. Although they disappeared, he could hear the faint sounds of them climbing the stairs to the first floor. It would seem the captives in his corridor were being supplied with food.

After breakfast Gregory informed him that Zhukov was arranging a formal meeting where the agreement on the participation in his smuggling operation would be discussed. This was scheduled for three o'clock, which would give him time to prepare any key points that he wanted discussed.

In the study next to his bedroom he sat down at the desk and started planning his own agenda for the afternoon meeting. Whether or not Zhukov would run the meeting formally was no big deal, as long as they reached agreement on the key points. He'd considered his situation carefully over the past couple of days and decided that, as long as he could remain in control of the situation, expanding it with Zhukov's resources could be of mutual benefit. However, he was still a captive and unless he could negotiate his freedom his operation would be severely compromised. Skill, diplomacy and courage would be called for.

Chapter 59

"Burton."

"DC Burton, this is Inspector David Fleming, Takapuna Police. We have a man in custody who could have a direct connection with your inquiry."

"My inquiry, inspector?"

"Yeah, into the disappearance of Fleur Lassiter."

"Fleur Lassiter. How—?"

"You need to be here asap."

"Oh. OK, sir, be with you in thirty minutes."

Burton, accompanied by Detective Young, arrived twenty-five minutes later.

"DS Burton, and DC Young," he said to the desk officer, who was immediately joined by a smartly dressed man. Introducing himself as Inspector Fleming, he ushered them into an adjacent office and seated himself behind a desk. Burton noted that, unlike his own desk, Fleming's was devoid of any stacks of paper save for a single folder placed neatly in the centre. The inspector leaned forward, placing his hand on the folder.

"Like I said, we have a guy in custody who may be of interest to you."

"How so?"

"Strange business really. He was stopped at a breath-testing checkpoint. When the officer started to question him, he became belligerent. Long story short, we booked him for resisting arrest. Under questioning he hinted that he had information on a missing woman and that he'd give us more details if we dropped the charges. He refused to say anything further until we agreed to his demands. We didn't, of course, but I'd heard about your investigation into Fleur Lassiter's disappearance so gave you a bell."

Burton nodded his thanks before asking, "What's his name?"

"Brusilov. Nicolai. He's a Russian immigrant."

Burton and Young exchanged glances.

"Zhukov?" murmured Young.

"Could be." He turned to Fleming. "We'd like to meet Brusilov."

"Thought you might." Fleming stood. "Come on."

They followed the inspector down a short corridor where he paused, opened a door on the right, and stepped back.

"After you," he said.

They entered a dimly lit room where a uniformed police officer was standing by the front wall. In the centre was a table with two empty chairs. On the other side of the table, a man sat hunched staring vacantly at the wall. He looked up quickly as the two detectives entered, straightened his back and lifted his chin in a transparent attempt to convey the impression of confidence.

After an affirming nod from Fleming they both seated themselves opposite the man.

"Mr Nicolai Brusilov?" asked Burton.

"Yes," he responded eagerly.

"I'm Detective Sergeant Burton and this is my colleague Detective Young."

"I am very pleased to meet you."

Burton suppressed a smile. The man's English was heavily accented and his expression of pleasure, straight from the pages of an *English for Dummies* textbook was, under the circumstances, faintly absurd.

He paused and studied the man. Although he was well-dressed, his nose was misshapen like a veteran boxer's. His hands were locked together, and he was nervously licking his lips.

"Would you like a cup of tea or coffee?" asked Burton pleasantly.

A little taken aback, Brusilov looked up at Fleming who showed no reaction, and then back at Burton.

"Coffee. Yes please. Black."

Fleming signalled to the constable, who left the room.

"Now, Mr Brusilov, we've been told that you might have some information about a woman that we are looking for."

The man hesitated then answered slowly, "I have. I say to inspector that I have information that I tell him, but only if he lets me go with no charge."

"You're seeking immunity from prosecution in return for information."

The Russian hesitated, processing the words before breaking into a smile. "Yes, of course, immunity from prosecution. Is OK?"

Young glowered at him. "Look, Brusilov, there's nothing for nothing round here. You have to—"

Burton grasped his colleague's arm and squeezed hard. Young glared but he ignored her.

"What my colleague means, Mr Brusilov, is that we need to know more about the information that you have. Immunity from prosecution is not given easily and, in your case, it will depend on its quality."

The constable re-entered and placed the coffee on the table. Brusilov began to reach for it but Burton quickly grasped the mug by the handle and pulled it back.

"We will cooperate with you if you cooperate with us, Mr Brusilov. Now, would you like to drink your coffee?"

"Yes," replied the Russian uncertainly.

"First, tell me the woman's name."

"I tell inspector I do not know name of woman."

Young gave a scornful snort. "You want immunity from prosecution because you have information on a woman who is anonymous? Not a chance!"

Brusilov's hands twisted tighter as he hesitantly addressed Young. "I not understand word 'anonymous'."

249

"It means nameless, no name and if you—"

"Mr Brusilov," interrupted Burton, "we need more information. A nameless woman is not enough."

"I give you more information and you let me go?"

"Like I said, that depends on its quality." He reached out and rested his hand on the Russian's right arm. "Now, Mr Brusilov, please give us all the information that you have, and we will see if we can help you."

Brusilov stared at Burton for a long moment before heaving a sigh of compliance.

"I have Russian friend. He tell me that he heard story about young woman who was killed and secretly buried in Auckland."

"Killed and buried," echoed Burton, leaning back in his chair. In a flash Brusilov reached out, seized the coffee, took a long drink and placed it back on the table, his hands wrapped round the mug.

"Tasty coffee?" Burton asked.

Brusilov, clasping the mug tightly, took another gulp.

"Yes, thank you."

Burton leaned forward.

"Who killed and buried her?"

Brusilov shook his head. "I say too much, already. I not say more until you are giving me immunity from prosecution."

Burton shook his head in turn. "Sorry Mr Brusilov, but you have told us very little. We need more hard information."

"Hard information?"

"Yes. You understand what this means?"

"I think so."

He stared hard at Brusilov then suddenly smiled and reached for the now empty coffee cup. "More coffee?"

Brusilov nodded slowly. "OK, I tell you information. And more coffee, please."

Burton nodded and the constable stepped forward and removed the cup as the Russian sighed and leaned back in his chair.

After studying him for a long moment, Burton spoke again in measured tones.

"You helped in the burial, didn't you, Mr Brusilov."

The Russian gasped and turned pale.

"How do you…?"

"What was her name?"

"I not know name of woman."

"You don't know her name. Then where did you meet her?"

"She was lying in lounge room of large house."

"Lying down. Asleep?"

"No," replied Brusilov looking hard at Burton. "Not asleep. Dead."

"Dead," echoed Burton, leaning back in his chair. "The woman was lying dead in the lounge?"

"Yes."

"You'd never seen her before," said Young.

Brusilov shook his head slowly. "Never before."

"Was she on a bed?" asked Burton.

"No, on carpet. There was blood on her head and on carpet."

"Had someone hit her?"

"I not know."

"Had there been a fight?"

The Russian shook his head. "I think not. No marks on her face, just blood on her head. Her clothes were OK.

"How old was she?"

"Hard to see in dark. Not very young, not very old."

"Hair colour?"

"Black."

"Who else was there?"

"Nobody. House was empty."

"See any weapons?"

The Russian shook his head. "No weapons. No mess. Just woman lying on carpet with eyes closed and arms by her side.

"So, why were you there?"

"I was told to go to house in Parnell. I went with three other men."

"Russian men?"

"Yes. Car took us there. Parked in driveway."

"Night time?"

"Yes. We go in and woman was on carpet, like I said. We pick her up and took her out of house and put her in trunk of car."

"You were told to do this?" asked Young.

"Yes. Before we went to house man gave us inst…"

"Instructions," prompted Burton.

"*Da*, instructions."

"Where did you take her?"

"I already tell you much information and—"

"Where did you take her?"

"I tell you already too much."

Burton leaned forward and fixed his gaze directly on Brusilov. His voice was slow and contained a hint of menace.

"I am asking you for the last time – where did you take her?"

At that point the constable entered and placed the fresh cup of coffee next to Burton.

Brusilov licked his lips, met the other man's eyes, looked down at the coffee cup, and then at the top of the table.

"We had instructions to…"

"To what?"

"To, to put her in ground."

"Bury her?" said Young, her face pale.

"Yes, bury her, deep."

"Where?" asked Burton.

"In some bush. On farm."

"Whose farm?"

Brusilov's complexion was turning pale and he began twisting his hands together. Slowly Burton slid the cup of coffee over to him. He seized it and lifting it to his lips, quaffed most of its contents.

Burton's voice was soft. "Whose farm, Mr Brusilov?"

Brusilov looked nervously around as if expecting to see a fearsome figure manifest itself in a dark corner of the room. His reply was almost a whisper.

"His name is Vladimir Zhukov."

Chapter 60

"Plane's all booked. We're due to take off in half an hour."

Matt slid his cell phone back into his top pocket and turned left into the aero club car park.

Sandy frowned. "Are you seriously suggesting you're going to try to land near the farm?"

"Yes. It's so risky I reckon there's a good chance that we'll get away with it."

"OK, Matt, let's look at it logically. We take off together in a light plane, circle the farm, and look for a suitable landing place."

"Which I'm pretty sure is on the flat area we saw near the house."

"And land there."

He nodded.

"Then we climb out, stroll up to the house and tell them we've come to visit, whereupon they'll welcome us warmly and invite us in."

Matt gave a thin smile as he parked the car and switched off the engine. "We take off from here, fly in the direction of the farm and, as we get closer I'll pull the mixture control to make it leaner."

"And what will happen?" Sandy looked doubtful.

"The engine will start misfiring, giving the impression that we're having mechanical problems.

"Is that safe?"

"Yes, the noise it creates will be an advantage to us." He smiled reassuringly. "If necessary, I can enrich the mixture by pushing the control back in. Anyway, we'll circle the farm and then land on the long paddock we identified earlier."

"You intend to land us on a paddock that'll probably have ruts and holes all over it. Could damage the plane, or even worse get us killed."

"Look Sandy, I'm trying to work out a way of rescuing Jenny and Sue and all you can do is raise objections. Zhukov's a bastard. Anything could happen to them. We've been warned not to contact the police. So it's up to us."

"But…"

"I know my plan frightens you. I'm going ahead with it but if you'd rather stay behind, I understand."

Sandy sighed. "OK, Matt, carry on with your explanation. I won't interrupt."

Matt reached over and squeezed her hand.

"So we land in the paddock. Some of Zhukov's men will probably meet us and they'll be very suspicious. I'll explain we're from the local flying club, that the engine keeps cutting out, I didn't want to risk trying to return to the club and when I saw the long paddock, decided to make an emergency landing. I'll apologise, of course. If we time it right, it'll be starting to get dark. I'll point that out and I'll explain I'm not authorised to fly at night."

"Then what?"

"Hopefully they'll take pity on us, and offer us a meal, or even better, a place to sleep. This will give us a chance to check out the location and to try to confirm whether or not Jenny and Sue are there."

"Or they could offer to drive us back to the aero club, or," she grimaced, "decide to shoot and bury us."

Matt shook his head.

"They won't shoot us. They'll assume we'll have contacted an airport and given our last position."

"So, won't the club be worried?"

"Not if we contact them on landing and tell them the plane's secure, we're OK and we'll be returning in the morning."

Sandy sat staring through the windscreen for a long moment before turning to face him.

"OK, Matt. Here's my take. Firstly, I agree that it's too risky to involve the police due to Zhukov's unpredictability. Secondly, the landing is also risky, but I'm prepared to trust you. The biggest challenge will be convincing the Russian and his thugs that our situation is genuine. That'll take a mixture of deference and diplomacy."

"Deference and diplomacy. Nicely put."

"Yes, but they're not your strongest suits, so you'll need to keep a civil tongue in your head. It will be up to me to work a little charm on all the males, Zhukov included."

Matt studied her for a long moment before replying, "Do you think you can do it?"

"If I commit myself to the operation, yes I believe I can."

"If?"

She paused and smiled grimly.

"OK. I'm in."

Chapter 61

They'd decided to travel light with only their wallets, cell phones and a couple of chocolate bars, so that if they were searched it would reinforce the impression that they had been out for a short flight.

Matt had compared his road map with the club's aerial photos of the surrounding countryside and had identified Zhukov's farmhouse and the long paddock where he intended to land. Its length looked about right and as there'd been little rain over the past month, he assumed that the surface would be dry. As to its smoothness, they'd just have to take their chances.

He decided to fly the Robin to the west of Zhukov's farm and then come in from the south to support their explanation that they were en route to the aero club.

At four o'clock they commenced their approach to the farm, about a kilometre ahead of them.

He reached out and, smiling in response to Sandy's anxious look, slowly pulled out the mixture control. Within a few moments the engine started misfiring. By this time, they had reached the outskirts of the farm. He pushed the stick forward which lowered the nose. With the engine sputtering he flew low over the house, circled back, lining the aircraft up for a landing, and pushing the mixture control back to normal.

He wanted to make some jocular remark to allay Sandy's fears, but his mouth had gone dry and his stomach muscles had tightened as he concentrated on landing the plane.

Sandy's voice crackled through the headphones. "Matt, there's two guys standing outside the house looking up at us."

He grunted and focussed on the ground that was rising to meet them.

"What if they're armed?"

Matt ignored her, adjusted the plane to the right to even up his approach and lowered the stick a little more. There was a thump as the wheels hit the ground and the plane shuddered, lifted again, re-settled and thumped its way towards the end of the paddock, coming to a stop about ten metres from a large hedge. Slowly Matt turned the aircraft in a half circle facing back the way they'd landed and switched off the engine. With eyes half closed he sat trembling and taking deep sucking breaths.

"What the hell you think you doing?" The voice was loud and the accent foreign.

Matt looked down to see two men standing by the cockpit door. They were glaring up at him and breathing heavily. He looked across at Sandy.

"You OK?"

Sandy nodded nervously.

"Get out of plane!" barked the taller man, angrily pointing towards the ground.

Matt lifted the canopy, unbuckled his safety harness and began to ease himself out of his seat. He needed to regain his equilibrium before trying to talk to the pair, so concentrated on clambering out of the cockpit and turning to assist Sandy. As he jumped to the ground the tall man seized his arms in a tight grip.

"What the hell are you doing?" Matt demanded, trying vainly to struggle free.

The other man grabbed Sandy as she clambered down and turning to his companion, muttered something. The language was foreign, but the meaning was obvious when the two men spun the pair round and began forcing them in the direction of the farmhouse.

"Our engine's not working! We had to make a forced landing! Let me go, you bastard!" protested Matt.

The response was a sharp blow to the side of his head followed by, "Shut your mouth!"

"Igor, no," muttered the other man.

Matt caught Sandy's eye. She frowned and shook her head.

They allowed themselves to be guided towards the back of the house. As they approached, a door opened, and they were pushed through. Two other men stood inside.

"The office. He is waiting."

The pair were steered down a corridor and halted in front of a closed door on the right. One of the men knocked and in response to "Enter" opened the door and pushed Matt and Sandy forward.

In the centre of the room Vladimir Zhukov sat behind a large desk staring fixedly at them, his eyes narrowed against the smoke that curled up from a cigarette held between the forefingers of his left hand. He gave the briefest of nods. Their two captors thrust Matt and Sandy in front of the desk and immediately positioned themselves behind them.

"So," began Zhukov, "why you land your plane on my farm?"

Matt opened his mouth, but Sandy spoke first. Her voice was low, and the tone, bewildered.

"Sir, the engine of our plane kept misfiring. We had to make an emergency landing on your long straight paddock. Sorry, but we had no alternative."

Zhukov frowned. "Were you flying plane?"

"No, sir." She glanced at Matt. "My friend Matt is the pilot. It was very difficult for him to land on—"

"Matt. And what is your name?"

"Sandy. I—"

"Where were you going in your plane?"

"Back to the aero club in Albany," said Matt.

Zhukov thrust the smouldering butt into an overflowing ashtray, slowly extracted another cigarette, tapped it on the back of the pack, placed it between his lips and lit it with the flame of his Zippo. He drew deeply and studied the pair standing before him.

"Your plane engine. You have trouble before?"

"No," replied Matt cautiously. "The plane belongs to the aero club. We hired it for a few hours."

"Why?"

"We thought we'd go joyriding."

The big Russian frowned. "What is this 'joyriding'?"

"Oh," smiled Sandy, "it's just flying for fun. The two of us enjoy—"

"Flying for fun?" He exchanged glances with his two henchmen. "You go nowhere for no reason?" His eyes narrowed and his voice slowed. "To me a very strange thing."

"Perhaps I can explain," said Matt, making a concerted effort to sound pleasant and reasonable. "I recently qualified as a pilot and it is important that I build up my flying hours." Seeing Zhukov frowning he hurried on. "I need to fly regularly to maintain my pilot's licence."

"Including flying for fun?"

Sensing the man's suspicions Matt smiled and replied, "It's recreational flying, where you take off to enjoy the flight and the scenery. Auckland has many interesting—"

"Tell me about trouble with engine," cut in Zhukov.

"I'm not sure what the problem is. It kept stopping and I had to re-start it each time. I was worried that it would shut down and wouldn't re-start and so decided I should put it down."

"Put it down?"

"Land it."

"On my farm."

"Yes, we saw that you had a long paddock."

"You say that already."

"I know." He half turned his head. "I began to explain it to these two men but one of them hit me on the back of the head."

Zhukov barked a question in Russian at the two men, one of whom muttered a reply. Zhukov looked back at Matt.

"Igor hit your head. He is sorry." He glared at the man. "Igor, say you are sorry to this young man!"

Igor walked slowly round and stood in front of Matt. His shoulders were lowered in an expression of contrition, but his eyes gleamed with anger.

"I am sorry I hit you on head," he muttered.

"Shake hands, Igor."

The man extended his right hand and Matt, after catching a look from Sandy, clasped it. The grip he received was vicelike and it took all his self-control to maintain a neutral expression and hold Igor's gaze.

Zhukov nodded his approval as the two men drew apart.

"Igor, Evgeni, chairs for our guests."

The men exchanged brief glances then quickly placed two chairs in front of the desk. Zhukov smiled expansively and stretched out his left hand with uplifted palm.

"Please."

Matt and Sandy, nodding their thanks, sat down.

"Coffee or tea?"

"Thank you," smiled Sandy. "Coffee for me."

"And me, thanks."

"Igor, two coffees."

"Two coffees, Mr Zhukov," muttered Igor and left the room.

His boss smiled and leaned forward.

"You were on your way back to aero club when engine had trouble."

Matt nodded.

"So, can you fix problem?"

Matt smiled uncertainly and looked towards the window.

"I might be able to, but unfortunately it is getting dark."

Zhukov frowned.

"Dark." He shrugged. "No problem. We have torches, lights and batteries."

"Unfortunately, Mr Zhukov, there is another problem."

"Another problem?" responded the Russian sharply.

"As I said, it is getting dark. I am not qualified, not permitted to fly at night."

The Russian slowly stubbed out his cigarette and gazed at his two visitors. Both Matt and Sandy felt a negative shift in the atmosphere.

"So, you can phone aero club and ask for mechanic to come and fix engine, and fly it away."

Matt slowly shook his head. "I'm sorry but the mechanic will be off duty now, and all the pilots, the instructors, will have gone home." He reached into his inside jacket pocket and produced his cell phone. "But I do need to phone the office and tell them that we are safe and the plane is undamaged."

Zhukov leaned forward.

"You said they have all gone home," he said softly.

"No, not everyone. The duty officer will be there. He cannot leave until all the aircraft return safely or he is notified of any delays."

Igor entered with two coffees on a tray with a jug of milk, a bowl of sugar and several biscuits. He handed a cup to Sandy with a, "Here you are, madam", and, moving to block Zhukov's view, handed a cup to Matt with no comment and a fierce glare.

They both took a sip of their coffee as Zhukov sat frowning. Abruptly he stood.

"Your plane does not work. You have no car. I cannot spare any of my men to take you to your flying club. You will stay here tonight and tomorrow morning your plane will be fixed, and you will fly away."

Sandy smiled warmly. "That's very kind of you…"

"Wait here," said Zhukov. He stood and signalled to the other two Russians who followed him as he strode from the room and shut the door.

The pair sat in silence listening to the fading footsteps, before Sandy turned to Matt.

"The first part of your plan has worked," she said softly.

Matt nodded and grinned.

He reached for his cell phone and tapped the keypad.

He pressed the instrument close to his ear. "Hi, Yvonne, it's Matt. Is Chris there? Thanks." There was a pause. "Chris, it's Matt. Look I've had to land the plane on a paddock near Coatesville. Yes. The engine kept cutting out and I didn't want to risk trying to bring it back to the club. The landing was a bit rough but the plane's OK. The owner says we can stay the night."

He listened to the response and then smiled.

"Sandy? Yes, she's fine."

He smiled at Sandy.

"Where are we? … We're at a farm. The paddock where we landed was near the farmhouse and two men escorted, er, took us to meet the owner. … What? … No, not really a farmer, a businessman who has other people to run the farm for him. … A foreigner? I think so. … Chinese?" Matt laughed. "No, not Chinese, Russian. He's OK with us staying here overnight. … Yes, I'll check the plane in the morning and—."

He looked up at the sound of approaching footsteps.

"Sorry, Chris, got to go. No, everything's fine."

He terminated the call as the door swung open and Igor and Evgeni entered.

Igor gestured with his head.

"Come," he said.

Chapter 62

"Burton."

"Sergeant, it's Chris Winstone from the North Shore Aero Club."

"Yes, Mr Winstone. How can I help you?"

"I thought I should phone you. One of our planes didn't make it back last night."

"Had it crashed?"

"No, it had to make an emergency landing."

"Anyone hurt?"

"No. The pilot phoned to report engine trouble. It was dusk so he said they were staying the night at the place where they'd made an emergency landing. It's at a farm near Coatesville."

"I see." Burton paused. "So why are you phoning me?"

"The pilot is Matt Bullock and Sandy Anderson is his passenger."

Burton looked up as the door to his office opened and DC Young entered. He pointed to the chair in front of his desk, and as his colleague sat, he pressed his phone's speaker symbol.

"Matt Bullock. The young man I interviewed?" asked Burton.

Young's eyes widened.

"Yeah. Look I don't want to sound alarmist, but I've just talked to Matt by phone. He assured me that he and Sandy are OK staying at the farmhouse where he'd landed."

"So, why are you worried?"

"When I asked Matt about the owner of the farmer he said that he was a Russian. I was about to ask for more details when he abruptly rang off. I tried to call him back, but he didn't pick up."

Burton paused and exchanged glances with Young before answering.

"You'll be interested to know we're also exploring a lead based on new information we obtained yesterday."

"New information?"

"Yes, a Russian individual who has links with another Russian named Vladimir Zhukov," said Burton. "Seems there's a link between this Zhukov and Fleur Lassiter."

"A link? How strong?"

"We're not sure. We've detained the informant and he's scheduled for further interrogation later today. However, in the light of your information we'll move the schedule forward and apply some additional pressure."

Young's eyes lit up.

"Further pressure?" asked Winstone.

Burton smiled. "Don't worry, Mr Winstone, we're not the CIA. But we do have some areas that can be further probed and should bring results. Now, please give me Matt Bullock's phone number."

He wrote it down.

"Thanks. We'll keep in touch. And if you receive any contact from the young man, notify us immediately."

"Of course. Thanks, Sergeant."

"You're welcome. Keep in touch."

He clicked off his phone and looked up at Young.

"Let's go and have a further chat with comrade Brusilov."

Chapter 63

"Zhukov wants to see you now."

Collins looked up to see Tony standing in the doorway of his room.

"Now?"

"Yeah, c'mon."

Collins scooped up his notes and stepped out behind Tony into the corridor.

"Back inside!" came a shout from the far end. Striding towards them came Igor, and behind him Collins could see Evgeni and what appeared to be a male and female figure. The opportunity was too good to miss and pushing past Tony he strode forward.

"What are you yelling about, Igor?"

Igor kept advancing.

"You not hear me! Go back inside your room!"

Within seconds the two men were face to face. Igor pointed down the corridor.

"You go back to your room, now!"

Collins didn't move.

"Listen, mate," he barked, "Vladimir has summoned Tony and me to a meeting with him, now. I take my orders from him, not from his minions!"

Although he was eyeballing the angry Russian, he also was able to shift his gaze down the corridor past Evgeni to the two figures. The light from an open door fell across their faces and he suppressed a gasp as he recognised Matt and Sandy.

Igor reached out his right arm and gripped Collins' shoulder.

"You trying to stop me seeing Mr Zhukov?" growled Collins.

Igor's eyes flickered with uncertainty.

"Step aside and let us pass." He held the man's gaze. "Now!"

Igor took a small step backwards and seizing his opportunity Collins called, "Come on, Tony," and walked purposefully down the corridor past a bemused Evgeni. As he passed Matt and Sandy, he raised his eyebrows in a flicker of recognition, shouted, "Can't keep Vlad waiting!" and kept walking, pausing at the corner for Tony to catch him up.

"Christ, was that—?"

"Say nothing. Don't look back. Just take me to Zhukov."

He stepped back and letting Tony move in front, followed him around the corner.

Igor jerked his head at Matt and Sandy.

"Follow me!" he barked, his face contorted with fury. He took a few steps forward and stopped by a door on his right.

"Wait!" He inserted a key, unlocked the door and stepped back. "In here."

Matt and Sandy entered a room with a large double bed, several chairs, a desk and an open door that led into an en suite.

"You stay here. Do not leave room until you are called down for dinner."

He swung round abruptly and stalked out. Evgeni, pausing to give them both a half-apologetic smile, followed him and closed the door.

Bewildered, Sandy stared at Matt.

"Jason bloody Collins. What the hell is he doing here?" she asked.

"He could be cooperating with Zhukov on his smuggling operation," murmured Matt. "That would explain why he dropped out of sight."

"And now he knows that we're here and—"

"He knows that we know that he's here. No wonder that other dude tried to order Jason and his mate back into their room."

"There'll be repercussions."

Matt frowned. "We know that Zhukov's here with at least four henchmen, plus Collins..."

"And presumably Jenny and Sue."

"Unless he's buried them in the garden," said Matt darkly, and seeing Sandy's reaction, hurriedly squeezed her arm reassuringly. "Only joking."

"Not funny." She paused. "I noticed three doorways in this corridor. Jason and the other guy came out of one, we've gone into another, and the third one's remained closed. Maybe that's where they're being held."

"Maybe," nodded Matt. "But in that case one of the Russians is probably outside on permanent guard during the night. And even if he isn't they'll be locked in the room. And if we do manage to get them out of their room..."

"OK, I understand. Maybe we'll get a clearer picture when we have a meal with Zhukov and any of the others." She eased herself into the nearest chair. "In the meantime let's just take a while to think the situation through."

Chapter 64

As the pair seated themselves in front of Zhukov, Collins noted that although the office stank of cigarette smoke there was no packet lying on the desk.

Gregory, seated at the end of the desk next to Tony, looked at Zhukov who nodded.

"So, Jason," asked Gregory, "have you read the proposal that I gave you last night?"

Collins nodded.

"Are you in agreement with it?"

Collins shook his head.

"You have problems with it?"

Collins nodded.

Zhukov, who'd been watching Collins intently, suddenly snarled, "Why you not fucking speak?"

"Let me, Vlad!" interrupted Gregory.

The big Russian sank back in his chair and glared balefully at both men.

"Now, Jason," began Gregory softly, "please tell us what problems you have with the proposal."

"I had made it clear that I was not interested in anyone taking over my operation. I did, however, make it clear that I was interested in an investment that would give me a cash injection enabling me to expand, while also giving the investor a handsome return on his money."

Zhukov frowned.

"What is this with handsome?"

"A good return on the money that you invested in the operation, Vlad," explained Gregory.

Zhukov grunted and eyeballed Collins. "What you are saying is that you want me to give you money that you will spend on making your operation larger and better and this will give me good profit on my money. Yes?"

269

"Exactly. That's what I explained at our meeting on—"

"How much money?"

"A hundred thousand dollars."

Zhukov began to reach into his inside jacket pocket, thought better of it and clenched his hands together.

"Hundred thousand. Lot of money."

"Lot of profit, too. I could increase the trans-Tasman trips thereby providing you with regular dividends on your investment – probably on a monthly basis."

Zhukov grunted and twisted his hands.

"There's one other matter that needs to be resolved," continued Collins.

"Yes?"

"I am happy to stay in this house in the meantime. However, I am not to be treated as a prisoner and will not be locked in my room again." He looked hard at Zhukov. "Agreed, Vladimir?"

Zhukov looked at Gregory who nodded.

"OK, no more locking. But you do not leave this farm without telling me where you are going and why. Agreed?"

"Agreed. And the investment?"

Zhukov paused for a long moment before he grunted and nodded.

"Give Gregory your bank account numbers and he will send money to you."

Collins nodded, rose from his chair and extended his right arm.

Zhukov gave him a long hard look.

"Do not try to cheat me, Jason."

"Understood, Vlad."

Both men shook hands.

"I need to look over some material before dinner," said Collins. He turned towards the door, noticing the obvious relief on Zhukov's face as he thrust his hand into his inside pocket and extracted his cigarettes.

Chapter 65

"But there's more to tell us isn't there?" said Young.

Brusilov rubbed his hand over a face.

"I tell you everything. I know nothing more."

"Nothing more, Mr Brusilov?" Burton smiled pleasantly. "Oh, I'm sure there's much more. For example, how do you know Vladimir Zhukov?"

"Know?"

"Yes, when did you first meet him?"

"When I first meet him?"

"Are you parrot, Brusilov?" barked Young. "In case you've forgotten, a woman has been murdered. Detective Sergeant Burton asked you a straightforward question. Now he wants a straightforward truthful answer."

Brusilov began twisting his hands together.

"I, I—"

"Yes, Mr Brusilov," smiled Burton. "Please continue."

"I met him in Russia, in St Petersburg."

Burton raised his eyebrows. "And?"

"I make documents for him."

"Documents, eh? Forgeries?" said Young.

Brusilov twisted in his seat.

"He tell me he wants exit visas. He wants to leave Russia and live in New Zealand. He tell me it is peaceful country, very long way from St Petersburg."

"He paid you well."

Brusilov shook his head.

"He only pay half of agreed price. I make high quality documents, but he insults and beats me." His eyes flashed with fury. "Zhukov is bastard!"

"So you decided to come to New Zealand to get revenge?" asked Burton.

Brusilov shrugged and shook his head.

"Not really. St Petersburg is dangerous place. New Zealand is good place. I apply for temporary work visa and come here one year ago."

"Have you met Zhukov since arriving here?"

"No, he not know I am in New Zealand."

"Yet you helped to bury the body of the girl that he may have killed."

"No, I only driver of car. I not help to bury body."

"But you know where the body's buried."

Brusilov nodded. "I was watcher."

"Watcher?" frowned Burton. "You mean you kept watch when they buried the woman?"

"Yes."

"And Zhukov hired you."

"No, other Russian person hired me. Zhukov did not know it was me."

"Are you sure that's the truth?" asked Young. Her voice was slow and menacing. "If it's not you will go to jail."

Brusilov's face paled.

"No! I cannot go to jail. I apply for permanent residency. I have Kiwi girlfriend. She is having my baby soon. I am good Kiwi citizen! I now have good job, I pay my taxes and am not criminal."

Burton reached out and placed his hand over Brusilov's twisting hands.

"It's OK, Mr Brusilov. I believe you. We'll say no more about your part in disposing of the girl's body, provided of course, that you help us further in our investigation."

"And from now on you keep your nose clean," added Young.

Brusilov reached up, touched his nose and frowned.

"My nose crooked but is not dirty."

Young laughed mirthlessly.

"It means, Brusilov, that you keep out of trouble in the future. Break the law again and we'll charge you with resisting arrest!"

"No, no not necessary. I keep my nose clean, I make no more trouble. I have girlfriend, and I have—"

"So you've said," interrupted Burton. "Now, if you continue to help us then you will have immunity from prosecution."

"If not, you'll be doing time," added Young darkly.

"Yes, yes I understand. I have Kiwi girlfriend and—"

"We know," interrupted Burton. "Now, I have one more question."

"One more?" replied the other man nervously.

"Why did you resist arrest at the police checkpoint?"

Brusilov hung his head.

"I very stupid. When policeman ask me to step out of my car I suddenly thought I was back in Russia where, if police say step out of car, then you are in big trouble."

The detective sergeant smiled, stood and thrust out his hand.

"Thank you for your cooperation, Mr Brusilov. We will be in touch with you shortly."

Brusilov blinked with surprise than grasped Burton's outstretched hand.

"Thank you, Mr Burton. You have my word. I will be good Kiwi citizen."

Burton nodded at Young. She also shook Brusilov's hand but did not smile. They watched as he hurried from the room.

"So," said Young, "what's our next move?"

Chapter 66

As he climbed the stairs to the first floor Collins smiled with satisfaction. He'd extracted a hundred grand from Zhukov and was no longer a prisoner. Not that he trusted the man. He knew he was a ruthless bastard who would betray anyone without a second thought. Well, two could play at that game. He'd provide a steady return on the Russian's investment but wouldn't be overgenerous. It was his field, his expertise, and therefore he could explain any delay in large profits with a plausible lie about temporary personnel, mechanical or delivery difficulties.

Deep in thought he began to walk slowly along the first-floor corridor. As he approached the door on his left, he frowned in puzzlement at the empty chair outside it. As he began to pass the door, he heard soft male and female voices. He paused, listened, and then looked up and down the corridor. No one was in sight. Reaching out he grasped the door handle and slowly turned it. He was mildly surprised to find that it wasn't locked.

Cautiously he pushed the door open. He'd half expected to see Matt and Sandy but instead Jenny and Sue sat gaping at him. Seated close to Sue was the young Russian Evgeni, who immediately sprang to his feet.

"Jason," he babbled, "I just helping these two ladies with some problems. They ask me—"

Collins smiled and held up his hand.

"It's OK, Evgeni, the door wasn't locked and so I thought…"

"Oh, not locked! My fault, I should have—"

"Evgeni, I've already said it's OK. Sit down and relax."

He turned to the two girls who were standing and staring open mouthed at him.

"Jason," began Jenny, "have you come…?"

"To help us," said Sue eagerly.

Collins, revelling in the unexpected attention, smiled beguilingly at both women.

"Jenny, this is a pleasant surprise." He slowly looked Sue up and down. "Who's your friend?"

"Sue," said Jenny coldly.

"Didn't realise you were visiting Mr Zhukov. Although, if the door was supposed to be locked, perhaps it's not a friendly visit."

"Kidnapped is the best description."

Collins stared at Jenny.

"Christ! Kidnapped. Why?"

"We paid Zhukov a visit."

"You visited Zhukov!"

"Yes," she replied. "We wanted to ask him about Fleur Lassiter."

Collins' eyes narrowed. "Fleur Lassiter. Why?"

"She's disappeared. We're worried about her and—"

"What did Zhukov say?" interrupted Collins sharply.

"He was quite friendly when we arrived. But as soon as we mentioned Fleur, his mood changed."

"Yes," continued Sue. "He virtually ordered us out of his house, then on the street two of his thugs seized us, threw us into a car and brought us here."

Collins stood staring at the two women for a long moment.

"When?"

"Yesterday. We arrived here early in the evening." She looked pleadingly at him. "What's going to happen to us?"

Ignoring her, Collins turned to Evgeni.

"Is your job to guard them?"

The young Russian nodded a nervous affirmation.

"By entering their room and chatting to them," continued Collins. "Obviously you couldn't resist two attractive Kiwi girls. Know how you feel." He looked Jenny up and down. "I asked Jenny out myself a few weeks ago."

Jenny swallowed nervously. She remembered the sleazy invitation, which had been abruptly terminated when she'd mentioned Fleur Lassiter. But she'd have to tread carefully. Jason Collins was in league with their captor, which meant he could be a help or hindrance to them.

She looked up into his eyes and forced herself to smile. "Yes, you did, Jason." She glanced round the room. "If we get out of this place, is the invitation still open?"

Collins studied her for a long moment before reaching out and touching her cheek. "Of course it is, sweetheart." He looked at both women and added, "But we just need to clear up a minor matter or two first."

Sue and Jenny exchanged glances before Sue gave him a shy smile.

"Jason, we've done nothing wrong. We paid Zhukov a non-threatening visit, and his reaction was to kidnap and bring us here. We don't know what's going to happen to us. We need your help."

"Excuse me, Jason and ladies."

The other three turned to Evgeni.

"I am supposed to be the guard. If Zhukov or Igor comes along the corridor and I am not in my chair there will be big trouble."

Collins jerked his head towards the door. "Yeah. Go."

Evgeni hesitated and looked at the two women. "Please, I have to say that I do not think it is right that you are prisoners here."

He stood, opened the door, and exited. They listened to the lock turning and the chair scraping. Jason broke the silence that followed.

"A conflicted young man," he said quietly.

"So, Jason, are you also conflicted?" asked Sue.

"How do you mean?"

"Our situation. We've been kidnapped by a man that we presume is your boss."

His head jerked upwards. "No," he responded angrily. "Zhukov's not my boss, he's an investor in my operation."

"I see," said Jenny. She stepped forward, took his right hand in hers and held it gently. "Jason, the key question is can you help us, and if so, how?"

"That's two questions." He grinned. "You asked me can I help you? The answer is yes, I can. The question however should have been, will I help you? The answer to that is, it depends."

"On what?" asked Jenny.

Collins looked at her intently. "Why did you think there was a link between Zhukov and Fleur?" he asked softly.

"It was a bit of a long shot," replied Jenny cautiously. "Matt had suggested that Zhukov might know something about Fleur and—"

"Matt Bullock?" His voice was sharp.

"Yes. He didn't know anything about her disappearance but thought that Zhukov might."

Collins took a step back and stood glaring at the pair.

"Zhukov knows nothing! He's never even heard of her!"

"How do you know?"

"I said he knows nothing," snarled Collins. "If you know what's good for you, you'll leave it at that."

Jenny stepped tentatively forward, and her hand hovered above his arm.

"You're right, Jason. It was a mistake for us to visit Mr Zhukov." She turned to her companion. "Wasn't it, Sue?"

"Yes, yes it was," responded Sue quickly. "We were both foolish but we meant no harm. Perhaps if you explained that to him, he will let us go."

"Yes," nodded Jenny eagerly. "Could you do that for us?"

Collins studied them both and gave a humourless smile.

"You two attractive women need me, don't you?"

They both nodded eagerly.

He ran his tongue slowly across his top lip.

"And will it be worth my while?"

They exchanged glances and then turned back to him with eager smiles.

"Of course," said Sue.

"You already said the offer was still open, so I'm ready," echoed Jenny, gripping his arm.

He slowly looked her up and down.

"In that case I'll see what I can do."

He shook off her grip, strode to the door, tapped, it was unlocked, he exited, and the door was locked behind him.

"Revolting bastard," shuddered Jenny. "What's his game?"

"Self protection. He's always been focussed on himself and his needs, with no sympathy or empathy for anyone else. He's obviously worried that we're looking into Fleur's disappearance and given Zhukov's reaction when we asked him about her, it would seem logical that they're both in league together. Neither of them wants us asking any more questions, so it suits them to keep us under lock and key – short term anyway."

"And long term?"

"A pessimist would say it doesn't look good. However, we have a few cards left in our pack." She gave Jenny a sympathetic smile. "Your suggestive promises had Collins flaring his nostrils."

"It was all I could do not to throw up!"

"Understand. But it means he'll keep sniffing around in anticipation."

Jenny grunted and Sue continued.

"Fortunately he's not our only option." She held up a hairpin. "Remember, we're now able to open our door at any time."

Jenny frowned.

"Provided there's no guard. But if the guard's Evgeni, he has potential – particularly if you flutter your eyelashes at him."

Sue shrugged and smiled.

"And," continued Jenny, "there's also that mysterious plane. We don't know who was on it."

"They could have easily been Zhukov's mates."

"Maybe. Bit odd though. The plane sounded like it was having engine trouble."

"True."

"And the passengers came in through a side entrance so we couldn't identify them."

"So they could be useful to us."

Jenny shrugged, walked over to the small sink, filled the jug with water and switched it on.

"Let's not forget the police and the aero club," she said.

"How so?"

"The two police officers who interviewed us seemed very keen to solve Fleur's disappearance. And, when I don't turn up for work tomorrow and they can't track me down, hopefully the club will notify the police."

"Who will hopefully see a connection? Sounds feasible, but I don't quite see how it will help them locate us here," frowned Sue.

"We both agreed that the plane sounded like an aero club Robin. If it is, then both the club and the police are going to start looking."

Jenny held up the coffee plunger and Sue nodded.

"So, all factors considered, there's room for cautious optimism," she smiled. "Now let's start working on a few possible scenarios."

Chapter 67

A long rumble of thunder followed the lightning flash that lit up the sky. The windowpanes vibrated and the lights in the room momentarily dimmed.

"Fucking weather," grunted Zhukov glancing out the window at the suddenly darkened sky. "Always the rain in winter."

"But no snow, and no freezing temperatures. Surely you're not missing Russia, Vlad," grinned Gregory.

Zhukov grunted, lit another cigarette, drew deeply and regarded his two colleagues through the expelled stream of smoke.

"So, Tony, what you think? Are they lying about the engine troubles of their plane?"

Tony frowned.

"I heard the plane when it flew above the house. I assumed that the engine was missing and—"

"Missing," snapped Zhukov. "How could you hear engine if it was gone?"

Tony suppressed a smile. "No, Vlad, when we say an engine is missing it means that it is not running well, it is coughing and cutting out."

The Russian nodded his understanding and Tony continued.

"Matt Bullock and Sandy Anderson are both members of the aero club. Matt has just gained his Recreational Pilot's Licence which means he can carry a passenger but can't fly at night. He would have been very worried when the engine began missing due to his lack of flying experience."

"Sounds OK to me, Vlad. This property is near the aero club so incidents like this could happen."

The big Russian drew deeply on his rapidly diminishing cigarette.

"Maybe, maybe not. And even if their engine is," he hesitated, "missing, they are now in my house where we have already two prisoners. If they find out anything about us and tell other people when they go back to aero club then police could come, how you say, sniffing around."

"Does Jason Collins know they're here?" asked Tony.

"No, I think not. He said nothing at our meeting," answered Zhukov.

Another long thunder roll followed a flash of lightning.

"This bloody storm. How long?"

"The weather forecast is not good, Vlad. The storm could last for two days."

"Two days! We have prisoners and the two people from plane, and Jason Collins who probably knows them."

"All in the same house," added Tony unnecessarily.

"So Gregory, the two plane people are to stay in their room. They are not to come out."

"How will we explain that?"

"Explain!" Zhukov's face began to redden. "Why I need to explain? This is my house! They were not invited, they invited themselves. My house, my rules!"

He glared at Gregory.

"So, tell them and also tell Igor and Evgeni they have two more people to guard. Rooms are all on same floor so will not be difficult. OK?"

Gregory opened his mouth, met Zhukov's glare, changed his mind, and stood.

"OK, Vlad."

Chapter 68

"Oh, hullo, is dinner ready?" smiled Sandy as Evgeni entered after a tentative knock.

The young Russian stood in front of them but avoided meeting their eyes. In his hands he held a tray of food.

"I bring your dinner for you," he said softly.

"Bringing dinner to us?" responded Matt sharply. "We understood we'd be having dinner with everybody else."

Evgeni shifted his feet uncomfortably.

"I am sorry, but Mr Zhukov has said you are not to join others for dinner."

"Really? Next thing you'll be telling us that he has ordered us to stay in our room for the rest of our stay," said Matt angrily.

Evgeni hung his head.

"Evgeni," said Sandy softly, "is Matt correct?"

Evgeni nodded. "You are not allowed to leave your room."

Sandy reached out and touched his arm.

"Why, Evgeni?" she asked.

The young Russian shrugged. "I think that he is suspicious of you. You belong to the same flying club as Jason Collins and—"

"I thought Zhukov and Collins were working together," interrupted Matt.

"They are," nodded Evgeni, "but I do not think Mr Zhukov trusts Jason. I was told that harsh words have been spoken between them."

Matt and Sandy exchanged glances before Sandy smiled at Evgeni.

"Thank you for your honesty, Evgeni. Can you also tell us about Jenny and Sue? Are they being kept here as prisoners?

A rumble of thunder rattled the windows and Evgeni started nervously.

"Yes, they are." He sighed deeply. "I do not think they should be prisoners. They are both nice girls and they have done nothing wrong." He shrugged. "But I can do nothing."

"Can you tell them that we are here?"

Evgeni's eyes shifted uneasily.

"Sorry, I cannot risk doing that. If Mr Zhukov—"

"Why is Zhukov keeping them prisoners?" interrupted Matt.

"I know they visited him and asked some questions that made him angry."

"What sort of questions?"

"I do not know. They do not tell me much."

"So, Evgeni, have you been told to lock us in the room?"

Evgeni nodded reluctantly.

"And will you?" Sandy's voice was soft.

He sighed deeply.

"Igor will check. If the door is unlocked, I will be in big trouble." His eyes narrowed and he slowly shook his head. "Big trouble," he murmured.

Sandy touched his arm.

"It's OK, Evgeni, we understand."

Hearing Matt's sharp intake of breath she turned and glared at him.

"Thank you," said Evgeni. He hesitated. "I will try to help you if I can."

He turned and with head lowered, left the room and locked the door.

Chapter 69

"Unlock the door, Evgeni. I need to talk to the prisoners."

"But, Jason, Igor has told me not—"

"Igor is not my bloody boss." His face reddened with anger. "Nobody in this place is my bloody boss." He thrust his forefinger into Evgeni's chest. "I'm telling you to unlock the door. Now!"

Evgeni turned, quickly inserted and turned the key. Pushing him aside Collins thrust the door open.

Jenny and Sue, seated at the table, looked up startled.

"There has been a development," said Collins.

"What sort of development?" asked Sue.

"An important one. I need to discuss it with Jenny."

Jenny put down her cup and lifted her head.

"With me, Jason?" She smiled and patted the seat beside her. "Sit down and fire ahead."

Collins hesitated, swallowed and then barked, "No, you are to come with me!"

"With you? Where?"

"And what about me?" demanded Sue.

"You stay here. Jenny comes with me." He reached down towards Jenny. "Come on!"

Jenny instinctively drew back.

"I don't understand, Jason."

Collins lowered his arm, took a deep breath and made an effort to smile. "Jenny, do you want to get out of here?"

"Of course, but..."

"Do you want to help me to help you?"

"Yes."

"Then I need you to come—"

"Jason," cut in Sue. "I don't understand why you need to take Jenny away to talk to her. Why can't you talk to us both together?"

"For Christ's sake," snarled Collins, "why all these questions? Do you want me to help you, or do you want to sit here wondering what perverted punishments that vicious bloody Russian has planned for you?"

Sue shuddered. "No, of course not. But what I don't understand—"

"All you need to understand is that I need to talk to Jenny. Alone. Now!"

"It's OK, Sue. If it will help us then I'll go with Jason, talk to him and then come back and tell you." She turned to Jason and forced herself to smile. "That will be OK, won't it?"

Collins sucked in a deep breath. "Yes." He stretched out his arm again. "Time to go, Jenny."

Sue opened her mouth, but Jenny caught her eye, frowned, shook her head and took his hand.

He smiled and pulled her upwards. Keeping his hand in hers he held her gaze. "That's it, Jenny," he smirked. "Come on."

Gripping her hand, he turned, walked towards the door and pulled it open. Jenny, her face pale, looked back at Sue.

"See you soon," she murmured before she was yanked through the door.

A flash of lightning was followed by a roll of thunder.

Evgeni jumped up as the pair emerged.

"Jason, what are you doing with Jenny?" he demanded.

"Out of my way," snarled Jason thrusting Evgeni back against the wall.

"Jenny, do not go with him. Do not trust him. He—"

A blow to the side of Evgeni's face sent him staggering.

"Shut your fucking mouth! This has nothing to do with you!" He tugged at Jenny. "Come on!"

Evgeni, blood seeping from his top lip, leapt forward and swung a blow at Collins. Ducking under it Collins slammed his right fist into Evgeni's solar plexus causing him to collapse, coughing and gasping for breath.

Leaning forward Collins turned the key to lock the door, dropped it on the gasping body of Evgeni, and tugged Jenny's arm.

"No, Jason!" she shouted. Wrenching her arm free she crouched down beside Evgeni.

"Jenny! With me! Now!"

Jenny raised her head and her words of protest died in her throat. In his right hand was a pistol pointing directly at her. Slowly she stood.

"You're coming with me." His voice was soft and menacing.

"Jenny!" The voice was Sue's. "What the hell's going on? Are you OK?"

Collins, keeping his pistol trained on her, jerked his head towards the door.

"Answer," he mouthed.

"It's alright, Sue, I, I tripped over and fell."

Collins swung his pistol towards Evgeni and held it for a moment before swinging it back to Jenny.

"So who was coughing?" came Sue's voice.

Jenny hesitated and Collins moved his pistol slightly forward.

"Oh, that was Jason. I, er, fell against him."

"You sure?"

Collins gestured with his pistol.

"Yes, of course. We're going now. See you soon."

Collins gave a malevolent smile. "Good girl." He pointed his pistol at Evgeni who was attempting to get back to his feet.

"Back on the bloody chair, and stay there," he ordered.

The young Russian reluctantly stood up and eased himself into the chair.

Thrusting his pistol inside his jacket, Jason reached for Jenny's hand. "Sorry about the weapon." He shrugged. "Blame it on bloody Evgeni."

Reluctantly Jenny took his hand and began to walk with him down the corridor.

Evgeni, gripping the door key, watched them go. His face was a mixture of fury and anxiety,

"Where are we going?" Jenny asked.

Collins grinned and stopped in front of a doorway. "Just here." He opened the door and stepped back, gesturing for Jenny to enter.

She stepped inside the room, which was identical to the one she'd just left. She noted that the bed was neatly made; the clothes hung tidily in the open wardrobe, and on the small table was a bottle of gin. Next to it were two small glasses.

"Make yourself comfortable," leered Collins, as he closed and locked the door.

Chapter 70

The scream startled him. It had come from further down the corridor. Evgeni leapt from his chair and looked rapidly up and down the deserted area. No sound, nobody.

Behind him he heard a scratching followed by a click. He spun round and saw Sue cautiously opening the door. They stared at each other for a moment before she said, "Evgeni, I heard a scream. It sounded like Jenny."

"Yes. I think it came from Jason's room."

"So let's go!"

"Wait." Evgeni frowned. "How did you open…?"

"Later! We need to help Jenny."

"Collins has a pistol."

"And don't you?"

"Yes, but he is behind a locked door, a good defensive position."

Sue thought for a moment.

"We need reinforcements. Where are the passengers from the plane?"

He hesitated before replying, "You mean Matt and Sandy?"

Sue's eyebrows shot up. "Yes. Are they on this corridor?"

He nodded, turned and pointed to a nearby doorway.

"We need them. Let them out!"

"But…."

She glared at him. "Do you want to help Jenny?"

He spun round and, with the key in his right hand, strode quickly down the corridor with Sue at his heels. Reaching a door, he inserted his key and pushed it open. Matt and Sandy scrambled upright from the bed where they'd been lying.

"Jenny's in trouble," barked Sue. "We need your help!"

"Sue! What the hell?"

"Later, Matt." She gestured to her companion. "This is Evgeni, one of Zhukov's men. However," she continued quickly, "he wants to help us. Jason Collins has Jenny in a room further down the corridor. We need to get her out!"

The pair looked at each other, were about to speak when they heard a scream and a crash.

"Come on!" ordered Sue. "Quickly and quietly."

The four of them followed Evgeni down the corridor and paused outside Collins' door. Sue leaned forward placing her mouth near Evgeni's right ear.

"Tell him you are Igor. Order him to open the door!"

After a moment's hesitation Evgeni nodded. He knocked loudly on the door and roughened his voice.

"Jason! It is Igor! Open bloody door!"

From inside, the four could hear shuffling and muffled voices.

"Jason! Open bloody door, now!"

Footsteps approached, it was unlocked and the opened crack framed Collins' angry face.

"What the hell?"

Matt's right foot slammed the door back, sending Collins sprawling. The trio burst in. Jenny was on the bed, bleeding from the mouth, and trying to tug her torn blouse back into place. Collins' attempt to regain his feet was thwarted by Evgeni who slammed him back to the floor with his right foot and stood over him. He held a pistol in his right hand.

"Lie still, you bastard, or I shoot."

Collins lifted his head. "How dare you crash into my room and bloody threaten me!"

He gasped in pain as Evgeni's right boot thudded into his ribs.

"I dare because I hate men who beat up woman," snarled the young Russian. "Shut your mouth and lie still, you dirty coward."

He swung round and thrust his pistol into Matt's hand.

"Guard him. He is not to move."

289

With a malevolent smile Matt took the pistol and stood over the coughing Collins.

"It'll be a pleasure."

Evgeni joined the two women who were comforting Jenny.

"Jenny, I am so sorry."

She gave him a weak smile. "No need for you to be sorry Evgeni. Thank you for coming to my rescue and," she looked around, "bringing reinforcements."

Reaching out he took her hand. "Did he hurt you?"

"Slapped me hard across my mouth and tore my blouse. I screamed and tried to get up. He pushed me back on the bed and knocked over the table lamp. I fought back and screamed again."

"We heard you," said Sue.

"And came running," grinned Sandy.

A brilliant flash of lightning that momentarily lit the figures in the room was followed by a long roll of thunder. Startled, they stood staring at each other before Jenny voiced their common thought.

"What do we do now?" she said.

Chapter 71

"Igor!"

Igor looked up from the Russian magazine he'd been reading.

"Yes, Mr Zhukov?"

"Remember, we have now four prisoners."

"Four prisoners. Yes, Mr Zhukov."

Zhukov looked up at the clock on the wall – framed on either side by two Russian female nude paintings. It showed 5.00 pm.

"Evgeni is upstairs on duty for two hours. Go and see him."

"See him?"

Gregory looked up.

"Check on him," he said.

"Da," nodded Zhukov. "We have to take extra care of prisoners. I have said already that if any of them escape—"

"I understand, sir," replied Igor, discarding his magazine and rising quickly to his feet. He paused for a moment, looking for a response from Zhukov, but the man had already looked away.

Igor paused outside the door, closed it and sighed. Although he had a grudging admiration for Zhukov's single-minded commitment to his organisation, he was becoming increasing irritated by the subordinate role to which he'd been assigned. He knew that Zhukov employed him for his muscle and his ruthlessness, but that didn't justify his being spoken to as if he were a clueless underling. Like Zhukov, he'd spent time in the Russian army where his superiors had physically and verbally abused him on a regular basis. He'd immigrated to New Zealand seeking a more peaceful existence, although he was quite prepared to apply the lessons gleaned from Russian military interrogation procedures to enhance his earnings where necessary.

His first encounter with Zhukov had been a promising one; a fellow countryman, financially successful, with flexible ethics, seeking some muscle. Igor had eagerly accepted the man's offer of employment, assuming that once he'd shown his abilities, he'd be increasingly involved within the organisation.

It hadn't happened. His role as one of Zhukov's heavies had initially involved some stand-over tactics against individuals who owed him money, and occasionally limited amounts of violence. He'd applied himself efficiently but the only thanks he got were occasional grunts of acknowledgment. His opinion was never sought, and he was always expected to carry out his assigned tasks without question.

A roll of thunder brought him back to reality and he sighed. He was about to spend the better part of the evening sitting outside a door in an empty corridor, guarding a couple of harmless women.

As the echo of the thunder died away, he lifted his head. Above him he heard the shuffle of footsteps and faint snatches of conversation. He moved quickly to the foot of the staircase and started to climb. Instinctively he softened his footfall, alert to any other suspicious sounds.

Reaching the top of the stairs he paused and gazed along the length of the corridor. The seat that should have been occupied by Evgeni was vacant. He frowned and reaching inside his jacket pocket, withdrew a Beretta 92 semi-automatic pistol and, his senses now alert, softly advanced towards the empty chair. Outside the door he paused and listened. His dark eyes narrowed as he heard a subdued mixture of male and female voices, two of whom he recognised as being Evgeni and Collins. Something dodgy was afoot.

His first instinct was to wrench open the door and confront the occupants over the barrel of his pistol. However, as he reached out his hand, he paused. He knew that Evgeni and Collins were armed and if they had decided to betray Zhukov, they would put up a fight. Similarly, the women, although unarmed, would be unlikely to meekly comply with any of his orders, a further factor in the development of a potentially dangerous situation.

He paused and smiled. Clearly, he needed backup and could use this situation to curry favour with Zhukov, and having alerted his boss to possible treachery, he could ensure that he was involved in the response.

He turned and as quickly and silently as he could, made his way to the top of the stairs. He paused and looked back. The corridor remained empty. Moving swiftly, he descended the stairs, advanced towards Zhukov's office door and wrenched it open.

Three startled faces of his boss, Gregory and Tony stared at him momentarily before Zhukov glared, thrust his chair back, and opened his mouth. Before he could speak Igor thrust his arm at the open door.

"Sir, the prisoners, Evgeni and Jason are all inside the room upstairs with the prisoners! They may be rebelling against you!"

"Are you crazy?" snarled Zhukov. "They—"

"No I am not," retorted Igor. "When I reached the top of the stairs I saw Evgeni was not in his chair. I walked up to the door and heard the voices of Evgeni, Jason, another man and some women. I—"

"You have a pistol! Why you not enter room and take prisoners? You are maybe a coward!"

Igor advanced two steps and stopped, his face inches from Zhukov. "You not call me a coward," he hissed. "I work hard for you, carry out orders without asking questions, get no thanks and now you insult me."

Zhukov, startled at the unexpected confrontation, took a step back. "You dare to speak to me like that!"

Tony and Gregory exchanged hasty glances before Gregory swiftly moved forward and thrust himself between the two glowering men.

"Quiet, both of you! If some sort of treachery is developing upstairs, we need a united response! Quarrelling with each other is completely stupid!"

Startled by the uncharacteristic vehemence of his colleague, Zhukov stared at him, grunted, sat down and signalled for Igor to sit.

"Now, Igor," began Gregory, "you say that Evgeni and Jason are together in the room upstairs with all the prisoners."

Igor glanced quickly at Zhukov, and then switching his gaze to Gregory, answered, "Yes. I think the two men were armed so I came to tell you."

"A wise decision, Igor, under the circumstances." He glared at Zhukov. "You agree, Vlad?"

Zhukov grunted and turned to reach for the cigarette packet on the table.

Gregory's voice was harsh. "Vlad, you agree?"

Zhukov's hand hovered over the packet, then his head slowly turned towards Gregory, and his eyes narrowed. Igor held his breath, but Gregory held his boss's gaze. Zhukov shifted in his seat, switched his eyes to Igor and said softly, "Yes, I agree."

The other three men sighed quietly as the big Russian, obviously keen to re-establish his dominance, quickly continued.

"Igor, you say you think Evgeni and Jason are armed?"

Igor, pleased that his opinion was being sought, nodded eagerly.

"OK," said Zhukov. "We need to make sure that all prisoners and two traitors are captured alive." His brow furrowed and his eyes darkened. "I will need to inter…"

"Interrogate them, Vlad," offered Gregory.

"Da, interrogate," agreed Zhukov. He smiled grimly. "I have experience in Russian army with captured prisoners." He extracted a cigarette from his packet and tapped it on his thumbnail. "We need extra men. Igor, go now to the gate and tell two sentries to come here immediately with their weapons.

Gregory, go to the sentries' room and bring the rest of them here also."

Igor stood and then hesitated. "Sir, if I bring in the two sentries then nobody will be guarding the house."

Zhukov glared at him for a moment before nodding. "You make good point, Igor, but we need all men." He shrugged exaggeratedly and smiled. "It will only take short time to complete our task."

Chapter 72

"So, are we going to check the place out?"

Burton smiled at Young and nodded slowly. "Thought it might be worth a look," he replied.

"Bit risky, isn't it? Zhukov sounds like a ruthless bastard who won't appreciate anyone sniffing round his property, particularly if he's keeping any prisoners."

"Yeah, fair enough. We've got the address, and viewed the aerial photos, but I still think we need to check it out in person before taking any further action."

"Are you suggesting we drive out there, knock on the door and ask for Mr Zhukov?" she asked.

Burton shook his head. "No, but it wouldn't do any harm to cruise slowly past a couple of times and check on the lay of the land."

Young shrugged. "If you say so. But I suggest we check out and carry a couple of handguns in the firearm security cabinet of your car."

"Good point. Will do." He looked at his watch. "Eight thirty. We'll leave at nine."

*

"Heard anything from Matt or Sandy?"

Chris Winstone looked up as Dale Salmond entered his aero club office.

"Not a word. I tried phoning him this morning, but the call went to voicemail."

"You notified the police?"

"Yes, they seemed pretty interested but I've heard nothing since then."

Dale paused. "Do you think, "he began hesitantly, "that…"

"We should follow his route and see if we can locate the plane?"

'Great minds think alike," nodded Dale. He looked up at the clock on the wall. "It's eight o'clock. The weather seems to have cleared. If we notify the club now, then carry out the pre-flight checks we should be off the ground by nine."

*

"Ray, I'm worried about Matt."

Ray Bullock looked up from his desk as his wife entered. In their sterile relationship both had made a point of keeping their feelings in check and addressing each other like business partners in a small but smooth-running company. However, Maryanne was making no attempt to conceal her feelings as she sat down opposite him, her hands clenched, and her eyes narrowed in anxiety.

"Yes, it's inconsiderate of him not to let us know if he's staying overnight somewhere," Bullock replied, endeavouring to maintain a casual attitude.

"Aren't you worried, Ray?"

"Not particularly," he shrugged. "He's a young guy who wants to have a little fun before settling down. I'm happy to let him get on with it."

"Christ!" exploded Maryanne, "just because you like to shag around with any passing female, don't assume that our son has followed your sleazy example! He didn't come home last night, hasn't phoned this morning, I've called several times, and all I get is his bloody answer phone. And you, his father, apparently don't give a shit!"

With an effort Bullock resisted the temptation to trade verbal blows. He knew full well that Maryanne, like him, had regular lovers but, by unspoken agreement, this aspect of their lives had remained off limits. However, his concern as to his son's whereabouts was growing. He too had made several unsuccessful attempts to phone Matt, and although he'd like to believe his son had spent the night with his girlfriend, he was unable to conceal his worry that somehow Zhukov or one of his hoods could be involved. However, it was essential that he concealed this from Maryanne whose present accusatory mood could easily turn more vindictive.

He looked at her, the woman he'd once found so attractive, now transformed into a furious shrew. He was about to speak when she leaned forward in her chair, locking eyes with him across the desk.

"And another bloody thing!" She paused and lowered her voice. "Last week the police came here and interviewed Matt."

Bullock shot back in his chair, as though he'd been slapped in the face. He gaped at her. "The police?" he asked softly. "Who? What did they want?"

She laughed harshly.

"No need to whisper, you stupid bastard. No-one can hear you in here, although the way things are moving, you too may have some questions to answer." She hurried on. "There were two police officers, mercifully in plain clothes and an unmarked car. Their names were Burton and Young. They wanted to talk to Matt about some missing girl." Her voice rose. "If the police are investigating her disappearance then it's obviously bloody serious! And if Matt's involved in some criminal—"

"Oh for fuck's sake, Maryanne you're becoming hysterical!"

Maryanne leapt to her feet. Her fury accentuated the sharpness of her features from which her eyes flamed.

"Me, hysterical? You, you bastard, I know that you're mixed up in some shady activities with some pretty sordid characters. You mask them with the term 'business dealings' but in reality, they're on the wrong side of the law." She thrust her arm at him, the silver and gold bangles jangling furiously. "You find Matt, you bring him home or you'll be the one answering questions from the police!"

She whirled round, stalked out the room, and slammed the large cedar door behind her.

298

Bullock stared after her for a moment before tapping his laptop's keyboard. He studied the screen for a moment before he reached for his pen and quickly jotted down some information. Tearing the page off the notepad, he tucked it into his top pocket. Unlocking a desk drawer, he took out a Walther p99 semi-automatic pistol and two clips of 9mm ammunition. Sliding them into his jacket pocket he exited his office, locking the door behind him.

*

The unmarked police Skoda swung off Highway 28 in response to Siri's electronic instructions, and on to a secondary road.

"It's a kilometre from here," said Young.

Burton nodded. His eyes were fixed on the road and he felt the tension building. Maybe this wasn't such a bright idea, but if all they did was to drive slowly past the property, then there'd be no harm done. On the other hand, having made the effort to come out here it would be a waste of an opportunity not to further progress the investigation into the disappearance of Fleur Lassiter.

"Coming up," said Young.

Burton slowed the Skoda. On the left was a wide gate that sealed off a winding driveway leading to a two-storied house. On impulse he pulled up a few metres from the gate. Two cars were parked outside the house but there were no personnel to be seen.

"Let's take a closer look," said Burton unbuckling his seat belt.

"You sure?"

"Yeah. Come on."

Both police officers climbed out of the car, walked up to the gate and studied the house and its environs.

"Looks peaceful enough," muttered Young.

Burton was about to reply when he heard the sound of a light aircraft coming towards them. It was flying slow and low.

"What's he up to?" said Burton.

The plane throttled back as it flew over the farmhouse, immediately went into a turn, dropped down further and repeated its pass over the property from a different angle before circling back for a third pass.

"Looks like he's preparing to land."

Burton spun round.

"We need to pay the inhabitants of the house a courtesy call. Get the revolvers just in case."

Keeping his eyes on the house, he unhitched the gates and the pair, having slipped their weapons into the inside pockets of their jackets, began to walk down the drive.

*

"Our only chance is to make a break for it," said Sandy. "The sun's up and the storm seems to have died down. There's a door at the other end of the corridor that's unguarded, and hopefully leads outside."

"Right," agreed Jenny. "Let's get out of here before Zhukov and his thugs come up to investigate."

"What about him?" asked Matt, pointing to Jason Collins who was propped up by the edge of the bed.

"Take him with us. If we strike trouble, we could use him as a bargaining chip."

"Bargaining chip," echoed Collins, lifting his head and giving a sneering laugh. "If you think that ruthless Russian bastard will bargain with you, you're bloody dreaming."

"Maybe he won't, but maybe you will – particularly if it's your life on the line." Matt prodded him sharply. "Now get up, and keep your mouth shut."

Collins, eyeing the revolver, clambered upright and stood glaring belligerently at the others.

"We'd better check outside before we move," suggested Sue.

Jenny nodded. "Evgeni," she said softly, looking at the young Russian, "could you please check outside."

Eager to play his part, Evgeni smiled briefly at her and moved quickly towards the door.

"Carefully, Evgeni," she said.

"Of course."

He reached for the handle, partially opened the door and looked through the gap. The corridor was empty.

"Nobody here," he said, widening the door and turning back to look inquiringly at the others.

They exchanged uncertain glances, each one reluctant to assume leadership over the others. Finally, Jenny broke the silence.

"Matt, you've got a pistol. How about you lead us out?"

"Sure you know how to use it, Bullock? Saw your hand shaking a few times."

Angrily Matt thrust his face at Collin's. "Listen, you bastard, I told you to keep your mouth shut!"

"Easy, Matt, he's just trying to rile you," said Sandy, reaching out and gripping his left arm.

"Evgeni, you and I will go next, with this loudmouth in front of us," said Jenny. "If he speaks or makes a false move then shoot him," she smiled mirthlessly, "in his balls."

Jenny was rewarded by the sight of Collins wincing and instinctively reaching down to cover his genitals, before hastily removing his hand.

"I think he very clearly understands you," muttered Evgeni, reinforcing Jenny's instruction by briefly flourishing his revolver at Collins' nether regions.

"We're wasting time," said Sandy sharply. "We should go."

Matt led the group out into the corridor, turning left towards the doorway at the corridor's end. By mutual agreement they moved forward slowly, opting for quietness over speed.

The house was silent, save for the sounds of their breathing and soft footfalls.

Matt kept his eyes flicking between the doorways on either side as the door at the end of the passage came nearer. Mindful of Collins' presence he was pleased that the man was keeping his mouth shut. It made sense to take him with them, but he'd need careful watching. Unknown variables crowded into his mind. Their immediate situation was perilous; even if they made it through the exit their chances of escaping from the grounds were slim. They only had two pistols and Zhukov's men would be armed with high-powered automatic weapons. Being wounded or even killed was a distinct possibility. A shudder went through him. How the hell had it come to this – a tortuous affair with Fleur Lassiter, a follow up relationship with Sandy that, despite a tempestuous start, was beginning to show some promise? Yet, where to from here? Who the hell knew?

At the rear of the group, Sandy watched the figures in front of her making their wary progress along the corridor. Ahead she could see Matt's head twisting, watching from side to side as the group slowly advanced. A brief smile flitted across her face. Originally writing him off as a gauche product of a prosperous but dysfunctional family, she was beginning to gain a new respect for him as he increasingly showed the ability to cope with their unprecedented situation. She sighed. If they ever got out of here intact, then who knew?

Her thoughts were interrupted by the sound of a door being opened on the lower floor and footsteps advancing towards the staircase.

"Matt," she hissed, "someone's coming!"

Matt whirled round, caught her apprehensive expression, and with a "Come on, faster!" increased his pace. Reaching the door, he grasped the handle and twisted it. It barely moved.

Footsteps could be heard on the stairs. Matt grabbed Evgeni's arm and pointed to the lock.

"Shoot it open!"

Evgeni pointed his pistol at the lock and fired. The shot echoed through the corridor, the door trembled and swung opened.

"Come on!" called Matt, seizing Collins by the arm, stepping back and urging the others forward.

Footsteps thudded up the stairs and, just as Matt followed Sandy through the doorway, there was a gunshot and wood splintered just above his head. He whirled round to see Igor racing forward, leading three other men. He levelled his pistol and fired. Igor stumbled and fell sideways causing the trio immediately behind him to trip and sprawl cursing on the floor. Evgeni fired two more shots before he and Matt scrambled through the door.

They exited onto an exterior staircase and hurried down it. As they gathered uncertainly at the base, Collins, seizing the moment, tried to dart away. Stretching out her left leg Jenny sent him staggering onto his hands and knees. Matt and Evgeni leapt forward and roughly hauled him upright. Jenny stepped forward and swung her right palm hard across his face.

"Don't even think about it!"

*

"Gunshots!" hissed Burton.

They both drew their revolvers and stood still near the front of the house, their heads darting from side to side seeking the source.

Two more shots sounded.

"It's from inside, up there," said Young pointing to the far side of the house.

"Come on!" ordered Burton.

Moving quickly they headed towards the right-hand corner and sidled round.

Another shot rang out.

Racing towards them came the escapees, led by Matt. At the sight of the two armed police officers the group slid to a halt. Matt, who had instinctively raised his revolver, hastily lowered it.

"Mr Burton," he gasped.

Above and to their left came a gun flash. Looking up, Burton saw three armed men descending the stairs. He lifted his weapon but two shots from Evgeni and Matt had already caused one of the men to stagger and tumble forward, crashing into the balustrades and bumping down the steps before lying motionless at the base. His two companions hastily retreated towards the door.

Momentarily nonplussed by the speed of events, the group hesitated. Their confusion was compounded as an aircraft swooped low above them, throttling back in preparation for landing on the paddock where Matt had landed his Robin.

"Follow me!" shouted Burton, over the aircraft's noise and an elongated roll of thunder. He spun round and started to move quickly towards the top of the driveway just as driving rain began pelting down.

"You go nowhere!"

The shout came from the front entrance of the house. They whirled round to see Vladimir Zhukov flanked by four dark-suited men. Two of them carried pistols, while the other two levelled AK 47 assault rifles at the group.

"Drop all your weapons!" commanded Zhukov.

The four men carrying revolvers exchanged glances.

A burst of automatic fire kicked up dust and stones at their feet.

"Now!"

All four dropped their revolvers and stood hunched against the driving rain.

"Now walk forwards towards me, slowly," commanded Zhukov.

"You'll never get away with this, Zhukov," shouted Burton above the noise of the storm. "My colleague and I are police officers!"

"Come forward, Mr Police Officer," snapped Zhukov grimly. "Here, the only person in charge is me."

Torn between fear of the guns and the need for shelter from the driving rain, the group shuffled towards the verandah over the entrance. Evgeni tried to keep his head concealed inside his coat, but Zhukov spotted him immediately.

"*Predatel*! Traitor!" he screamed. Leaping forward he slammed Evgeni hard up against the exterior wall and began to rain blows on the young man's head.

Jenny jumped forward and seized Zhukov's flailing right arm. "Stop!" she shouted. "Stop!"

The big Russian whirled round, wrenching his arm free from Jenny's tight grip. His left fist was about to smash into her face when Matt, his head lowered, rammed into Zhukov with a rugby-style tackle, sending him sprawling. As he fell, he collided with Evgeni, sending him and Jenny crashing down in a tangled heap of bodies.

Zhukov's henchmen twisted and turned with weapons at the ready, trying to isolate their boss from the jungle of arms and legs. From the writhing heap came Evgeni's voice.

"You men drop your weapons and step back!"

A clap of thunder rolled across the sky.

Jenny and Matt twisted away from the others revealing Zhukov lying on his back. Underneath him was Evgeni holding the blade of a flick knife to his throat.

"Order them to step back, Zhukov," hissed Evgeni.

Zhukov twisted his shoulders, only to feel the clamp of Evgeni's right arm across his neck and the prick of the blade on his windpipe.

"Order them, Zhukov!"

The Russian hesitated then croaked, "Step back."

"And drop your weapons," rasped the voice in his ear.

He hesitated again until he felt the blade probe a little further.

His voice was virtually inaudible. "Drop your weapons!"

"Louder!"

The blade drew a trickle of blood.

"Drop your weapons!" he snarled huskily.

With a clatter the weapons fell to the ground and Burton, seizing a pistol, gestured for the men to move back to the opposite side of the verandah. He looked down at the sprawling forms of Evgeni and Zhukov. "Get him on his feet. We'll cover you."

Slowly Zhukov rose to his feet, shadowed by Evgeni who maintained his grip and the blade's position.

Burton looked at Matt, Sandy, Sue and Jenny who had also picked up weapons.

"Take these men inside. We need answers to questions." He turned to Evgeni. "Zhukov first."

The scrape of rapid footsteps caused Burton to turn and see the fleeing form of Jason Collins disappearing through the driving rain. Momentarily he raised his revolver before shaking his head and lowering the weapon.

"He won't get far," he muttered before turning to the rest of the group. "Get this lot inside."

*

The propeller shuddered to a halt, and Winstone and Salmond sat peering out of the cockpit window at the sheeting rain.

"A hairy landing, mate, but you made it. Well done," grinned Salmond.

"Probably against all the best flying procedures, but needs must," shrugged Chris.

"Can't see a bloody thing now. You only just beat the worst of it."

Winstone gestured to the other aircraft parked about fifty metres away. "We guessed right," he grinned.

Their plane shuddered as a gust of wind swept past its westerly side.

"So you're suggesting that we now venture out into this bloody weather to try and track Matt and Sandy down?"

Before Winstone could reply there was a loud thump and a lurch on the left-hand side of the plane followed by frantic hammering on the cockpit canopy. Startled, they turned to be confronted by the drenched wild-eyed figure of Jason Collins gesturing for them to open the cockpit door.

Reaching forward Salmond slid it back a crack.

"Jason, what the hell?"

"Open up! I'm soaking bloody wet!" came Collins' bellow above the howling of the storm.

The two men exchanged glances.

"The bastard's mad," said Winstone. "We can't let him in. There's no bloody room."

Nodding his agreement Salmond turned to Collins, vigorously shook his head and gestured for him to dismount from the plane's wing. Collins immediately thrust his hand inside his jacket pocket and brandished the Russian Nagant 7-shot revolver that he'd scooped off the ground as he'd escaped.

"Now!" he bellowed.

"He looks insane," said Winstone. "Better open up."

Salmond reached forward and tugged at the sliding door. It refused to budge. He glanced up at Collins' distorted face and the barrel of the revolver pointing directly at his head. He tugged harder and the door slid open with a rush.

"Get out! I need the fucking plane!"

Salmond, hunched against the rain pelting into the cabin, peered at the figure crouched on the wing.

"You're mad! You can't take off in this storm!"

He saw Collins lift the revolver and tighten his finger on the trigger.

307

"OK, take it easy." He looked down at the man's feet. "But you'll need to get out of the way."

Collins looked round and keeping his revolver trained on the cabin, carefully moved two steps back. Hunched against the wind, he gestured with his revolver. Reluctantly, Salmond started to ease himself out of the seat.

"Get a bloody move on!" Collins shouted.

As Salmond stepped onto the wing Collins pointed downwards.

"Down on the ground. Now!"

Salmond turned and looked back at Winstone. Collins gave a jeering laugh. "Don't worry about our brave General Manager. He's going to fly the plane for me!"

In spite of the precarious circumstances Winstone burst out laughing.

"You're insane, Collins! It'll be impossible to take off in this wind!"

Angrily Collins swung his revolver towards Salmond, shouted "Get down!" and then swung it back towards Winstone.

"We will wait for a break in the weather. Then we'll take off."

There was a thump as Salmond landed on the ground by the wing and stood looking up at Collins. "And what am I supposed to do in the meantime, you bloody madman! Stand here getting soaked to death?"

Collins hesitated, realising that once he entered the cockpit, he'd no longer be able to control Salmond's movements. As he prepared to enter he gestured with his revolver.

"Stand under the wing, but make sure I can see you at all times."

Chapter 73

The late model Mercedes slowly rounded the corner, the driver peering through the wipers working at full speed to keep the rain-swept windscreen clear. The vehicle slowed by the large double gates and, reading the number screwed to the gatepost, the driver gave a grunt of satisfaction.

He stopped the car, gave a curious glance at the Skoda parked nearby and, squinting through the rain beyond the gates, was able to make out a driveway that led to a two-storied house. Moving the vehicle forward, he parked it by a roadside grove of tall trees, out of sight of the house. Zipping up his parka he pulled the hood over his head and tied it tightly. He reached into the glove cabinet, removed a revolver, slipped it into the right-hand pocket, opened the door, and stepped outside. A strong gust of wind sent him staggering back against the car and, with a curse, he hunched low and hurried towards the trees.

Inside the grove he found a reasonably sheltered position that enabled him to view the house and its environs. He noted the various buildings but was not surprised by the absence of people, all of whom were presumably inside sheltering from the elements. His eyes slowly swept the scene, taking care to memorise any important details. He noted the fencing around the small paddocks and a larger single-levelled building that could be a woolshed. As his view moved on, he also noted that the paddocks increased in size. He was about to end his visual inspection when a flash of lightning penetrated the curtains of rain and showed a momentary reflection from a metallic surface. He narrowed his eyes and fixed his gaze on the spot. Another lightning flash revealed a tail fin.

"A bloody plane," muttered Ray Bullock.

He kept his gaze focussed on the spot hoping for another flash. A few moments later several flashes revealed what appeared to be the fuselage of a second aircraft.

"Two bloody planes." Hunching his shoulders and thrusting his right hand into his parka's right pocket, he fingered his revolver and moved cautiously forward.

A line of pines provided some shelter from the relentless elements as well as shielding him from the prying eyes of the large house. Every few metres he stopped and checked but, apart from the noise of the rain and the wind shaking the branches of the trees, there was neither sight nor sound to worry him. Reaching the last of the trees he paused behind one and peered across the saturated paddock where a light plane was parked. He frowned. There was a strange shape underneath the nearest wing. He watched it carefully, and when the rain curtain lifted for a moment, he saw it move.

"A bloke," Burton muttered. "Why the hell is he standing there in the pouring rain?"

Twenty metres in front of him was a large tree stump. Forsaking the shelter of the pine he dashed forward and slithered to a stop, hunched down by the stump and stared at the craft. He saw the man, who was clearly uncomfortable, shuffle forward from under the shelter of the wing, look up at the cabin and gesticulate with his arms. Bullock followed the man's gaze. The canopy door slid open and another man thrust his head out and, pointing a revolver at the drenched figure, gestured for him to move back under the wing. The man on the ground gesticulated again and the other thrust his head further out, pointed his weapon and shouted again.

"Jason bloody Collins," gasped Bullock, recognising him from the photographs that had been provided to him by Zhukov. Reaching inside his pocket he withdrew his Walther. He looked closer and managed to make out a second figure seated next to Collins. The figure appeared to speak, and Collins abruptly turned to reply, pulling his gun arm back inside the cabin. A series of thunderclaps began to roll across the heavens. The man on the ground hesitated then suddenly dashed away from the plane, heading towards Bullock. Collins thrust his face out of the

310

canopy, shouted and then aimed his revolver at the fleeing figure. A shot rang out but the man didn't falter. Instinctively Bullock lifted his pistol and, squinting through the rain, fired at Collins. He heard the whine of a ricochet and saw his target hastily duck his head.

"Over here!" shouted Bullock waving his left arm in the air.

The running figure jinked right and moments later slid into place next to Bullock's crouching figure. The two men studied each other for a long moment before the man said, "Dale Salmond, North Shore Aero Club. That bastard's taken over my plane."

"Ray Bullock." He jerked his head towards the plane. "That's Jason Collins, isn't it?"

The man frowned and nodded. "Yeah, how do you—?"

The sound of a bullet thumping into the stump caused them both to hunch lower.

"Who's the other guy?" asked Bullock.

"Chris Winstone, our General Manager. Collins is trying to escape by forcing him to fly the plane out of here."

"In this weather?"

Salmond shrugged and drew a circle on the side of his head with his forefinger.

A second bullet thumped into the stump.

"Bastard's mad!"

"Or desperate," responded Bullock. Cautiously he peered round the edge of the stump. "They're both still in the plane."

"Yea, Chris is in there with an armed madman. We've got to get him out!"

Abruptly the rain ceased, and the clouds reluctantly parted to reveal a weak sun.

"Do you think they'll try to take off now?"

"If he's desperate enough. The surface'll be soaking, and the takeoff length is probably too short. Both of them—"

The sputtering of an engine drowned the rest of his sentence. Peering over the top of the stump both men saw the propeller gathering momentum in response to the increasing roar of the engine. In contrast to his companion's look of despair, Bullock smiled. Resting his gun arm on the top of the stump he squinted along the barrel and squeezed the trigger. The report from the gun was immediately followed by a smaller report of a burst tyre and the plane's sagging to its left.

"Great shooting!" exclaimed Salmond as they both ducked in response to the whine of a bullet passing close to their heads.

"Keep low. Don't think the bastard's very happy," smiled Bullock grimly.

This view was reinforced by a further shot and overhead whine.

The pair remained crouched and listening to the sounds of water dripping from the pine branches, the gurgling rivulets and the fluttering of wings as the birds began to enjoy their rain-free freedom. From the plane they heard the sounds of an angry conversation followed by several thumps. Bullock peered cautiously round the base.

"Collins is on the wing. He's forcing Winstone to follow him."

"Could you…?" Salmond's voice tailed away.

"There's the chance I'd hit Winstone."

Salmond nodded.

"They've jumped down. They're heading this way."

The squelch of the approaching footsteps suddenly stopped.

"Come out with your hands high or I'll shoot Winstone," came Collins' command.

Bullock thrust his pistol in his right-hand pocket, looked at Salmond, they both shrugged and slowly stood, their hands held above their heads.

Facing them was Chris Winstone. Behind him Jason Collins held a pistol close to his head.

"Afternoon, Jason."

"Who the hell are you?"

"Ray Bullock." He lifted his head and gave a sardonic smile. "Causing problems for yourself and others with your big new gun."

"Where's your weapon, Bullock?" snarled Collins.

"On the ground behind the stump."

Collins considered this for a moment before asking, "What the hell are you doing here?"

"Looking for my son Matt. Is he here?"

Collins shrugged and grinned. "Maybe." He gestured with his weapon. "Both of you step forward and stand in front of Chris."

"Then what?" demanded Bullock.

"Just do as I say, Bullock."

Bullock stood glaring at Collins for a long moment before starting to move forward. Abruptly he stopped and, switching his gaze above Collin's head, gasped and his left hand flew up to cover his mouth. Taken by surprise, Collins snapped his head round in the direction of Bullock's stare. Bullock's hand immediately plunged into his right pocket, withdrew his weapon and pointed it at Collin's head.

"Drop your gun, Collins!"

The two men locked eyes before Collins thrust the barrel of his pistol into the side of Chris Winstone's head.

"Drop your gun, Bullock," he countered.

The four stood stock still, each man rapidly considering the scenario in front of them that seems certain to end in the severe wounding or death of at least one of them.

"You heard me, Bullock, drop your gun or I'll shoot!"

"You shoot Winstone and I'll shoot you," replied Bullock his voice icy calm. "I'll aim to wound you, which will mean that you'll live to be charged with murder. No more than a sleazy sky jockey like you deserves." His voice rose. "So, drop your bloody gun!"

Collin's eyes flickered and he licked his lips nervously.

"Drop your weapon, Jason," said Salmond softly.

313

Collins cleared his throat several times, took a deep breath and said, "OK, we've got a stalemate. I'll make a deal."

"We're listening," replied Bullock.

"The other plane over there. Let me fly it out of here."

Bullock laughed scornfully. "Not a chance. I came here to find my son. I need you to tell me where he is."

"If I do, do we have a deal?"

"Maybe."

Collins jerked his head in the direction of the house.

"Your son's in the house, with Zhukov and his thugs."

"Who else?"

"I think they've got a couple of the women from the aero club as well."

"Are they being kept prisoner?

"They were."

"What do you mean?" frowned Bullock.

"Two plain clothes cops turned up and they captured Zhukov and his cronies."

"How come you got away?"

Collins grinned. "This sleazy little sky jockey saw his chance and made his escape during a downpour. Would have got out of here if you hadn't interfered." He looked directly at Bullock. "But now I've got a second chance, so what do you say, Ray?"

"No chance!"

"I'll take Mr General Manager with me. He'll stand there as my guarantor while I start the plane. If you shoot at me, I'll shoot to wound him," he smiled grimly, "hopefully."

"Look," said Winstone, "I don't like the idea of letting him fly away, but short of some sort of OK Corral shootout it's the best option."

"Chris, surely—"

"He'll only shoot me if Bullock tries to shoot him." He twisted his head round and looked at Collins. "Right?"

"Yeah, I've already said—"

"OK, let's go," said Winstone turning and striding in the direction of the plane. "Come on, Collins, get a bloody move on or you'll miss your flight!"

Salmond and Bullock watched as the pair walked quickly towards the parked plane and stopped underneath the near side wing. They saw Collins wave his pistol in front of Winstone's face before mounting the wing and climbing into the cockpit while he moved to stand alongside the nearside wheel.

"He'll be pissed off if the pilot took the keys with him," muttered Salmond who then shrugged as the engine sputtered into life. The prop began to turn and increased its revolutions in response to the engine's roar as Collins prepared the plane to move forward.

"Hey, what's going on?"

Bullock and Salmond spun round at the shout from behind. Two men were hurrying towards them. One of them paused briefly and then, with a shout of, "Dad!" ran towards Bullock. The two men surprised themselves and each other by exchanging a tight hug.

"Who's in that plane?" shouted a voice behind them.

They turned to see Burton striding towards them, pointing at the Robin that was starting to move forward on the soggy surface.

"It's Jason bloody Collins!" shouted Matt above the roar of the engine.

"Collins! He's wanted for questioning! Can't we stop the bloody plane?"

The watchers saw that Collins was pointing his gun outside the cabin window at Winstone who was keeping pace with the slowly advancing aircraft.

"He's forcing Chris to walk alongside the wheel to prevent us getting a shot at the tyre," shouted Bullock. "And if we try to shoot Collins he'll shoot back and—"

He broke off as Matt suddenly dashed away from the group, ran across the path of the aircraft and ducked down under the right-hand side wing.

"Matt!" shouted his father.

He spun round as Burton seized his arm.

"Collins hasn't spotted him, he's too busy flying the plane and trying to watch Chris. Keep him focussed on this side." He cupped his hands round his mouth and shouted, "Collins! Give yourself up!"

"You've got no show!" shouted Bullock. "Stop the plane!"

The pair continued shouting and waving their arms as the plane revved loudly and shuddered its reluctant way across the soggy ground. As they watched they saw Matt move quickly alongside the far side wing, seize it and swing up and over onto its angled surface. Bullock noticed that Collins showed no reaction, the noise and the vibrations obviously covering Matt's efforts. Both men held their breath as Matt crouched and began to move toward the cockpit.

The young man concentrated on advancing towards Collins whose head was alternating between facing forward and turning to his left to watch Chris and the shouting men. The plane's speed was slowly increasing, with a corresponding increase in the vibrations of the wing – still slippery from the recent storm. Above the noise Matt heard shouting and, risking a glance between the nose and the spinning prop, he could see his father and the detective shouting and waving their arms. "Go, Dad," he muttered as he inched closer to his quarry. The plane lurched left and he dropped on his stomach, scrabbling for a handhold on the surface. He glanced up at the cabin, but Collins continued to show no interest on his right-hand side but, judging by the engine's revs, was concentrating on increasing his ground speed. Matt hauled himself upright and, throwing caution to the winds launched himself at the cockpit window. He crashed against it and groped for the catch, Collins' head spun round and stared at him in disbelief.

"He's seen him!" shouted Burton.

Bullock immediately raised his pistol and fired two quick shots well above the cockpit. They had the desired effect, causing Collins to whip his head to the left and thrust his pistol out the window. Seizing the latch, Matt wrenched the window open and flung himself into the cockpit, causing the shot that Collins had fired to hum well above the heads of the men on the ground.

"You bastard!" he snarled trying to swing his gun towards Matt who, in anticipation, seized Collins' right wrist in an effort to wrest the weapon from his hand. As Collins twisted and turned, his feet lifted from the rudder pedals causing the plane to start veering left towards the main building. Matt, seeing the danger, wrenched his right hand free, reached out and shut off the engine master switch. The plane rolled forward on its own momentum then shuddered to a stop alongside the main building. Collins, realising that the plane was immobilised, cursed, cracked Matt across the face, wrenched open the left side window, fired two wild shots at Bullock and his companions, clambered out, dropped down via the wing and headed for the house, his escape given additional impetus by the crack and whine of a bullet passing over his head.

"No need to shoot him!" shouted Burton, seizing Bullock's arm. "He won't get far."

The three of them looked round as Matt scrambled out of the plane to join them. Bullock hurried over to his son.

"You OK?" he asked, reaching out and touching the cut on his son's upper lip.

"Yeah, I'm fine, Dad." He looked round at the other men. "Now let's get the bastard."

"Just a minute," said Burton holding his right hand. "This is a police matter and as such will be dealt with by my colleague Detective Young and me. We won't need any vigilante backup."

"You were happy enough to have our help just now," growled Bullock. "Matt certainly did a great job. Now you just want to push us aside!"

Salmond and Winstone nodded in agreement.

"Now listen—" Burton began.

"Where is Detective Young?" interrupted Matt.

"She's inside the house where we have Vladimir Zhukov and his cronies under guard."

"And Jason Collins armed and on the loose," said Bullock. He turned to Matt and shrugged. "But Mr Burton thinks he's got the situation under control so we may as well leave him to it."

Burton reached out and touched Bullock's arm. "OK, I spoke too hastily. What I meant was that this is primarily a police matter. However, there are only two of us, so I'd appreciate your help until our reinforcements arrive. I just didn't want you charging off and getting involved in a shootout with Collins."

Matt and his father exchanged looks.

"OK by me, Dad. In any case, I don't want to leave without making sure that Sandy is alright."

Bullock nodded and smiled. "Sandy, of course. Cherchez la femme." He turned to Burton. "We're at your disposal, Sergeant. Surely Collins won't hang around here, anyway. He's probably long gone."

"He couldn't get too far on foot, though."

"True," agreed Burton. "You four go round the front of the house and see if you can see any sign of him. But don't approach him or fire at him. Understood? If you spot him, one of you follow him and the other return to the house and inform me. OK?"

The four men nodded and turned, heading towards the front of the house. Matt suddenly stopped and pointed.

"There he is! Top of the driveway. Looks to be heading for the road."

"That's where I parked the bloody Merc."

"That's OK, it's too difficult to hot wire," said Winstone.

"Bloody hell!" gasped Bullock. "I think I left the key fob inside. I was in a hurry and it was pissing down and—"

Collins paused at the top of the driveway and then suddenly turned left and moved quickly forward.

"He's seen the Merc," muttered Bullock.

As confirmation they heard the sound of a car door slam, engine turn over and the squealing of tyres.

"Christ!"

"We need to tell Burton."

Chapter 74

Collins gripped the steering wheel as the big Mercedes roared off down the road. He checked in the rear-view mirror. Nobody. He checked the petrol gauge. Three quarters full. A sharp corner loomed up ahead and he lifted his foot off the accelerator.

"Easy," he muttered. "Road's still wet."

Where to next? His mind raced. He could go to the aero club and try to talk his way into taking a plane, but they'd probably been alerted and could phone the police. Best idea, head north and make contact with one of his team and arrange for a plane to come over from Australia, pick him up and take him back there where he could disappear. He had sufficient funds to cover the costs, although there'd be bugger all left by the time he reached Oz. Still, he had contacts there and his flying skills would be of use to those who needed a pilot who could keep his mouth shut. Yeah, things could take a turn for the better if he didn't do anything foolish.

He grunted and smiled. What a piece of luck finding a late model Merc with the key inside! And the bloody rain had stopped. He turned on the radio and grinned at the sound of The Highwaymen singing "*On the Road Again*". Yes, his luck was surely changing!

*

"He's stolen my car and headed north."

"I'll alert my colleagues who'll set up road blocks once we get a fix on his position," nodded Burton.

"How long will that take?" asked Matt.

"Hopefully before the sun sets tonight. If not, it could take longer. We'll also release his photo and details to the press and social media outlets. Don't worry, we'll track him down."

As Burton started tapping his phone, Sandy turned to Matt. "I'd hate to see him escape, Matt. I'm sure he was going to try and rape Jenny."

Matt nodded and looked round the room. Zhukov and his henchmen were hunched in a corner being guarded by Evgeni. All eyes were on Burton who was talking rapidly into his phone.

Matt grabbed Sandy's arm.

"Follow me," he whispered.

Moving quickly the pair slipped through the lounge door into the corridor.

"Matt, what—?"

Matt held his finger to his lips and moved towards the back entrance. He opened the door, let Sandy through and quietly closed it.

"Matt? What's going on?"

"Do you want Collins to get away?"

"No, but the police—"

"May get him, but may not. We're going to give them a helping hand."

He reached out, took her hand and walked swiftly towards the long paddock where the Robin had been abandoned. Reaching its side, he turned to Sandy.

"Hop up and climb into the cockpit."

"Are we going after him?"

"Yes, we are. He has a head start but we have an aircraft."

"You're crazy, Matt," she grinned as she climbed up onto the wing.

*

The traffic was light and consequently Collins was able to make unimpeded progress on his northwards journey. Although eager to put as much distance as possible between himself and the farmhouse, he was careful to keep his speed at 100 kph, having no wish to attract the attention of any road patrols.

Feeling the pangs of hunger and thirst he risked pulling into a roadside café where he bought a couple of bottles of orange juice, several sandwiches and small cakes. Exiting with his supplies he checked the road but saw no sign of any suspicious vehicles or personnel. With increasing optimism, he started the car and sped away.

The Mercedes had a Satnav system that enabled him to select a route north on the west side of Highway 1, the main motorway. He'd take Highway 16 which primarily went through rural areas. Although it would take longer, he would be less likely to encounter any highway patrols on the lookout for him.

He bit into his ham and cheese sandwich and grunted with satisfaction; tasty food, refreshing drink, a powerful car, plenty of petrol and a good plan of action – so far, so good.

*

Knowing that they'd soon be missed, Matt wasted no time in starting the engine and easing in the throttle. The plane had veered near a couple of pohutukawa trees and he had to work the foot pedals to manoeuvre around them, before heading down the paddock. Collins' initial approach had reduced the distance so taking off presented a challenge. Matt increased the engine's revs and felt the aircraft respond. Working the foot pedals to keep the Robin as straight as possible, he continued to incrementally increase the speed. With every turn of the prop a tall hedge at the end of the paddock was looming larger. It was going to be tight.

Sandy, aware of the challenge, bit her lip and gripped the sides of her seat as Matt pulled back on the stick. The plane started to lift and he increased the power. The nose continued its upward movement as it sped towards the hedge. Matt dragged harder on the stick and the hedge disappeared under the aircraft accompanied by a jolt and a shudder.

Matt glanced at Sandy, grinned and gave the thumbs up.

He continued the climb and then lowered the nose bringing the aircraft into a straight and level position.

Two helmets and a pair of binoculars were lying on the cockpit floor at Sandy's feet. Matt signalled for her to retrieve the helmets, put one on, and hand him the other one. He then spoke to her through the microphone.

"My guess is that Collins will head north."

"Probably. On the main motorway?"

Matt started to swing the Robin in a wide half circle that would take them northwards over the farmhouse.

"Doubt it. He'll probably figure that the road patrols have been alerted and therefore he'll take an alternative route. My guest would be north west near Highway 16."

"Will that make it harder for us to find him?"

"Yes and no. The motorway would be more predictable, but we could lose him in the traffic. The side roads offer him more choice, but he'll be easier for us to spot."

"What colour is your dad's car?"

"Red. That helps."

Sandy looked down as they approached the farmhouse.

"There's your dad, Burton, Chris and Dale and a couple of others outside. They seem to be signalling for us to come back down."

"I'd better answer," replied Matt.

As he swept low over the farmhouse, he waggled his wings and waved.

"They may have ordered a chopper up so let's see if we can be the first."

"Sounds like a plan. But if we find him what will you do?"

"I could radio his location, or…"

"Or what?"

He shrugged. "Depends on the circumstances."

"Matt, you're not planning any fancy heroics are you?"

"Moi?" he grinned, putting his hand over his heart before increasing the height of the aircraft and levelling off again.

"We'll follow the road he took and maintain a northerly direction, west of the motorway. Keep your eyes skinned and use the binoculars if you see anything promising."

Sandy nodded as she put the binoculars round her neck. Maybe this was not too mad an idea, and in any case, Matt was unlikely to risk both their lives by swooping in and buzzing the plane. She'd always been a fan of vintage Alfred Hitchcock movies, and had seen *North by Northwest* several times. She vividly recalled the sequence featuring Cary Grant hitting the prairie dirt as the light crop duster plane bore down and repeatedly swept low over him. But Matt, of course, would never do anything as crazy as that. She glanced at him, noting his eyes sweeping both sides of the road unfolding beneath them, his whole being concentrating on the task he'd set himself. Well, a challenge like this doesn't come every day, so she might as well enjoy the ride.

With a tiny smile she lifted the binoculars and studied the road ahead.

*

The hum of the tyres complemented the gentle growl of the motor, a combination that gave Collins a growing sense of security. He'd passed through several small towns but no one on the roadside had shown any interest as his car swept past. Similarly, there had been no reaction from the occasional slower vehicles that he'd overtaken, and his rear-view mirror remained free of anyone closing in on him. Staying off the main highway had been a wise choice.

He smiled as the radio reached the chorus of an Eagles' song. Reaching out he increased the volume, and enthusiastically joined in.

So, put me on a highway and show me a sign,
And take it to the limit one more time.

324

Take it to the limit, take it to the limit,
Take it to the limit one more time.

The high-powered escape car was his sign and he would take it to the limit, one more time.

*

Sandy, scanning the road ahead through her binoculars reached out and gripped Matt's arm.

"Red car, Matt." She lowered the binoculars. "About five hundred metres ahead."

"I see it."

"Is it Collins?"

"Not sure yet."

The Robin rapidly drew level with the red car.

"It's my dad's Merc," said Matt excitedly. "We've got him!"

As the final chorus died away an unfamiliar noise caused Collins to lift his head. Above him he saw the shape of a low-flying aircraft. He slowed, thrust his head out of the car window and looked up. He immediately recognised it as the Robin he'd almost managed to escape in earlier in the day.

Matt, after quickly checking for roadside telegraph poles and power lines, eased the plane down above the car's right-hand side, pulled back on the throttle and tipped the left wing.

"It's Collins, Matt! He's stuck his head out of the window."

"Bet he's not happy to see us."

"Bastards!" shouted Collins. He ducked back inside the car, clicked open the glove cabinet and grabbed his Nagant revolver. Thrusting his right arm out the window, he fired up at the Robin.

The report of the gun was followed by the whine of a ricocheting bullet.

"Jesus, he's shooting at us!" shouted Matt, pulling the plane to the right and lifting it above and behind the Mercedes.

"You've got a gun," replied Sandy. "Shall we shoot back?"

325

Matt shook his head. "Too dangerous."

Sandy looked out at the car that had increased its speed

"Don't know why he's speeding up. He can't shake us off. All we need to do is just follow him and radio his position to the police."

Matt didn't answer.

"Matt? That's the best option."

Matt pulled back and flew upwards in order to view the surrounding countryside.

"He's heading towards the town up ahead. What is it?" asked Matt.

"Kaukapakapa. If he maintains that speed, he'll cause an accident."

"A fast car, a pistol and a furious driver. A lethal combination," said Matt. "We need to stop him."

Sandy opened her mouth, but the question died in her throat as Matt lowered the Robin and drew level with the left side of the speeding vehicle. He eased the plane to the right and felt his right wheel graunch against the roof. The plane faltered and the nose dipped, causing him to haul back on the stick.

"His car swerved across to the other side of the road," exclaimed Sandy. "Don't do that again. He could smash into something coming the other way."

"It's harder for him to fire at us if we're on the left hand side. But you're right. Back to Plan A." He lowered the stick and pulled Robin to the right and behind the car.

"Matt, don't be bloody stupid! He'll fire at us again! Radio the police for God's sake!"

Matt tightened his grip on the stick. Sandy was right, of course. The sensible course of action would be to radio the police and then remain in the air maintaining a watching brief and providing any additional information. But the arrogant bastard had shot at him. It was time to even the score.

Collins had managed to bring the car back to the left-hand side of the road but realised that if Matt tried the same tactic he could be forced into the face of an oncoming vehicle. He also assumed that back up had been summoned and his options were now severely limited. Once he arrived in Kaukapakapa he'd ditch the car and try to escape using the cover of buildings or trees. He looked up at the sky. Twilight was about an hour away. If he could last until then he could escape under cover of darkness. Maybe steal a car…

The roar of the plane's engine brought him back to reality. He glanced in his rear-view mirror and saw the wheels advancing towards his right-hand side. The bastard was going to try to run him off the road! He could be seriously injured or killed. Instinctively he slammed on his brakes and the car screeched to halt. He flung open the driver's door and leapt out, gun in hand.

"Tricky bastard," muttered Matt as he saw the Mercedes disappear beneath him. "He'll not get away."

The engine surged as he climbed and swung round in a tight turn, facing back towards the stationary car, behind which he could see Collin's crouching figure. He brought the plane down parallel with the road and flew directly at the car.

"Matt, what the hell are you doing?" screamed Sandy. "He's got a bloody gun! Enough of this! I need to notify the police. Collins is a danger to everyone on the road."

Before Matt could protest, she pulled her cell phone from her jacket and hit 111. When the voice answered she requested the police.

"Jason Collins, the man who is wanted by the police, is heading towards Kaukapakapa in a red Mercedes," she said loudly and clearly above the noise of the plane. "You need to take action immediately." She terminated the call just as the police officer began to ask for her identity.

"All done, Matt. Now let's go home and leave Collins to the authorities."

"Leave him? Like hell!"

Collins hunched behind the car's right rear wheel, listening to the increasing roar of the approaching plane. As it came nearer, he stood, and holding the pistol at arm's length with both hands aimed towards the cockpit and fired two rounds. He ducked down as the plane roared overhead and spun round to watch its progress.

For a brief period, the aircraft continued to fly straight and level but then started to veer from left to right. Collins raised his right fist skywards, let out a whoop of triumph, turned, and climbed back into to his car. His heart was beating rapidly, and his face was soaked with sweat. He drew several long, deep breaths. He needed to take the time to calm down.

"Matt! You're bleeding," gasped Sandy.

"It's above my right eye. I think his bloody bullet shattered part of the Perspex." Matt attempted to wipe away the blood that was seeping into his eye and gestured with his head. "The first aid kit. Should have a bandage in it. Wrap it round my head."

He shut his right eye and, trying to ignore the throbbing pain in his head, made an effort to steady the plane that was flying an increasingly erratic course. Eventually he was able to settle it into a straight and level position.

"I think I can keep her steady," he said, the tremor in his voice reflecting the effort he'd made to get the Robin under control. "Can you clean me up a bit?"

"OK. I've got some antiseptic that I'll put on the wound and then wrap a bandage round it. Might sting a bit."

"That's fine. Just get on with it," snapped Matt.

Sandy bit back a curt response and, pouring the antiseptic onto a cotton ball, dabbed it on the cut. Matt winced and gasped but kept his eyes on the skyline. Sandy began to wipe away the small drops of blood on his cheeks, but he shook his head.

"Just put the bandage on," he ordered.

Sandy pursed her lips but said nothing as she wrapped the bandage around the cut above his right eye and fastened it with a clip.

"OK?" she asked curtly.

He glanced at her and seeing the anger in her eyes reached out for her hand and gripped it. Her hand remained limp.

"Sorry, Sandy. My head's throbbing, like hell, I nearly lost control of the plane and..."

She gave his hand a brief squeeze.

"I understand, Matt. Just don't take it out on me." She reached out and squeezed his shoulder.

He shrugged her arm away, reached out, increased the throttle, swung the plane into a tight arc and headed back following the contours of the road.

"Matt, don't be a bloody fool. You're in no condition—"

"Not another bloody word, Sandy!"

Moments later the red Mercedes came into view. With a whoop of triumph Matt dropped the plane to a position a few feet above the road and, his eyes gleaming, headed straight towards the vehicle, intending to smash it off the highway.

Sandy, all colour drained from her face, screamed, "Matt you bloody fool! You'll kill us!" Reaching out she tried to wrest his hands from the stick, but he shoved her sideways.

"Leave it, Sandy! I'm going to get him!"

Hearing the unexpected sound of the plane's engine Collins panicked and seeing a clear road on either side began to zigzag the car across the highway.

"No you don't, you bastard," growled Matt, concentrating all his efforts on mirroring the car's movements. Eyes glittering with triumph, he steered the plane straight towards the car as it reached the far-left hand side of the road. He saw the wheels turn sharp right as Collins desperately resumed his zigzag and, with a howl of triumph he swung the plane towards the side of the turning vehicle.

Sandy cried out in horror as she realised that Matt had misjudged his height and was too low. A split second later, with a sickening crash, the plane slammed into the turning car.

Chapter 75

Confused by the strange sounds all around him, he tried to open his eyes, but only one responded. To his right he saw a bottle suspended upside down, with a long tube hanging from it. He lifted his right arm but felt a slight tug and realised that it was attached to the tube.

There was a similar resistance when he moved his left arm. He slowly turned his head and saw wires of various colours leading up to a boxlike instrument that was displaying a variety of ever-changing digital numbers on a small screen.

He moved his left foot and wriggled his toes. Relieved that they moved easily he tried his right foot. He let out a gasping moan at the pain that immediately shot through him.

His head sank into the pillow and he tried to consolidate his thoughts. He remembered flying low along the highway, aiming to clip Jason Collins, but instead there'd been a giant jolt, he'd been flung forward and...

His eyes closed for a moment and then snapped open. He gave a hoarse cry. "Sandy!" He tried to sit upright and shouted again. "Sandy!"

A young female nurse hurried in and quickly placing her left hand behind his head and her right hand on his chest began gently but firmly easing him back onto the pillow.

"It's all right, Matt. You had a bad accident."

Matt stared at her for a long moment before asking, "Where am I?"

"The intensive care unit, North Shore Hospital. I'm Olivia, your day nurse." She smiled reassuringly. "You've had a long sleep, just what you needed."

Matt reached out and gripped her right arm.

"Do you know what happened to me, Olivia? I was in a plane..."

"Yes, apparently it crashed."

"Sandy was on the plane with me." He looked wildly around the room. "She's not here. What happened to her?"

Olivia smiled sympathetically. "You're safe, Matt. That's the important thing."

She winced as Matt's grip on her arm tightened and his eye stared wildly at her. "Sandy! I want to know what's happened to her."

Chapter 76

"So, plane crash, yes?" He expelled a stream of smoke and drummed his nicotine-stained fingers on the table. "Anyone dead?"

"Can't tell you at this point, Mr Zhukov. Maybe later when you've shown us that you're prepared to be more cooperative."

The big Russian spread his arms wide and regarded Burton quizzically.

"You think I am not cooperative. I have nothing to hide. I run business that is leg, er leg..."

"Legitimate, Mr Zhukov?" said Burton with a thin smile.

"Da, yes. I am legitimate businessman, I make no trouble, I like living in this beautiful country with its very friendly people and—"

"Been reading travel brochures, have you?" grunted Young.

She and Burton were seated opposite Zhukov at a table in an interview room. The Russian had been informed of his rights and that the interview was being visually and audibly recorded. He had been offered a lawyer and had immediately contacted Christian Frost, a middle-aged man whose immaculate suit contrasted strongly with his client's tousled appearance.

"Can we get to the main issue, here, gentlemen," said Frost in a voice of contrived exasperation. "Obviously Mr Zhukov was nowhere near the plane crash so questioning him about it is clearly futile."

Zhukov lifted his head and grinned mockingly.

"Clearly futile," he echoed.

In a swift movement Burton thrust out his right hand, seized the near new packet of Camel cigarettes and handed them to Young.

"No smoking," he barked.

"But you said—"

"I changed my mind, Mr Zhukov." He glanced at Frost. "Now Mr Frost has suggested we address the main issue." He looked down at his notes, turned several pages and then looked directly at Zhukov.

"Fleur Lassiter?" His voice was soft. "Tell us what you know about her."

Zhukov looked at his lawyer and, with an obvious effort, contrived an expression of innocence.

"Fleur Lassiter. This is a woman, yes?"

"Obviously," snapped Young.

Zhukov gave an exaggerated shrug. "I am not familiar with all the English names for man and woman so I ask you."

"What do you know about her?" interrupted Burton, his voice still soft.

"Of this person I know nothing."

Burton fixed Zhukov with an unwavering stare. "Mr Zhukov, are you acquainted with Nikolai Brusilov?"

Zhukov frowned and turned to Frost. "What means acquainted with?"

"He means...?"

"Do you know Nikolai Brusilov?"

Zhukov appeared to be searching his memory, and then shook his head slowly.

"Answer please for the recording. You've never met Nikolai Brusilov?"

"Never."

Burton and Young exchanged glances before the older man reached into his folder, extracted a 6x8 photograph and slid it across the table. In the silence that followed, Zhukov studied the photo. Burton noted that his face was expressionless, but his hands were starting to make small restless movements.

Finally, Zhukov pushed the photograph back across the table.

"Sorry, I not know this man."

Burton's voice was slow. "You don't know Nikolai Brusilov."

"Look, Sergeant, he's already told you he doesn't know this man."

Ignoring Frost, Burton continued to address Zhukov.

"Then let me jog your memory. Cast your mind back to St Petersburg and to a man who forged documents that enabled you to leave Russia and ultimately enter New Zealand. A man to whom you owed money, a man you beat up." His smile was devoid of mirth. "Remember him now, Mr Zhukov?"

The big Russian turned pale and automatically reached forward for his cigarettes, and finding nothing, began to twist his hands together. He turned to his lawyer with a desperate look.

Frost cleared his throat and asked, "Mr Burton, you have proof of the relationship with this Brusilov person?"

Burton nodded.

"Have you personally met Brusilov?" asked Frost.

Burton smiled. "I have personally met Brusilov."

"Where?" croaked Zhukov.

"Here in Auckland." He looked at Frost and then at Zhukov. "I'm sorry, Mr Zhukov, you don't seem to be aware that your Russian colleague is living in New Zealand. That really surprises me. I thought the Russian diaspora was a closely-knit community. That they helped each other in all sorts of ways, including gardening jobs."

"Gardening jobs?" frowned Frost.

"Yes, digging holes in the ground and burying evidence of crimes committed by their Russian friends and colleagues."

"What has this to do with Mr Zhukov?"

"He's your client. Why don't you ask him?" suggested Young.

Zhukov suddenly leapt to his feet and confronted the two police officers.

"I know nothing about Brusilov in New Zealand! Yes, I said I not know him because last time I saw him was years ago in St

Petersburg, on other side of world. If he came to New Zealand I not know." His voice increased to a shout. "I not know!"

He remained there, his eyes flicking desperately from left to right, his face covered in sweat, his fists clenching and unclenching, and his body trembling.

"Tell your client to sit down, Mr Frost," commanded Burton.

Frost stood and put his left hand on Zhukov's right shoulder.

"Mr Zhukov, shouting at the police officers will not help your case. Please sit down and, if you can, answer their questions."

Zhukov whirled and thrust his face inches from Frost's.

"You are my bloody lawyer. I pay you much money to help me, not to tell me to help policemen. Maybe you not really work for me. Maybe you are spy for police." He reached out, seized Frost by his coat lapels, slammed his head into the bridge of the luckless lawyer's nose and flung him backwards onto the floor. Burton reached under the desk and pressed the alarm button before joining Young and the duty constable who had immediately leapt forward and, with some difficulty, wrestled the enraged Russian face down to the floor.

"Cuff him," gasped Burton, seizing Zhukov's wrists and forcing them together.

With practised ease Young clicked the handcuffs into place and the trio continued to hold him down as he twisted and turned, gasping out a stream of Russian invectives.

Two police officers burst into the room.

"Get this man immediate medical attention, then report back to me," commanded Burton, indicating Frost who had staggered to a chair in the corner and was moaning and clutching his nose from which blood was steadily seeping. The pair moved quickly to help the shaky lawyer to his feet and lead him from the room, muttering threats of legal retaliation.

Slowly Zhukov's struggles subsided, and he lay still, breathing heavily and muttering to himself. At Burton's signal the three men eased themselves off the Russian's prone frame and stood looking down at him.

"Get up, Zhukov. Now."

Zhukov made an attempt to stand but was handicapped by his handcuffed arms. At a nod from Burton the other two men lifted him to his feet, forced him back to his chair, and pressed him into a seating position. Initially he slumped forward breathing heavily. Then, in an obvious effort to recapture some of the initiative, he sat up, straightened his back and met the eyes of each of the three men in turn.

"I need new lawyer. Other guy was useless prick."

"You deliberately assaulted the man in front of witnesses, Zhukov. We'll add that to your charge sheet."

Zhukov shrugged.

"A new lawyer, I need." He coughed. "And some water," he paused, "please."

"We'll get you some water," replied Burton, "but we also have further questions for you."

The Russian glared at him. "Water, yes, but questions, no. Not without lawyer."

Chapter 77

"Any problems with Comrade Zhukov?" asked Young, sitting down in front of Burton's desk.

"Apparently not. He went quietly to his cell last night and ate all his breakfast this morning."

"So we'll proceed as discussed."

"Yes. And the Russian. You've contacted him?"

"Yeah." Young looked at her watch. "He's being collected as we speak."

"Going to be an interesting morning." He stood. "Let's go."

As Burton reached the door his cell phone sounded. "Burton."

As he listened his face began to darken. "What do you mean, he's not there! Young has contacted him and he agreed—"

"Are you talking about Brusilov?" frowned Young. "I spoke to him early this morning and—"

He held up his hand. "You've searched his apartment and checked to see if his car's there?" He looked at Young. "You know the make and model of Brusilov's car?"

"Toyota. Green. About ten years old."

Burton repeated the information and added, "Find the rego number and notify all mobile patrols. He must be found!"

*

Brusilov cruised slowly along busy Wairau Road that was full of car dealers, searching for one that had older cars on display. His eye was caught by a line of small plastic flags drooped indifferently around a sign that read, Stellar Autos: Super Star Deals. Pulling up near the entrance he looked over the stock, noting the usual collection of low budget vehicles that included two Toyotas that were of a similar age and condition to his own. He licked his lips nervously. He had bought his car

337

from a Russian friend and had no experience of car dealers. However, he needed to quickly rid himself of his Toyota.

Earlier that morning he'd answered a call on his cell phone.

"Hullo?"

There'd been no response.

"Hullo? Who is there?"

"Is this Nikolai Brusilov?" The male voice had been harsh and low.

"Yes, it is. Who is this?"

There had been a pause and then the caller had rung off.

Brusilov had stared at the silent instrument for a long moment. Although the caller's question had been short, the accent was eastern European. His stomach had tightened, and he'd felt fear beginning to crawl over the surface of his skin. It was eight o'clock and the police were due to collect him at ten. Yet if the caller knew his cell number, he probably also knew his location. His fear had increased. If Zhukov had fingered him, he had to get out immediately.

He had wrenched open his desk drawer, pulled out his wallet and passport, lifted his car and apartment keys from their hook, slammed and locked the door and hurried down the stairs to the interior car park. Entering, he'd glanced round nervously but the tenants' cars were all parked silently in their bays. Swiftly he'd unlocked his Toyota, and with motor revving, swung out onto the street into the passing traffic. He'd glanced in the mirror, noted a car that appeared to be following him, and suddenly swung left down a side street. His squealing tyres had blended with the angry horn blast from the other car. He'd pulled up further along the street and nervously glanced round and in his rear-view mirror. Apart from an elderly lady leading an equally elderly spaniel, the street was deserted.

He gave a long sigh and then took a deep resolute breath. Whoever was after him would know his car. He had to get rid of it.

The car dealer approaching him was wearing a cheap suit, shoes in need of a clean, and a dazzling smile.

"Good morning, my friend. Eric Teagle's the name." He reached out and gave Brusilov a hearty handshake.

"And your name, sir?"

"Nikolai Brusilov."

"Good to meet you, Nick. I'm sure that—"

"Nikolai," said Brusilov sharply. "My name is Nikolai."

Teagle retained his dazzling smile. "Nikolai, of course. Are you looking to trade in your car, Nikolai?"

Brusilov shook his head. "No, I need to sell my car."

The dealer looked at it and frowned. "Sell your car," he said. "Not much call for this model at the moment, Nikolai. I could—"

"But, you have two of these models already here in your yard. There are many such models on the road. Toyota is very popular brand."

Teagle's smile was smoothly reassuring. "I'll give you the best price I can, Nikolai. How many kilometres on your clock?"

"About ninety thousand."

Teagle passed his hand over his chin, frowned, shook his head and began to circle the Toyota like a predator seeking his prey's weakness.

"Rather high, Nikolai, for a ten year old model." He walked over to the Toyota, scrutinising it carefully. He paused, then ran his hand over a small scratch on the right mudguard. "Nasty scratch. Any others?" He paused by the passenger's door, drew his finger along another minor imperfection, made a tut-tutting sound and continued his circumnavigation, followed closely by an increasingly agitated Brusilov.

They reached the driver's door, which Teagle opened. He ran his hand over the two front seats, looked into the well and shook his head. "Rather worn and a little grubby, I'm afraid, Nikolai. But I can take if off your hands for five thousand, which is a very generous—"

"Grubby, you say!" expostulated Nikolai, seizing the other man by his shoulder and spinning him around. "I take care of my car. Is not grubby, is clean! And marks on body are small, very small." He thrust his face close to the car salesman. "I know men like you. They say my car is dirty, is old, offer me cheap price and then sell car at much higher price to some sucker person!"

Teagle wrenched himself from Brusilov's grip. "Don't you bloody speak to me like that! I was assessing your car, before I offered you a fair price."

"Fair price! You are liar. You say bad things about my car."

"What's going on here, Eric?"

Both men turned to see a small older man with receding hair and a pencil thin moustache. With hands clasping the lapels of his shiny suit coat, he addressed Brusilov in a heavy South African accent.

"I'm Brian Herbst, the owner of this establishment. Is there a problem here, sir?"

"Brian, I was just giving this man an appraisal, a fair appraisal in fact, of his vehicle when he started to abuse me and—"

"Abuse him! No, he say my car is grubby and has many scratches. He offers me very cheap price—"

"Sir," interrupted Herbst firmly, "that's not right. We offer fair prices for cars at our establishment."

Brusilov thrust his arm towards the two Toyotas in the front of the yard.

"Look! Two cars like mine. Both over eight thousand, and this man only offer me five thousand. He is a liar and a cheat!"

"Listen to me you bloody Polack, no bastard calls me a liar—"

"Polack! You call me Polack!" shouted Brusilov, reaching forward and seizing Teagle by the lapels of his jacket. "I am Russian, from St Petersburg, you dumb bloody Kiwi!"

"Take your grubby hands off me, you bloody foreigner!" With both hands he thrust Brusilov backward – the momentum causing him to hit the side of his Toyota and fall to the ground.

"Ach, Eric, for Christ's sake take it easy, man," shouted Herbst seizing him by the arm and looking round nervously at the increasing group of passers attracted by the altercation.

Brusilov angrily scrambled to his feet, shouldered Herbst aside, rushed at Teagle and swung a right hook that caught him on the side of the face.

"You insult my car, and then you attack me!" He shook both his raised fists. "You want some more, you lying cheat!"

Teagle wiped the back of his hand across his mouth and, at the sight of the smear of blood, advanced towards the other man with fists clenched. As some of the watchers shouted encouragement, Herbst stepped between them starting to spread his arms wide like a boxing ref. In doing so he received simultaneous blows from both men that sent him staggering back into the watching spectators.

In the noise and the fracas, nobody noticed the vehicle that pulled up on the opposite side of the road and the uniformed man and woman that hurried across.

"That's enough!"

"Step back, all of you!"

The sight of two police uniforms immediately resulted in an uncertain silence.

"Now then," began the young policewoman, "what's the problem, here?"

On seeing the police Brusilov had began to move backwards into the crowd, but Teagle, pointing at him accusingly, shouted, "This man attacked me, officer. He asked me for an appraisal of his car here, which I gave, and it was a fair appraisal, but suddenly, for no reason, he attacked me."

The other police officer held up his hand and turning to Brusilov asked, "Is this your car, sir?"

Brusilov nodded.

"And did you attack this gentleman?"

"He insult me and my car. He try to cheat me with cheap price for my car and—"

"Listen you bloody Polack, I did not—"

"I not Polack, I am Russian man from St Petersburg."

"Just a moment, sir," said the female officer, holding up her hand. She caught her colleague's eye and muttered, "That car. We had a call about a green Toyota this morning."

"I'll check," replied her companion. The female officer turned to the group and waved her arms. "All of you go on about your business," she paused and looked at Brusilov and the two car dealers, "except for these three men."

The small crowd quickly melted away as she turned first to Brusilov.

"Now, you, sir. You are from Russia?"

Brusilov nodded, his eyes flickering nervously.

"And this is your car, sir?"

He nodded again and watched apprehensively as the other officer stepped forward and murmured in his companion's ear.

"Brusilov, and a green Toyota. We have a match. Let's bring him in." He turned to the Russian. "Please come with me, sir." He gripped the man's arm firmly. "Now."

Accepting the inevitable, Brusilov allowed himself to be escorted across the street, as the other officer turned to the remaining pair.

"If you want to make a complaint you have the right to do so. However, you could also be charged with fighting in a public place. My advice would be to keep your heads down and stay out of any further trouble."

Both men exchanged glances and nodded. As the police officer crossed the road, she heard Herbst say, "I need a serious word with you, Teagle."

Chapter 78

"Good work, both of you," smiled Burton, reaching out and shaking the hands of the two young officers standing in front of his desk.

"Thanks, Sarge," replied Indie Simpson. "We just happened to be passing the car yard, saw an incident and decided to investigate."

"Just as well," grinned Finn Wylie. "A big fish I believe, Sarge."

Burton nodded. "He's a key witness in a murder investigation that could lead to other criminal charges." He paused. "Did he say much on the way in?"

"Only that the dealer tried to cheat him by offering a very low price for his Corolla."

"We asked him why he wanted to sell it but he just shook his head and refused to answer any more questions," added Simpson.

Burton smiled. "We'll see about that." He looked up as Young entered. "All set?"

"Yes, Sarge."

Burton stood. "Excellent. Let's go." He turned to the two officers. "Thanks again for your excellent work."

"Sarge?" asked Simpson hesitantly.

He raised his eyebrows.

"Could we, you know, come and observe the next stage?"

"We'll keep quiet and give you any extra help," added Wylie. Seeing Burton hesitate he hurried on. "We're assigned for patrol duty, but as we've nabbed Brusilov we could be assigned to participating in the follow up, couldn't we?"

"For the next couple of hours?" asked Simpson. "It would contribute to our professional development."

Burton smiled. "OK, I'll accept your offer, and square it with your supervisor."

Zhukov and his lawyer looked up as three police personnel entered the interview room.

"Mr Zhukov, Ms Randall, let me introduce Officer Wylie who is here to observe proceedings."

As Wylie took a chair behind Burton, Zhukov looked inquiringly at his lawyer.

"Don't see why not," she shrugged.

Zhukov nodded. He'd had some doubts about the female lawyer that had been recommended to him. A sharp dresser, who looked ridiculously young, but in their preliminary interview she had exhibited a complete grasp of all the relevant details and assured him that any case against him would have flaws that she could exploit. Regarding the disappearance of Fleur Lassiter, she'd pointed out that the lack of an actual body would considerably handicap any attempt to bring a case against him. He hadn't told her about Brusilov, as he was confident that the man had been kidnapped and disposed of – thanks to the phone call he'd been permitted before being locked up for the night. The price had been high, but worth paying to ensure that Zhukov's involvement in the Fleur Lassiter's death would be very hard to prove.

He watched Burton and Young as they seated themselves on the other side of the table where Burton switched on the recording device and made an identification of the participants, the date and the time.

Burton looked at Zhukov and smiled.

"I'd just like to re-cap on a couple of points that were dealt with in our first interview."

Zhukov grunted and nodded.

"You have denied any knowledge as to the disappearance or death of Fleur Lassiter."

Zhukov nodded again.

"For the recording please, Mr Zhukov."

Zhukov looked at Christine Randall who said quietly, "Just say that you have no knowledge of her disappearance."

Speaking slowly Zhukov said, "I have no knowledge of this woman's death."

Burton looked at him for a long moment before turning around and signalling to Officer Wylie. He stood, turned, opened the door and stepped back. Officer Simpson and Nikolai Brusilov entered the room.

Zhukov stared at the pair in stunned horror.

"Brusilov," he stammered. "I thought…" his voice trailed off.

"You thought what, Mr Zhukov?" asked a smiling Burton.

Christine Randall leaned over and whispered in his ear. Zhukov straightened his back and shrugged.

"I am surprised. It is long time since I see Nikolai."

"How long?"

"Many years ago in St Petersburg. He did some work for me there."

"And you haven't seen him since then?"

"No."

Although Zhukov's face remained resolute, Burton noticed that his hands were tightly gripped together, and his breathing was becoming heavier.

"Then," continued Burton, "you'll be pleased to hear that you'll have the chance to renew your acquaintance with him."

Zhukov frowned. "What means 'renew acquaintance'?" he asked.

"You and Mr Brusilov will be able to start your friendship all over again," smiled Young mirthlessly.

"Mr Burton, you are talking in riddles," said Christine Randall sharply. "Both my client and I would appreciate it if you would clearly state your purpose in bringing this Mr Brusilov to this interview."

"Of course, Ms. Randall," replied Burton smoothly. "We are taking him and your client on a short journey where we hope to uncover some additional evidence which we anticipate being of considerable interest to both of you."

Zhukov and his lawyer exchanged an urgent whispered conversation at the end of which she asked, "My client would like to know where you intend taking him and why."

"Be assured, Ms. Randall, that all will be revealed shortly." He stood. "Transport has been arranged. Please follow me."

As he led the group out of the door he turned to Young.

"Have the others arrived?" he asked.

"Yes, Sarge. And very keen to help."

"Great. We may not need them, but they'll be able to strengthen our case against Zhukov. Put them in the second car."

Young nodded, left the office and walked out to the reception area.

"Ready to go?" she asked.

Jenny, Evgeni and Sue smiled simultaneously. "Whenever you are," Jenny replied.

The group was divided between two police cars, each one driven by officers Wylie and Simpson. Burton, Zhukov and his lawyer, accompanied by an additional uniformed officer, occupied the lead car. Brusilov, Young, Sue, Evgeni and Jenny followed in the second car.

As the two police vehicles pulled away from the police station a large police van that had been parked outside swung round and joined them.

"Who are they?" demanded Christine Randall.

"Colleagues who will be assisting us," replied Burton without turning round. "I suggest you just relax and enjoy the ride."

*

They headed north. At first Zhukov sat hunched in the back seat glancing occasionally out the window, but when the car turned onto Highway 28, he sat up and began to look agitated.

He then turned to his lawyer and began a whispered conversation that seemed to do little to calm his demeanour. In fact, his concern increased considerably when a few minutes later the car headed up a road that was obviously familiar to him and stopped at the gates of his farm. He gasped as the two police officers standing guard moved quickly to swing the gates open. As the cars drove towards the house Zhukov noticed several other police cars parked outside the front.

"What is happening here? Why so many police cars?" he asked, barely able to conceal his fear.

"Stay in the car," was the only response from Burton as he opened his door and stepped out.

The second police car drew up alongside and Zhukov saw Brusilov exit and stand alongside Young. Two other uniformed officers from the van quickly joined them. Watching the group intently, he caught his breath when he saw a man lead four other men, all dressed with protective clothing that covered their heads, and wearing gloves and gumboots. Each pair carried a large crate between them.

"*Der'mo! Sukin syn!*" he expostulated.

"I'm sorry, Mr Zhukov, what did you say?"

Zhukov glared at Christine Randall. "I said, 'shit, that son of a bitch!'"

"Who?"

"Brusilov, of course." His glare intensified. "You, Ms Randall better be shit hot lawyer."

Before she could reply the door was pulled open by a police sergeant who ordered them out of the car. Four officers immediately moved alongside them. Burton, accompanied by Brusilov, led the group of men to the grove of trees near the front of the farm. The sergeant signalled them to follow and flanked by the quartet of officers they moved forward.

Standing by the police car, Evgeni watched the group intently.

"Mr Burton has not explained why he wanted us to come."

347

"No, Evgeni, but with all these police personnel, I'd think they're looking for some important evidence," said Jenny.

Evgeni looked ahead at the figure of Zhukov trudging reluctantly behind Burton.

"Why do you think they've brought Zhukov with them?"

"Not sure but we'll find out soon enough. Mr Burton told us to stay at the back of the group but I'm sure we'll still have a good view."

"Come on," said Sue as she reached out, took Evgeni's hand and they moved quickly to follow the others.

The ground was still damp from the recent rain and the group in front had created a muddy pathway – to the lawyer's annoyance, as the hem of her expensive skirt and her shoes quickly become spattered in slush. Heedless of the mud, Zhukov's eyes darted nervously to either side of the track as he groped inside his pocket and extracted a packet of Camels. He felt a grip on his arm and looked up to see the tall police sergeant slowly shaking his head and urging him forward.

After walking for about five minutes, the group, on a signal from Burton, paused at the edge of a small clearing and watched as Brusilov moved to the centre and looked upwards at the tall trees that cast long shadows over the ground. Slowly he walked backwards and forwards before pausing, studying the dirt at his feet and finally lifting his head.

"Here," he said.

"Here?" echoed Burton.

Brusilov nodded.

Burton signalled and the five-man group moved forward. At the direction of their supervisor they marked out an area of ten square metres using yellow tape. Police personnel took up positions at each corner while Brusilov and Burton remained in the centre of the area until the process was completed. They were then joined by the supervisor and, after a brief conversation with Brusilov, they exited and joined other watchers.

Two pairs entered the area, placed the crates on the ground and took out spades, shovels and long probes. Alongside them they placed bottles and sprays, groundsheets and a body bag.

A plain-clothed woman, wearing protective clothing, joined the group. She was carrying a small black bag and had a camera slung around her neck.

At the supervising Detective Sergeant's signal each of the pairs took up a position in a line on the right-hand side of the marked-out area and began slowly moving forward and inserting their probes deep into the ground. Silence descended over the other personnel. The only sounds were the squelching footsteps of the men, and the grunts as they pulled their probes out of the soil before moving a few more steps forward. Their advance was slow and meticulous. The spectators watched the proceedings intently, while stealing surreptitious glances at Zhukov whose shoulders were sagging and his face glistening with sweat.

"Sarge!"

The shout caused Zhukov to raise his sagging head and, with the rest of the spectators, stare at the man who had shouted.

"You hit something?"

"Yes, Sarge. Something hard."

"Ok, start digging – carefully."

The other three quickly picked up their spades, formed a square around the area and began carefully digging and removing the sods of earth. After a few minutes there was a clunk as one of the spades hit a solid object. The men exchanged glances and then began inserting their spades to widen the area around the object's edges

Burton and Young moved up to stand alongside the supervisor as he told the men to stop. They peered down into the cavity.

"As expected, a long box," said the supervisor.

Burton turned and signalled Brusilov who reluctantly joined him.

"Recognise it?" asked Burton.

Brusilov nodded, shifting uncomfortably. "Yes. Young woman is inside box."

"Fleur Lassiter?"

"I say before, we were not told her name. But is probably her."

The men began clearing the dirt from around the four edges of the box until it was completely exposed in the bottom of the small pit. A murmur rose from the spectators as two of the men lowered themselves into the pit and secured ropes around both ends of the box, before being assisted out by their colleagues. Each then grasped a rope's end, hauled the box upwards, guided it onto the ground and stepped away. Two of the men picked up crowbars and, on a signal from Burton, began to ease the lid off the box. The resistant screech of the nails added to the mounting tension as the lid was slowly prised free and lifted clear.

Burton swallowed hard and nodded to Young and Brusilov who stepped over to the coffin. Staring upwards with unseeing eyes was the body of a young woman. The skin was stretched tightly across the skull, which bore the scar of a gash above the right temple. Burton gazed at the body for a long moment, speculating on the events that had resulted in her sudden death. Young, her lower lip trembling, reached out and grasped Burton's arm. He squeezed her hand before turning to Brusilov.

"Is that the girl?"

The Russian took a deep breath. "Yes," he nodded.

At Brusilov's nod a sigh went around the spectators. This was quickly replaced by a shout and a snapping of twigs and branches as Zhukov, taking advantage of the momentary distraction, spun round and dashed away at right angles into the trees surrounding the clearing. Immediately all the police personnel set off in hot pursuit. Burton, resisting the temptation to follow them, muttered, "He won't get far," and signalled to the forensic photographer to begin her task.

"Come on!" hissed Evgeni.

He spun round and followed by Jenny and Sue, strode straight ahead.

"Why are we going this way?" demanded Jenny, striving to keep up with him.

"I think he will lead the policeman through the bush and then try to head back to the farmhouse. Maybe we can catch him there."

Moving quickly, they soon reached the front of the house. Jenny looked around at the various vehicles parked in the driveway.

"We should get out of sight. Come on."

She quickly led the way to the large police van and crouched by the right mudguard.

"Keep your eyes skinned," she muttered.

"Eyes skinned?"

"It means, watch carefully, Evgeni."

"Of course."

She grabbed his arm. "Listen," she hissed.

In the distance they could hear the faint sounds of the excavation personnel. Above it came rapid footsteps followed by Zhukov's appearance at the side of the house. After a quick look around he moved to the front door, opened it and disappeared inside.

"Damn, he must have had a key concealed. We've missed our chance," muttered Sue.

"I do not think he will stay in the house. We should wait a few minutes," said Evgeni.

"OK, eyes skinned," said Jenny.

They remained crouched behind the van, staring at the closed front door.

Suddenly Evgeni gripped Jenny's arm.

"Look."

Zhukov appeared from a side door grasping a pistol in his right hand.

"He's heading this way."

They crouched lower as Zhukov hurried towards the van. As he drew level Evgeni flung himself forward, seized the Russian round the shoulders and tried to drag him to the ground. But Evgeni, in spite of the element of surprise, was not as strong as his former boss, who slammed his left elbow back into the younger man's stomach causing him to fall to the ground, gasping for breath. As Jenny and Sue dashed forward Zhukov stepped back with eyes blazing and his pistol levelled straight at them.

"Move back, bitches! You not get in my way!"

Jenny stared at the unwavering gun barrel, thinking that the last sounds she'd ever hear would be Evgeni's gasps for breath.

"Zhukov!"

At the shout she and the others rapidly spun round.

"Top floor!" shouted Jenny.

Looking up they saw a figure standing at the window aiming a rifle downwards.

A shot rang out.

Jenny heard a thump and looked down to see Zhukov crumpled at her feet, with blood beginning to seep from a chest wound. As she stood staring, Evgeni gained his feet.

"Who fired the shot?"

Jenny pointed up to the window where figure waved briefly before disappearing from sight.

"Tony," gasped Evgeni. "He saved us."

"But why?"

"Zhukov always bullied him. When he killed Fleur Lassiter that was…" he hesitated.

"The last straw."

Evgeni nodded. "Yes, the last straw." He turned to the two women. "But we say nothing. Tony is a good man and he saved us."

"Our secret, Evgeni," nodded Sue.

"We arrived to find Zhukov already dead. OK?" said Jenny.

"OK," agreed Evgeni.

A harsh cough caused them both to look down. Zhukov's eyes were open, and blood was trickling from the left side of his mouth. Slowly his head turned, and he stared up at Evgeni.

"Evgeni," he croaked.

The young man crouched down, his face close to the dying Russian who reached up, grasped his wrist and pulled him closer. The frequency of his rasping breaths increased, but with an obvious effort he gained sufficient control to gasp, "*Tot, kto ne ishchet druzey, yavlyayetsya yego sobstvennym vragom.*"

The effort had cost him dearly. With a final gasp his head snapped back and his eyes stared sightlessly at the darkening sky. Released from the man's grip, Evgeni slowly stood.

"What did he say?" asked Jenny softly.

"Russian proverb – One who seeks no friends is his own enemy."

They stood together staring down at the lifeless body before the sounds of footsteps caused them to turn and see a group of police officers hurrying towards them.

Chapter 79

"Sit down, son," said Ray Bullock, indicating the seat in front of his desk. "How's the leg?"

Matt sat down and gently eased his right leg forward.

"The surgeon seems happy with the x-rays, but warned me it's going to take a few more months."

Bullock grunted. "Not surprised. You got off bloody lightly, considering your reckless flying and—"

"Yes, Dad. I've said I'm sorry, and that it was a bloody stupid action on my part. Do you think we can drop it now?"

"OK, fair enough." His father paused. "Now while you were in post op I had a long talk to DS Burton. He's consulted with the Air Accidents Office investigation and the consensus of opinion is that if you accept full responsibility and plead guilty then you'll probably get off with a heavy fine. You'll be notified officially, of course."

"And my pilot's licence?"

"Revoked. Permanently. No arguments."

Matt's shoulders slumped but he made no protest.

"Now, Matt, as to your future." He paused and looked hard at his son. "I'm prepared to take you into my business and, if you perform well, to make you a partner. I'll pay you a generous salary that will help with your impending fine and legal costs."

Matt returned his father's direct gaze and then slowly shook his head.

"No, Dad. Thanks for the offer but I'm going back to uni to finish my degree. I'll get part-time work to pay the fine and other costs." Seeing his father about to interrupt, he held up his hand. "The only way I'll be a success is to gain qualifications that are the result of my own hard work. So, thanks, Dad, but I'm determined to be my own man."

The long silence that hung in the air was broken by Bullock.

"Does Sandy agree?" he asked, his voice tense with suppressed anger.

"She does." Matt smiled. "She's recovering well and has accepted my sincere apologies. She's not yet convinced that there's a future for us, but she's OK to keep discussing it with me."

His father opened his mouth, but Matt stood.

"Need to go, Dad. I've arranged to meet her in an hour."

He turned and walked purposefully from the room.

Chapter 80

"Take seat. How are the ribs?"

Jason Collins grimaced slightly as he eased himself down into the chair.

"Healing steadily, if I take it easy."

"And don't do anything stupid," said Burton.

"Not likely. I've learnt my lesson. Easy money is a contradiction in terms."

Burton grunted. "Neatly put and, based on my experience, very accurate." He leaned forward and opened a large folder on the desk between them. "Now, there are several matters that still need to be discussed.

Collins nodded.

"Firstly," continued Burton, "there's the theft of the Mercedes automobile."

"I understand," began Collins hesitantly, "you were going to speak to the owner, Ray Bullock who—"

"Won't press charges. He's prepared to settle out of court; doesn't want the publicity."

Collins tried not to look too relieved.

"Next," continued Burton, "The collision of the car and the aircraft. The findings are that there is insufficient evidence to show that you were in any way responsible for the collision. It looks like charges will be brought against Matt Bullock, so you can count yourself lucky."

Collins said nothing.

"And the discharging of a weapon at the plane. You still deny it?"

"I do."

Burton shrugged. "It's your word against Matt Bullock's and the young woman's. The plane was damaged in the crash but there's no sign of any damage that could be attributable to bullets." He paused. "No gun was found either, so, although we have our suspicions, as there's no proof, at this stage we won't be taking it any further."

Collins raised his eyebrows and remained silent.

"Now," continued Burton, turning over several pages, "the question of the death of Fleur Lassiter. You've already admitted that you were involved in the accident that led to her death."

"Yes, the accident."

"You've stated that it was a blow from Vladimir Zhukov to the side of her head that caused her to collapse, that you tried to catch her as she fell, you slipped and her head connected with a sideboard."

"Yes. That's correct."

"You've further stated that Zhukov warned all those present that they were to keep quiet, speak to no-one and that he would arrange for Ms Lassiter's body to be taken away."

Collins shifted in his chair and shuddered at the memory.

"Yes," he said softly, "that is how it happened."

"You had no part in the disposal of her body," asked Young, locking eyes with him.

Collins shook his head vigorously. "Absolutely none. I was in shock and intimidated by that Russian thug."

"Yet you subsequently became part of his organisation," she replied.

"I joined briefly in order to exploit his weaknesses for my own purposes, to try to discover what had happened to Fleur's body, and possibly get revenge for Fleur's death."

"Get revenge? How?" asked Burton.

"It depended on what I discovered. The most effective revenge would have been to inform the authorities and let the law take its natural course."

Burton exchanged glances with Young.

"And you say that you took no part in any of Zhukov's illegal activities," he continued.

"None whatsoever."

Burton tapped his pen on top of the paper in front of him.

"We've discussed your case in detail higher up the justice sector. The decision is that at this stage there'll be no charges against you." He paused and looked hard at Collins. "However, we now come to the matter of coercing Chris Winstone and Dale Salmond at gunpoint, firing shots at several other men as you tried to take off in your plane, then threatening them with a firearm, obviously with the intent to cause grievous bodily harm."

Collins shifted uneasily in his seat.

"Look, Mr Burton, I was under stress. I had no intention of shooting anyone, I just used my pistol to threaten them. When I did fire, my shots were aimed over their heads or into a large tree stump. No-one was injured." He spread his arms appealingly. "I was desperate to get away from Zhukov. He'd already beaten me up and I knew he'd try to kill me. I'm sorry I threatened the other men, but I knew that unless I escaped my life would be in danger."

"We can't ignore that fact that you threatened and shot at men with a weapon. As to your motivation and any mitigating circumstances, we'll leave that to the courts."

"The courts?" echoed Collins, his face drained of colour.

Burton turned to his colleague. "Detective Young, charge him."

Chapter 81

Four years later, in a quiet bar in central Auckland, Jason Collins glanced at his watch, released the hand of the pretty young woman sitting opposite him and smiled winningly.

"The waiter said the meal would take about fifteen minutes, sweetheart. Meantime I just need to make a quick business call and then I'll be back to enjoy the rest of our evening together."

She frowned briefly and took a sip from her glass of Chardonnay. "Must be a very important business call, Jason."

"It is, darling. I need to arrange the special delivery of a shipment of expensive imported items. It's a lucrative opportunity for me and one which will also be to your advantage if you play your cards right."

He reached out, smirked and squeezed her thigh.

Acknowledgements

Motivation, inspiration, support and assistance came from many sources in the writing of *Low Flying*.

It all began a decade or so ago when Bess shouted me a trial flight at the North Shore Aero Club for my birthday. Flying in a two-seater plane was an exciting and exhilarating experience as on a cloudless day the pilot and I took off and flew over Auckland's beautiful Waitemata Harbour with its pristine marine park that provides so much pleasure to locals and visitors from all over the world.

What was also a revelation to me was the vulnerability of flying these small, noisy aircraft, and the consequential adherence to a range of safety checks, prior to and during flying. The sense of adventure and, even though air accidents are comparatively rare, the sense of potential danger were a revelation to me.

I clocked up 15 hours of flying time with the aero club instructors but was forced to give it up for various reasons. However the experience had stirred my imagination. The adventure, the danger, the unpredictability, the individualism, the flexibility combined with the personalities of the pilots and support personnel provided me with an intriguing platform from which *Low Flying* was eventually launched.

All my works of fiction, including my musicals and novels, have provided me with adventurous journeys. They start with a few ideas and, once I start tapping on my keyboard, I embark on a road untravelled. At times it leads down blind alleys causing me to retrace my steps and change direction. At other times I collapse exhausted by the roadside and crawl metaphorically into a nearby copse where, after sipping a high-quality Kiwi Chardonnay, I fall asleep – for days, weeks or even months.

Minor pathways are not always dead ends. For example, the decision to make my chief antagonist a Russian triggered off a raft of ideas and concepts. In my twenties I'd driven a mini from London behind the Iron Curtain via East Berlin to Warsaw where I'd spent three weeks driving round and meeting the locals. The following year I'd taken a coach trip from London to Moscow, following the same route as Napoleon's ill-fated Grande Armée, and Hitler's Wehrmacht forces 130 years later. These two trips, supplemented over the years by readings, research and wide-ranging conversations, provided me some insight into Russian society which Churchill famously described as "a riddle wrapped in a mystery inside an enigma". A subsequent trip that Bess and I took to St Petersburg in 2018 added to my insight into post-communist Russia. All these experiences I drew on in weaving the story around fictional Vladimir Zhukov and his compatriots; Russian hard men living in democratic New Zealand on the other side of the world.

Of specific note are colleagues and family members who provided me with insightful criticism into the novel as it took shape. My membership of a local writing group, The Mairangi Writers, was of great assistance to me as, at our fortnightly meetings, I would read my latest efforts and receive insightful comments from other writers. So, special thanks to Vicky Adin, Barbara Algie, Pam Laird, Evan Andrew, Gabrielle Rothwell, Maureen Green, Erin McKechnie, Michael Hansen, Trish Devine and Norma Riley.

Bev Robitai, a former member of Mairangi Writers who now lives in Ohakune, deserves a special mention for her editing, formatting and cover design. Her prompt and informative responses were crucial in putting the finishing touches to the plot and characters.

Other friends included Alan Dormer, Brad and Heather Bradley, Gary and Ann Jenkin, whose particularly detailed analysis of the first draft was much appreciated, and our three sons Christian, Shane and Justin, and all other acquaintances who provided encouraging comments while making suggestions for improvement.

Thanks to Ross Hindman, a pharmacist friend for his informed advice and information on medical drugs vis-a-vis 'snake oil', and Brooke Mackley for his information on matters related to trans-Tasman flights by light aircraft.

Of particular note is Elena Stepanova, who lives in Moscow. She is a former distance student of mine with whom I have maintained regular contact over the years, and whose insight into the passages describing Zhukov's years in Russia was invaluable.

To my flying instructors, for their patience, humour and companionship; although I never completed the course, your influence was a key factor in the writing of this novel. (Needless to say, none of them bears any resemblance to the novel's more nefarious characters.)

And finally, to Bess, my wife, my lover and my muse, whose continued love and support has been a crucial factor in the completion of so much of my writing.

The Author

John Reynolds was born in Auckland, New Zealand. He is a qualified teacher and has lived and worked in many parts of the world including England, Saskatchewan Canada, Zimbabwe, USA and Australia.

After completing a BA in History at the University of Auckland he completed an MA in Instructional Technology at San Jose State University, California (with the support of a Creative New Zealand grant) and a PhD at the University of Auckland on the life and works of New Zealand pioneer filmmaker John O'Shea.
As well as being a freelance author and scriptwriter he has lectured in Media Studies and related areas at a number of tertiary institutions.

John has extensive experience in TV, radio and public speaking. He is available to talk to schools and community groups about various aspects of his writing (either in person or through social media) and can be contacted directly at jbess@xtra.co.nz or through his website:
https://drjohnreynolds.wixsite.com/dr-john-reynolds

Other works by John Reynolds

Publications

Uncommon Enemy https://goo.gl/NyQbu5

Uncommon Enemy (audiobook narrated by John Reynolds)
https://audiobooksnz.co.nz/book/detail/236142/uncommon-enemy

Robyn Hood Outlaw Princess
https://www.amazon.com/Robyn-Hood-Outlaw-Princess-Reynolds-ebook/dp/B071CQNNJZ

Writing Your First Novel https://goo.gl/YUlCPU

Starblaze shorturl.at/zGJLQ

Musicals

Robyn Hood Outlaw Princess (music: Gary Daverne)

Starblaze (music: Shade Smith)

Windust (Music: Shade Smith)

Valley of the Voodons (Music: Shade Smith)

Sink the Warrior (Music: Shade Smith)

Pirates and Petticoats (Music: Mal Smith)

www.ingramcontent.com/pod-product-compliance
Lightning Source LLC
Chambersburg PA
CBHW062005170626
46813CB00001B/45